WHITETHORN WOODS

WHITETHORN WOODS

Maeve Binchy

First published in Great Britain in 2006
by Orion Books,
an imprint of the Orion Publishing Group Ltd,
Orion House, 5 Upper St Martin's Lane,
London, WC2H 9EA

Earlier versions of some chapters of this novel have appeared in *Ageing
Matters, Books Quarterly, Woman's Own* and *Woman's Weekly. June's Birthday*
was read on BBC Radio 4. Copyright © Maeve Binchy 2004.

A CIP catalogue record for this book
is available from the British Library.

Printed in Great Britain by
Clays Ltd, St Ives plc

The Orion Publishing Group's policy is to use papers
that are natural, renewable and recyclable products and
made from wood grown in sustainable forests. The logging
and manufacturing processes are expected to conform to
the environmental regulations of the country of origin.

www.orionbooks.co.uk

For dear good Gordon.
Thank you for the great happy life we have together.

Contents

Chapter 1   The Road, the Woods and the Well – 1   3

Chapter 2   The Sharpest Knife in the Drawer   19

Chapter 3   The Singles Holiday   43

Chapter 4   Friendship   64

Chapter 5   The Plan   89

Chapter 6   Bank Holiday Party   114

Chapter 7   The Last Word   131

Chapter 8   The Road, the Woods and the Well – 2   155

Chapter 9   Talking to Mercedes   176

Chapter 10   June's Birthday   198

Chapter 11   Tell Me Why?   215

Chapter 12   The Anniversary   234

Chapter 13   Going to the Pub   249

Chapter 14   Your Eleven O'Clock Lady   270

Chapter 15   The Intelligence Test   293

Chapter 16   The Road, the Woods and the Well – 3   317

CHAPTER I

The Road, the Woods and the Well – 1

Father Brian Flynn, the curate in St Augustine's, Rossmore, hated the Feast Day of St Ann with a passion that was unusual for a Catholic priest. But then as far as he knew he was the only priest in the world who had a thriving St Ann's Well in his parish, a holy shrine of dubious origin. A place where parishioners gathered to ask the mother of the Virgin Mary to intercede for them in a variety of issues, mainly matters intimate and personal. Areas where a clodhopping priest wouldn't be able to tread. Like finding them a fiancé, or a husband, and then blessing that union with a child.

Rome was as usual unhelpfully silent about the well.

Rome was probably hedging its bets, Father Flynn thought grimly, over there they must be pleased that there was *any* pious practice left in an increasingly secular Ireland and not wishing to discourage it. Yet had not Rome been swift to say that pagan rituals and superstitions had no place in the Body of Faith? It was a puzzlement as Jimmy, that nice young doctor from Doon village, a few miles out, used to say. He said it was exactly the same in medicine: you never got a ruling when you wanted one, only when you didn't need one at all.

There used to be a ceremony on 26 July every year where people came from far and near to pray and to dress the well with

...nds and flowers. Father Flynn was invariably asked to say a few words, and every year he agonised over it. He could not say to these people that it was very near to idolatry to have hundreds of people battling their way towards a chipped statue in the back of a cave beside an old well in the middle of the Whitethorn Woods.

From what he had read and studied, St Ann and her husband St Joachim were shadowy figures, quite possibly confused in stories with Hannah in the Old Testament who was thought to be for ever childless but eventually bore Samuel. Whatever else St Ann may have done in her lifetime, two thousand years ago, she certainly had *not* visited Rossmore in Ireland, found a place in the woods and established a holy well that had never run dry.

That much was fairly definite.

But try telling it to some of the people in Rossmore and you were in trouble. So he stood there every year mumbling a decade of the rosary, which couldn't offend anyone, and preaching a little homily about goodwill and tolerance and kindness to neighbours, which fell on mainly deaf ears.

Father Flynn often felt he had quite enough worries of his own without having to add St Ann and her credibility to the list. His mother's health had been an increasing worry to them all, and the day was rapidly approaching when she could no longer live alone. His sister Judy had written to say that although Brian might have chosen the single, celibate life, she certainly had not. Everyone at work was either married or gay. Dating agencies had proved to be full of psychopaths, evening classes were where you met depressive losers; she was going to come to the well near Rossmore and ask St Ann to get on her case.

His brother Eddie had left his wife Kitty and their four children to find himself. Brian had gone to look for Eddie – who had now found himself nicely installed with Naomi, a girl twenty years younger than the abandoned wife – and had got little thanks for his concern.

'Just because you're not any kind of a normal man at all, it doesn't mean that the rest of us have to take a vow of celibacy,' Eddie had said, laughing into his face.

Brian Flynn had felt a great weariness. He thought that he *was* in fact a normal man. Of course he had desired women, but he had made a bargain. The rules, at the moment, said if he were to be a priest then there must be no marriage, no children, no good normal family life.

Father Flynn always told himself that this was a rule that would one day change. Not even the Vatican could stand by and watch so many people leave the ministry over a rule that was made by Man and not by God. When Jesus was alive all the Apostles were married men, the goalposts were moved much later.

And then all the scandals in the Church were surely making the slow-moving conservative cardinals realise that in the twenty-first century some adaptations must be made.

People did not automatically respect the Church and Church-men any more.

Far from it.

There were hardly any vocations to the priesthood nowadays. Brian Flynn and James O'Connor had been the only two ordi-nations in the diocese eight years back. And James O'Connor had left the Church because he had been outraged by the way an older, abusive priest had been protected and allowed to escape either treatment or punishment by a cover-up.

Brian Flynn was hanging in there, but only just.

His mother had forgotten who he was, his brother despised him and now his sister Judy was making a trip from London to visit this cracked pagan well and wondering, would it work better if she came on the saint's Feast Day.

Father Flynn's parish priest was a gentle elderly man, Canon Cassidy, who always praised the young curate for his hard work.

'I'll stay on here as long as I can, Brian, then you'll be considered old enough and they'll give you the parish,' Canon Cassidy often said. He meant very well and was anxious to spare Father Flynn from the indignity of having some arrogant and difficult parish priest brought in over the curate's head. But at times Brian Flynn wondered would it be better to let nature take its course, to hasten Canon Cassidy to a home for the elderly religious, to get someone, almost anyone, to help with the parish duties.

Admittedly attendance at church had died off a great deal since he was a young man. But people still had to be baptised, given first communion, have their confessions heard; they needed to be married and buried.

And sometimes, like when in the summer a Polish priest came along to help him, Brian Flynn used to think he might manage better alone. The Polish priest last year spent *weeks* making garlands for St Ann and her well.

Not long ago he had been in the junior school at St Ita's and asked if any of the pupils wanted to become nuns when they grew up. Not an unreasonable question to ask little girls in a Catholic school. They had been mystified. No one seemed to know what he meant.

Then one of them got it. 'You mean like the movie *Sister Act?*' Father Flynn felt that the world was definitely tilting.

Sometimes when he woke in the morning, the day stretched ahead of him, confused and bewildering. Still he had to get on with things, so he would have his shower and try to pat down his red hair which always stood in spikes around his head. Then he would make a cup of milky tea and a slice of toast and honey for Canon Cassidy.

The old man always thanked him so gratefully that Father Flynn felt well rewarded. He would open the curtains, plump up the pillows, and make some cheerful comment about how the world looked outside. Then he would go to the church and say a daily Mass for an ever-decreasing number of the faithful. He would call to his mother's house, heart in his mouth about how he would find her.

Invariably she would be sitting at her kitchen table looking lost and without purpose. He would explain, as he always did, that he was her son, a priest in the parish; and he would make her a breakfast of porridge and a boiled egg. Then he would walk down Castle Street with a heavy heart to Skunk Slattery's news-agents where he would buy two newspapers: one for the canon and one for himself. This usually involved some kind of intellec-tual argument with Skunk about free will or predestination or how a loving God could allow the tsunami, or a famine. By the time he got back to the priests' house, Josef, the Latvian carer, had arrived and got Canon Cassidy up, washed and dressed him and made his bed. The canon would be sitting waiting for his newspaper. Later, Josef would take the old man for a gentle walk to St Augustine's Church where he would say his prayers with closed eyes.

Canon Cassidy liked soup for his lunch and sometimes Josef took him to a café but mainly he took the frail little figure back to his own house where his wife Anna would produce a bowl of something home-made; and in return the canon would teach her more words and phrases in English.

He was endlessly interested in Josef and Anna's homeland, asking to see pictures of Riga and saying it was a beautiful city. Josef had three other jobs: he cleaned Skunk Slattery's news-agents, he took the towels from Fabian's hairdressers to the Fresh as a Daisy Launderette and washed them there, and three times a week he took a bus out to the Nolans' place and helped Neddy Nolan look after his father.

Anna had many jobs too: she cleaned the brasses on the doors of the bank, and on some of the office buildings which had big important-looking notices outside; she worked in the hotel kitchens at breakfast time doing the washing up; she opened the flowers that came from the market to the florists and put them in big buckets of water. Josef and Anna were astounded by the wealth and opportunities they found in Ireland. A couple could save a fortune here.

They had a five-year plan, they told Canon Cassidy. They were saving to buy a little shop outside Riga.

'Maybe you'll come to see us there?' Josef said.

'I'll look down on you and bless your work,' the canon said in a matter-of-fact tone, anticipating the best in the next world.

Sometimes Father Flynn envied him.

The old man still lived in a world of certainties, a place where a priest was important and respected, a world where there was an answer for every question asked. In Canon Cassidy's time there were a hundred jobs a day for a priest to do. And not enough hours to do them. The priest was wanted, expected and needed at all kinds of happenings in the lives of the parishioners. Nowadays you waited to be asked. Canon Cassidy would have called uninvited and unannounced to every home in the parish. Father Flynn had learned to be more reticent. In modern Ireland, even a town like Rossmore, there were many who would not welcome the appearance of a Roman collar on the doorstep.

So as Brian Flynn set out down Castle Street, he had half a dozen things planned to do. He had to meet a Polish family and arrange the baptism of their twins the following Saturday. They asked him, could the ceremony take place at the well. Father Flynn tried to control his annoyance. No, it would take place at the baptismal font in the Church of St Augustine.

Then he went to the jail to visit a prisoner who had asked for him. Aidan Ryan was a violent man whose wife had finally broken the silence of years and admitted that he had beaten her. He showed no sorrow or remorse, he wanted to tell a rambling tale about it all being her fault as many years ago she had sold their baby to a passer-by.

Father Flynn brought the Blessed Sacrament to an old people's home outside Rossmore with the ridiculous name of Ferns and Heathers. The owner had said it was nicer in a multicultural Ireland not to have everything called by a saint's name. They seemed **pleased to see him and showed him their various gardening** projects. Once upon a time all these homes were run by Religious, but this woman Poppy seemed to be making a very good fist of it.

Father Flynn had an old battered car to take him on his travels. He rarely used it within the town of Rossmore itself since the traffic was very bad and parking almost impossible. There had been rumours that a great bypass would be built, a wide road taking the heavy trucks. Already people were in two minds about it. Some were saying that it would take the life out of the place, others claimed that it would return to Rossmore some of its old character.

Father Flynn's next call was to the Nolans' house.

The Nolans were a family that he liked very much. The old man, Marty, was a lively character full of stories about the past; he talked about his late wife as if she were still here, and often told Father Flynn about the miracle cure she had once got from St Ann's Well that gave her twenty-four years more of a good life. His son was a very decent man, he and the daughter-in-law Clare always seemed pleased to see him. Father Flynn had assisted the canon at their marriage some years back.

Clare was a teacher in St Ita's and she told the priest that the school was full of gossip about the new road that was coming to Rossmore. In fact she was asking her class to do a project on it. The extraordinary thing was that from what you heard or could work out, the road would be going right through here, through their own property.

'Wouldn't you get great compensation if it did go through your land?' Father Flynn said admiringly. It was pleasing to see good people being rewarded in this life.

'Oh, but Father, we'd never let it go through *our* land,' Marty Nolan said. 'Not in a million years.'

Father Flynn was surprised. Usually small farmers prayed for a windfall like this. A small fortune earned by accident.

'You see, if it came through here it would mean they'd have to

9

tear up Whitethorn Woods,' Neddy Nolan explained.

'And that would mean getting rid of St Ann's Well,' Clare added. She didn't have to say that this was the well that had given her late mother-in-law another quarter-century of life. That fact hung there unspoken.

Father Flynn got back into his little car with a heavy heart. This insane well was going to become yet again a divisive factor in the town. There would be still more talk about it, more analysing its worth, claims and counter-claims. With a deep sigh he wished that the bulldozers had come in overnight and taken the well away. It would have solved a lot of problems.

He went to call on his sister-in-law, Kitty. He tried to visit at least once a week, just to show her that she hadn't been abandoned by the whole family. Only Eddie had left her.

Kitty was not in good form.

'I suppose you'll want something to eat,' she said ungraciously. Brian Flynn looked around the untidy kitchen with its unwashed breakfast dishes, the children's clothes on chairs and a great deal of clutter. Not a home to welcome anyone.

'No, I'm great as I am,' he said, searching for a chair to sit on.

'You're better not to eat, I suppose, they feed you like a prize pig in all these houses you visit – it's no wonder you're putting on a bit of weight.'

Brian Flynn wondered, had Kitty always been as sour as this. He couldn't recall. Perhaps it was just the disappearance of Eddie with the sexy young Naomi that had changed her.

'I was in with my mother,' he said tentatively.

'Had she a word to throw to you?'

'Not many, I'm afraid, and none of them making much sense.' He sounded weary.

But he got no sympathy from Kitty. 'Well, you can't expect me to weep salt tears over her, Brian. When she did have her wits, I was never good enough for her marvellous son Eddie, so let her sit and work that one out for herself. That's my view.' Kitty's face was hard. She wore a stained cardigan and her hair was matted.

For a fleeting moment, Father Flynn felt a little sympathy for his brother. If you had the choice of all the women around, which apparently Eddie had, Naomi would have been an easier and more entertaining option. But then he reminded himself of duty and children and vows, and banished the thought.

'The mother can't manage much longer on her own, Kitty, I'm thinking of selling up her house and moving her into a home.'

'Well, I never expected anything out of that house anyway, so go ahead and do it as far as I'm concerned.'

'I'll talk to Eddie and Judy about it, see what they think,' he said.

'Judy? Oh, does her ladyship ever answer the phone over there in London?'

'She's coming over here to Rossmore in a couple of weeks' time,' Father Flynn said.

'She needn't think she's staying here.' Kitty looked around her possessively. 'This is *my* house, it's all I have, I'm not letting Eddie's family have squatters' rights in it.'

'No, I don't think for a moment that she'd want to . . . to . . . um . . . put you out.' He hoped his voice didn't suggest that Judy would *never* stay in a place like this.

'So where will she stay then? She can't stay with you and the canon.'

'No, one of the hotels, I imagine.'

'Well, Lady Judy will be able to pay for that, unlike the rest of us,' Kitty sniffed.

'I was thinking about Ferns and Heathers for our mother. I was there today, the people all seem very happy.'

'That's a Protestant home, Brian, the priest can't send his own mother to a Protestant place. *What* would people say?'

'It's not a Protestant home, Kitty.' Father Flynn was mild. 'It's for people of all religions or no religions.'

'Same thing,' Kitty snapped.

'Not at all, as it happens. I was there yesterday bringing them Holy Communion. They are opening a wing for Alzheimer's patients next week. I thought maybe if any of you would like to go and look at it . . .' He sounded as weary as he felt.

Kitty softened.

'You're not a bad person, Brian, not in yourself. It's a hard old life what with no one having any respect for priests any more or anything.' She meant it as a kind of sympathy, he knew this.

'Some people do, just a little bit of respect,' he said with a watery smile, getting up to leave.

'Why do you stay in it?' she asked as she came to the door.

'Because I joined up, signed on, whatever, and very occasionally I do something to help.' He looked rueful.

'I'm always glad to see you anyway,' said the charmless Kitty Flynn, with the heavy implication that she was probably the only one in Rossmore who might be remotely glad to see him anywhere near her.

He had told Lilly Ryan that he would call and tell her how her husband Aidan was getting on in prison. She still loved him and had often regretted that she had testified against him. But it had seemed the only thing to do, the blows were so violent now that she had ended up in hospital and she had three children.

He didn't feel in the mood to talk to her. But since when was all this about feeling in the right mood? He drove into her little street.

The youngest boy Donal was in his last year at the Brothers School. He would not be at home.

'Aren't you a very reliable man, Father?'

Lilly was delighted to see him. Even though he had no good news for her it was at least consoling to be considered reliable. Her kitchen was so different to the one he had just left. There were flowers on the window sill, gleaming copper pans and pots;

there was a desk in the corner where she earned a small living by making up crosswords: everything was in order.

She had a plate of shortbread on the table.

'I'd better not,' he said regretfully. 'I heard in the last place that I was as fat as a pig.'

'I bet you did not.' She took no notice of him. 'Anyway can't you walk it all off you in the woods above? Tell me, how was he today?'

And with all the diplomacy that he could muster, Father Flynn tried to construct something from his meeting with Aidan Ryan that morning into a conversation that would bring even a flicker of consolation to the wife he had once beaten and now refused to see. A wife that he seriously believed had sold their eldest baby to a passer-by.

Father Flynn had looked up newspaper accounts over twenty years ago of the time that the Ryan baby girl had been taken from a pram outside a shop in town.

She had never been found. Alive or dead.

Father Flynn managed to keep the conversation optimistic by delivering a string of clichés: the Lord was good, one never knew what was going to happen, the importance of taking one day at a time.

'Do you believe in St Ann?' Lilly asked him, suddenly breaking the mood.

'Well, yes, I mean, of course I believe that she existed and all that . . .' he began blustering and wondering where this was leading.

'But do you think that she is there listening at the well?' Lilly persisted.

'Everything is relative, Lilly, I mean, the well is a place of great piety over centuries and that in itself carries a certain charge. And of course St Ann is in heaven and like all the saints interceding for us . . .'

'I know, Father, I don't believe in the well either,' Lilly

interrupted. 'But I was up there last week and, honestly, it's astonishing. In this day and age all the people coming there, it would amaze you.'

Father Flynn assembled a look of pleased amazement on his face. Not very successfully.

'I know, Father, I felt the same as you do, once. I go up there every year, you know, around Teresa's birthday. That was my little girl, who disappeared years before you came to the parish here. Usually it's just meaningless, but somehow last week I looked at it differently. It was as if St Ann really was listening to me. I told her all the trouble that had happened as a result of it all, and how poor Aidan had never been right since it happened. But mainly I asked her to tell me that Teresa was all right wherever she is. I could sort of bear it if I thought she was happy somewhere.'

Father Flynn looked mutely at the woman, unable to summon any helpful reaction.

'But anyway, Father, I know people are always seeing moving statues and holy pictures that speak, and all that kind of nonsense, but there was something, Father, there really was something.'

He was still without words but nodding so that she would continue.

'There were about twenty people there, all sort of telling their own story. A woman saying so that anyone could hear her, "Oh, St Ann, will you make him not grow any colder to me, let him not turn away from me any more . . ." Anyone could have heard her and known her business. But none of us were *really* listening. We were all thinking about ourselves. And suddenly I got this feeling that Teresa was fine, that she had a big twenty-first birthday party a couple of years ago and that she was well and happy. It was as if St Ann was telling me not to worry any more. Well, I *know* it's ridiculous, Father, but it did me a lot of good and where's the harm in that?

'I just wish that poor Aidan could have been there when she said it or thought it or transferred it to my mind or whatever she did. It would have given him such peace.'

Father Flynn escaped with a lot of protestations about the Lord moving in mysterious ways and even threw in the bit of Shakespeare about there being more things in heaven and earth, Horatio, than are dreamed of in your philosophy. Then he left the little house and drove to the edge of Whitethorn Woods.

As he walked through the woods he was greeted by people walking their dogs, joggers in tracksuits getting some of the exercise he obviously needed himself according to his sister-in-law. Women wheeled prams and he would stop to admire the babies. The canon used to say that a playful greeting of 'Who have we here?' was a great get-out when you came across a child in a pram. It covered both sexes and a failing memory for names. The others would fill you in and then you could take it up from there – grand little fellow, or isn't she a fine little girl?

He met Cathal Chambers, a local bank manager, who said he had come up to the woods to clear his head.

He had been flooded by people wanting to borrow money to buy land round here so that they could sell it at a huge profit once the new road was given the okay. It was very hard to know what to do. Head Office had said he was the man on the ground so he should have a feel for what was going to happen. But how could you have a feel for something like that?

He said that Myles Barry the solicitor was exactly in the same predicament. Three different people had come into him asking him to make an offer to the Nolans for that smallholding they had. It was pure greed, speculation and greed, that's what it was.

Father Flynn said it was refreshing to meet a banker who thought in such terms, but Cathal said that was not at all the way they looked at things in Head Office.

Skunk Slattery was walking his two greyhounds and came up to sneer at Father Flynn.

'There you go, Father, coming up here to the pagan well to hope that the gods of olden times will do what today's Church can't do,' he taunted the priest, while his two bony greyhounds quivered with what seemed like annoyance as well.

'That's me, Skunk, always one for the easy life,' Father Flynn said through gritted teeth. He nailed the smile to his face for the few minutes it took before Skunk ran out of rage towards him and moved the trembling dogs onwards.

Father Flynn also went onwards, his face grim as he headed for the first time ever on his own to visit St Ann's Well. He had been here as part of parish activities, always resentful and confused but never voicing his opinion.

A few wooden signs carved by pious local people over the years pointed to the well, which was in a big, rocky, cavernous grotto. The place was damp and cold; a little stream ran down the hill behind and around the well and it was muddy and splashed where many of the faithful had reached in to take scoops of the water with an old iron ladle.

It was a weekday morning and he thought that there would not be many people there.

The whitethorn bushes outside the grotto were festooned, yes, that was the only word Father Flynn thought suitable, literally festooned with bits of cloth and notes and ribbons. There were medals and holy cures, some of them encased in plastic or cellophane.

These were petitions to the saint, requests for a wish to be granted; sometimes they were thanks for a favour received.

'He's off the drink for three months, St Ann, I thank you and beg you to continue to give him strength . . .'

or

'My daughter's husband is thinking of getting the marriage annulled unless she gets pregnant soon . . .'

or

'I'm afraid to go to the doctor but I am coughing up blood,

16

please, St Ann, ask Our Lord that I be all right. That it's only some kind of an infection that will pass . . .'

Father Flynn stood and read them all, his face getting redder.

This was the twenty-first century in a country that was fast becoming secular. *Where* did all this superstition come from? Was it only old people who came here? A throwback to a simpler time? But many of the people he had met even this very morning were young and they felt the well had powers. His own sister was coming back from England to pray here for a husband, the young Polish couple wanted their babies baptised here. Lilly Ryan, who thought she heard the statue tell her that her long-disappeared daughter was all right, was only in her early forties.

It was beyond understanding.

He went inside the grotto where people had left crutches and walking sticks and even pairs of spectacles as a symbol of hope that they would be cured and able to manage without them. There were children's bootees and little socks – meaning who knew what? The desire for a child? A wish to cure a sick baby?

And in the shadows, this huge statue of St Ann.

It had been painted and refurbished over the years, making the apple cheeks even pinker, the brown cloak richer, the wisp of hair under the cream-coloured veil even blonder.

If St Ann existed she would have been a small dark woman, from the land of Palestine and Israel. She would *not* have looked like an Irish advertisement for some kind of cheese spread.

And yet kneeling there in front of the well were perfectly normal people. They got more here than they ever did in St Augustine's Church in Rossmore.

It was a sobering and depressing thought.

The statue looked down glassily – which was a bit of a relief to Father Flynn. If he had begun to imagine that the statue was addressing him personally he would really have given up.

But oddly even though the saint was not speaking to him, Father Flynn felt an urge to speak to her. He looked at the young troubled face of Myles Barry's daughter, a girl who had failed to get into law school to her father's great grief. *What* could she be praying for with her eyes closed and her face so concentrated?

He saw Jane, the very elegant sister of Poppy who ran the old people's home. Jane, who, even to Father Flynn's untutored eye, seemed to be wearing high-fashion designer clothes, was mouthing something at the statue. A young man who ran an organic vegetable stall in the marketplace was there too, his lips moving silently.

As he gave a last look at what he considered an entirely inappropriate representation of the mother of the mother of Jesus, he wished he could ask the saint through the statue whether any of these prayers were ever heard and ever answered. And what did the saint do if two people were seeking conflicting favours?

But this way fantasy lay, and madness. And he was not getting involved.

He stroked the walls of the cave as he left the grotto, damp walls with messages carved on them. He made his way past the whitethorn bushes crowding the entrance, bushes that no one had cut back to give easier access because they felt the hopes and prayers and petitions of so many people were attached to them.

Even on the old wooden gates there was a note pinned:

'*St Ann, hear my voice.*'

All around him Father Flynn could almost hear the voices. Calling and begging and beseeching down the years. He heard himself make up a little prayer.

'Please let me hear the voices that have come to you and know who these people are. If I am to do any good at all here let me know what they are saying and what they want us to hear and do for them . . .'

CHAPTER 2

The Sharpest Knife in the Drawer

Part 1 – Neddy

I've heard people say about me, 'Oh, Neddy Nolan! He isn't the sharpest knife in the drawer . . .' But, you see, I never *wanted* to be the sharpest knife in the drawer. Years ago we had one sharp knife in the kitchen and everyone was always talking about it with fear.

'Will you put the sharp knife up on a shelf before one of the children cuts the hands off themselves,' my mam would say, and 'Make sure the sharp knife has the blade towards the wall and the handle out, we don't want someone ripping themselves apart,' my dad would say. They lived in fear of some terrible accident, and the kitchen running red with blood.

I was sorry for the sharp knife, to tell you the truth. It wasn't its fault. It didn't set out to frighten people, that's just the way it was made. But I didn't tell people how I felt, they'd just say again that I was being soft.

Soft Neddy, they called me.

Because I couldn't bear to hear a little mouse squealing in a mousetrap, and I had cried when the hunt came near where we lived and I saw the eyes of the fox as it fled by and I shooed it into Whitethorn Woods. Yes, I suppose other fellows thought it was soft but the way I looked at it, the mouse hadn't asked to be born in the scullery instead of out in a field where he could have lived peacefully to be an old happy mouse. And the lovely red fox certainly hadn't done anything to annoy all those hounds and horses and people dressed up in red who galloped after him with such fury.

But I'm not quick and clear at explaining things like that, so often I don't bother. And nobody expects too much from Soft Neddy so I more or less get away with my way of looking at things.

I thought it would be different when I grew up. Adults didn't get all silly about things and sorry for them. I was sure this would happen to me too. But it seemed to take a very long time.

When I was seventeen a crowd of us – me, my brother Kit and his pals – all went off from Rossmore in a van to a dance, oh, miles away beyond the lakes, and there was this girl. And she looked very different to the others, like they were wearing dresses with straps over their shoulders, and she was wearing a thick polo-necked jumper and skirt, and she had glasses and frizzy hair, and no one seemed to be asking her to dance.

So I asked her up, and then when the dance was over she shrugged and said, 'Well, at least I got one dance out of tonight.'

So I asked her again, and then again; and then I said at the end, 'You got fourteen dances out of tonight now, Nora.'

And she said, 'I suppose you want the going home.'

'The going home?' I asked.

'A court a ride,' Nora said in flat resigned tones. This would be the price she would pay for having been asked to dance fourteen times.

I explained that we were from the other side of the lakes, from near Rossmore, and we'd all be going home together. In a van.

I couldn't work out whether she was relieved or disappointed. The others were slagging me in the van.

'Neddy's in love,' they kept singing all the way home.

There was very little singing four months later when Nora and her dad turned up at our place and said that I was the father of the baby she was carrying.

I could not have been more shocked.

Nora didn't look at me, she just looked at the floor. All I could see was the top of her head. Her sad frizzy perm. I felt a great wave of pity for her. Even more pity when Kit and my other brothers laid into Nora and her dad.

There was no way, they said, that their Neddy had spent ten seconds alone with Nora. They had a hundred witnesses for this. They were going to get Canon Cassidy to come to the house as a character witness. Red-faced, they confronted Nora's dad and swore that I hadn't even kissed the girl goodbye when they were bundling me into the van. This was the greatest scam they had ever heard.

'I never made love with anyone,' I said to Nora's dad. 'But if I had, and it resulted in a child being conceived, then I'd certainly live up to my responsibilities and I would be honoured to marry your daughter, but you see . . . that's not the way things happened.' And for some reason everyone believed me. Everyone. And the situation was over.

And poor Nora raised her red, tear-stained face and looked at me through her thick glasses.

'I'm sorry, Neddy,' she said.

I never knew what happened to her.

Somebody once said that it was all the fault of her grand-father, but because he was the money of the family, nothing had been done about him. I didn't know if her child got born and if she brought it up. Her family lived so far away from Rossmore, there was never anyone to ask. And our family didn't encourage me to enquire.

They were very scathing about it all.

'A bold rossie,' my mam said.

'Palming off someone else's bastard on our Neddy,' my granny said.

'Sure, not even Soft Neddy could fancy that poor ibex,' my dad said.

And I felt a lump in my throat for the poor young woman, who had said so proudly that at least she had got one dance out of the night and offered herself to me in abject thanks for having had the luxury of fourteen dances.

It was all very sad.

Not long after this, I left Rossmore and went off to London in England to work on the buildings with my eldest brother Kit. He had found a flat over a shop, there were three of them there already and I made the fourth. It wasn't very clean or tidy or anything but it was near the Tube station and in London that's all that mattered.

At first I just made the tea and carried things for people on the site, and they had such cracked, broken old mugs that on the day I got my first wages I went to a market and got a dozen grand new ones. And they were all a bit surprised at how I washed the mugs properly and got a jug for the milk and a bowl for the sugar.

'A real gent is Neddy,' they said about me.

I'm never quite sure whether people are praising me or not. I think not. But it's not important anyway.

But there was this way they had of doing things on the site, like every sixth dustbin wasn't filled with rubbish at all – there were bags of cement and bricks and spare tools. Apparently it was some kind of system, an arrangement, but nobody told me, so naturally I pointed out to the foreman that perfectly good stuff was being thrown away and I thought everyone would be pleased.

But they weren't.

Far from it.

And Kit was the most annoyed of all. I was ordered to stay in the flat next day.

'But I'll be sacked if I don't go into work,' I begged him.

'You'll be flayed alive by the other fellows if you *do* go in.' Kit was very tight-lipped. It was better not to argue with him.

'What will I do here all day?' I asked.

Kit always knew what everyone should do. Not this time.

'Jesus, I don't know, Neddy, do some bloody thing, clean the place up a bit. Anything. Just don't come near the site.'

The other lads didn't speak to me at all which made me realise how serious this whole dustbin thing had been. I sat down to think. It wasn't working out nearly as well as I had thought it would.

I had been planning to save lots of money in London. So that I could get my mam a holiday and my dad a good overcoat with a leather trim. And here I was being ordered not to go into work.

Clean the place up a bit, they said. But with what? We had no cleaning stuff. No bleach for the sink or the bath. No polish for the furniture. No detergent to wash any sheets. And I only had nine English pounds left.

I got an idea and I went down to the shop where the Patels worked hard day and night.

I picked out cleaning stuff and a tin of white paint worth ten pounds in all and put them in a box. Then I spoke to Mr Patel.

'Suppose I was to clear up your yard there for you, sweep it, stack all your boxes and crates. Would you give me those cleaning things as a wage?'

He looked at me thoughtfully as if adding up and weighing the cost and the amount of work I would do.

'And would you clean the shop window as well?' he bargained.

'Certainly, Mr Patel,' I said with a big smile.

And Mr Patel smiled too. A slow unexpected smile.

Then I went to the launderette and asked them if I could paint their door which looked a bit scruffy.

'How much?' Mrs Price, the woman who ran the place and,

they said, had many gentleman friends, was wise in the ways of the world.

'I want to have two loads of washing and extra drying,' I said.

It was a done deal.

When Kit and the lads came back from the site they couldn't believe the transformation.

They had clean beds, the shabby linoleum on the floor was polished, the steel sink was gleaming. I had painted the cupboards in the kitchen and the bathroom.

There were more jobs I could do for the Patels next day, I told them, and they would give me a thing that restored the enamel on baths. And there was more painting to be done in the launderette and that meant we could have loads of things washed there – shirts, jeans, anything – and I'd take the bags of stuff and pick them up again, what with not being able to go to the site and everything.

And because they all seemed to have calmed down and become so admiring of the nice new clean flat, I felt I could dare to ask them about the other business. Had the foreman cooled off any?

'Well, he has apparently,' Kit said. 'He can't believe that you would shop me, your own brother! I put it to him that no one would do a thing like that, nor the lads you lived with. That he'd have to look elsewhere for the culprits. So now he is looking elsewhere.'

'And do you think he'll find them?' I asked, excited.

It was like living in a thriller.

They looked at each other confused. There was a silence.

'Probably not,' Kit said after a time.

'And will I come back to work next week?' I wondered.

Another silence.

'You know, you're doing such a great job here, Neddy, making this a real smart place for us to live, maybe *this* is what you should do. Do you know?'

I was very disappointed. I thought I'd be going out to work with them every day like mates.

'But how will I earn my living, my deposit on a house, if I don't have a job at all?' I asked in a low voice.

Kit leaned towards me and spoke to me man to man.

'I think we should regard ourselves as a company, Neddy, and you could be our manager.'

'Manager?' I said, feeling overawed.

'Yeah, suppose if you were to cook us a breakfast, even make us a packed lunch and keep this place looking shipshape. And of course handle our finances, put our money in the post office for us. Then you'd be taking a load off our backs and we'd all kick in with a wage for you. What do you think, lads? Nice clean place for us to live in, we could even bring people back here once Neddy puts his mark on the place.'

And they all thought it was a great idea and Kit ran out for fish and chips for everyone to celebrate the day I became their manager.

It was a great job altogether and much less confusing really than working on the site because I made my own arrangements and knew what I was doing. I wrote all this on my weekly letter home and I thought Dad and my mam would be pleased. But they sent me warning letters telling me to be sure that Kit and the others didn't work me too hard and make use of me.

'You're such a decent, gentle boy, Neddy,' my mam wrote, 'you must look out for yourself in this life. You'll promise me that, won't you?'

But actually it wasn't hard at all because everyone was so nice and I could make everything fit in. After serving a good, cooked breakfast for the lads, I'd take the Patel children to their school. Then I'd open up the launderette because Mrs Price who had a lot of men friends wasn't good in the early morning.

Then I'd go back to the Patels and help them stack shelves and **take their rubbish down to a dump. Then I'd get to work on the** flat, clean it all up, and every day I tried to do something new for them, like put up a new shelf or do a bit of cleaning in the television repair shop in exchange for a second-hand telly. Then Kit found a video that had fallen off a lorry but hadn't got broken so it was like having our own cinema in the kitchen-sitting room.

I'd pick up the Patel children from school; do the shopping for Christina, an old Greek lady who made our curtains in return.

And every year I would organise the tickets back to Ireland. Kit and I went back home to the little farm outside Rossmore to see the family.

The place changed all the time, the town was growing and spreading out very far. There was even a bus now that came to the corner of our road. I never heard a word about that poor girl Nora and her problems. Kit said it was wiser not to ask.

I always did a bit of work in the house when we came home for the two weeks. Well, Kit would be out at dances, and he didn't really notice anything wrong, like the place getting shabby and needing a coat of paint here, a few shelves there. Dad was out with the cattle and he hadn't the time or the energy to do it.

I would suggest to Kit that we get them a nice television set or maybe even a washing machine, but Kit said we weren't made of money and to stop pretending we were returned millionaires, which was enough to give everyone the sick.

I used to worry about our mam. She had been delicate always, but she always said that St Ann had given her those extra years to watch her family grow up and she was very grateful. One summer I thought she looked very frail, but she said that I was not to worry about her as everything was fine and they lived comfortably now that Dad had sold off a field and had fewer cattle so he was at home more often to hand her a cup of tea. She had no worries about anything except would Dad be all right when she eventually did go.

And then Kit and I went back for Mam's funeral.

And all our friends in London sent flowers because I had told them about Mam. People said that Kit must be very well thought of over in London to have so many friends. Actually they were *my* friends, but it didn't matter anyway.

Poor Dad looked like a bloodhound. His face was all set in lines of sadness as he waved us goodbye.

'You look after young Neddy now,' he instructed Kit at the railway station. Which was odd really as I did all the looking after.

'Wouldn't you think he'd have given us our fare,' Kit grumbled. But I had our fare so it didn't matter.

And then because I fixed up all Mr Patel's outhouses for him to give him more storage, the Patels let us have another entire room included in the same rent, and one of the lads had moved out and got a girlfriend and a real shacked-up relationship so now we were only three in the flat and we had a room each.

The others brought girls back sometimes, nice girls all of them, and they'd have breakfast and be very nice to me.

And honestly it was all so very busy that the time just passed by and I was thirty-seven years old but I'd been saving for nearly twenty years so I had a fortune in the building society. I mean, if you're putting away twenty pounds a week at first and then that goes up to thirty and fifty, well, it all adds up to a huge sum.

I managed to get Kit to come back home with me every year, which wasn't always easy. He said being in Rossmore was like spending time with the living dead. So this particular year, anyway, when we went back home our dad really wasn't well. He hadn't mended the fences of the chicken run and the fox had all the hens. He wasn't able to go to the market any more and relied on people coming to him and making an offer for the beasts, which broke his heart.

He'd grown very in on himself and wasn't keeping the place right at all. I said to Kit that he couldn't live much more on his own like this. Kit said that he'd hate to be sent to the County

Home. As if I'd send our dad to the County Home!

No, I said, I thought I should come back and mind him. Try to run the place for him.

'And take all our inheritance for yourself?' Kit said in a horrible voice.

'Oh no, Kit, I'd get someone to value the place, maybe Myles Barry the solicitor in town, and then give you and the others your share. Wouldn't that be fair?'

'You'd live here with Dad?' Kit was open-mouthed.

'Someone has to,' I explained, 'and anyway, I might get married soon if I could find a nice girl.'

'Buy this house? Give us all a share? In your dreams,' Kit laughed.

But I could buy it and I did, the very next day, and my dad was delighted but Kit wasn't pleased at all.

He had no savings, he said, and yet I, who had never done a day's work in my life, was able to put my hand in my pocket and draw out enough to buy a small farm and a gentleman's residence. It was a strange state of affairs.

'But what do you mean I've never done a day's work in my life, wasn't I your manager?' I cried, very upset at the false accusation.

He didn't seem to accept that explanation.

'I *was* your manager,' I insisted. Because I was. I had been a great manager, made a smashing flat for them all to live in. I would have put their money away every week like I put my own, if they'd only have given it to me. It had to go into post office accounts with a whole lot of different names, something to do with accounting apparently. But I couldn't snatch the money from them on a Friday if they were going up west to clubs or taking girls out or buying classy gear.

The reason I was able to save was because I didn't drink. I bought my clothes in Oxfam and anyway I worked so many hours that I didn't have *time* to go out and spend money – so I **saved it for a house.**

And I told all this to Kit patiently and explained it to him carefully in case he hadn't understood. I watched his face and he stopped being angry. You could see it. His face got all soft and kind like it was the night he had made me manager. The night he had gone out for the fish and chips. And he put out his big hand and laid it over mine.

'I'm sorry, Neddy, I spoke out of turn. Of course you were our manager and a very good one. And I don't know how we'll replace you if you come back here. But then we'll have a lump sum from this place and we'll know Dad's being looked after and that will be a great relief in itself.'

I smiled with relief. It was all going to be all right again.

'You know, the getting married bit might be harder, Neddy, you won't get upset if that isn't as easy for you as everything else. Women are very difficult to understand. Hard to work out. You're a great fellow but you're not the sharpest knife in the drawer and you wouldn't be up to what women want these days.'

He was being kind so I thanked him as I always thanked people for advice whether I understood it or not. And I set about finding a girl to marry.

It took seven months. Then I met Clare.

She was a schoolteacher. I met her when she came home to our parish church outside Rossmore for her father's funeral. I thought she was very nice indeed.

'She's too bright for you,' they all said.

Well, my dad didn't say that because he loved living with me, and he didn't want to say anything that would annoy me. I made him porridge every morning, and I employed a man to look after the few cows we had. I minded the chickens and the ducks. I went for walks with him up to the woods to keep his legs mobile. Sometimes he went to the well to thank St Ann for all those extra years he had with my mam. And I brought him to the pub every day to meet his friends and have a pint and a hot lunch.

Dad used to say about me, 'Neddy's not soft as you all think ...'

And Dad thought Clare would be fine for me. He said I should spend money on a few nice shirts and get my hair properly cut in the salon in Rossmore. Imagine Dad knowing words like 'salon'.

Clare was ambitious, she told me this from the start. She wanted to get on in teaching and maybe become a principal sometime, and I said that would be fine because the way I saw it I could be the manager in the house and have everything done when she got home. And suppose, just suppose, we had a little baby, I could look after the baby while Clare went out to work. And to my delight she said it all sounded very good and very restful and she'd be honoured to be my wife.

Kit wasn't able to come to the wedding, because he was in jail in England over some misunderstanding. The real culprits weren't found this time either.

And Dad was much stronger and better now. All it had been really was loneliness and neglect that had him feeling so low.

So we got in a great builder and fixed a price and he did a marvellous job dividing up the house so that Clare could feel that, when she came to live here when we were married, she would have her own home for herself and myself and not that she had come to live with Dad and me. And this way everybody would be happy.

I encouraged Dad's friends to come and see him of an evening. And I bought him a great big television which they all loved when the sport was on.

Our wedding day in Rossmore was just great.

Canon Cassidy did the actual wedding bit, but the new curate Father Flynn was very helpful too. And we had a reception in the hotel where people made speeches.

My dad said that as far as he was concerned his beloved wife who had been cured by St Ann was in this room with us to celebrate the day and I was the best son in the world and would be the best husband and indeed father too when that time came.

I made a short speech and said that I wasn't the sharpest knife in the drawer. I wanted people to know that I *knew* that's what they said. But I was the luckiest knife. I had got everything I wanted all my life and I could ask for no more.

And Clare said that she would like to make a speech. She knew it wasn't usual for the bride to speak but there was something she wanted to say.

I had no idea what it was going to be.

She stood up in her beautiful dress and said to everyone in the room that the drawers were full of sharp awful old knives. So many that she had almost despaired of opening a drawer again. And that then she had found me and her whole life turned around. And as I looked around the big room in the hotel I saw everyone was half crying as they clapped and cheered and it was simply the happiest day of my life . . .

Part 2 – Gold Star Clare

When I was at school at St Ita's, Rossmore, I used to get the gold star every week.

Once when I had flu, another girl, my friend Harriet Lynch, got it but otherwise it was always mine.

I used to take it off my school tunic every Monday morning and lay it back on the Principal's desk and then an hour later, when the gold stars in each class were being read out, I would get it back again.

It was a reward for a combination of good marks, good behaviour and school spirit. You couldn't just get one for studying hard. No, you had to be an all-rounder, a balanced person, as they saw it.

And it was easy really to make them see it like that. Because I liked being at school. I was in early and I left late. They had plenty of time to see me and my good school spirit in their environment. I mean, if you came from *my* home, any environment was preferable. Who wouldn't prefer to be at school than at home.

It wasn't entirely my mother's fault. Not entirely.

Women were different then, they did literally everything not to rock the boat, no matter how dangerous and unpleasant that boat was. Any marriage was better than no marriage, any humiliation was better than the ultimate humiliation of being an abandoned wife. They went up to St Ann's Well to pray that things might get better but they didn't try to make them better themselves.

And I wasn't the only child in the school that had trouble like that at home. There was a poor girl – Nora Something – who was a bit soft in the head. In her case it was her grandfather who bothered her. And she got pregnant and she said that it was some fellow she had met at a dance, but apparently the fellow brought all his brothers and proved that he was never with her alone. And poor Nora went to the nuns, had her baby and gave it up for adoption and her grandfather went on living in that home. And they all knew. All the time. And said nothing.

Like they knew about my Uncle Niall in our home. And said nothing.

I put a lock on my bedroom door and no one asked me why. They knew too well that my father's brother fancied me. But he owned most of the farm, so what could they do?

I asked God a lot if he could stop Uncle Niall from trying to do these things. But God was busy back in those days or there were a lot of cases worse than mine, I suppose. The really hard thing was that they all knew and did nothing. They knew why I did my homework up at the school lest he approach me when the house was empty, and why I didn't come back until I was certain that my mother had come back from the creamery where she worked and my father in from the fields and that there would be other people to protect me. Sort of, anyway.

I was both proud and ashamed when I was a schoolgirl. Proud

that I was able to stay out of my uncle's messy clutches. And ashamed because I came from a family that wouldn't look after me but left me to fight my own battles against things I didn't understand.

And I suppose it did make me grow up quickly. And then when I passed my exams I announced firmly that I was going to university miles away.

There was a bit of grumbling about this. Where would they get the money to pay for all this? my father wondered. He had wondered about money all his life, it was his greatest curse.

Why couldn't I stay at home and do a secretarial course and mind my sister? my mother said, as well she might.

My sister Geraldine *did* need to be minded and I would warn her well before I left. Maybe I'd go to the bad in a big city? Uncle Niall said that, even though he knew and I knew and my parents knew. I'd go to the bad much quicker here had I not got a lock on my bedroom door.

But I was much tougher than they all thought.

I was really quite grown up for my years.

I'd survive, I told them, I'd get a job to pay for a flat and my fees. I was a gold star girl. An all-rounder. I could turn my hand to anything.

And I did. I went to Dublin two weeks before term started and I fixed myself up in a flat with three other girls, and got a job in an early morning breakfast place, which was terrific because I had nearly a day's work done and a huge breakfast eaten by the time I went to my 10 a.m. lectures, and then I worked a shift in a pub from six to ten every night, which kept me out of the way of spending money and I had the whole day to myself.

And because of Uncle Niall and all that sort of thing I wasn't all that keen on fellows like my flatmates were, so I could put my mind to my studies as well. And at the end of the first year I was in the top five of the whole group, which was an achievement.

I never told them any of this when I went back home to Ross-more. Except for my sister Geraldine because I wanted her to know we could do anything, *anything*, if we wanted to.

Geraldine thought I was wonderful and she told me too that she was well able to deal with Uncle Niall now by shouting aloud, 'Oh *there* you are, Uncle Niall, what can I do for you?' at the top of her voice, alerting the whole house and he would slink away. And she had announced one day in front of everyone that she was putting a giant padlock on her door.

And then in the middle of my second year at university a lot of things went wrong. My mother got cancer and they said they couldn't operate. My father coped with it all by drinking himself senseless every night.

My sister went to stay with my friend Harriet Lynch's younger sister in order to study and to get away from Uncle Niall since there was no one to protect her.

Back in Dublin they put up the rent on our flat. Seriously high. And just then I met Keno who ran a nightclub down a little cobbled street in Dublin and asked me to dance there. I said, nonsense, I couldn't dance, and he said there was nothing to it. And I said it would be dangerous, wouldn't it be sort of flaunt-ing yourself at people and then not letting them touch you?

But Keno had bouncers who looked after all that sort of thing.

And then my mother died.

Yes, it was awful, and I tried to mourn her properly but I could never forget that she had turned aside and left Geraldine and me to our fate. And shortly after the funeral Uncle Niall sold the farm over my father's head and Geraldine hadn't done any work at school because she was so upset about everything and if I did do the bloody dancing it meant I could have my own flat in Dublin, finish my university degree, put Geraldine into one of those sixth form Leaving Certificate colleges and keep an eye on her. So I said okay to Keno and wore this ludicrous thong and danced around a pole every night.

It was silly. Just mainly silly and a bit sad really.

And the music sometimes would do your head in.

But the tips were enormous, and the bouncers were great and there was always a taxi home at 3 a.m. and God, why not?

I told Geraldine that it was a gambling club, and I was a croupier taking in the money, and that the law said she was too young to come in, and that was fine. And then one night of course, wouldn't you know, Harriet Lynch's father and some friends were there and recognised me. They nearly dropped dead.

I went to their table to have a drink and said very sweetly that everyone earned their living and took their pleasures in an entirely individual way and I didn't see any need to inform Harriet Lynch's mother or daughters back in Rossmore of the nature of these business trips to Dublin. They got the message and Keno told me afterwards that I was the brightest girl he ever had in his stable. I didn't like the word 'stable'. I felt we were all like performing prancing horses or something. But I did like Keno. A lot. He was very respectful to us all and he was doing all this because he had a very poor family who needed support back in Morocco. He would really like to have been a poet but there was no money in poetry. His little sisters and brothers wouldn't have had an education if he were busy writing verses so he had this club instead.

I understood so well.

Sometimes we'd have a coffee, Keno and myself – my friends from college thought he was gorgeous. He always talked about poetry so they thought he was some kind of student. He never told any actual lies, I noticed, but he never told the whole truth either.

But I wasn't going to criticise him for that, I didn't want him to tell my friends from the BA honours group that he knew me from my dancing nearly naked five nights a week in his club.

He was the same with Geraldine, who was now also at university, and mercifully having too good a time to want to investigate my so-called life as a croupier in a casino. I didn't fancy Keno and he didn't fancy me, but we often talked about love and marriage and what it might be like. He was cynical that any romance ever really lasted. His business experience told him so much the contrary.

He said he would like children and in fact he had a child, a daughter in Marrakesh. But she was being brought up by her grandmother. Her mother was an exotic dancer in one of his clubs there. That was the first time I knew he had any other establishments than the one where I worked in Dublin.

But I said nothing and never brought the matter up again.

'You're a great girl, Clare,' he said to me often. 'A real star.'

'I was a gold star at school,' I explained and he thought that was very endearing.

'Little Gold Star Clare! Give up this nonsense of becoming a teacher and manage my club for me instead,' he begged.

But I told him that in fact when I did become a teacher I'd actually give up the club. Too much danger that the pupils' fathers might see me!

'Well, as you said yourself, they shouldn't be there,' he laughed.

He came to my graduation and sat at the conferring ceremonies with Geraldine. I smiled as I took my parchment in my hand. If they knew that the girl with the First Class honours was a topless dancer . . . Only Keno knew and he was clapping loudest of all.

A year later I was a fully-fledged teacher with my diploma and I got into exactly the kind of school I wanted to. I took Keno out to lunch to say goodbye. He didn't believe it when I told him what I was going to be earning. For me it was plenty.

Geraldine had won a scholarship, I had my savings and hardly any outgoings.

I thanked him from the bottom of my heart for having made it all possible. He was dark and moody looking, and he said I was ungrateful.

'Over the years, Keno, if there's anything I can do to help you I will,' I promised and I meant it.

I didn't hear from him for three years. And by the time he got in touch again a lot had changed.

After years of drinking my father eventually died and at the funeral I met an old man in a wheelchair called Marty Nolan, who had known my father once. Like back in the days when it had been possible to talk to my father. A long time ago. A nice old man. His son, who was pushing the chair, was a really good-natured fellow called Neddy. Neddy had worked in England on the buildings, he said, well, more as manager for his brother and their friends, and now he had come home and looked after his father.

He was an oddly restful person and I liked talking to him.

Harriet Lynch said to me, I should see his elder brother Kit, a real hunk. Take the sight out of your eyes, he would. And where was he now, I wondered? Apparently he was banged up in jail for something, Neddy was the one who had the decent streak in that family.

Not the brightest mind, a bit slow, a minute late, she said. Harriet Lynch was always sorry she had volunteered this information to me.

Very sorry.

I saw Neddy again because I came back to Rossmore over and over to get what I considered were Geraldine's and my just portions of my father's estate. If you could use a word like 'estate' to describe what was owing to a drunk who had died in the County Home. Over the years I had tried to contribute to my father's keep from my earnings in Keno's club, but the doctor told me to save my breath. He said that my father didn't know where he was and would only spend any money that came his way on cider. People had been discouraged from giving him anything at all.

I faced my Uncle Niall after the funeral when he was busy accepting sympathy about his unfortunate poor brother. The one with the drink problem, people said, shaking their heads sadly.

I asked for his attention for a moment.

He looked at me witheringly.

'And what can I do for you on this sad day, Miss Clare?' he said.

'Just a third of what you got for the family farm,' I said to him pleasantly.

He looked at me as if I were mad.

'One third is fine. I have written down the bank account number.'

'And what makes you think I am going to give you one single Euro?' he asked.

'Let me see, I think you won't want Geraldine and myself to tell the local doctor, the priest, half of Rossmore and, even more important, a top lawyer the reason why she and I had to leave home at a very young age,' I said.

He looked at me, unbelieving, but I met his stare and eventually it was his eyes that moved away.

'It will be no problem, there's a new young curate here who would give Canon Cassidy the courage to stand up to you. Mr Barry would get us a hot-shot barrister from Dublin, the doctor will confirm that I asked his help to get Geraldine away from your clutches. The world has changed, you know. The days are gone, Niall, when the uncle with the money can get away with anything he likes.'

He spluttered at me. I think my calling him Niall was about the clincher.

'If you think for one moment . . .' he began.

I interrupted him. 'One week from now, and a decent gravestone for my father,' I said.

It was surprisingly easy. He lodged it.

It was blackmail, of course, but I shrugged. I didn't see it as that.

Then I was going out with Neddy. He came to Dublin once

a week to see me. And I went down to see him once a week. And we hadn't slept together because Neddy wasn't like that.

And in the middle of things in Dublin, which were always a bit pressurised, he was very restful indeed.

And then I heard from Keno.

They really needed me back at the club, he wouldn't ask if he wasn't desperate. He'd been having a bit of trouble with some of the girls from abroad. Visas and red tape and form filling. He needed someone reliable to be in there, dancing, yes, and keeping an eye on things for him.

I explained how impossible it was for me, or I tried to explain. I even told Keno about Neddy and the kind of man he was. I shouldn't really have told Keno about Neddy.

When he put the pictures down on the table, he mentioned Neddy.

I hadn't known there were any pictures being taken, and it was very obviously me, and the positions were very suggestive indeed. It was sickening, looking at them.

It didn't bear thinking what the board of the school or dear innocent Neddy would make of them.

'It's blackmail,' I said.

'I don't see it as that,' Keno said, shrugging.

'Give me a week,' I said. 'You owe me that.'

'Right.' Keno was always agreeable. 'But you owe me too. For your start in life.'

During the week, of course, wouldn't you know, Neddy asked me to marry him.

'I can't,' I said. 'Too much baggage.'

'I don't care about the past,' Neddy said.

'It's not just the past. It's the future,' I said.

And I told him. Everything. Every single thing – like my awful Uncle Niall and Geraldine and how boring and tiring the dancing had been. I had left the envelope of pictures on the table and he just threw it into the fire without opening it.

'I'm sure you are very beautiful in the pictures,' he said, 'and why shouldn't people pay to look at you?'

'He'll have more,' I said in a despairing kind of voice.

'Yes, of course he will, but it won't matter.'

'Ah, come on, Neddy, these are nice respectable girls I teach – do you think anyone would let me near them if they saw those pictures?'

'Well, I was hoping that if you married me you'd come back to Rossmore and teach near by.'

'But he could still show them,' I said. I wondered if Neddy might really be soft in the head.

'But you could tell them in advance. You could say at the interview you had to pay your way through college by doing various jobs including exotic dancing,' he said.

'It won't work – we won't get away with it, Neddy.'

'It will work because it's true.' He looked at me with his honest blue eyes.

'I wish things had been different,' I said to him.

'Would you have said yes and married me if it weren't for this little problem?' he asked me.

'It's a big problem, Neddy.' I sounded weary.

'Would you, Clare?'

'Well, yes, I would, Neddy. I would have been honoured to marry you.'

'Right then – we'll sort it out,' he said.

And he came with me to Keno's that night. We walked right through the dancers and the punters to the office at the back. To say Keno was surprised is putting it mildly.

I introduced them formally and then Neddy spoke.

He told Keno that he sympathised with the situation, and how it must be hard running a business with all the staff problems and everything, but it wasn't fair to take away my dream, as I had *always* wanted to be a teacher ever since I was a schoolgirl.

'Clare was a gold star at school,' Keno said, more to make conversation, I think, than anything else.

'I'm not at all surprised,' Neddy said beaming at me proudly. 'So, you see, we can't make Clare do anything else except concentrate on her teaching. Neither of us can.'

Keno pulled a big brown envelope from his desk drawer.

'The pictures?' he said to Neddy.

'They're very beautiful, Clare showed them to me earlier tonight,' he said.

'She did?' Keno was amazed.

'Of course, if we are to be married we must have no secrets. I have told Clare about my brother Kit who has been and still is in prison. You can't keep quiet about things that are part of you. And I know that Clare is very, very grateful for the start you gave her. So that's why we are here.'

'Why exactly are you here?' Keno was totally bewildered.

'To know was there any *other* way we could help you.' Neddy spoke simply as if it were obvious.

'Like what way, in God's name?'

'Well, I have a great friend who does wrought iron, he could do you really nice windows outside which would look well and also be good and strong against unwelcome visitors. And let me see, what else could we do? If the dancing girls were tired and wanted somewhere to stay, it's very peaceful by the woods where we live . . . Perhaps some of your dancers might need a nice restful holiday. They could come to stay with us. There's lots to see in Rossmore. There's even a wonderful well in the woods. People can wish there and it comes true.' His good-natured face was straining with good ideas for Keno.

I begged God not to let Keno mock him, or tell me I was marrying a simpleton. I spoke to God very strongly in my mind. 'I never bothered you about things, did I, God? I didn't go up to that well rabbiting on to your grandmother, St Ann, now did I? No, I sorted out my own problems and looked after my little sister. I didn't go round doing much sin, unless the dancing is a sin? But it's so silly, it can't really be a sin, can it? And now I want to escape from all this and marry a good man. So that's the kind of thing you're meant to be *for*, isn't it, God?'

And God listened. This time.

Keno turned on the shredder and put the pictures into it.

'There aren't any more,' he said. 'Get your wrought iron man to give me a ring, Neddy. And now get the hell home, the two of you, to plan your wedding. I have an ailing business to run here.'

And we walked out of the club together hand in hand and down the cobbled street.

CHAPTER 3

The Singles Holiday

Part 1 – Vera

It was very clear from the moment I saw the advertisement:

Holiday for Singles
fun, sun, sea and relaxation

That was exactly what I wanted.

And they were so slow back at the Active Retirement Association, and they were so scornful at the cardiac exercise class. They were positively hostile at the Gardening in Later Years Group. My cousins back in Rossmore were the most disapproving of all. They said that sort of holiday was only for young people. Undesirable young people who would probably have sex on the plane on the outward journey, and be drunk for fifteen days when they got there.

But where did it say anything about that in the advertisement? Nowhere.

I paid my two hundred Euro deposit and then the rest when they sent the invoice. At no time did anyone ask me my age. And proper order too. I had not asked them *their* ages. I turned up at the airport with my little purple and yellow label saying *Holiday for Singles*.

That's what I was, single.

I could easily have married Gerald, and quite possibly I could have married Kevin. But Gerald was very, very dull. So I didn't marry him. And the woman who *did* marry him went sort of mad from the tedium of it all. And I didn't try to make Kevin infatuated with me or anything because truly he was very unreliable. I wouldn't have had a moment's peace with him.

And I never regretted being single. Never for one moment – except sometimes on holidays.

You had to pay a single room supplement. You were often given a very small, poky table away from other people's eyes. It was a bit lonely not having anyone to talk to like other people had, someone to laugh over the day with. That's why I was thrilled to see a holiday that catered for exactly what I needed.

At the airport I saw lots of those purple and yellow labels and, yes, the fellow travellers did seem to be very young, like about forty years younger than me, but then that was just who I saw now. The older crowd would turn up later.

They didn't as it happened. And as I stood in the line waiting for check-in, I got a few odd glances. But then I have always had a few odd glances. A sixty-something woman in jeans and a big floppy sun hat does often attract a second look. People often look again just to check that they haven't imagined all those lines and wrinkles under a floral, cotton hat and over a trim pair of jeans.

The check-in girl asked me if I was sure I had booked the right holiday and I assured her that I was indeed single and greatly looking forward to it. On the plane they were all introducing themselves to each other, so I joined in too.

'I'm Vera,' I said and shook hands heartily with those nearest to me. They were nice young people called Glenn and Sharon and Todd and Alma. None of them had ever been on a singles holiday before, and neither had I, so we had that in common anyway.

'Where did you go last year, Vera?' Glenn asked.

I told them about the Active Retirement Association's walking holiday in Wales, and the year before the bus tour of Scotland for the cardiac exercise class. I had been planning to go on the Gardening in Later Years Group trip to Cornwall and the Eden Project but suddenly I had seen this advertisement and decided that it had everything I really wanted.

Sharon, who was a very pretty girl with a lovely smile, asked did I have family at home and I said sadly, no, I had been an only child, I had never married but I had lots of good friends. And plenty of time to see people nowadays since I had retired.

Todd wanted to know where I was from. I explained Dublin nowadays, but originally from Rossmore – they probably wouldn't have heard of it. It turned out they all had.

There had been some kind of documentary on television about it. There was what they called a cool kind of wishing well, which gave you whatever you wanted. Alma said maybe we should all be going there on holiday rather than Italy, imagine getting what you wanted from a holy well. I thought of telling them that the well wasn't really holy, it had been there for years before St Patrick ever came to Ireland. But it was a mistake to give young people too much information.

Glenn asked had I been to Italy before and I told them a bit about Rome and Florence and Venice but said that I'd never been to this place, Bella Aurora, where we were heading. In fact I had never heard of it until I got the brochure which said it was full of places of interest. I was eager to see what they were.

'Mainly clubs, I think,' Alma said. Her friend had been here last year, and said it was great, that she had been locked day and night.

Locked? I wondered but didn't say. Young people get so irritated if you sound bewildered.

'Sounds good,' I said with a bright smile and maybe it was only my imagination but they seemed to look at me with more interest.

After we arrived and got our luggage at the airport, two almost naked girls with purple and yellow bikinis checked us all off on clipboards and put us on a bus. We went through several very big resorts until we got to Bella Aurora. All had huge white hotels, facing the sea, lines of cafés, pizzerias, ice cream parlours, bars. And Bella Aurora looked just the same.

Hard to see where all the interesting things were. But I never start by complaining. Hard to know how it could be exactly relaxing either – very loud music blaring everywhere – but no point in finding fault before you have settled in. There might well be fun, though not much room for it, the beach looked very crowded. But they had promised fun and no doubt it would be delivered.

Three more near-naked courier girls with clipboards were waiting for us at the hotel to assign us our rooms and we were told we had half an hour to unpack and then there would be welcome drinks by the pool.

So I hung up my clothes and had a shower, put on a nice clean T-shirt with my jeans and down I went.

To my surprise almost all the people who had travelled on the plane were almost naked too, like the courier girls. A lot of them were very white-skinned but some, like Alma and Sharon, had been on electric tanning beds. Sharon looked very beautiful, like someone from Hawaii. They looked as if they had been here for weeks.

There was a kind of fruit punch served and very nice and refreshing it was too; and we were all quite thirsty what with the heat and the travelling and everything. And the almost naked courier girls told us of all the interesting things to do, which was mainly a list of clubs that opened at midnight and were lively, and cool, and full of action. And then I began to feel a bit odd and as if the swimming pool had started to slide away so I lay down for a while and closed my eyes.

When I woke up it was much darker and the others seemed

to be dancing beside the swimming pool. There was very loud music.

Todd was lying on one of those slatted wooden sunbeds beside mine.

'They put a fair whack of vodka in that punch all right,' he said appreciatively.

Vodka? I had been drinking vodka in the afternoon, in this heat?

'You're a great old stayer, Vera, I'll give you that,' said Glenn who was holding his head. 'I like a woman who can hold her drink. Personally I think I'm going to have to pace myself a bit. See you at dinner . . .'

Dinner? I thought I had slept through it. I thought it was bed-time. But maybe food was what I needed.

The dining room was decorated with paper flowers and you could sit where you liked. I sat beside Sharon, who was depressed and didn't want to eat. She told me that she fancied Glenn. But in the way of things, he didn't seem to see her. Only that noisy Todd came on to her and then he had passed out at the cocktails. Life was very hard, wasn't it?

I said it was, but that it was early days yet, maybe she was better off not to be fancied too soon. She brightened up at this and ate a huge dinner.

Just after midnight they all headed off to one of the interesting clubs down the road and I went to bed and passed out again.

Next morning I went down and swam three lengths of the pool and felt much better. I looked around for my new friends but none of them showed up. So I went back to the pool and read. I would normally have taken a walk and found an old church or museum but I didn't want the Singles people to think I was being aloof. So I waited and waited and nobody turned up at all.

Then I thought there must have been Something Interesting arranged and I had missed it when I had sort of passed out from

47

the vodka fruit punch the night before. One of the near-naked courier girls had given us her card in case of any problems, so I phoned her and wondered had I missed anything Interesting.

The near-naked girl sounded upset, annoyed almost, to be woken so early. Early? It was past midday, I had been up since eight. No, of course nothing was planned for the morning, she said. People didn't want anything in the *morning*. There would be a seafood buffet lunch any time after two-thirty, which would be followed by water polo. It was all written up on the hotel notice board. And now if I would excuse her, she had to get back to sleep.

So I read my book and waited for the seafood buffet lunch. About 3 p.m. everyone started to appear, very tired still and hung-over. They all had about three cups of black coffee and an occasional orange juice, which must have been breakfast, then they moved on to cold beers and ate mountains of prawns, squid and mussels. And then amazingly they all had the energy to play water polo. I don't think there were many real rules, it had a lot to do with removing the tops of other people's bikinis.

I watched it and said that I didn't usually take exercise for two hours after a meal. It used to be the way in the olden days. And they listened, interested, as if I were telling them news from the planet Mars.

And Sharon said that Glenn did fancy her a bit now, which was terrific, and I had been right to tell her to hang in there. And Todd told me that Sharon was a proper little slapper. And Alma said she thought that Todd was divine. And Glenn said to me that he thought this was a fantastic holiday and wondered, was I enjoying it? And because I was brought up to be polite and always to say that things were great even when they weren't, I said that I was loving it.

But the truth was that I didn't think there were all that many interesting things to do, and I was a bit too old for their kind of fun. Still there was the sea and the sun and nice people to have meals with, so while they were playing what they called water polo I went off and got postcards and sent them back to my friends in the Active Retirement Association, and to my cousins in Rossmore, to the Gardening in Later Years Group and the cardiac exercise class, saying it was all delightful. Which it mainly was.

I watched the fruit punch carefully the second evening and at dinner Sharon confided that Glenn wanted to be with her even when they got back home. Todd said that Sharon was a tease, Alma said that Todd was only loud because no one had understood him. They all went to another cool club this time and I went off to bed.

I realised of course that I had the whole morning to do my kind of interesting things. Just as long as I was back for the seafood buffet lunch at three no one would miss me. I went to the museum in the Old Town, which was delightful, and I saw a really old-fashioned hotel, completely unlike the rest of Bella Aurora. It was so different to all the very noisy places along the seafront, full of near-naked people, that I decided to go in and have a cup of coffee.

They served it in a big shady garden. This was much more my sort of place really, except that it would have been lonely here. And nobody's lives to get involved in as I had on my Singles holiday.

In the hotel garden there was an older man in a sun hat doing a sketch. He nodded at me graciously and I nodded back hoping that I was being gracious in return. Forty-eight hours with these wild young people had made me speak differently, think differently almost. Eventually he came over and showed me the drawing.

'What do you think?' he asked.

I said it was excellent and that he had a great sense of detail.

He said that he was called Nick and he had been here for two days. It was a lovely hotel but quiet, and then of course everyone

49

else was a couple. I sighed with him and said it was always a problem. He told me he was a widower with no children, he quite liked his own company but was not entirely happy as a retired person. I told him I had never married, and that because of discrimination against solo travellers I had signed up for a Singles holiday.

He was astounded.

'Aren't they for much younger people than us?' he said.

'It didn't say in the advertisement,' I explained and this seemed to please him. He laughed and said I was a fine person.

I explained that of course they didn't get up until 3 p.m.

'And what are they doing?' Nick wondered.

I said that I honestly didn't know. I couldn't believe that they would *all* be having sex all morning, I assumed that they must stay up so late all night at these clubs that they were all exhausted.

Again Nick said I was a very interesting person and he wondered if I would have a late lunch with him. I explained that I had to be back for the seafood buffet lunch at three.

And he patted my hand as if I were an old friend.

'Well, please say you'll come back here tomorrow morning and we'll explore somewhere while the Singles all sleep on?' he asked.

I said that would be great.

At the buffet lunch, Alma said she and Todd had got together last night and it was great. I didn't enquire exactly what 'got together' might mean. I just nodded enthusiastically. Sharon didn't know whether she should be easy or hard to get with Glenn. It was so difficult to know. I advised them as best I could. There was a wet T-shirt contest instead of water polo but it seemed more or less the same. At dinner Todd said that Alma was a slapper and Glenn seemed to have eyes only for one of the near-naked courier girls. They went off to another club and I went to bed and listened to the music coming from all over Bella Aurora.

I was looking forward to meeting Nick next day. And then the days got into a very nice easy rhythm.

Nick and I went out every day together. Sometimes we took a bus to various inland villages and on two occasions I skipped the 3 p.m. buffet lunch but I never missed the dinner.

'Could I come to the dinner one night?' he asked.

Nobody had ever brought a guest in so I said I'd have to enquire.

'I'd pay, of course, and bring some wine,' he said.

'I'll tell them that,' I reassured him.

One of the near-naked courier girls said it was not normally allowed but that it was no problem in my case. So I invited Nick.

'I'm a bit nervous, as if I were meeting your family,' he said. I had told him about Todd and Glenn and Sharon and Alma and their complicated lives. I had told them nothing about Nick.

The night he came to dinner Glenn was kissing the near-naked courier girl instead of eating his dinner, Sharon was crying, Alma was telling everyone that Todd was a toe-rag.

'What is that exactly?' I asked.

'A scut,' Alma said, which didn't make things any clearer.

Nick took it all in.

'It's the climate and the drink,' he told Sharon. 'Get Glenn away from the booze and the heat for a day, up to a nice shady village where you can talk without all this flesh around. You'll be fine.'

And he told Todd to stop behaving like a horse's ass or he'd end up going home a total loser, and that nice girl was only calling him a toe-rag because she fancied him. And Nick came to dinner all the nights except the last one where we went out by ourselves and discussed all the things we had in common.

He had a little car but he was nervous of motorways and only liked driving on back roads. Maybe he could drive me down to Rossmore and I could show him these famous woods that everyone was getting excited about.

'And I could meet your cousins,' he said tentatively.

'They will disapprove of you, they disapprove of everyone and everything,' I told him.

He thought this was great.

'What will I talk about to them?' he asked.

'They will interrogate you,' I explained. 'And then when they have found out enough they will blind you with their views about a new bypass being a National Disgrace, and they will ask you to write letters to the papers about it.'

'And is it a National Disgrace?' Nick asked.

'No, it's totally necessary, Rossmore is like a car park except you can't get in or out of it. Should have been done years ago.'

'But this holy well?'

'It's a pagan shrine. The whitethorn is meant to have some kind of magic about it – farmers never want to cut it down. The whole thing is hysterical rubbish of the highest order.'

Nick said he found me very entertaining. And wasn't it great that he only lived a short bus ride away from me in Dublin, and how he had always wanted to learn about gardening but thought it might be too late and how I had always wanted to sketch but didn't know how to begin, and how liking your own company was good but liking someone else's was better.

The next day when we were leaving, Glenn and Sharon were arm in arm, and Todd was carrying Alma's suitcase for her.

When the near-naked girl courier was checking us back into the bus she asked me would I be coming back on another Singles holiday. I looked at her from under my flowery sun hat and said that next year I might well not qualify for a Singles holiday at all.

Part 2 – Chez Sharon

Well, I just hated coming home from that holiday. Hated it, I tell you. When we were pushing the trolleys through Dublin airport I had a big knot in my stomach. I was dead sure it was all over now, a summer romance kind of thing. He'd say, 'See you around,' or he'd call me and then it would be finished. No lovely places to go like in Bella Aurora. Only desperate work and rain, and I'd never liked anyone as much as Glenn, not in my whole life, and I'm twenty-three now so that's been a fair old life.

Anyway they were all shouting goodbyes and kissing each other and swearing that they'd see each other in this club or that, and Glenn just stood there looking at me. I wished to God I could think of something to say instead of what was racing through my head, things like *don't dump me, please, Glenn*, or *we will be all right even back home when we have to go to work and all* . . . I could only think of awful tying-down things – the things fellows dread to hear.

So I said eventually, 'Here we are then,' which wasn't very bright. I mean, of course we were here. Where else would we be?

Glenn just smiled. 'Indeed we are,' he said.

'So it was great fun.' I hoped I didn't sound too intense, too tying down.

'Yeah, but it's not over, is it?' Glenn asked anxiously.

'No way,' I said and I knew I had this big silly grin all over my face.

Just then Vera came up to say goodbye.

'Nick will be coming back next week, he had a week longer than we all did, and I was going to have a few people round for a get-together in my house – a sort of a reunion. You will come? Todd and Alma are coming. You have my address so it's Chez Vera, Friday of next week then? About eight o clock?'

'Shay Vera?' I asked foolishly.

She's dead nice, Vera, she'd never make a fool of you.

'It's a silly expression. It means . . . at the house of someone, Chez Moi at my house, Chez Vous at your house . . . It's just something we used to say a hundred years ago.' She was apologetic under her ridiculous hat and with her faded jeans.

She waved as she went off to catch her bus. Funny little figure, yet everyone was mad about her – *and* she'd pulled on the holiday, too.

Glenn said that his brother and some mates were coming in from Santa Ponsa in an hour's time and he was going to meet them in the bar. They'd give him a lift back to Chez Glenn. Would I like to wait and they'd drive me to Chez Sharon too?

I would have liked to wait very much, to have given our holiday romance some kind of base in Ireland as well as out there under the blue skies. But there was no way I could let him see Chez Sharon. Now Glenn isn't posh, it's nothing like that, but there's about a month's work to be done tarting up our house before I'd even let him see it. This is not putting on airs or anything, this is survival.

The garden is full of dandelions and bits of old metal that can never be thrown out. The kitchen window is boarded up after the last time Dad started throwing things, and they're unlikely to have got any glass in it since I went away. The paintwork is all peeling. Whatever chance I had with Glenn it would be wiped out if he saw Chez Sharon.

So I said no, that I had to run and that I'd hear from him soon, and I sat on a bus and cried the whole way home.

My mam was getting the supper. She looked tired, as she had always looked tired for as long as I could remember.

'Don't upset your dad tonight,' were her first words.

'Is he on the piss again?' I asked.

'He had a bit of bad luck, Sharon, be a good girl now and don't upset things, you've just had a lovely holiday, what have the rest of us had?'

It was unanswerable.

My mam had had nothing but dog's abuse, and a desperate job cleaning offices from 4 a.m. until 8 and then turning round and going out to be a washer-up in a place that did all-day breakfasts. I had just had fourteen days of sunshine and sangria and great laughs and I'd met a fabulous fellow. I wasn't going to upset things.

I nailed a smile on my face when my dad came in, fulminating about some horse and some false friend who had told him wrong things about this horse.

'Well for you, Sharon, out in foreign parts,' he said looking at me resentfully.

'I know, Dad, I was very lucky,' I said and saw my mam's face relax. In fact I wasn't lucky at all, I was just hard working. I had saved twenty Euro a week from the money I earn at the dry-cleaners for thirty-seven whole weeks! All to pay for this holiday and a few outfits to wear on it.

Dad had never saved anything. Mam saved all right, but then she spent it all on us and the house and getting him a few decent shirts in case he ever had an interview and might ever get a job again.

My young brothers came in for their tea and I gave them all the big box of Italian biscuits I had brought home and my dad dipped them into his tea because his teeth weren't good and he hated chewing things.

Suppose I had brought Glenn home here? To this room draped with clothes drying on the backs of chairs with newspapers open at the racing page thrown around the floor. With no cloth on the table. I gave a shiver at the thought.

Next day it was back to work in the dry-cleaners in my uniform and it was as if I had never been on holiday. The girls who worked there did comment on my tan all right but the customers never noticed. They only cared about getting a red wine stain out of a white lace blouse without leaving a trace or how to get tar out of an expensive skirt where someone had sat on something that couldn't be shifted.

Then I looked up and Glenn was standing there at the counter. 'You look beautiful in yellow,' he said, and suddenly I thought it might well be all right. He hadn't forgotten me, he wasn't going to dump me.

He worked for his uncle who was a builder and had a job which was quite near by. We could meet every day, he said. The question of where we might meet every night was one that could be dealt with later. He was one of six children so no space in his house, and there was no way he was going to be let within a mile of Chez Sharon.

And then even the customers began to notice me – they said I was all smiles and good cheer. The girls who worked with me told them I was in love, and they loved to hear that. In a world of grease-based stains, water stains and fabrics that crumpled up as soon as you looked at them, it was pleasant and distracting to think about love, just for a moment or two.

We went to Vera's on the following Friday. It was in a very smart part of town, I don't suppose the residents had ever seen people like Glenn and me and Todd and Alma visiting that area before. Vera had a three-storey house, much too big for her and Rotary the ginger cat who lived with her. Of course Nick might be going to live with her too the way things were working out. They got on together like a house on fire and he had obviously been visiting her every day since his return. He laughed so much at her jokes and told us that she was a wonderful woman. He closed his eyes when he said 'wonderful'.

Nick, it appeared, lived in rented accommodation a bus ride away. Surely he would come and live in this big place. They would be company for each other and they might even get married.

Vera had made us a big spaghetti bolognese, and Nick had made a great pavlova full of strawberries, and everyone had a great time except Alma, who whispered to me that Todd had suggested they cool it a bit, which was bad news. And then when Todd said he had to leave early, Alma said she'd go with him, which I thought was a bad idea, it looked clinging. You could see that he was annoyed and that made poor Alma more anxious than ever.

Anyway Vera and I were doing the washing up and Glenn was helping Nick to cut back some of the worst briars and brambles that were threatening to take over the back door of the house.

'You two look nice and cosy together,' I said as I dried the plates.

'Yes, he's a very, very good man,' Vera said, pleased with it all.

'So will you be moving in together?' I asked. You could ask Vera that sort of thing even though she's nearly ninety or something.

'No, no, that wouldn't do at all,' she said unexpectedly.

I was sorry I had asked now. 'I didn't mean for *sex*,' I said, trying to take the harm out of it. 'I meant for companionship.'

'No, there's no problem with the sex part of it, we'll probably have sex again after you've gone,' Vera said matter-of-factly.

I wondered what the problem was. Could he have a wife, another woman hidden away somewhere? Did he have a rake of children who wouldn't let him get together with Vera?

Apparently not. It had all to do with being set in their ways. When you get old it seems that you don't want to change your way of going on, in fact you can't change it, much as you would like to. It has to do with space, and having your own things where they've always been.

'I wouldn't mind *where* my things were if I was with a fellow I was mad about,' I said.

'Yes, but then you probably don't *have* all that many things and they haven't been in place as long as ours have.'

'What sort of things?' I wondered.

'Oh it's all cracked, Sharon, there's things I couldn't bear Nick to touch like my collections of pressed flowers, and my boxes of things I'm going to put into a scrapbook one day. And he is very odd about his tubes of paint, almost worn out with hardly a squeeze of anything left in them, and torn sketchbooks and boxes of letters and cuttings that he will throw out sometime but not now. We couldn't merge all that, Sharon, we'd be fighting in a week. What we have is much more important. We can't risk losing that by moving in together.'

Glenn and I talked about it when we left. It seemed a waste of two nice people not getting together for the time they had left. We sighed. No one had everything. We were just dying to live together and no problems about being set in our ways. It was just that we had no money, and we'd never find a place to live.

'Could I not move into your house, Sharon? Share your room? At least you *have* a room – I have to share with my brother,' Glenn pleaded.

'No, Glenn, believe me, no. It won't work. My dad's a wino and a gambler.'

'Well, sure, mine is a religious nutter, I told you, it doesn't matter.'

'It would if you were living there.'

'I could bring in some money, couldn't I?'

'Ah, no, Glenn, it would just go towards getting more drink for my dad.'

'So what will we do then?' He seemed defeated.

'We'll think of something,' I said, sounding much more confident than I was. I watched my mam's life and was determined I would never settle for anything remotely like it. She cooked and washed and cleaned up around my dad and the boys every hour that she wasn't working cleaning office floors or washing greasy plates.

'I'm happy enough, Sharon,' she would say if I questioned it. 'I mean, I love him and we've got to remember that he didn't walk away when I was expecting you.'

A lifetime of gratitude that he had acknowledged what was after all *his* child too. Twenty-four years of saying thank you and calling that love.

I met Alma from time to time. She said that Todd was definitely seeing someone else, but she loved him and would do anything to get him back. He was seeing another woman and she *knew* it but whatever she felt for him she called love.

And then I would talk to Vera as well and she talked about loving Nick and what a delightful person to meet in the late afternoon of her years, yet at the same time she was prepared to lose it all over books of pressed flowers or his tubes of paint. It seemed a very peculiar definition of love to me. And there were Glenn and myself who really *did* love each other and wished the best for each other and we hadn't a chance of getting a place to live together.

It didn't seem fair or just somehow. But there was some old wan on the radio going on about how we have to *make* our own luck, that it doesn't come by magic and she had known people whose life turned out fine – they had got whatever they wanted. So I said to Glenn that's what we'd have to do. Make something happen.

I wish I could say that he was full of ideas – but then neither was I.

I asked Vera, did she think this holy well thing in Rossmore might work. She said it wasn't very likely. If there was a St Ann, and St Ann was listening, which was more problematical still, then she might be slow to bring about a situation where a couple could live in sin and have lots of extramarital sex. I said that I was desperate and might try it so Vera said she'd come with me to point me to the Whitethorn Woods and go and visit her hatchet-faced cousins.

It was a lovely walk up to the well but once I got there I felt kind of ashamed. I mean, it's not as if I knew who this St Ann was or went to Mass or anything. And there were nearly a hundred people there. Some of them had children in wheelchairs or on crutches and some didn't look in good shape at all. And they were all asking desperately for favours. I felt I couldn't ask for a **place for Glenn and me to . . . well . . . it didn't seem right.**

So I sort of said, 'If you get a chance and the matter comes up it would be nice. But to be fair maybe you should deal with these people first . . .'

And I told Vera this on the way home and she said I might well get what I want because I was far nicer than lots of people including herself.

I asked her about the cousins, and she said they were like weasels. Weasels with small minds, pointed teeth and horrible voices. All they could talk about was the price of land and what compensation people would get when their homes were disturbed. When we got off the bus Glenn and Nick were waiting for us, Glenn with his motorbike and Nick with his little car.

'We missed you girls,' Glenn said, and I hoped that St Ann was listening. Glenn was so decent, any old saint would want you to be living with him. I must look St Ann up and see what kind of a private life she had herself.

I asked Glenn what kind of things he and Nick had talked about when the four of us went out for a pint together. Apparently it was all about the basement in Vera's house.

Nick said he thought that despite the looming presence of Rotary the ginger cat, there might well be an r–a–t in it, and Glenn had said there were probably dozens of them. Nick wondered, was it the kind of place that could ever be done up to live in, and Glenn said he'd ask his uncle to look at the place and give an estimate.

So I realised that they were still mulling over the possibilities of it all. But that crashed to the ground eventually because apparently it would cost a small fortune to get it done up right and Vera didn't really like the notion of Nick living below stairs and they were both droning on about being so old and maybe needing someone to look after them in even later years. When they got older still.

God, they'd make you sick. The two of them have twenty times more life in them than people half their age and now suddenly they start talking like geriatrics. It was the thought of change that had done it, they were fine as they were with their old paint tubes and books of pressed flowers.

It's only the thought of the merger that has unhinged the pair of them. The waste, the sheer waste of it all.

And there, looking us all in the face, was a perfectly good rat-filled basement which Glenn and his uncle could clean up in three weekends for *us* to live in. We wouldn't be picky – we'd do it up in time.

It was hard to concentrate on work in the dry-cleaners when there were so many things churning through my head. I realised that this woman was going on and on about something and I hadn't been paying any attention at all. It was about this outfit she had borrowed from her sister to wear to a wedding and some eejit had spilled an Irish coffee over it. Was there *any* way of getting the stain out completely? Her sister was like a lighting devil about most things but in particular about clothes that would be described as ruined.

'And you wouldn't mind, only that's what I do, solve problems for a living, I'm an agony aunt and I don't even know how to face my own sister.'

I did a deal with her there and then, I'd get the manager on the case, we'd get the stain out if she could solve *my* problem. I told her about Vera and Nick who loved each other but hated each other's possessions, and about Glenn and me who wanted to get into the rat-filled basement and live there.

She asked how many bedrooms were in the house. Four, I explained.

'Far too many for them, they're not going to be hearing the patter of tiny feet at their age. Give them a study each, get your fellow to put up shelves and things for all the paint tubes in one and the pressed flowers in the other. Do up the basement, tell them you'll mind the house, scare away the burglars, give Rotary the cat a bowl of something and fresh water when they go on holidays, and look after them when they're old. It's obvious, isn't it?'

And amazingly it was.

And even more amazingly there was some kind of terrifying solvent that got the stain out of the borrowed dress.

Glenn and his uncle shelved the two studies in no time, and as the wise agony aunt realised, Vera and Nick had no objection to sharing bedroom, bathroom, sitting room or kitchen as long as their precious belongings were safe.

Then they attacked the basement with Rotary looking on loftily as some rodents were removed. Rotary was the kind of cat who didn't exert himself unnecessarily. Why attack something big and menacing when you had humans who could do it for you? And I asked Vera about St Ann's private life, and she said that St Ann was married to a fellow called Joachim.

Happily, I asked?

'No better or worse than anyone's marriage, I'd say,' said Vera who had never tried marriage at all.

I think she saw I was disappointed at that. I wanted a better ending.

'Oh, go on then,' Vera said grudgingly. 'Happily, I'd say. If there had been any sacrificing the children or pestilence, we'd have heard about it.'

There was plenty of room for us in the basement. It was just gorgeous, so we made a grand little nest for ourselves. Mam gave us some old saucepans from home and some cleaning materials which she came across when doing the offices in the early mornings. Glenn's mam gave us some curtains. My dad gave us a lawnmower so that he would never have to use it again, not that he had ever used it much. Glenn's dad gave us a tip for a greyhound, which won at five to one.

Nick gave us his bed, since he would be sharing Vera's now. Alma gave us a bunch of flowers and a lecture about there being **No Good in Men. Todd had gone his way.**

Glenn is terrific when he comes up to my parents' house, once called Chez Sharon. He gives my dad a hand with all the work my dad didn't do during the week. Glenn and I are getting married next year when we have enough saved to have a nice wedding day. Vera said if it was in the summer we could have it in the garden and she could be my bridesmaid. She said she only meant it as a joke but I said that it would be great, I'd love it. I said I could be *her* bridesmaid, maybe at St Ann's Well when she and Nick finally got it together. But she laughed at the very idea of it.

She and Nick aren't going to get married at all, apparently. That's oldies for you. And people laugh when we say we met Vera and Nick on a Singles holiday.

'You *are* funny, you and your fancy tales,' they say.

As if you could make up something like that.

CHAPTER 4

Friendship

Part 1 – Malka

I met Rivka Fine, let me see, oh, it was years and years ago now, back in the 1960s. We were on a kibbutz in the Negev desert for the summer. I was the first person from Rossmore to do such an adventurous thing, head for the Middle East and pick oranges and pluck chickens. I remember that way back then poor Canon Cassidy said that though it was a great thing to go to the Holy Land and walk where Our Lord had walked, I would have to be careful that I didn't lose my faith when I met so many people of other beliefs.

I didn't know that Rivka and I would be friends at first – she seemed a bit sulky, moody even – while I was delighted with everyone and talked to them all. They came from so many countries: Morocco, Romania, Turkey, Germany. They had all learned to speak Hebrew. There were only a few English speakers around, so we had to manage, Rivka and I, learning that *tapoosim* meant oranges and *toda raba* meant thank you. I tried to learn ten words a day but actually with the heat and the hard work in the kitchen and everything, it was too much and I settled for learning six.

We had to share a hut so we learned quite a bit about each

other. She was there because her parents back home in New York felt guilty about not emigrating to Israel, so they wanted to be able to say, 'Our daughter is out there as a volunteer in the desert.' I was there because I had taught Latin to two little Jewish boys back in Rossmore and their parents, Mr and Mrs Jacobs, had given me a trip to Israel to thank me. It was the holiday of a lifetime, they had even found me this kibbutz to work in because a cousin of Mrs Jacobs had been there one summer and had enjoyed it.

And I thought it was really great. I fell in love with Shimon who was originally from Italy and he loved me too and we were going to set up our own business growing gladioli when his National Service was over.

I suppose Rivka may have been a little bit jealous because Shimon was always coming and hanging round our hut. Not that we slept with each other or anything. I know, I know, but we just didn't in those days. Afraid, I suppose. Anyway that's the way it was.

Rivka asked me was I *really* going to work in a gladioli farm, and I said I sure hoped so, all I had to do now was go back home to Rossmore and sort of soften up my family for the whole idea, which wasn't going to be easy. There was bound to be interference from Canon Cassidy about marrying a non-Christian. Then we'd have to deal with *his* family – which was going to be another day's work, what with the Jews believing that the line sort of passed down through the woman and they wouldn't care for him bringing a non-Jewish girl back to them.

And then Rivka fell in love with Dov who was Shimon's friend and that made everything more cheerful and the four of us could go off for drives. Rivka had no long-term plans to live with Dov in Israel back then. She said she had to go back to New York and marry a dentist or a doctor. It was as simple as that. No, she couldn't take Dov with her when he had finished his National Service. Dov was from Algeria. His people lived in a hut. No,

Rivka didn't mind that – but her mother would. Big time.

It was a magic summer. We were busy taking oranges from trees, and feathers from chickens, and stray hairs from our eyebrows. We rinsed our hair in lemon juice, we both lost tons of weight because we hated the margarine they used so we just ate oranges and pieces of grilled chicken. If they could see me now, all those people back in Rossmore, I kept thinking.

Then, quicker than we could have imagined, it was all over and time for me to go back home, back to being a teacher in St Ita's in Rossmore, and it was time for Rivka to go back to working in a travel agent's office in New York. We were firm friends by then and hated saying goodbye. No one else would understand the summer we had and how we loved the Friday night dance and the red rock of the desert. We both knew that tales of Shimon and Dov would sound like foolish holiday romances to our friends and would be like a red rag to a bull if mentioned to our parents.

We swore that we would keep in touch and we did.

I wrote a tear-stained letter to Rivka when I heard from Shimon that there was no future in gladioli. Or anything else. Rivka wrote in rage to say that Dov's brother had been in touch to say that Dov couldn't read English writing and please to stop pestering him. I told Rivka about how my mam had offered to pay for golf lessons in the hopes that I would meet a lawyer or a banker at some golf resort. Rivka explained that *her* mother was taking her for a week to this mountain place which was like a marriage market. She must look her very best, it was make or break time.

It must have been break time. It certainly wasn't make time.

Rivka was promoted to become office manager but there was nothing moving in the marriage stakes. This was a heavy stress factor at home apparently. It was stress time with my mam too. Several serious rows, with fairly unforgivable things said: 'When I was your age, Maureen, I was married and pregnant,' and, 'You don't think you are going to get *better* looking once you've passed twenty-five, do you?' I said that I'd prefer to die wondering than to put myself up to be chosen by these bog-ignorant, so-called professional men of her choice who preferred drink and golf to female company anyway. My dad just said that it would be very nice to have Peace in his Time, which was all he asked.

Back in Rivka's place things were getting really serious, she told me.

Her mother was now advertising for a husband for her in some suitable magazine. I knew that if I had to spend the summer vacation at home this year I would go mad.

My mam would be sending me up to St Ann's Well in Whitethorn Woods to pray for a man and I would probably kill my own mother with my bare hands and go to jail, and this would not be Peace in his Time or anyone's time for my quiet gentle dad. So I applied for a summer job teaching in a children's camp in America.

First I was going to stay with Rivka for a week in New York.

'What kind of a name is that? *Rivka?* my mam asked.

'It's her name,' I heard myself say mutinously, as if I were a six-year-old.

'But where does it come from? I mean, was she baptised Rivka?' My mam was in one of those moods. I was too weary to explain that Rivka was very unlikely to have been baptised at all.

'I don't really know,' I said glumly.

I allowed my mind to drift away while my mam went on about the fact that for all my great education I actually never really knew anything. Men liked a woman who was alert, awake, alive – not dreamy and drifty like I was.

I thought it was a small miracle that my mam didn't know just how alert and alive I had been out in the Negev desert with Shimon. For all the good it had done me. Anyway I would be out of here soon in New York with Rivka.

She met me at the airport and we hugged each other in

delight. On the way to her house she told me that she was very sorry to lay all this on me but she had implied to her mother that I was Jewish and would I mind pretending that I was? Just for a week?

It was idiotic, I said. It wasn't as if Rivka was going to marry *me*!

'It's just for an easy life, just for one less battle to fight,' she begged. *Snap!* It was the same situation at home for me. We sighed over mad mothers.

'So I said your name was Malka,' she confessed.

'*Malka?* I shouted.

'It's the Hebrew for queen,' Rivka explained, as if that made any difference.

'Right,' I said.

The 1960s were meant to be a decade of change, of looking forward. Not for me, not for Rivka. I couldn't be Maureen for her mother, she had to have been baptised for mine.

Heigh-ho.

It was a great help having worked for Mr and Mrs Jacobs, and having been in Israel. At least I knew about Seder, and Pesach, and High Holidays. I knew about Hanukkah instead of Christmas, I knew about milk and meat dishes being separate, even the plates they were served on, and about not eating things that had cloven feet.

Mrs Fine was beautifully dressed and very pretty. She fussed a lot, as Rivka had warned me. But one thing I hadn't been told. She absolutely adored her daughter.

I said this to Rivka when we were alone up in the amazing frilly bedroom.

'Maybe,' Rivka said, 'but what's the use if it's only a suffocating kind of love. I'd prefer not to be loved at all.'

We got through the first days without too many problems. Mrs Fine wanted to know did my mom keep a kosher kitchen. So I said she did and I even heard myself describing the synagogue that the Jacobs family went to when they went up to

Dublin, not that I had ever been inside it. I had to excise from my conversation the fact that I taught with nuns in St Ita's convent and make the school into a secondary school for the small but active mythical Jewish community in Rossmore. In fact there were only three Jewish families in Rossmore, but no need to burden Mrs Fine with this.

They were pleased with me, and they were happy that I, like their Rivka, lived with my parents at home. They thought it was fast for young girls to live in apartments, they said.

Young girls! – Rivka and I sighed to each other when we were on our own. As if we were young! Pathetic old maids, nearly a quarter of a century on this earth and no sign of a husband or even a fiancé.

When they addressed me as Malka or called out that name, I feared that I never responded quite quickly enough, but Rivka told me I was doing so well, and she apologised again for what was even in those days a totally ludicrous farce.

And then it was time to go and I took a long, tiring train journey to the summer camp where I was called Maureen again, not Malka, which I had begun to get accustomed to. It was all much more sporty than I had thought, lots of hikes and field trips with the kids and baseball, and endless consoling of girls who thought their mothers hated them because they had been sent away for the summer.

'Mothers don't hate us,' I explained over and over. 'They just think they are doing the best for us. It's always wrong, but honestly they don't know that.' I think I mended a few fractured relationships and calmed down a few troubled hearts but then teachers are always thinking they do that anyway. Maybe they didn't take a blind bit of notice.

And I was doing it by mail too.

Rivka wrote constantly to say that her mother had really admired me and it was Malka this and Malka that since I had left. Malka had such a sunny disposition and Malka never ate between meals and was interested in all the people who lived near by instead of dismissing them like Rivka did.

I wrote back saying that I had decided life was mainly an act. There was I, a complete fake, passing myself off as a member of their community. They had been taken in. There was a lesson there somewhere. We must put on a show for people, pretend that we were calmer, happier, more in control than we really were.

Rivka wrote back to say that she had thought about this a great deal and that I might indeed have found the Secret of the Universe.

And about a week later, when our camp was playing a series of games against another camp, I met Declan who was a teacher from a small country place a few miles outside Rossmore and we fell madly in love.

So much so that he said he wanted to come and meet my parents the moment we got back to Ireland. And even though he wasn't a doctor or a lawyer, only a teacher like myself, he was everything my mam wanted: a Catholic, from a nice family, and had really good manners.

By Christmas he said he wanted to marry me.

I wasn't too sure about wanting to go and live in the wilds of the country and maybe getting absorbed into his huge family network; but they were all very welcoming and in those days no self-respecting man made any lifestyle changes for a wife or anything.

So that's what I did – marry him and go to live in the wilds of the country. I kept Rivka informed every step of the way and, as luck would have it, she had met Max who was not exactly a dentist but was a very successful businessman who owned travel agencies, and *her* mother was utterly delighted with him, and *she* would be getting married too. So she came to my wedding in Ireland first and it was lovely to have her, and my mother was so excited about what she would wear and the fact that Declan had

an uncle who was a judge coming to the wedding that she managed not to interrogate Rivka about her odd name, and didn't
even notice that Rivka's mother had sent a wedding gift addressed to 'Dear Malka'.

Rivka got everything wrong in Rossmore. She kept calling the
statue in the church the Holy Heart instead of the Sacred Heart.
She was astounded by the length of the nuptial Mass and the
papal blessing, and the fact that a lot of the women wore head-
scarves and mantillas on their heads during the ceremony rather
than splashing out on hats.

She couldn't take in the amount of drink served at the wedding, and the number of people who had songs that they insisted
on singing . . .

But it was all a great occasion and Declan kept squeezing my
hand and I had never believed I could be so happy.

Declan and I went to Spain for two weeks for a honeymoon
and then came back to live in his part of the world, which was a
sort of mountainy place where nothing much happened. Because
I was a married woman I couldn't teach any more so time hung
heavy on me. Days seemed very much the same except that we
went to lunch with his mother every Sunday and his sisters called
around every week to enquire whether or not I was pregnant.

My letters from Rivka were a lifeline in this odd backwater.
She told me what books to read, she suggested that I set up a
kind of amateur mobile library and drive around to people who
were housebound. And everyone liked my doing that. Declan
went so far as to say that I was inspired.

But he wouldn't come to Rivka's wedding with me. It was too
far, too expensive, he wouldn't know where to put himself with
all these Jewish people and their customs. No, really he wanted
to pass on this one. Well, you know when you're not going to
win. I cheered myself up, I told myself that if I were to be Malka
there again it would be easier to be without Declan. And indeed
it was.

It was all so different – the canopy in the Fines' huge garden and the singing and chanting in Hebrew, and the smashing a glass which was something to do with the destruction of the Temple or something, but I couldn't really ask, what with my being Malka and meant to know all this already.

Max was very cheerful and friendly and whispered to me that he knew my little secret. I had no idea what he was talking about. Did he know that I had gone to a doctor in Dublin to get the contraceptive pill because I didn't want to get pregnant until I had the library up and running? Did he know that I found Declan's mother and three bossy sisters a hundred times worse than my own mother had ever been and that I went to huge lengths to avoid meeting them?

No, it turned out that he knew I wasn't really Malka, that I wasn't even a little bit Jewish.

'Rivka and I have no secrets, never will,' he said.

And for some reason I felt a bit uneasy. Which was ludicrous, of course. Why should I be uneasy about Max? He was gentle and kind, he loved Rivka. In fact he was a pussycat.

Rivka and I still wrote to each other. For a while. Then she began to call me from the office from time to time. She said it was easier, more immediate, one to one. Well, it was, of course, but it was also much more expensive. I mean, there was no way I could afford transatlantic calls. But Rivka said it didn't matter, she could call free from her office where she was manager. She didn't mind that I wasn't able to make calls from my end.

I missed our long rambling letters, but it wasn't that she was keeping anything from me, she told me every heartbeat of what seemed to be an exhausting life. Rivka seemed to be permanently on some crucifying diet. She was always wasting a long-distance call telling me about some big benefit night that was coming up and she had to drop twelve pounds in fourteen days to get into a dress. She said she was always tired these days.

And I told her how horrific Declan's sisters were and that I should be canonised in my own lifetime for not telling him what a trio of mad bats they were.

'Will you?' she asked with interest.

'Will I what?' I said.

'Be canonised in your own lifetime?' Rivka asked. She must have been *very* tired. Even Jewish people should know that was a joke and that you can't be made a saint until you're dead.

And then we both had a crisis at the same time.

Rivka's wasn't that big a crisis as it happens, she was just desperately tired at some travel conference they went to in Mexico and fell asleep when everyone thought she was getting dressed for the awards banquet where they were giving Max a lifetime achievement award, and she had to be woken up and arrived flustered and looking terrible. And it was somehow an insult to Max, and to the travel industry, and to Mexico. God, you'd think the Third World War had begun.

Compared to what had happened to me it was nothing. *Zilch, nada*, as they say in Mexico.

My beautiful sister-in-law felt that she had to tell Declan what she found in our medicine cupboard in the bathroom where she just *happened* to be looking. Poor Declan wouldn't have known that these pills I was taking were *abortifacient*. That was her word: they prevented conception and killed the incipient baby. They wouldn't tell their mother – she would be too shocked, she might not survive hearing the information. Declan was very upset and said I had been holding out on him. I said my fertility was *my* business and he said, no, it was *our* business and he should have been consulted, and what kind of fairness and equality in marriage and the future did we have if I behaved in this secretive way?

And there was a bit of me that agreed that he had a point, but sadly I didn't say that: I said instead that his sisters were a pack of interfering hyenas and that I hated them with a passion almost equal to that which I felt against his mother. This was not a sensible or good thing to say, and things were very cool between us for a long time. The sisters smirked all over the place. I threw the pills into the fire but Declan said he didn't want to force a child on me so we didn't have sex and the sisters seemed to guess this and smirked even more.

So I spent more and more time driving the mobile library up into the mountains, and Declan spent more and more time talking about hurling and firing pints into himself down in Callaghan's with that awful fellow Skunk Slattery, and to be honest times weren't great at all.

And I tried to tell Rivka about all this, but she thought with some reason that Declan's sisters were from the funny farm and even though she tried to understand she just didn't.

And I tried hard to understand why Rivka simply had to go to all these functions when she was so tired. It was a rulebook that I had somehow missed, and I knew she wanted to explain it but there weren't any words.

When we talked on the telephone I just kept on advising her. 'Tell him you're really tired.'

And she kept advising me.

'Tell him you're really sorry.'

Eventually Declan came back to our bed. It wasn't the same as before but it was less lonely and the atmosphere wasn't hanging around the house any more. Meanwhile Rivka found some marvellous vitamin supplement that gave her more energy, and amazingly we both got pregnant at the same time.

They had a girl called Lida, after Max's mother, and I hoped we would have a girl too and we would call her Ruth and that she and Lida would be friends for ever. Declan said it was a bit far-fetched as an idea, and anyway he'd prefer a son who would play hurling for the county.

Brendan, named after Declan's father, was born two weeks after Lida, and now that Rivka wasn't in the office any more she and I began to write to each other again about labour pains, about breastfeeding, about disturbed nights, about tiny fingers and toes. We seemed in a veiled way to be telling each other that life wasn't quite as good as we had hoped it might be.

But we never said that. Why would we say such a thing? We had our children.

I suppose I *should* have noticed how late Declan came home at night and how he wasn't drunk, which he ought to have been if he had spent four hours in Callaghan's, and I *should* have noticed that Skunk Slattery often asked me how Declan was, which was odd since he was meant to be drinking every night with him, but I didn't because I was so taken up with little Brendan who was an angel. I spent busy days putting toddler Brendan into the mobile library van and driving him round to meet all the readers in small villages and to be admired. I was also concentrating very hard on keeping him well away from his awful aunts.

The months went on and on. We still went to see Declan's mother every Sunday, each of us bringing a dish as she became more frail. It made her happy to see all her children around her, so I went along with it. Rivka often sent me recipes from America. When Declan's mother eventually died it was very peaceful and she sort of slipped away.

On the evening after her funeral Declan told me in a very calm voice that of course I must know he was seeing someone else. Her name was Eileen, she was the school secretary and they were going to England at the end of term. Brendan was seven then. Quite old enough to come and visit his dad regularly, Declan said casually. And he added reassuringly that Eileen would be like a second mother to Brendan.

I looked at Declan as if I had never seen him before. It felt very unreal, like fainting or the sort of shock you get if you bang your head suddenly. I said that Brendan and I had to go to Dublin on the train the next day and we could talk about the visits and everything when I came back. I had put Brendan on my passport two years ago when I thought we might be going to America to see Rivka and Lida, but Max had something on that time and we couldn't go.

I left a note for Declan saying that I had taken enough money from our bank account to go to New York and for a little spending money when we were there; he could make the arrangements about the house and telling people about the situation. He wasn't to think I was taking his child away for ever, I would be back.

No need to call Interpol.

I didn't mention what a rat he was, how upset I was, or even a word about the lovely Eileen.

Rivka had said she would be delighted to see me.

'What about Max?' I asked fearfully.

'He's hardly ever at home, he won't notice if you are there or not,' she said.

We cried in each other's arms when we met, big heaving sobs. It was the first time I had cried since the night that Declan had told me. I wept for all that there might have been. But no, I wouldn't take him back now even if he were to beg me. Possibly he was right, it was over, long over.

The two seven-year-olds played happily with Lida's toys. My blond boy and her beautiful little girl with the dark ringlets. We gave each other advice as we had always done: Rivka said I must get him to sell the house, and I should move. My father was dead now, Rivka said I should live with my mother.

'But I can't go back to her house, I spent so long trying to get out of it,' I heard myself bleating.

'Well, you can't stay *there* in that place way out of Rossmore, with all the sisters, and the dreadful Eileen, and the whole place talking about you. This is the time for courage, Malka, up and out. Go back to Ireland, you could even move to Dublin, and take your mother, find a place of your own. Start again.'

Yes, it was all very well for her, Americans are accustomed to doing that, new frontiers and covered wagons, but not in Ireland. Living with my mam and all the I-told-you-sos? Not really.

I advised *her* to throw in the job at the office, which was cutting across her busy social life, and to go into the travel business like Max, build up an aspect of the holiday business that he hadn't yet done. Let her mother help more in looking after Lida. Her marriage wasn't over yet but it could be, the way she was going.

Of course she resisted that terribly too but we laughed over it.

As the days went on, I felt stronger and better than I had for years. Brendan loved it all there.

'Why do they all call you Malka out there, Mammy?' he asked on the plane coming home.

'It's American for Maureen,' I explained.

And he was perfectly satisfied. As he was when we moved to Dublin, and when my mam turned out to be miles better than we all thought, and never said I told you so once.

I got a job teaching in a school where I set up a real library and Brendan grew up big and strong. I did make sure he went from time to time to see his dad in England, and learned with some pleasure that Eileen was very sharp-tempered and told Declan that he drank too much, and then the Principal of the school told him he drank too much.

I wrote to Rivka every week, and then she got a fax machine, which was quicker still.

And finally e-mail.

She was in Europe four times a year now because she ran an art tours section of Max's business and brought people to galleries and exhibitions. They included Ireland in the itinerary so that Rivka could come and see me. Well, there *were* nice art things to visit too, I suppose.

Rivka talked less and less about Max and more and more about Lida. Max went to a lot of business meetings and came home only rarely. We didn't *think* he had another woman but we agreed that he had lost interest in Rivka. Somehow it didn't really matter all that much, any more than Eileen with her sharp temper mattered, nor the fact that Declan had been sacked from his job in England and was back in his place outside Rossmore, helping out his brothers-in-law where he earned so little that he had to ask Eileen for drinking money to go to Callaghan's every night. But Lida mattered to us and Brendan mattered to us.

They were our future.

When Lida was seventeen she came to me for a holiday in Dublin. She wanted to be away from her mother for a bit and, well, Rivka and I understood *that*. We could write the textbook on that sort of thing.

She said that her mother and father hadn't slept in the same room for as long as she could remember; she wondered whether that was natural? Normal?

I said I hadn't a clue about America, it was probably different there. And that maybe it was all for the best anyway. I had slept in the same bed as my husband for years and it hadn't done me all that bit of good since he left me for another woman.

She was very sympathetic. She sat and stroked my hand. She said men were hard to fathom. That a man had said to her she was frigid when she wouldn't have sex with him. Then he had said she was queer like her father. She hadn't said it to anyone.

I told her she was right, best to forget it, the guy was obviously just mad to have sex with her and was flailing around because she wouldn't.

We kept in touch over the years, but she never mentioned it again and neither did I.

Now Lida was in her twenties and headstrong, dark and beautiful. She had studied law. And then this summer she announced that she was going to Greece for two months before she settled down in a big law firm. Nothing her mother said would make her go to Israel. Oh no, she objected to this about the place and that.

Rivka and I were very disappointed.

My Brendan was also in his twenties: fair-haired, leisurely and, I thought, very handsome.

He was almost qualified as an engineer but before his career began properly he would take a long holiday in Italy.

How Rivka and I would have liked them to go to the Negev desert, to 'our' kibbutz. They could have checked whether the gladioli farm had ever come to anything and what kind of women Shimon and Dov had married in the end. They could have fallen in love with each other, Brendan and Lida, against the romantic backdrop of those red cliffs and valleys. They would marry and give us three grandchildren, which Rivka and I could share. The young couple and their family would live six months of the year in America and six months in Ireland.

Well, stranger things have happened, you know. Like both our own mothers turning out to be quite reasonable in late middle age, people you could talk to, not automatically lie to. That had never been on the cards.

And though we sometimes sighed wistfully when we heard the radio play tunes for couples whose thirtieth wedding anniversary it was or saw a big celebration in a hotel, mainly we were fairly contented with the way things had turned out for us.

We were fiftyish, trimmer and better dressed than when we were twenty-five and not too bad looking. If we were to put ourselves out in the marriage market again we might not do too badly. But we didn't need to, we each had jobs we enjoyed, we each had a child we adored and for decades we had shared a friendship with no secrets, no disguises, and the wisdom to know that such a great friendship was rare.

I remember reading once that your enjoyment of something doubled if you realised how lucky you were to have it. If everyone had a huge diamond on their fingers, or if sunsets were universally scarlet and gold, then we wouldn't value them at all. It was like that with us.

Part 2 – Rivka

I sometimes give little talks, nothing too demanding, but you know the kind of thing – either for charity or to get publicity for Max's company. Or both, even. Anyway I have learned over the years that there are two subjects that never fail to hold an audience. One is how to drop five pounds painlessly before your vacation, and the other is the positive power of friendship.

The five pounds one is easy, it's got to do with having exotic fruits for breakfast and supper, mangoes, papayas and the like. And small portions of grilled fish or chicken for lunch. I sort of intersperse it with funny stories about times things went wrong, and I ate a box of chocolate chip cookies or a tub of ice cream. They love that.

But they love even more my stories about my great friend Malka. I call her that, even though her real name is Maureen. I tell them how we met on a kibbutz and remained friends for a lifetime, and how love could come and go but friendship survived. That friendship was *better* than love in a way, it was more generous. You didn't object if your friend had other friends, you even encouraged it. But you did object violently to your love having other loves and did everything possible to discourage it.

I could see the audience nodding in recognition.

I always smiled when I talked about Malka.

We had great times together after that chance meeting on a kibbutz. My mom thought she was a nice Jewish girl and didn't realise that she came from a town of mad Catholics who all worshipped some well in the middle of the woods. I mean, if you only *saw* it. Cherish friendship, I advised them, and then I gave them the hard sell about going on vacation with a friend rather than a spouse.

If your spouse didn't want to visit art exhibits, go shopping, and sit in a piazza or a square watching strangers and making up stories about them – your girlfriend would.

When I started working for his family firm, Max always admired the way I built up this side of the business: the art tours, the painting classes and the ladies' bridge clubs or reading groups. But he admired this and indeed admired me very distantly and objectively.

You see, looking back on it all, Max never really loved me, not *loved* as people write about and sing about and dream about. I never thought that he loved anyone else. I told myself that possibly he didn't have a high sex-drive, not like Malka's husband sure did over in Ireland. No, I am sure that he didn't love anyone else, he just thought of what we had as a sort of business partnership. That's the way he was made.

For a while I thought that if I tried harder, dressed better, got thinner, developed more sparkle, he would grow to love me. But oddly it was my friend Malka who convinced me that this was not really the way it worked. Otherwise all thin, groomed, sparkly people would be very happy and we all knew – because we saw them all round us – that most of them were totally miserable.

And Malka told me I was a scream, and as bright as a button, and sharp as a tack, and a dozen other insane Irish phrases, and I started believing it all and became unreasonably confident about almost everything. And I was happy, most of the time, when I look back on it.

I wasn't happy in those years when my mom was on my case screeching at me about getting married. And there was that time when I was wearing myself out, eating nothing and putting in a ten-hour day at the office followed by social functions: I wasn't happy then.

But when Lida was born, my beautiful, beautiful daughter, I was happy then and never stopped being happy. And I had a notebook where I wrote down all the things my mom had done to irritate me and break my heart, and I tried not to do any of them myself.

But the world had changed.

Imagine my asking Lida to consider her marriage options before she lost her looks.

I mean, *imagine* it! It would be like living on a different planet.

And oddly, my mom had changed around that time too, she became normal and knew a lot of the world's wisdom. She certainly had not been normal or wise when I was young and could have done with it, still it was nice that she had discovered it in later life.

Malka said the same thing about her mother too, that she had calmed down since she had a grandchild. But I had never thought that Mrs O'Brien was all that bad. Very superstitious, of course, and caring about what other people in Rossmore thought or would say, like all people of her age. But basically a nice person.

Yet Malka said Mrs O'Brien had been quite horrific when she was younger, so I guess that generation just improved with age.

Malka's little boy Brendan was a darling, which was just as well since her husband turned out to be a lot less than we had all hoped he would be. I loved it when she brought Brendan over to stay with me for a few weeks that time, the time that Declan, the roving husband, had roved off with Eileen the school secretary. Malka was very depressed when she arrived first, she cried a lot. She said she hadn't cried back home – she wouldn't give her sisters-in-law nor her own mother the satisfaction of seeing her down. But she cried in my kitchen, and in my garden as we watched our children playing in the pool, and she cried when we went out to a piano bar one evening, she and I, and the pianist played 'Blue Moon', which had been their song, hers and Declan's.

'I never thought he'd fancy another woman,' she wept. 'He always said I was the only one. I thought that if I ever lost him it would be to the drink, I believed it was a battle between Callaghan's licensed premises and myself for his attention.'

I patted her hand in the piano bar, and passed her tissues. This was not the time to tell Malka that her intended had tried to jump me for three evenings before their wedding.

If I hadn't told her back then just on the eve of her wedding day when it might have been helpful, useful, wise, then there was no point in telling her any time afterwards.

I had told myself that maybe it was just high spirits. I didn't know these people and their culture, did I? Maybe for him and his friends it was just meaningless to press me, the bride's best friend, up to a wall in a grip I couldn't get out of and to kiss me. So I either spoke then and ruined her wedding and our friendship, or I shut up.

You might have done it differently but I made my choice and was stuck with it.

And I always told myself that if I had said anything that time, then maybe Brendan would not exist and her life would have been greatly the less.

Brendan has been a fine son for her – won't listen to advice, of course, but then what young person does listen these days? He was never any trouble to her, all that time he grew up in Dublin, with his father away from home. He always got himself a holiday job to help to pay his tuition fees. One summer Max gave him a position in one of the travel agencies and he worked so hard they were prepared to offer him a full-time post. But I said, no way, imagine if my friend Malka were to be deprived of saying, 'My son the engineer'!

Unfortunately he didn't get to know my Lida that summer; she was in Ireland of all places. She and Malka had loved each other from the word go, but then I knew they would so that didn't surprise me a bit. And I liked her Brendan too, very much, when he came to stay here at weekends. He was easy and relaxed and had no hang-ups about his father.

'Dad was over-interested in women always, one was never **enough for him,' Brendan told me. 'I think he felt he had to try** it on with everyone to prove he was alive or something.'

I nodded in agreement, he had it right. That's exactly what Declan was doing, proving something.

'And are you the same?' I asked. Sort of joking.

Apparently not, it's like the children of a wino being teetotal. Brendan told me that his mates said someone would have to light a fire under him to get him going.

'I expect my father made a pass at you, Rivka?' he said.

'Way back, it wasn't important,' I heard myself say.

'Did you tell my mam? You know, later, when they split?' he asked.

'No,' I told him. 'As I said, it didn't seem important.'

He nodded approvingly.

It was the only secret we had, Malka and I, that's a fact. We told each other everything. I don't think she had any secrets from me. I don't think so, but then if she were to be asked had I kept anything back, she would have said no.

And what could she have known or experienced that she couldn't tell me? Max certainly never leaped at Malka like her husband-to-be had leaped on me. Max has a low libido, that's what my mom says to explain his long absences. It might be true. She says I should be grateful. I suppose that tells me more about her life with Father than I want to know.

It was never great sex with Max by my reckoning but I realise that he felt that it was never great with me.

Malka always said that she had loved it with Declan but had always been nervous in case she got pregnant. His sisters had five children each and these were regarded as *small* families.

Malka was the only person I ever talked to about sex and not very often. When you think of wars starting over sex, and murders being committed, and people breaking up families and getting publicly disgraced, it's really very hard to understand.

Lida, I gather, has had plenty of sex so far in her young life. She told me a long time ago that she went to a women's clinic to get herself sorted out. When I imagine myself saying that sort of thing to my own mom, well, I almost feel faint. But times change.

And who would have thought that I, Rivka Fine-Levy, would have my own specialist art tours agency and be highly thought of as the wife of the great Max Levy. Unlike so many women I knew, I never had a day's worry about Max being unfaithful to me, I just sort of knew. It was the way he was with women, not interested, not like Declan who was always up for it, as even his own son recognised.

Who would have known that I would become someone who loved my mom instead of hated her, and that I would really enjoy going shopping with her? That I would love my own daughter more than life; that I would still remain such a friend of Malka whom I had met plucking chickens all those years ago when she was going to convert to Judaism, marry Shimon and run a gladioli farm? The time when I was too timid to let that Algerian boy, Dov, get to first base.

I do wish Lida had gone to Israel, but of course there was no point in mentioning it.

She was proud of Israel, she explained, but she disapproved of something or other they were doing out there at the moment and she wouldn't lend support by visiting.

Lida was like that, taking stands, concerned about issues, standing up and being counted.

Very laudable, admirable even. But it didn't always make for an easy life.

Max was hardly ever there to discuss it with. If I tried he just kept repeating that he was astounded to have a daughter at all, which wasn't much of a help, and a bit repetitive.

After nearly a quarter of a century you'd think he might have got used to the fact by now.

So this summer I planned a little trip for Malka and myself. We would go for a week to Florence and a week by the sea in Sicily to recover from all the sightseeing and the pounding round art galleries. It was so odd to think that our two children would be also on the Mediterranean, swimming in the same sea. But we knew we must make no plans to meet them, nothing claustrophobic that would make them resent us. We had been through enough of that in the old days when *our* mothers were bad, suffocating people. We knew all about the long rein and letting them be free. Don't let them know you miss them.

I was so busy getting ready for the trip, I really didn't miss Lida. I can pack two cases very quickly and scientifically now. Another of my talks on the breakfast or ladies' lunch circuit is 'intelligent packing'. People just love it.

I tell them about having the typed master list and adding items like a small torch, your own favourite pillowcase, and a little wooden wedge to keep doors open – you won't believe how useful that is.

Anyway, out of a clear blue sky when I was folding the dresses between sheets of tissue paper, this young man called to the house, about thirty-something. I wondered if he had called for Lida. But no, he was looking for Max.

Max was away, coming back tonight, I said. I was leaving for Europe next day, we would be having a rare dinner at home together – I could give him a message. What name would I say?

The man said I was to tell him that Alexander had called by, and that he was very sorry, he thought I was leaving for Florence today, not tomorrow. He knew I was going to Florence this week and yet I had never even heard of him. I felt alarmed somehow. He refused tea, gave no details of what his business was with Max, then left very quickly.

'Alexander came today,' I said to Max that evening. 'He thought I would already have left for Florence.'

Max looked at me levelly.

'I'm so very sorry you had to find out this way,' he said.

I had no idea what I had found out. None at all, as Malka would say. I looked at him blankly.

'About Alexander,' he said.

And then suddenly it was all clear. Everything made sense. The long absences, the discretion, the way I was worn on Max's arm for public occasions, the separate bedrooms.

Malka asked me afterwards, did I behave well, did I react as I would like to have done.

The answer is yes, I behaved perfectly out of sheer shock. I sat wide awake in my bedroom all night piecing things together. Of course that was the explanation. Why had I been so blind? But it's not something you'd expect.

Then I'm afraid I began to worry whether everyone else knew. Was I the only fool who didn't realise that my husband played for the other team? And as the clock ticked on and dawn came to the sky, I decided that it was *not* generally known, that I was *not* a laughing stock. And that helped. Perhaps it shouldn't have but it did. At least I wasn't a public fool.

I dressed carefully and did my face. My car was coming to pick me up at 10 a.m.

Max looked terrible, white faced and unkempt. He hadn't slept either. He looked at me like a puppy that knows it's going to be punished.

'What will you do?' he asked fearfully.

'I'll tell you my plans when I get back, Max.' I was cool, polite and slightly distant.

I left everything else, the weeping, the railing, the questioning, the rage, until I got to Florence, and to Malka.

She knew at once. You can't fool Malka. She poured some duty-free and I told her everything, left nothing out. I can't remember anything that we did on that holiday that didn't involve both of us bawling, crying, deciding to kill Max, to sue him, to take him for everything that he had. We were going to 'out' him, make him look ridiculous, or we were going to be noble and say it didn't matter.

By the time we got to Sicily we were completely exhausted.

We rented a car and drove around the island. We swam in the bright blue sea, we drank more wine than I had ever thought possible.

'I'll have to go into detox when I get back to real life,' I said, not really wanting to think about getting back.

'Shouldn't you contact your office?' Malka suggested.

Normally I'm on my cellphone and picking up e-mails everywhere. The office was, of course and irritatingly, surviving fine without me.

There was an e-mail from Lida:

'Dad says he doesn't know where you are in Italy, your office says you'll call in but you haven't, so it's not my fault. I tried to find you everywhere to tell you my plans have changed and I am going to Israel after all. I met Brendan in Rome. We always planned to meet there, we've been in touch with each other for the past two years and meet a lot. We didn't tell you and Malka because you'd fuss so much, and we wanted to be sure before we said anything. And now we are. Very sure.

'And he asks me for you to tell his mom, because apparently she is hopeless about technology and expects a pigeon to come in carrying a letter. And there is to be none of this nonsense about culture and tradition and history and differences and all that kind of shit. You are to square it with Grandmother and Dad. You will, won't you? You've always been terrific about everything. Brendan says the same about his mom. Can you tell us where this bloody gladioli farm is and we'll go look for it and examine these guys who could have been our fathers if things had been different.'

Malka and I know the letter off by heart. Well, you would, wouldn't you? A letter that turned everything round and made sense of it all.

CHAPTER 5

The Plan

Part 1 – Becca

Mother was always saying to me, 'Becca, you could do simply anything in this world if you had a proper plan.' She would say this as we walked down Castle Street doing the shopping together or waited for the sheets and towels to dry at the Fresh as a Daisy Launderette or had coffee in the Jumping Bean.

Mother did have lots of plans as life went on. Like when I was twenty-one and Father wouldn't hear of paying for a big party, Mother developed a plan. She went to the new hotel that had just opened in Rossmore and showed them our guest list with lots of very important people on it. She insisted to the manager that they should give her half-price because of all the introductions she was giving them over her daughter Becca's party. And she eked this bit of money out of Father and that bit. And there you were. A stunning twenty-first with just *everyone* there! Just because she had a plan.

Dear Mother was so right about lots of things. Well, not always entirely right about Father, of course. But then, how could anyone have known what he was going to do? You'd need to have been some kind of mystic to have known. Father went off with Iris, this perfectly awful, common woman, when I was twenty-five and Mother was fast approaching fifty. The awful woman Iris wasn't even young. She was a woman who wore a cardigan and walked through the Whitethorn Woods with a mongrel dog. Mother said it wouldn't have been quite so bad if she had been a silly young girl with a huge bosom. But no, she was the same age as all of them. Humiliating.

I foolishly suggested to Mother that she might go to St Ann's Well, a lot of people got their wishes answered there. She was horrified at the very thought of it. Ludicrous place, pagan super-stition, a place maids and women from cottages went. I wasn't even to mention it again.

Mother said that if she had the energy, she would kill Iris.

I had begged her not to. 'Please, Mother, don't kill Iris. You'll get caught, and arrested, and go to jail.'

'Not if I did it properly,' Mother said.

'But you wouldn't do it properly, Mother, and suppose for a moment that you did, imagine how terrible it would be if Father were to pine over this Iris. Think how terrible that would be.'

Grudgingly Mother agreed. 'If I were younger and could make a proper plan, then I could easily have killed Iris,' she said calmly. 'But Becca darling, I should have started much earlier and it would all have been fine. I think you are right and that I'd probably be wiser to leave it now.'

Mercifully she did.

Father didn't really stay in touch. He wrote from time to time to say that Mother was bleeding him dry. Mother said that he and that terrifying Iris had taken every penny she was entitled to – all she had left was the falling-down house in Rossmore. She sighed and sighed, and said that to hire yet another lawyer on top of Myles Barry was like throwing good money after bad.

'When you grow older, Becca darling, I beg you to have a plan. Do nothing without a plan, and do it sooner rather than later.'

And it always seemed a very good idea because everything

Mother did later, having waited around, had gone belly up, while all the things that had been done sooner had been fine. She must have been right about striking when the iron was hot.

So I tried to have a plan about most things. I worked in Rossmore's new fashion boutique that catered for rich clients and I planned to get to know these people socially. Sometimes it worked, sometimes it didn't. I also made a friend of Kevin the van driver, who drove a taxicab on the side, and he often gave me lifts to places – which was nice because I was fairly broke and I wouldn't have had money for taxis.

Kevin was nice. He had a terrible cough and he was a frightful hypochondriac, always thinking that a headache was meningitis, that sort of thing, but he was very fond of me and said that I could always ask him to come out and collect me on a wet night and he would. I never abused it but I did ask him from time to time.

Mother was in bad form a lot but to be very honest I didn't get too involved with Mother and her problems because there was so much going on in my own life. You see, I'd just met Franklin and everything changed then.

You know the way people find it impossible to describe some huge event in their life, like seeing a film star, or the Queen of England, or the Pope, or the President of the United States, or something earth-shaking? You can remember all kinds of unimportant details but not the thing itself.

It's as if it was too big to take in.

It was just like that when I met Franklin.

I remember the dress I was wearing: a red silk dress with a halter neck that I had got at a thrift shop. I remember the perfume I wore: it was Obsession by Calvin Klein. I couldn't afford it myself but amazingly a customer had left it behind her in the boutique.

I can't remember why I went to that particular party. It was to launch a new restaurant in Rossmore. The town was so big now and so different to the way it was when Mother was young. New restaurants, hotels, art galleries opening all the time. I hadn't been invited or anything but I knew that if you turned up looking well dressed they always let you in. So about two or three times a month I would show up at a party and mingle a little. It got me out from under Mother's feet and you never knew who you might meet.

Well, up to now I had only met a lot of frogs actually and was beginning to despair of meeting a prince at any of these dos and then that night I met Franklin. It was at 7.43 p.m. on the huge pink neon-lit clock. I had been thinking I might go home at eight. I wouldn't call Kevin tonight, there was a bus stop outside the door, and just then Franklin said hallo.

Blond, blue eyes, tousled hair, perfect teeth. He was startlingly good-looking. And so nice and easy. It began almost immediately between us. We discovered we had literally everything in common, just everything. We both loved Greece and Italy, we loved Thai food, and skiing, and re-runs of old movies on television. We liked big dogs, and tap dancing, and long brunches on a Sunday.

Mother had been going through a depressive stage at the time and she was very doubtful about my new romance.

'Everyone likes those things, Becca, you silly girl. Do stop getting your hopes up, darling, he's only stating the obvious. Imagine anyone not liking Italy, or *Sergeant Bilko*, or *Dad's Army*, or skiing! Be sensible, darling. Please!'

Then she met Franklin and like everyone else she was bowled over.

He was charming to her. She loved everything that he said.

'I see where Becca gets her wonderful cheekbones.' 'You must be fearfully intelligent to play bridge so well.' 'You *must* let me call you Gabrielle, you're much too young for me to call you "Mrs King".'

Now if I had been cynical, I could have said that it was just a line, he knew what to say to older ladies. But I'm not cynical – I'm sunny and optimistic and I said nothing. Just smiled.

And because Franklin, the poor lamb, had nowhere proper to stay at the moment, he came to stay with us. There was a fiction for a while that he stayed in the guest room, but actually we soon needed the spare room for all his gear so he moved into mine.

Franklin didn't have a job, not as such, but he and another man called Wilfred, a friend of his, were developing an idea, a concept. They were going into business together. It had to do with mobile phones and was very hard to explain and, indeed, to understand. But Franklin and Wilfred were like two bright schoolboys with a project. Their enthusiasm carried them along.

Mother said to me many times that I should have a plan to keep him because treasures like Franklin didn't come along every day of the week. I should be more domestic for one thing, and cook for him. Also I should dress up more, borrow clothes from the boutique, get them dry-cleaned and give them back. Show him what an asset I was and could be in life.

We were all so happy together. Mother taught us all, Franklin and Wilfred and me, how to play bridge, and then I would make us a supper. It was a wonderful four months.

Franklin and I had a terrific understanding. We were both twenty-nine years old so, naturally, we had a bit of a past but we had never ever loved anyone else in the past, not one tenth as much as we loved each other. And if for any reason our love began to diminish or we met someone else, there would be no deceit, no lies. We would tell each other straight out. We pealed with laughter at the very idea! It was so unlikely that it would ever happen.

Then one evening Franklin told me that he had met this girl called Janice and that they had feelings for each other, so true to our promise and our understanding he was telling me immediately. He smiled at me his heartbreaking smile.

He had a look on his face as if he should somehow be *praised* for telling me about this damn Janice. As if his honesty and trustworthiness had somehow been proved. I gritted my teeth and forced a smile on to my face. There was an ache at my cheekbones, so like my mother's cheekbones apparently.

'Maybe you only think you have feelings for her,' I said. 'Possibly, when you get to know her, you'll find it's quite different.' I admired myself so much for staying so calm.

But then he explained that he did know. He was very sure.

'Shouldn't you wait till you've slept with her to be sure?' I was so proud of how I was handling this.

'Oh, I have,' he said.

'That wasn't exactly part of our understanding, having sex before telling each other, was it?' I hoped my voice didn't sound quite as steely outside as it did from within.

'But you weren't there, I couldn't ask you,' he said, as if it was the most reasonable thing in the world.

'Wasn't where exactly?' I asked.

'In the hotel. Wilfred and I were there meeting some investors and there happened to be a bridge session on, so we joined it and that's where I met Janice.'

I realised that my own mother had delivered the weapon of destruction herself. Why couldn't she have left Franklin ignorant of how to play bridge? If she had, then he would never have met this Janice. Our lives would have been perfect.

But I knew that I must have a plan. And that until I had one I must remain calm.

'Well, if that's the way it is, that's it, Franklin,' I said with a huge smile. 'And I truly hope that you and Janice will be very happy together.'

'You are marvellous!' he cried. 'You know, I told Janice that you and I had this understanding but she said you'd never honour it. I knew you would, that we both would. So I was right.' He stood, beaming at me, delighted that his faith had been justified.

Was he insane? Could he not see what had happened to me – that the light had left my life? Did he not hear the sound that went click in my head and the rush like a great wind that seemed to be blowing all around me? Maybe it was shock. Or a break-down. Or the beginning of madness. I had never felt that way before, it was like you feel before you faint. As if the world was advancing and receding at me.

But I couldn't faint, I must not show any signs of weakness. This was a turning point in my life. Now I still had to work out the plan to get him back, he must have no idea how my world was crashing down around me.

I told Franklin I had to rush, there was a late-night crisis at the boutique and that I simply had to leave. I wished him every happiness with this Janice and I fled. I hadn't smoked for five years but I bought a packet of cigarettes. Then I let myself into the boutique and sat down at a table and cried and cried.

Kevin was there. Always a heavy smoker, he joined me at the table and patted my hand.

Before I could tell him what was wrong he started to tell me his troubles.

'I'm not in great form myself, Becca,' he said and I noticed that his face was haggard and gaunt.

'What's wrong, Kevin?' I asked politely even though I couldn't have given a damn.

Something wrong with the van probably, not much work in the cab business, only two numbers off winning the Lotto – who cared? Who gave a blind damn about it, when Franklin was leaving me for Janice and the world was coming to an end?

'I've got really bad cancer, Becca. No point in operating, they say. I've got two months at the most.'

'Oh, Kevin, I'm so very sorry,' I said and I was. For thirty whole seconds I forgot Franklin and Janice and the plan. 'They're very good in hospitals nowadays,' I reassured him. 'They'll give you plenty of painkillers.'

'I'm not going to wait, Becca, I couldn't wake up every day wondering, is it going to happen today.'

'So what will you do?'

'I'll drive quickly in the van straight into a wall. Splat,' he said. 'Much quicker, no waiting, no worrying, no hanging about waiting for it to happen.'

And that's where I got my plan.

Suddenly my brain was working overtime – I felt I could cope with a hundred things at the same time. It was a daring mad plan. But it had a great deal going for it. It would solve everything in a stroke.

If he were going to kill himself, then he could take Janice with him.

If he were going to die anyway, and he was afraid of waiting, well then, why couldn't they both leave this life together?

I must be very, very clever, he must never know. He must not have an inkling what I was thinking.

'I think you're quite right, Kevin, that's just what I'd do if it were me. Well, it will be me one day, of course. And I'll do just that. Leave at my own time, not someone else's.'

He was completely surprised. He had expected me to beg him not to.

'But do you know what I think, Kevin? I think you should do it in a cab rather than your own van. Cabs are always crashing. It would look more natural when people investigate it, better for your life insurance policy. For your mother or whatever.'

'I see,' he said slowly. 'So they wouldn't pay up if they thought it was suicide?'

'Apparently not.'

'You're very good to be so interested, Becca, but what has *you* so upset?'

'Oh nothing, compared to your problems, nothing at all, Kevin, a silly quarrel with my mother, it will blow over.'

'But everything's all right with you and Franklin?' he asked.

I think Kevin was always a little bit in love with me. Not, of course, that I showed any sign of noticing that. But he must never know what Franklin had done.

I reassured him. 'Oh, Franklin and I are fine, not a cloud on the horizon,' I said. Just thinking that made me stop crying. Kevin gave me a tissue and I wiped my eyes. It was all going to be all right.

I could afford to spend time being kind to Kevin. 'Come on, Kevin, I'll take you out for a Chinese supper,' I said, and he looked so pathetically grateful.

'Won't Franklin mind?' he asked.

'Franklin lets me do what I want to do,' I said.

'If you were mine I'd be just the same,' Kevin said.

And we went and had a long and terribly depressing meal where he told me about his diagnosis and his wish to end it all. I nodded sympathetically and told him he was absolutely right. I didn't listen to one word of what he said. I sat there thinking about my plan. Kevin would do it for me. Kevin would see it through.

I would pretend to be enthusiastic about this awful Janice, I would become her friend.

Then I would give her Kevin's number as a reliable taxi driver. Of course Kevin naturally wouldn't want to take a perfectly innocent passenger with him, kill her, so to speak. So I'd have to tell him some story that Janice was also suffering from a terrible incurable disease and she had asked me to arrange a swift exit from the world. It was going to be a challenging role for me. It was if I had to write it and act it. But it had to be done. It was the perfect plan. No one would ever suspect me because I was going to be Ms Nice Guy, full of human kindness.

'I don't know what I'd do without you, Becca,' Kevin said to me a dozen times during the Chinese meal.

'And I don't know what I'd have done without you, Kevin,' I said to him truthfully.

97

Wilfred, who was Franklin's friend and business partner, was astounded by me.

'You're really full of surprises,' he said. 'I thought we'd have the full hell hath no fury bit – but I was totally wrong.'

I laughed a tinkling laugh. 'Franklin and I always had an understanding, Wilfred,' and as I saw him looking at me in awe, I gave him a smile that I hoped would break his heart as well as Franklin's.

My mother was astonished when I told her that there was no point whatsoever in trying to hold on to Franklin if he didn't want to be held. She shook her head in wonder and said that I had always been even more unbalanced than she was, so it was amazing to see me so rational.

I told Franklin that he must be in no hurry to move out. But that, of course, he would sleep in the guest room now that things were different. I went out a lot myself. Often with Kevin. It seemed only fair. But of course the real part of the plan was getting to know Janice.

The first blow was that she was only nineteen.

Then she wasn't interested in clothes, so I couldn't offer her cheap things from the boutique. She didn't care about cookery so I couldn't give her recipes. *How* was I to get to know her?

As so often in life, the solution was to be found in the game of bridge. I asked the loathsome Janice to do me a favour and be my bridge partner at a ladies' social evening for charity. Since I'd been so nice to her and so desperately decent about handing her Franklin without any grumbling, there was really nothing she could do but accept.

We got on fine that first night and several times she told me that she admired me and my generation for our attitude to love. Some day she hoped she would be as mature as that.

I resisted choking her to death at the bridge table with my own hands. After all, I had a much better plan.

We actually won the competition and agreed to play together

again the next week at another charity function at the Rossmore Hotel. In many ways she was a fairly pleasant companion. A university student with far too much money and time for her own good, but nice manners and, I have to say, a good bridge player. Very young and silly of course, like a niece or a neighbour's child.

And naturally I had a few pangs, a little remorse, a concern, I suppose you'd call it, about sending a nineteen-year-old girl to her death. I mean, I am human. Who wouldn't feel something? But then she had come between me and my one true love, there was no way he could be talked out of her or she of him.

It was this or nothing.

So on and on we played, Janice and I. We had been out together several times before I chose the night.

Franklin was talking about moving out of our home but I begged him to stay for a few more days. 'You can always go and spend nights with Janice,' I purred at him. 'But don't move all your gear yet.'

The plan would only work if he were still living with us when she died.

Kevin was very troublesome these days.

He was beginning to have second thoughts. He had become most concerned about taking another passenger with him. He thought he should discuss it with her first, ask her what preferences she had. Maybe she would like to be sedated before the crash, he suggested?

I said that I thought that she would very definitely not change her mind. As Kevin and I went through the details over and over again this was always his sticking point. Suppose she changed her mind at the last moment? He wouldn't be able to stop. It would be too late.

No, I said, this was definitely not going to happen. Again and again I explained that Janice had this terrible illness that was already beginning to take its toll, the pain would be unbearable. And in addition to this wasting disease she was developing a personality disorder. She had asked me to arrange it so that she wouldn't have to think about it or discuss it.

Well, he only wanted to do what was best, Kevin said. He really was such a kind and considerate man. Sometimes I allowed myself to think how much easier life would have been to love someone like that. But I didn't waste time going down that road of speculation. Since the incident when Franklin had told me about Janice I had become very focused.

Sometimes Kevin wondered was he right to take his own life. Was it his to take?

I dealt with that too. People preached about a loving God who understood everything. If this was so, then this God would understand that Kevin couldn't hang about and wait for what was inevitable. That he was just speeding things up. For everybody. Usually it worked after about ten or fifteen minutes but it was utterly exhausting.

During this time, Mother, Franklin, Wilfred, people at work and even poor Kevin himself told me I was not looking myself. Wild, somehow. Unhinged, Mother said. But I put on more make-up and smiled a nightmarish grin.

The big night eventually came, the date that would be the night of the accident. I had met Kevin earlier that day and reassured him that he was doing the right thing about himself, and that we were both doing the right thing about Janice. He turned up just as we had planned outside the door of the hotel where the charity bridge function was taking place.

'Oh, here's a taxi for you, Janice!' I said, sounding pleased.

'You are marvellous, Becca, everyone else is rushing about looking for them and you find one immediately.' She looked genuinely admiring.

Kevin got out of the driver's seat and came to open the passenger door. He and I gripped each other's hands.

Janice was going back to her flat where Franklin would join her later. He and Wilfred were out at yet another business meeting.

I said that I must run now as my bus was just coming and we were going in different directions anyway.

'Bye, lovely Becca,' Kevin said.

'See what I mean, Becca, everyone's mad about you,' Janice said enviously as she waved me goodbye.

And I went home and I talked to my mother for a long time and then went to bed. Franklin telephoned to know what time we had all left the bridge function because Janice wasn't back yet. I said I couldn't understand it, lots of people had seen her getting into a cab hours ago. And in the morning he telephoned again and said she hadn't come home all night.

I was so sympathetic but I had no idea what could have happened.

In the afternoon he rang to say that poor lovely little Janice had been killed and the taxi driver too, they had ploughed into a wall. Everyone was shocked. Franklin didn't move out because he was so shattered, and soon he began to love me again. The whole thing should have been perfect, it *would* have been perfect if it hadn't been for Kevin.

I was right.

He did love me.

And he had insured his life in my favour. I was going to get a small fortune. This of course destroyed the whole plan. No one would ever have connected it with me if it hadn't been for this policy.

That and the letter Kevin left thanking me for all I had done for him.

Now everyone was investigating it. Insurance people, police, everyone. And the whole of Rossmore is talking about me. They say that Janice's mother and sisters went up to that ridiculous well in the woods and a kind of procession went after them. As if that was going to bring her back!

People say I am as hard as nails. I never used to be, I was always as soft as a kitten.

Of course I may not get charged with anything. But Franklin is nervous of me. He didn't say so but he started to move all his things out last week.

It had been such a perfect plan – if only Kevin hadn't tried to be generous. Tried to give me something as he ended his life.

Instead of which he managed to take my whole life away.

Part 2 – Gabrielle

All my friends at the bridge club have been very kind. Very kind indeed.

They glare at each other if someone accidentally mentions prison, or murder, or convicts, or anything. They think I am very brave to go to visit Becca in jail every week and to hold my head up everywhere I go in Rossmore. It's not all that hard to have confidence actually. It depends really on how you look. I always knew that but I never had the money to look well.

My ex-husband, that bloody Eamon, left me penniless when he went off with that appalling, vulgar woman, Iris. The upkeep of the house was amazing, so I was always very stuck for cash when it came to it. Which, of course, was why I was so grateful to the tabloids.

Now I know we have to pretend to think they are terrible and that we only let them into the house for the maid sort of thing, but they were hugely interested in what poor Becca had done and in fact I was secretly delighted with them. One of them bought the story of Becca's childhood and the 'What Made Her the Woman She Became' angle. Another bought stuff about her life in the chic fashion boutique. I should have got a retainer from that hoity-toity madam who owns the place – I bet I doubled her business.

Then there was a piece about how Becca had changed after her father, bloody Eamon, had left home. I enjoyed helping to write that. Nowhere did they say that I was collaborating but I gave them all the information and all the pictures. It made a magnificent set of articles.

Of course I didn't like titles like 'In the Mind of the Murderess' but on the other hand it did sell papers, and in many people's minds that's exactly what poor silly Becca actually was.

Every time I visited, she would ask how had the reporters found out all these details. I reassured her that I had told them nothing new, they knew it all already. What they didn't know, they made up. Like all that silly business about poor Becca going up to the well in Whitethorn Woods to pray to St Ann that Franklin would love her.

'I never did, Mother, you know that,' she had wept at me.

I soothed her and patted her down. Of course everyone knew it was nonsense. They just made it up out of their heads . . .

I had been very well paid for that particular story. It gave the newspapers freedom to take pictures of the terrible shrine. And did that sell papers! Obviously Becca knew nothing of this and I reassured her and reminded her that I *had* managed to keep Franklin out of the story and she was naturally very grateful. When she came out of jail she would marry him, of course, so she didn't want him attracting unpleasant limelight and attention until then.

She had begged him to come and visit her until I told her that the reporters were outside the jail all the time and they would spot him and the careful privacy we had all been keeping would be blown. She saw the sense in that.

They're quite nice in the jail, really. Basically out for the prisoners' good – which must be quite hard when you think of the kind of people they have to deal with normally. Of course, Becca is different, and they see that, naturally they would. She's a lady for one thing and she hasn't the *mind* of a criminal for another. She's so far above everyone in the place and yet gets on perfectly pleasantly with them all, which is a true sign of good breeding.

She's learning embroidery at recreation time, from one of the warders, a nice woman called Kate. Becca says it's very restful, therapeutic even. She gave me a perfectly horrid little cushion cover she had made and I told her it has pride of place in the sitting room. Poor dear Becca! She thinks she'll be home any day to see it. She has risen above her whole terrible situation by refusing to acknowledge it. It's a way of coping and for Becca it's working very well.

She has started a huge coverlet for her bed with the words 'Franklin' and 'Rebecca' intertwined.

I have to remember not to wear my best finery going to see her because Becca can spot a designer outfit at half a mile, it was all those years working in the boutique. She would know I couldn't ordinarily afford Prada or Joseph jackets. I have what I call my prison visiting outfit, so that she wouldn't make the connection between the publishing of the tabloid stories and her mother's new wardrobe.

Becca herself looks a lot better as the weeks and months go by. She walks straighter, she doesn't fuss about her hair and sort of twiddle with it like she used to, it's just straight now and classy looking. There's one of the warders, Gwen, who is a friend of Kate, the nice one, and apparently she trained as a hairdresser and still works part time in a beauty parlour and she gives them all a regular trim. They're not allowed to hold a pair of scissors themselves of course. Which is idiotic in Becca's case, I mean, what harm would she do to anyone with a pair of scissors?

She seems less anxious these days than when she was out in the real world, somehow much calmer. Very interested in shading and matching threads, and whether she'll be chosen for a netball team. Becca! Interested in sports and embroidery! Who would have thought it? Well, who would have thought any of it really?

Sometimes the tabloid people ask me, do I have any sympathy for poor Janice who went unsuspecting to her death because of Becca, but I remind them that I cannot be quoted; my opinions and my natural, deep, deep sorrow cannot be entered into. And then before they start to turn against me I feed them another picture of Becca or titbit about the parties she used to go to, launches, receptions, to which she hadn't even been invited. They would run another story describing her as a good-time party girl.

Imagine!

You know the way they talk about people becoming institutionalised? Well, I think it's absolutely true. Becca has few interests now outside the terrible place where she is. She tells me of horrid lesbian affairs between the prisoners, and sometimes between prisoners and warders. The only thing that unites her to the world outside is her future with Franklin.

It's marvellous, of course, that she is so positive about everything but then she does seem to have lost touch with reality since she doesn't realise how long she is going to be in there. Nor did she ever refer to the enormity of what she had done. She sort of waves it away.

And yet it was a terrible thing. Killing Franklin's fiancée – or getting her killed, which was just as bad. 'A deliberate and cold-blooded killing,' as the judge said when he sentenced her after a unanimous verdict from the jury. She never once spoke of Janice or, indeed, that sad chap, Kevin, who did the driving, or anything at all about that night.

And I didn't want to distress her. Poor lamb, her life hadn't turned out at all as she had hoped.

So when she talked about Franklin and the future I did nothing to discourage her. Once she realised he couldn't come to see her, she stopped asking about him and what he was doing.

This was a great relief.

A huge relief in fact. It's been getting more and more difficult to field her questions about him. I tried to tell her about the bridge club but Becca had lost all interest – she barely reacted when I told her about the grand slam that I had got. I think she barely takes on board that Wilfred and Franklin and I play regularly together, getting a fourth where we can find one. But then I suppose bridge might have been a bit of a sore subject, what with Janice's having met Franklin there, being a bridge partner and everything.

So maybe better not mention bridge.

Trouble is that there are so many things it's better not to mention. I talk on about whether this thread is cerise or fuchsia, and how hard it is for Kate the warder to support two children on her wages, and I listen to stories about how Gloria's romance with Ailis is over, and how it's all political getting on the netball team.

And I listen to stories about women who are prostitutes, drug dealers, or have murdered their husbands in self-defence. It's such an uncanny sort of an existence. That bloody Eamon, my ex-husband, asked would Becca like him to visit and I said certainly not. He had been no help to her before all this business and he would only upset her further now. So that softened his cough.

Kate draws me aside from time to time when I visit and tells me that Becca is adapting very well and is very popular with the other prisoners. As if I would somehow be pleased that these terrible women liked my Becca or not! But Kate meant well, she couldn't help it if she had no advantages when she was growing up, and from what Becca said, Kate too had been a victim like I was, her husband had left her. Bastards, really, all of them when you think about it.

So I took to bringing Kate little presents as well when I visited. Nothing huge, just a nice soap or a glossy magazine, or a little jar of tapenade. Poor dear, I don't think she knew what it was, but she was pleased all the same. And as I say, it wasn't her fault that she didn't grow up in a proper home. And she was very kind to my Becca.

Franklin was relieved that I had sorted out that he shouldn't visit. Very relieved, I imagine. But Wilfred, who was so polite and always tried to do the right thing, asked, should he come and see Becca. I thought about it for a while but I said, not really, what would there be for him to say? And he too was frightfully relieved. I could see it. I didn't want Wilfred in there anyway, blabbing and saying the wrong thing. He was only offering to be polite.

He was still Franklin's partner in this mysterious mobile phone service they were doing, downloading or uploading or offloading something on to people's cellphones, impossible to understand.

Then the mother of that poor Janice asked could she visit Becca, but I told Kate to tell the authorities that this would be the wrong thing. This poor woman was Born Again or something very dubious and she thought Becca would find peace if she went to tell her she had forgiven her, but I think Becca has actually forgotten about Janice, to be honest, so I discouraged it and Kate must have passed the message on because she never went.

And life went on in the funny way it does, everything changed and yet finding a similarity in the days. We continued to play bridge two nights a week. Becca's father, bloody Eamon, would telephone me every time there was something new in the tabloids – his frightful wife apparently reads nothing else.

'How do they know these things?' he would cry at me into the phone.

I shrugged, I had no idea, I told him. I never saw him so he wouldn't know that I had such smart clothes and that I had bought a sports car. Or that there was a cleaner every day now and a gardener once a week. It was none of his business anyway. Little he had cared when he abandoned his wife and daughter.

I would take a taxi to the prison each week, and ask it to wait at the bus stop around the corner and then join the rest of the prison visitors, opening my bag for examination and accepting a body search before visiting my own daughter. I didn't want anyone to tell Becca that I kept a taxi waiting. She would wonder where I got the funds. And in the end it was all for her own good, her peace of mind, and enabled me to visit her every week without too much stress and strain.

'Kate is very good to me, Mother,' she said one day.

'Yes indeed.' I was wondering where this was leading.

'I was wondering if you could ask her for tea sometime on her day off, Mother?'

'No, darling, that wouldn't do at all,' I said.

'Please, Mother.'

Becca had lost touch with the real world. How could I ask such a sad, poor woman, who lived in a council flat and worked as a prison warder, to my house?

'Sorry, Becca, out of the question,' I said briskly.

Becca was very disappointed. I could see by her face. But the whole thing was totally impossible. She said no more, just resumed her stitching at a feverish pace. I wondered as I got back into my taxi why I had bothered to come and see her at all. She was really so ungrateful for all I had done. Wasn't it enough that I had bought all these little gifts for Kate? Not a word of thank you from Becca. Maybe the woman had never told her.

It was so hard to know! I mean, Kate was just a prison warder. Imagine Becca thinking I could entertain her at home. I couldn't possibly let her see how we lived.

As the taxi pulled away, I thought I saw Kate standing there looking at me thoughtfully but it must have been my imagination. If she had seen me she would have come over and talked, not just stood there watching as she was. I hoped that she wouldn't say anything to Becca about my taking a taxi. But then I shook myself and told myself not to be fanciful. Being in that awful prison would make anyone fanciful, really.

When I got home the chaps were waiting for me with a scotch and ginger. Such dear boys. They always ask about Becca and I always say that it's too dreadful to talk about and that I must go and have a long bath. Just the very fact of *being* in that place makes you feel defiled. I lay in the warm scented bubbles and drank my long cool scotch and ginger. Life was a great deal better these days than it used to be. Amazing, really, how having enough money can take the edge off things.

I never worry these days about the roof slates, or getting a new handbag to tone in with a new outfit, or having good wine when we go out to dinner. I am beginning to accept as my right that I have a silk dressing gown and a redecorated bedroom. Tonight I would wear the really smart dress that had cost what we spent on our first car. It looked nice certainly but I needed better shoes. Perhaps I can come up with another little story for the ghastly papers. Something like 'Stitching Her Way to the Future' and a description of the counterpane Becca is making. Yes, that would be good, it would throw suspicion on some of the people in the prison. That boot-faced Kate, for example.

I looked at myself in the mirror.

Not bad at all for my age. New shoes would make it perfect.

Franklin stood at the bottom of the stairs. Wilfred had gone ahead to be at the table to greet us. A special dinner out in a new restaurant. My treat. Always my treat. But then don't be all bitter and twisted, Gabrielle, I told myself. The boys' business is still in the foothills, it hasn't risen to great heights yet. They actually don't have any real money yet, poor darlings.

'You look lovely,' Franklin said. It really was a pleasure to get dressed for people who appreciated it. Bloody Eamon wouldn't notice what I was wearing.

'Thank you,' I purred at him.

'Does she not ask about me at all?' he said unexpectedly.

'No, well, you know, we all agreed that it was better for her not to get in touch until . . . you know . . . until she comes out.'

'But, Gabrielle . . .' he looked at me astonished. 'She's not going to get out for years and years.'

'I know,' I said. 'But you'd be amazed at how strong she is. You and I would go under in a place like that, but not Becca, she's brave as a lion.'

He looked at me affectionately.

'You make all this so much easier for me,' he said, his eyes full of gratitude.

'Come on, Franklin, let's not be late,' I said, and we walked down the steps of our home, past the new wrought iron railings with the sweet peas and honeysuckle entwined. Just before we got into the car I thought I saw that Kate in our road.

But it must have been a hallucination.

What could she have been doing in our neighbourhood?

And then next day I thought I saw her there again. It couldn't have been, of course. But it made me uneasy for some reason and I decided to get her a little present and have a chat with her on my next visit. Possibly foolish Becca had already invited her to tea in my house. And now she was annoyed because the invitation had not been followed up.

Ridiculous, but who knows what kind of thoughts people like her have.

I brought Becca some roses from the garden, and some sweet peas for that Kate. Also a silly little lace-trimmed handkerchief with a letter K on it. She accepted the flowers and handkerchief silently with a nod of her head and left almost immediately without any little chat.

'Is everything all right, Kate?'

'Never better, thank you,' she said, reaching to the back of the door of her office for her overcoat and leaving immediately. It was very mystifying.

Becca looked just as usual but there was something watchful, wary about her. It was as if she were examining me.

'We are always talking about me,' she said. 'And really nothing much changes here. Tell me all about your days and nights, Mother,' she said.

I was a bit wrong-footed here. I hadn't expected this. Up to now I had been vague and she had never wanted to know.

'Oh, you know me, Becca darling, drifting from this to that, a little bridge here, a little reminding your bloody father to give me some support there. The days pass.' She reached for my hand and lifted it to admire my nails.

'Some of them must pass at the beauty parlour,' she said.

'Oh, I wish, darling, just cheap enamel I put on myself.'

'I see. Like your hairdo. Do it yourself with the kitchen scissors, do you?'

I was very annoyed. These were things I couldn't hide from her, the expensive styling and shaping of my hair every five weeks with Fabian. The weekly manicure at Pompadours.

'What are you saying?' I asked.

'Not very much, Mother. You learn not to say anything here until you're quite sure what it is you are trying to say.'

'That would make the world a very silent place,' I twittered at her.

'Not really, no, just a more certain place.'

I tried to change the subject. 'Kate seemed in a hurry today, she almost brushed past me.'

'It's her half-day,' Becca said.

'Yes and I know that you did want me to invite her to after-noon tea, darling, but you're a little out of touch, Becca. It would be so inappropriate. I hope you don't mind.'

'No, that's all right, I understood, and so did she.'

'Well, that's good,' I said doubtfully.

'Do you get lonely at all, Mother? What with Father having left you and my being in here and everything?'

I couldn't imagine why she was asking this question. 'Well, lonely isn't the right word. I don't ever think about that bastard Eamon these days. I miss you, darling, and wish you were at home. And you will be. One day.'

'Not for years and years, Mother.' She was matter of fact.

'I'll be there for you,' I said firmly.

'I doubt it very much, Mother, I really do.'

She still looked totally calm but this wasn't the way she normally spoke. A little silence fell between us. Then after what seemed a long, long time Becca spoke.

'Why did you do it, Mother?' she asked.

'I don't know what you're talking about,' I began. And I didn't really – there were so many things it could have been. Was it the taxi? Had that really been Kate in the road who would have told her about the house being all painted up? That there were definitely signs of money, ill-gotten money, around the place? Or had she told her anything else?

I stood up as if to leave but her hand shot out and pinned my wrist to the table between us. One of the warders moved towards us but Becca smiled and reassured her that everything was fine.

'My mother is just about to tell me something, she's finding it a bit difficult, but she will find the words.'

I rubbed my wrist. 'Well, you see . . .' I began.

'No, I don't see, Mother. I hear that you are living with Franklin. That's what I hear.'

I began to bluster a little.

'But I'm doing it for you, Becca darling. Wilfred and Franklin had to live somewhere, I live in a big falling-down house – why shouldn't they have rooms there?'

'Not so falling-down now, I hear,' Becca said.

'But, darling, they just have rooms there – don't be so silly.'

'Do you sleep with Franklin?' she asked calmly.

'Now how can you say that?' I began.

'Because Kate told me, and Gwen told me.'

'Gwen?'

'One of the warders here, you go to her every week for a manicure. Dressed very differently than you are dressed today . . .'

For once I was speechless. Becca wasn't speechless, however.

'It's disgusting, he's thirty years younger than you.'

'Nineteen,' I said with spirit.

'He'll move on,' she said.

'Maybe,' I agreed. 'One day, yes, maybe.'

'Sooner than you think,' my daughter said.

And Becca told me her plan. She reminded me that I had said everyone should have a plan. Becca's plan was to put Kate in touch with the tabloid papers. Kate and Gwen didn't think that it was fair, the way Becca had been treated, and had alerted tabloid photographers to lie in wait for Franklin and myself.

'Murderess Betrayed by Her Own Mother' was going to be a much, much better story than anything that I had sold them so far. They would really pay Kate well for this.

She looked very calm and in control as she spoke to me. I wondered suddenly whether, if I had put aside all my principles and invited the damn woman to afternoon tea, all this would never have happened. But we'll never know . . .

CHAPTER 6

Bank Holiday Party

Part 1 – Barbara

You see, I was always such fun and so much the centre of things in the office, I obviously assumed that I was part of the Bank Holiday party. It never occurred to me that they would all go off without me. Not without me, Barbara, life and soul of the party. I mean, I was the one who had told them about it in the first place, this hotel in a place called Rossmore, miles away in the country where they had a big swimming pool with a patio where they let you grill your own steaks or pieces of chicken. I found the website and I printed out all the information and showed it to them.

So naturally I thought I was part of it all.

Then I heard them all talking about it and who they were going to be sharing rooms with and what time they were all getting together to have a drink before they set off to catch the train. And there was some kind of wishing well in the woods where a saint had kept appearing and they were going to investigate it and see could they catch her in mid-apparition.

And then suddenly it dawned on me that I wasn't part of it.

At the start, I thought it was a mistake, you know the way things are. Everyone thinks that someone else told me. They just couldn't be going without me. But you get a sort of gut feeling when you are being left out of things and this is what I had.

Well, at first I was totally furious. How dare they take my idea and not include me? Then I became upset. Why did they not like me? What reason could have made them leave me out? Tears of self-pity had to be beaten back. Then I started hating them all. People I had thought were my friends. Laughing behind my back. I hoped they would have a really awful Bank Holiday weekend, and that the hotel would be a disaster. I wished them downpours of rain, and wanted the patio to be crawling with awful beasts that would get into their clothes and hair.

They were leaving on Friday at lunchtime, catching a two o'clock train. They all brought their bags to the office that morning. What was really amazing was how they talked about it so openly in front of me. They weren't even embarrassed that they had stolen my holiday and then left me out of it. They didn't lower their voices or turn away, just discussed it as if I had assumed I would be no part of it.

On the Friday morning Rosie, who was one of the nicer ones, confided to me that she had great hopes of getting together with Martin from Sales during the weekend.

'Do you think I might stand a chance with him, Bar?' she asked.

'I don't know why you ask me,' I said coldly.

Rosie seemed surprised. 'Because you're so cool, you know everything, Bar,' she said. As far as I could see she wasn't mocking me. Which made it all the odder that she hadn't wanted me to join them.

'I think you have every chance of winning Martin's affections,' I said. 'Best keep him away from Sandra, though, she's meant to be a bit of a man-eater.'

'Oh Bar, you're just wonderful, I wish you were coming with us, you could advise me the whole time. Why will you not come? Just this once?'

'Wasn't asked.' I shrugged, trying not to show how much it mattered.

Rosie pealed with laughter. 'As if you would have to be asked,' she said. 'You just didn't want to come, we knew that from the word go, the way you talked about the place and sneered at it. We knew you had something much better to do.'

'I *never* sneered at Rossmore, I suggested it,' I cried, outraged.

'No, not sneered exactly, but, Bar, we all knew it wouldn't be your kind of thing. A bit beneath you. Not in a snobby way but that's the way it is.'

'I don't believe you,' I said.

'Well, ask anyone then,' said Rosie. And I did.

I asked the man-eating Sandra.

'I don't suppose it would be your scene,' Sandra said. 'All right for us ordinary folk but not for you, Bar.'

'Why not for me?' I asked in a voice of steel.

'You're sort of classier than we are, Bar, you know – no one could see *you* spending a weekend in jeans grilling sausages.'

I was astounded.

Well, yes, I do dress well. I take care of my appearance. I consider myself well groomed. I have had some elocution lessons to improve my accent. But too classy to go on an office outing? Come on. They couldn't all be so humble and in awe of me as not to include me? Surely?

But I wasn't going to let them see how startled and upset I was. No way.

'Have a good time anyway, Sandra,' I said cheerfully. 'Got your eye on anyone in particular for the weekend?'

'Not really. That Martin fellow in the Sales Department is a bit of a looker. But we'll see.'

Sandra could have any man she wanted, Rosie wasn't so fortunate. Even in the middle of my own disappointment I decided to even things up.

'I wouldn't waste my time on him, I heard he's as dull as

ditchwater when you get to know him,' I said.

'Thanks, Bar,' Sandra said, putting on more lip gloss. 'Good to have your card marked. What are you doing for the Bank Holiday by the way?'

'Me? Oh, I'm not doing much,' I said, confused.

'I bet you are,' Sandra said.

'I'm giving a big lunch party,' I heard myself say.

'Ooh, Barbara, aren't you something else? How many people?'

'Twelve including me.' Was I mad? I don't *know* twelve people. I couldn't cook for them even if I did.

'Twelve people! You're fabulous, Bar, will you have photos next week?'

'Very probably,' I said miserably. I could always say the camera had jammed. Not only was I pathetic and unpopular . . . I was mad and dishonest as well. Great start to a Bank Holiday weekend.

I waved them all goodbye as they left the office for the two o'clock train. People I had thought were my friends – sexy Sandra, innocent Rosie, that nice, gentle Martin from Sales, and half a dozen others who all thought I was stuck up and superior. I looked at myself in the mirror in the ladies room. A pale face, framed with an expensive haircut, a well-cut jacket, which I sponged and brushed every night. I wore cheap T-shirts underneath, a different colour every day. There was nothing upper class, snobby about me. Was there?

Two cleaning women came in with their buckets and mops. They greeted me pleasantly with big smiles and a lot of gold teeth. They weren't Irish but there are lots of overseas people working in Ireland now and I didn't know where they were from. They were remarkably good-humoured with three hours of scrubbing and polishing ahead of them.

And yet I dared to feel sorry for myself, I, who had a good job in marketing, a big garden flat, a flat-screen television and a designer jacket!

'Are you looking forward to the Bank Holiday weekend?' I asked them.

'Not very,' said one.

'Sunday often a sad lonely day in a big city,' said the other.

I knew how she felt.

'Would you like to come to lunch with me?' I heard myself say.

They looked at me open-mouthed.

'To eat a lunch with you?' they asked astounded.

'Well, yes. On Sunday at about one o'clock in my house. Look, I'll write down the address for you.'

I got out my little leather-bound notebook. The two women in their yellow working overalls looked on as if I were writing them an invitation to fly to the moon.

'Oh, and I'd better know your names, to introduce you to other people,' I said.

'There will be other people?' They looked alarmed.

'Oh, indeed, about twelve of us altogether,' I said cheerily.

They were from Cyprus, sisters, they told me, they had Greek names: Magda and Eleni.

Nobody had ever invited them to a home before, Eleni said, excited.

Magda was worried about it all. 'You like us to clean the house for you maybe?' she said.

I felt so ashamed I could hardly speak. 'No, no, as my guests,' I mumbled.

'We will make some baklava . . . beautiful Greek dessert,' Magda said, now that it had all been cleared up.

I left them talking excitedly in Greek, nothing so marvellous had happened to them before in their new country.

On the way back to my own office, before I had even time to think about what I had just done, I met my boss Alan, a tense, anxious workaholic of about forty-five, I suppose. We knew nothing about his private life except in bursts when he announced that he hated his ex with a great passion. This was one of these bursts.

'She is an evil vicious woman,' Alan told me in the corridor. 'A foul and very bad person.'

'What has she done now?' I asked. Alan was quite handsome and he could be good company apart from all this droning on about his ex.

'She's only gone and dumped Harry and two of his ten-year-old friends on me for the whole of the weekend, and instructions about no fast food. I'm to cook them proper meals apparently.'

'Oh, bring them round to my place on Sunday – about one o'clock,' I said, casually writing down my address.

'I can't do that, Bar,' he said, though it was obvious that he wanted to.

'Ah, why not?' I shrugged. 'There'll be twelve of us, and plenty of home-cooked food.' I began to wonder, was I going mad?

'I'll bring you some wine then,' Alan said, eagerly bursting with gratitude.

Back in my office and gathering up my things I took a last look at my diary. I would be away from it until Tuesday, better see was there anything I should remember. It was my Aunt Dorothy's birthday on Sunday – my father's elder sister. Disapproving of everyone, she had rarely been known to utter a pleasant remark.

There was still time to fling a birthday card into the post so that she couldn't accuse me of neglecting her when next she saw my parents. Then I thought, better still, I'd ask her to lunch. She couldn't make it any more ludicrous than the way it was shaping up to be.

Aunt Dorothy was in a black humour when I called. Her three bridge friends had forgotten her birthday, she always remembered *their* birthdays, but oh no, they hadn't said a thing about celebrating it.

'Why don't you return good for evil, Aunt Dorothy, and ask

them all to lunch at my house,' I suggested. I was now completely insane, I realised. Aunt Dorothy liked the idea a lot. She would embarrass them, humiliate them even, make them feel ashamed.

'What can I bring with me for lunch, dear?' she asked in tones that almost approached civility. I thought for a moment. I hadn't even planned what we were going to eat but we'd need a salad. I suggested it.

'For five?' Aunt Dorothy asked.

'No, for twelve actually,' I said apologetically.

'You can't seat twelve,' she snapped.

'We'll eat in the garden,' I said. And hung up.

I did a count, we had now reached eleven. Only one more. Larry the security man came in. He was about to lock the place up for the weekend. So naturally I invited him to lunch and naturally he said he'd love to, and that he'd come over early in his van with some planks and set up a table in the garden.

So there was my party.

I went home by a bookshop where I looked up a book on very easy entertaining. On Saturday I went shopping and bought three cheap tablecloths, packets of crisps and dips, some brightly coloured balloons as well as the ingredients for an Easy Chicken Pie and an Easy Vegetarian Special. That and the Greek desserts, Aunt Dorothy's salad and Alan's wine should cover everyone.

I slept well on Saturday night and never thought at all about my colleagues on their patio in Rossmore, grilling their lamb chops and sausages amongst the mosquitoes and visiting walking statues in the woods.

Larry, true to his word, was round with the wooden planks, and he had put half a dozen folding chairs in the back of his van, borrowed from the office penthouse. I had no seating plan: let them sit where they liked.

At half past twelve I wondered whether any of them would come. At one o'clock sharp they all arrived and Alan had brought enough wine for half the neighbourhood. There was a roar of conversation from the moment they came in.

Magda and Eleni had brought olives as well as dessert.

Alan's son Harry and his two friends turned out to be hugely interested in money. 'How much will you pay us to be waiters?' they asked as soon as they arrived.

I looked at Alan helplessly. 'They're worth two Euros each, no more,' he said.

'Five,' I said, and then I settled back while they did all the work.

Aunt Dorothy lorded it over her friends very happily. 'Oh, Barbara has a wide circle of acquaintances,' she said proudly, and wept a little tear when I got everyone to sing 'Happy Birthday' to her.

Magda said that Eleni had always needed a strong helpful man like Larry and did everything to throw them together. Harry and his friends finished the washing up and wondered, would they be paid for weeding the flower beds.

'One Euro each,' Alan said.

'Three Euro each,' I said.

Magda and Eleni taught Larry to do a Zorba dance; Aunt Dorothy and her friends all sang 'Just a Song at Twilight'.

Alan said to me, 'You know, I always fancied you a bit but I thought you were rather toffee-nosed. I never in a million years thought you were like this. You are absolutely wonderful.'

So I forgot about the people who hadn't invited me to grill things on a patio on a holiday that I had more or less set up for them, and Alan forgot about his ex.

And I think somebody took some pictures but it didn't really matter. Because no one would ever forget the day.

Part 2 – Someone from Dad's Office

Lots of people at school have parents who are divorced. Well, it stands to reason, you don't always want the same thing all the time, do you? I mean, I don't like the things I liked when I was seven, not now that I'm ten. Those awful Playstations that I liked then, well, of course they were fine then, but they are so boring now.

So I quite see why Mum and Dad got tired of each other and wanted different things. It's nothing personal. Or at least it shouldn't be. But that's not the way it is in this family. Mum never stops talking about how mean Dad is, how he keeps us in poverty.

I don't think we are in poverty but it doesn't do to say that so I don't say anything really.

Dad is always saying to me that that mother of mine will have us all in the workhouse before long and that can't be true either because Dad drives a big car and he is very high up in his office, but it's not a good idea to say that we don't look like the workhouse people you see pictures of in Charles Dickens' time. So I say nothing about that either.

They both keep telling me that they love me. Too much really.

Mum says, '. . . the one thing that can be said about that monument to selfishness is that he gave me you, Harry.'

Dad says, '. . . if there's one thing to be said about that dizzy self-obsessed woman it's that she gave me a fine son.'

I don't know why they think that, because I am always the problem, or the worry, or the person to be parked here or collected there.

George doesn't see his father at all, so he says I'm lucky compared to him. Wes says that his family are rowing all the time and we are both lucky compared to him. So obviously the whole family thing isn't really meant to work.

Anyway Mum has a new fellow. He's awful, of course, trying

to be nice to me and pretending to be interested in me when he isn't a bit. His name is Kent, he's not from Kent in England or anything. Kent is what he is called.

George says that Kent has a very expensive car and so he must be loaded and that we should make as much money from him as possible while he lasts. He said I should say that I was saving for a new ipod, or a mobile phone, or computer updates. I should concentrate on something that sounded as if I would get myself out of his hair and Kent would be likely to hand over a tenner or whatever.

I was nervous at first but it worked like a dream. I kept my part of the bargain: I stayed out of his way and was very polite to him when I was in his company. Mum asked me, did I like him and I opened my eyes very wide, which is a good thing to do if you're telling something not exactly true, and I said I thought Kent was just fine and Mum said I was a good son, a very good son indeed, and her eyes got watery so I took myself off.

George says that mothers go ahead and marry these kind of people anyway whether we like them or not, his mother certainly had. So George says, make life easy on yourself, say he's the greatest thing since sliced bread and make sure that he keeps contributing to various projects. Wes said that he would just love his parents to split up and he'd have someone to get him an MP3 player.

So anyway for this Bank Holiday we were going to work on Kent to take all three of us to a theme park. There were plenty of things for old folks to do there like sitting in restaurants and we could go on the rides. I had the spiel all ready to give him when suddenly he said to me in a very serious voice that he was going to take my mother away for a long weekend to a beautiful hotel by a huge whitethorn wood. I didn't want to go to a beautiful hotel by a wood. Not one bit. But I reminded myself to be very polite. I could hear George's voice as clearly as if he were standing beside me hissing warnings into my ear.

'Won't it be very expensive for you if we all come – Wes, George and me?' I asked.

A sort of shudder went over his face at the thought of taking us all to a beautiful hotel by a river and the Whitethorn Woods.

'Well, no, Harry, this is it, I'm going to take your mother by herself; I want to ask her a question, you see.'

I explained that she was in the kitchen and he could go out and ask her the question now, but no, it was a question that needed to be asked in the proper setting. I could see the theme park fading into the distance, theme parks weren't a place you could ask a question, apparently.

But I had invited Wes and George to stay. That had to be sorted. Was there any hope that they'd let us stay on our own? No, apparently that wasn't on. We were to go to Dad.

'But it's not his weekend,' I began.

'It will be,' Kent said.

From the kitchen I could hear Mum screaming down the phone. 'You were always selfish, Alan, that was never in dispute but unable to take your own son for a bonus weekend – most men would be delighted, but not you. It doesn't *matter* where I am going or with whom. I am not married to you, Alan Black, something I thank the Living God for every day of my life. Marriage is something that leaves me very cold indeed. So listen well. Harry and his friends will be dropped at your house on Friday. It doesn't matter about there being enough beds, they have sleeping bags, and they *must* have proper food, not take-aways, do you hear me . . .'

Half the neighbourhood must have heard her.

Kent was hovering nervously waiting for Mum to finish. He looked embarrassed. 'It's all right, Kent, they go on that way, it isn't important,' I explained.

'I don't like that – she says marriage leaves her cold. I don't like it one bit,' he said in a worried voice. I thought I understood about the holiday in the one-horse town called Rossmore.

I thought about it for a bit. He was better than any of the others.

'Oh, that's just marriage to Dad, I'd say. I don't think she's against it in general.' I nodded wisely as if I understood the problems of the world.

'It's just that Rossmore in this weather would be a perfect place – I don't want to say anything inappropriate.' He was biting his lip.

'Rossmore? Is that the place they have the big row about a road going through some woods? The teacher at school made us have a debate about it: some of us were to be for the road, some against it . . .' I was only saying this to distract him, but it seemed to please him.

'Yes, there was a big documentary about it on television. Your mother said it was a romantic place and I was hoping . . .'

'Okay, Kent, go on hoping, I'm sure it will all be fine,' I said cheerfully. 'Enjoy the hotel and the woods and the question and all that. Compared to us you'll have a great time. I'll have my dad grizzling and complaining from now until Tuesday,' I said with a real hangdog expression.

Kent gave me twenty Euros out of pure guilt to spend on anything I wanted.

When we arrived at Dad's house I thought Dad looked very grey and old and tired compared to Kent. Kent has a sort of permanent suntan and Dad looked as if someone had run over him with a garden roller. He cooked a chicken and we had frozen peas.

'It says *fresh* frozen peas on the packet,' he said defensively and we all said it was fine.

There was an apple tart, which he said was home-made at the local bakery, and ice cream.

Next day he agreed he would take us to the theme park.

'Do you have any current squeeze that you could bring to entertain *you*, Mr Black?' Wes asked politely.

'Current what?' Dad asked, mystified.

'Squeeze. Female companion is what Wes meant,' George explained.

'No, no, indeed,' my father said, embarrassed.

'Never mind – you might find one there,' Wes consoled him.

We didn't push Dad for as much money as we would have Kent but he was reasonably generous and of course I did have Kent's unexpected money so we had a great day.

Then on the Sunday it turned out that we had to go to lunch with someone from Dad's office. I asked, did he have a big house, this man, and Dad said it was a woman. Wes and George exchanged knowing glances. But I knew they were barking up the wrong tree. Dad goes off to work and comes back and fusses, and fights with Mum on the phone. Dad doesn't have lady friends. It must be business.

We wondered, might we skip the lunch, but it seemed that we mightn't. We asked, had this woman any children, would there be babes there, and Dad said he didn't know who would be there but he gravely doubted that there would be babes. So we set out without much hope.

Dad was bringing all the wine, boxes of it. They must be a fairly drinky crowd, we thought. It didn't bode well when we got there and saw a terribly old woman called Dorothy sitting on a chair. She had a face like a handbag that kept snapping open and shut and she had other old people beside her all full of disapproval. Then there were two foreign people putting out dishes of olives and a man called Larry laying out chairs who kept saying, 'Oh my God, Mr Black is here, he'll see the chairs.' I mean, why shouldn't my father have seen the chairs like everyone else? Where was he going to sit? Really, it couldn't have been a more crazy crowd.

Dad was busy setting up a bar with Larry on a side-table while Larry kept saying, over and over, that it was a surprise to see Mr Black.

'How are we going to be polite all day here?' I asked George who was very wise about the ways things should be done.

'We'd better find the hostess and start with her,' George said.

She was in the kitchen. Much younger than anyone else we'd seen but still old, if you know what I mean. She looked worried. Her name was Barbara.

'We'd like to help,' George said.

'We're not expensive,' Wes added.

'I thought you were guests,' Barbara said, confused.

'What my friends meant was that of course we are guests and delighted to be here but we wondered, would you like any help with the waiting and serving, we're quite experienced in fact.' I saw George making awful faces at me but I didn't understand: I thought he was urging me on. 'We've done quite a few functions actually . . .' I went on. And then I realised my father was in the room.

'Illegally, I suppose,' he said.

'Informally, Mr Black,' George corrected.

'Not more than two Euros each then, and they have to work properly,' Dad said. A rate of five was suggested by Barbara, who said we would have to work like slaves. Dad went out to pour wine for people and we got our instructions.

We were to make a terrific fuss of that woman who sat upright in the chair. We were to tell her that this party was in her honour and to call her Aunt Dorothy.

'But she's not our aunt,' George said logically.

'I know, George, but it's what's called a courtesy title,' Barbara said. Which explained nothing.

'But she wouldn't want *Wes* to call her aunt, would she?' I wanted to get this clear, Wes was black.

Barbara seemed not to have noticed this or to think it was irrelevant.

'I don't exactly look like her nephew,' Wes said.

'None of you are her nephews. I told you it was a courtesy title. Now are you going to argue everything down to the bone or are you going to help?'

Aunt Dorothy said that we were extraordinarily nice, helpful boys and compared to the youth of today we were a delightful exception. Wes said that it was our privilege to be at this party and to get to know the guest of honour, and all Aunt Dorothy's awful friends sort of twittered with envy and rage at this. Back in the kitchen I reported all this to Barbara and asked, was there anything else that needed sorting, and she wondered, could I try to tell Magda and Eleni that we were the paid help and they weren't.

'Why do they think they are doing it?' I asked resentfully.

'Because people are mad, Harry, most of them stark raving mad. You'll realise that when you're older.'

'I realise it now,' I said and she laughed with me like a friend.

I went off to deal with these two mad women from Greece or wherever, and I sat them down and filled their glasses.

'You no work today, we work,' I said several times until I thought they understood.

George found an atlas and asked them to show us where they lived in Cyprus and apparently nobody had ever asked them this before and they were delighted. It turned out that nobody was vegetarian and Barbara seemed upset by this because she assumed that half the guests would be but I said we should ladle a bit of both dishes on every plate and that would mean plenty for everyone and she was very pleased.

'You're a complete treasure,' she said. 'What happened that your mother couldn't have you this weekend? I'm very glad about it by the way, but I just wondered.'

'She's gone to a place called Rossmore to be asked a question by Kent,' I explained. 'I don't know what the question is but it has to be asked by a river and a wood, it seems.'

She nodded as if she understood.

'He might be asking her to marry him,' she suggested. 'That's the kind of thing you might ask by a river.'

'It did cross my mind that it might be that, but if that's all it is, couldn't he have asked her in the kitchen at home?' I said. I was thinking that she was totally right – everyone was getting madder by the moment.

'Harry, would you do one more thing for me, could you tell Larry that Mr Black, I mean your dad, wouldn't recognise those chairs if they came up and bit him in the face – tell him to stop fussing.'

'It's hard to tell a grown-up to stop fussing,' I said. 'I've been trying to tell my dad to stop fussing for years and he won't and he says that it's impudence on my part even to say it.'

'All right, you keep chopping parsley and sprinkle it over these plates and I'll talk to Larry, while I'm getting them to sit down.'

Wes and George came into the kitchen. 'They're all mad,' Wes said.

'They're meant to be mad, she knows that, she talked about it. Stop eating that parsley,' I said.

'Maybe they're from a home.' George was thoughtful.

'What are we all doing here, and your dad, then?' Wes wanted to know.

It was unanswerable.

And the chicken pie was very good indeed, everyone praised it and said the sauce was delicious, and Barbara said that it was nothing really. I knew it was all cans of mushroom soup, a half-bottle of wine and frozen pastry because I had been helping her tie up the rubbish. But I said nothing. Dad ran round filling people's glasses and suggesting that he and Larry take off their jackets if the ladies didn't mind. Larry had stopped fussing and started fancying one of the Cypriot ladies. Aunt Dorothy had relaxed greatly and was telling everyone that there were no songs like the old songs. And when we were clearing the pudding plates away, George, who always says the right thing, said to Barbara that it was going very well and that she must be pleased with herself.

He reported that she took him by the lapels and for an awful sickening moment he thought she was going to kiss him so he shouted at her that the flower beds were in a terrible state and for an extra few Euro we would weed them for her. And then she released him and the deal was done.

Wes said that of course all these people must be from some kind of a home, Barbara included, and that my father was very decent to have spent the day looking after them. But I saw Dad sitting at the table in his short sleeves, singing 'Mad Dogs and Englishmen Go Out in the Midday Sun', and somehow I didn't *think* the whole thing was some massive work of charity.

Then the mad women began Greek dancing and Aunt Dorothy started singing old songs with her friends joining in the chorus, and we were all digging the flower beds with trowels and hoes that Barbara found for us. It was all pretty terrible, to be honest.

But we had eaten a good lunch and drunk all the dregs of people's white wine before they went on to red wine, and we were making a decent income out of the whole day. Dad wasn't fussing a bit and this woman, who apparently is called Bar, not Barbara, was very nice. She was drunk as all get out, of course, but very pleasant. Do you know, I saw her holding Dad's hand as he began another song, 'Bye Bye, Miss American Pie', and everyone joined in the chorus.

I said to Wes that Mum would never believe it.

'She won't be interested,' Wes said. That was odd because she was always interested in what Dad, or that bastard Alan as she called him, did or said.

'Not now that she has had the question asked,' George explained. And I felt terrific for some reason. It might have to do with all the ends of white wine we had drunk. Or how we had washed up very well and left the kitchen tidy *and* done the flower beds. But I think the others might have been right all along about Bar being Dad's squeeze.

And that would be absolutely fine with me.

CHAPTER 7

The Last Word

Part 1 – Dr Dermot

I know everyone in the place, that's a fair enough thing to say. If they're thirty-five or under, then I delivered them into the world, and if they're any other age I listened to their chests and coughs and cured their measles and mumps, sewed up their torn ears, took glass out of their cut knees.

Doon is only a small place, twenty miles from Rossmore, along a narrow, bumpy road but we don't need to go into the big town much. We have everything we want here, and it's just a small quiet country place where I know the story of every man, woman and child.

I've closed the eyes of their mothers and fathers and grandparents, I've told them good news and bad news, I've found the words that others don't find. These people owe me, for God's sake. That's why I was so betrayed and let down over the way they all flocked to this new young doctor.

Dr Jimmy White.

A young whippersnapper who called me Dermot as soon as look at me. Everyone here calls me Dr Dermot but, oho, that's not good enough for Dr Jimmy White. Oh, very eager and anxious to please he is, running here and there. Of course he does house calls any time of the day and the night, and of course he has a mobile phone so you can find him anywhere. And he's thorough, sending people halfway across the country for scans, blood tests for everything, X-rays. These are simple people, they think that's a kind of magic in itself.

Even the hospital in Rossmore isn't good enough for Dr Jimmy White. Oh, no, he sends them to specialists, to teaching hospitals in Dublin, no less. Rather than relying on years of experience, and someone who has known them inside and out for generations.

Like myself.

Not that I let them see I was upset or anything. No indeed. I always spoke well of Dr Jimmy White. Very bright young man, I said, plays it by the book and, indeed, consults his medical books, he won't have to do that when he's older and more experienced, but very thorough, of course, always checking things out when he's not sure.

People thought I liked and admired him while I managed to sow the seeds of doubt, like why he was checking books, getting second opinions, sending blood to be tested and people to have scans.

There was an over-talkative American man called Chester Kovac – staying in the hotel, must have been made of money. His grandfather was called O'Neill, came from round here once, not that anyone remembers him or anything. Sure, the country's coming down with O'Neills. I told him several times that the young doctor had to learn his trade somewhere, but in a way it was hard to see him make his mistakes on the people of this parish. Chester said, surely he had to be a qualified medical man and I said yes, but that there was qualified and there was experienced. Chester nodded a lot as if the idea had sunk in.

Then he told me he was buying land in Doon and going to build. He wanted my advice about what kind of services this little town needed. What were we lacking, where were the gaps . . . He had a real over-concerned look on his face. It would sicken you. All that kind of sensitive stuff that has no place here. I pretended to be interested, you know, the way you have to in a small place like this. Some rambling on about social housing, affordable housing. You know the kind of thing they go on with, moaning over the past, saying that if his poor grandfather had only owned a house, then he wouldn't have had to emigrate.

I nodded and sipped my pint. And I thought to myself, if his grandfather hadn't got up off his arse and gone out to somewhere where he could find a living, Chester wouldn't be wearing designer suits and handmade shoes. But better not to say that. Let them live their dream. Oh and he was going to build a hall, and a centre of some sort. Here in Doon, no less! Terrific, I used to say to him, before going back to the subject of Dr White and the gaps in his learning.

For a while my way of coping with my rival worked and there was enough business for both of us. Well, for me anyway. But then things took a turn for the worse.

It was all to do with that stupid woman, Maggie Kiernan, who was having a baby, and let me tell you there was no baby ever born in the world except to Maggie. Her pregnancy was endless, no mammoth could have had a longer gestation period. She was in twice a week, she was sick and then she wasn't sick, the baby was moving – was that natural? or it wasn't moving – did that mean it was dead? What she needed was a private team, gynaecologists, obstetricians, all in a waiting room in her house.

Three weeks before she was due, she rang at two in the morning to say that the baby was arriving. So I told her to have a nice cup of tea and we'd talk about it in the morning. She kept on and on that the baby was definitely coming and wouldn't I come out. Four miles out, halfway up a mountain! Was she mad? I was soothing but she just slammed down the phone.

It wasn't until halfway through the next morning I heard the story: she called Dr Jimmy White and of course he went out there. And wouldn't you know? The child was half born and there were complications and he got an ambulance up that mountainy road and if he hadn't accompanied her to Accident and Emergency in Rossmore, then the baby would have died, and Maggie would have died, and half the population hereabouts would have died out of sympathy.

I must have heard it fifteen times that morning, poor Maggie Kiernan and how frightened she must have been, and was not it the mercy of God that young Dr White had been able to attend her. And always the unspoken words that I had let Maggie Kiernan down.

I was annoyed of course, but I didn't show it: instead I showered praise on Dr Jimmy White and concern about Maggie, and said several times that babies had minds of their own and wouldn't life be easy if they'd only let us know. I never explained, never apologised. And I thought that eventually the message was getting over to them. I was still their wise, good Dr Dermot.

Now, every Saturday at lunchtime, Hannah Harty, a single lady, comes to do the books for me. She is a qualified bookkeeper, the soul of discretion, and does books for a lot of people in town. Just five Saturdays after all Maggie Kiernan's shenanigans, Hannah cleared her throat and told me straight out that I was losing a great many patients to the new young Dr White. And therefore a fair amount of income.

At first I didn't believe her. Hannah has always been a bit of a gloom merchant. Word was that she had set her cap at me, long, long ago. But I don't think that can be true.

I certainly never gave her any encouragement. I had looked after her old mother for years. Well, Hannah actually looked after her old mother, but I would call and reassure them a lot, and if they were eating a supper I was made part of it.

I myself had never married. I had my heart set on a woman once but she told me I was too easy going, and that she could never settle down with a small town doctor. Well, I am who I am. I'm not going to change for anyone so I spent little time thinking back on her and what she had said.

I listened carefully to Hannah as she spoke and, indeed, less than half an hour after she had told me about our takings being down, I had begun to take action.

I called on the Foley family for a chat. Their old father was on his last legs; he wouldn't last much longer. But I was full of cheer about him, said he had the heart and constitution of a lion and that he was in fine fettle. When I left them the Foleys all felt vastly cheered. And I told myself as I so often do that *this* is what a doctor is meant to do, cheer people, buoy them up, carry them along. Not frighten the wits out of them with statistics and tests and scans.

On my way home I met the young Dr White.

'All that business about Maggie Kiernan . . .' he began awkwardly.

'Yes?' My voice was cold.

'Well, I wouldn't want you to think I was muscling in on your territory or anything like that . . .' he said, shifting from foot to foot.

'Do you feel you were?' I was still icy.

'Well, technically of course she is your patient but I had to decide whether it was an emergency or not. And, well, I decided it was.'

'So you feel you did the right thing, Dr White?'

'I do wish you'd call me Jim, I call you Dermot.'

'I know, I've noticed,' I said with one of my smiles.

'There's plenty of work for both of us, Dermot,' he said with a familiar kind of leer. 'Neither of us will go hungry in this place.'

'I'm very sure of that, Dr White,' I said and went on my way.

When I got back home I sat and thought further and deeper. Hannah Harty telephoned and suggested that she bring me over a steak and kidney pie she had made. Since her mother died she had not asked me to supper in her house, which I missed, especially at weekends, which can get lonely.

I do have a housekeeper, a weary-looking woman, but she just keeps the place clean, washes and irons. She shops, of course, and prepares the vegetables but there's never anything tasty like Hannah makes. I said that I'd be honoured to eat the pie with her and would produce a bottle of claret. When Hannah came in bearing her dishes of food it was clear that she had been to the hairdresser since we had met in the morning. She was wearing a smart white blouse and a cameo brooch. She had even put on make-up, which was most unusual.

Could it possibly be true that she still had notions about the two of us?

Best thing possible was to ignore all the finery in case that was what was at the back of it all. No point in complimenting her or anything. That would be just asking for trouble. We talked about the famous Rossmore bypass and would it ever happen. It had been talked about for years. Would it make any difference to our little quiet backwater, or would they just ignore our bumpy little road to Rossmore? Nobody seemed to know.

We had a pleasant meal and since Hannah had brought a plate of rather good cheeses I opened a second bottle of wine.

'What in God's earth are you going to do about young Dr White, Dermot?' she asked me straight out. Her face was anxious. She really cared what was going to happen to me when most of the town had deserted and gone to the opposition. I reached forward and patted her hand.

'I wouldn't worry at all, Hannah my dear,' I reassured her. 'It's always important to stay calm in a situation like this and wait until it all blows over.'

'But it might not blow over, Dermot. You know, I work in several different establishments around the place, and a lot of them are moving. Mr Brown in the bank is going to consult Dr White because of his father's pneumonia. Mr Kenny the solicitor is worried about his mother not being able to walk properly and he thinks young Dr White might get her some better drugs, newer, modern things. You can't just sit here, Dermot, and watch all your hard work, setting up this practice, trickle away into the ground.' She looked really upset on my behalf. Or maybe on her own behalf if she really saw a future with me.

'No, indeed, I won't sit here and watch, Hannah. I was thinking actually that I might take a little holiday.'

'A holiday? Now? In the middle of this crisis? Dermot, you must be going barking mad,' she gasped.

But I refused to respond or react. Just smiled at her.

'I know what I'm doing, Hannah,' I said over and over.

And over the next week I made several house calls. I decided that old man Foley had about two weeks to live; that Mr Kenny's mother should be allowed to live out her last months peacefully without any new medication, which would only unsettle her; that Mr Brown's father was entering his last bout of pneumonia, which would take him peacefully away from this world.

Then I announced that I was taking a little holiday. I encouraged the Browns, the Foleys and the Kennys to attend that nice young Dr White while I was away. No, of *course* I didn't mind, what was life about except give and take, and the young man was extremely well qualified. He would look after them perfectly.

Then I put my golf clubs into the back of the car and drove a hundred and fifty miles away to a nice quiet hotel by the sea. It was easy to find a four-ball so I played eighteen holes a day.

Every night I played bridge in the hotel lounge and at breakfast each morning, with my second cup of tea, I turned the pages to the Deaths column.

First I read of the death of old man Foley, then of Mrs Kenny, and finally of Mr Brown. I said a swift goodbye to my new golfing and bridge friends and drove straight back home to Doon.

I called on the homes of the bereaved, shaking my head in bewilderment over their great losses. I said I couldn't understand it – old man Foley had been in great form when I left, there had been plenty of life in him still; and in Mrs Kenny and Mr Brown. How sad and ironical that they should all die when I, who had known them for so much of their lives, was far away. Then I would shake my wise old head again and say it was a total mystery.

It didn't take long. In fact it all happened much quicker than I had expected. People began to talk.

They said that it was very odd that three perfectly well people had died during the ten days that Dr Dermot was on holiday. They said it was a pity to be hasty and to run to the new instead of staying with the tried and tested. With the man who had known them young, old, well and sick, all their lives. Little by little they came back to me, even those who had asked for their medical records to take to Dr White. Some of them had been annoyed about the scrappy nature of the records and had not accepted that it was all in my head. I knew which child had had mumps and which had had measles, for heaven's sake. No need for computers and print-outs in my case.

I was very generous, talking to them. I showed no hurt, not even a trace of sulking in my face. They were all so relieved that I was taking them back, they wanted to denounce Dr White. But here again I was noble. I wouldn't hear a word against the boy. I called him a boy, as I smiled about him forgivingly, and said he was very young and that he had to make his mistakes somewhere. They marvelled at my great generosity.

He called on me before he left town, Dr White did. A courtesy call, he said, to tell me that he was moving on. I knew already but I pretended to be surprised. I wished him well and said I would be sorry to lose him as a colleague.

'You'll find somewhere more suitable,' I said.

'Yes, I'm sure I will,' he said.

'And you have a nice manner, which is what it's all about,' I added to praise him.

'Which is what *some* of it's about, certainly, Dermot,' he said.

I winced as I did every time he was familiar like that. But I don't think it showed. I offered him a drink but he refused.

'It won't last, of course, Dermot, it can't. Would you like a little bit of advice from me before I leave?'

To humour him I said that I would. After all I had run him out of town. I could afford to be gracious.

'When the next young fellow comes in, Dermot, make him your partner, sell this house and take a room in Chester's clinic, go into semi-retirement, marry Hannah Harty, go and live in that big house of hers. It's better that way than a big malpractice suit or one of your old friends thinking you had been negligent.'

He stood up, impudent young pup, and left without looking back.

I thought for a little while about what he had said. There was no wisdom in it. None at all. And what was this that he was babbling about – Chester's clinic? Chester had been organising some kind of a medical centre, a ludicrous place with expensive machinery where people could waste time and money. They were even going to have rooms for aromatherapy or some kind of New Age nonsense. And what a mad time he had chosen to do it! Just when a new road would come to take the patients straight into Rossmore from here. As a project, it was doomed before it even began. That was nothing for me to worry about.

People round here had their feet on the ground, they wouldn't go for this kind of nonsense all in the name of Danny O'Neill, some loser whom none of them could remember. But one thing was definitely clear and was much more important: my name was definitely up with poor Hannah Harty's. That was something that must be nipped in the bud. She was meant to be making me a fancy salmon dish in pastry tomorrow. Better ring her now and tell her I wasn't free.

Everything was going so well now, it would be a pity to complicate things.

Part 2 – Chester's Plan

I had always promised my Irish grandpa Danny O'Neill that I would go to Ireland but I didn't make it while he was alive. He used to tell tales of his home in Doon, which was some miles from Rossmore. And of the huge Whitethorn Woods and how there was a holy well there where miracles had happened. But somehow I never got to Ireland when he was alive. There was too much else to do like get an education, and make a living.

My own father, Mark Kovac from Poland, had been a carpenter but he had TB and was never strong, and so as the eldest I had to support the family. I used to say to my mom that life would have been a bit easier if they hadn't felt it necessary to have nine children. But she only laughed and asked which of them would I send back. We worked hard, got good grades at school, and we each got a job from the moment we were high enough to stack shelves in a supermarket or collect cardboard and fold it in neat piles.

And I had a bit of luck and met a banking guy who offered me money to start my own building contractor's business, and then I was able to give jobs to all the brothers and sisters, and I put my father on the board. He was so delighted to see 'Mark Kovac & Family Building Contractors' on the trucks.

I didn't need to put my own name on the company, I *knew* it was mine, and it looked more established somehow to have the father of the family on it anyway. Gave us credibility, a pedigree.

My father's people had all left a village in Poland that didn't exist any more but my mother's father went on and on about this lovely place in Ireland. So when I was fifty I decided to reward myself with three months' vacation.

I had never married. No time really. It sounds a bit hopeless, I suppose, but I never thought of it like that. I was too busy getting everything up and running in the business and now that was done I found I had left it a bit late. My brothers and sisters were all well married with children and so I had plenty of family life around me if I needed it.

But then my doctor said that I was suffering from hypertension and therefore should take it easy. After Grandpa died, and there was all the Irish music at his funeral and the chat about Rossmore and the woods and everything, I got thinking about his country and I decided it might be a good time to go to Ireland and have a rest there, away from the business.

But at the same time, since I wasn't a person who was used to doing nothing, I could investigate this idea I had of building a tribute to Grandpa O'Neill. Something that would show to the people of his native place that his life and his travelling to America had all been worthwhile.

Everyone thought this was a good idea, and they assured me that Mark Kovac & Family Building Contractors could manage to stagger along without me.

'And maybe you might even find an Irish colleen over there,' my mother said. I thought she'd have to be a fairly long-in-the-tooth colleen to fancy me, but I said nothing like that. Over the years I got used to smiling at people and agreeing with them rather than having to have the last word. The last word isn't all that important really.

And so I came here to my grandpa Danny O'Neill's place. A very good place to take it easy. Nobody in Doon remembered my grandpa, which was disappointing.

They knew the line of little cottages he came from but these had all been long knocked down because they had fallen into disrepair. And it was all so long ago, and O'Neill was a very common name in Ireland anyway.

So I decided that he *would* be remembered. I would see to this. I would make a monument to him, but not something vain, something that would be of great use in his home town. I asked around for suggestions. They were many and varied. People thought of a little theatre. Or an art gallery. Or maybe a small park where the children could play and the old people sit in the evening. Or a church hall or a museum. There were as many ideas as there were people offering them.

One old lady said I should go to pray at the well in the woods outside Rossmore and then I would see as clear as daylight what I should do. So I drove in and parked my car near the edge of the woods and went in. I met a big friendly dog that accompanied me and seemed to know his way to the well as he made the correct turning at every little wooden signpost. Then he sat outside respectfully while I went into the damp dark cave.

The well was extraordinary. That was the only word. I'm as religious as the next man, I mean, as the son of an Irish Catholic mother and a Polish Catholic father, I wouldn't have much chance of escaping it, would I? But this was beyond anything I had ever seen.

People had put their petitions on the walls of the cave for all to see, they had left children's tiny shoes and socks with notes attached, praying for a recovery from rheumatic fever, or rosary beads with notes begging for the recovery of a beloved mother.

It was grotesque in many ways and yet so touching in others. Such a collection of frail hopes all gathered in one little space. It didn't give me any sense of well-being, holiness. There was no wisdom coming towards me from that statue. Instead I felt uneasy and wanted to be away from there. Yet as I came out I found the big dog again – a kind of sheepdog or a collie, I guess; he had been waiting for me as if I were his long-lost friend. I scratched his ears and walked back through the woods deep in thought.

Then an idea formed in my mind.

I would build a health centre so that the people of this area wouldn't have to be on their knees in this cold wet place praying to a saint who was two thousand years dead that a cure would be found for a loved one. Maybe, I thought to myself, this is the way the well worked: you got your problem solved once you left it.

The dog trotted along beside me happily.

He was never going to leave me now.

I took him to the nearest Garda station. They looked at him thoughtfully. He had no collar and he wasn't well kept. Someone had brought him to lose him in the woods.

I was shocked.

A lovely, friendly dog like that.

'You might give him a home yourself?' suggested the young Garda.

'Come on then,' I said to the dog and he leaped eagerly into the car.

I decided to call him Zloty. It was the old Polish currency. He answered so readily that you'd think it was his original name.

Back home again in Doon, I was determined that the place would have some kind of medical centre. If anyone needed specialist treatment, or a scan, or an X-ray, they had to take the bumpy road into Rossmore. Yes, I had heard all about this bypass road that was meant to be built. But it could all be just dreams for the next decades. And anyway in Rossmore they didn't have all the facilities that patients needed – sometimes they had to make the long journey to Dublin, adding to their stress and strain.

Wouldn't it be great to have all these opportunities on their doorstep?

The people in this place were all very nice and easy to talk to. I stayed in the local hotel, and Zloty slept in a big outhouse. I met Ciaran Brown from the bank, and Sean Kenny the local attorney, and the Foley family, and Maggie Kiernan who told everyone how desperately she wanted to have a baby and eventually she did. There was a very ladylike woman, Hannah Harty, who was a bookkeeper and the soul of discretion in a very gossip-prone place. So when I bought a plot of land through Sean Kenny, he suggested that I should ask Hannah to look after the paperwork for me, and nobody would know my business.

And there were two doctors in the town, a very crabby sort of fellow, Dermot, and a much younger smarter lad called Jimmy White. Unfortunately I had registered with Dr Dermot before Jimmy White came to town so I had to stick with him. He was a slow, lazy guy, just looked at my prescribed medication and told me to continue with it. Then he went off on a vacation. After a bit I felt short of breath. I consulted Jimmy White who sent me for a stress test and an ultrasound. And a heart specialist changed my beta blockers and I was fine again.

That was a bad time for everyone. Old man Foley died, then Sean Kenny's mother and Ciaran Brown's father died, all within ten days. We had a path worn to the churchyard for funerals.

Poor Jimmy White was distraught.

'It would have to happen on my watch,' he confided to me one night. 'The people here think that the sun shines out of Dermot's arse and that all those old people wouldn't have died if he had been here.'

'But that's impossible,' I said. 'I mean, they were old and frail, their time had come.'

'Tell that to the Foleys, the Browns and the Kennys,' he said glumly.

'That was certainly bad timing,' I sympathised.

'Yeah, or maybe – as I think in my more paranoid moments – it was planned,' he suggested.

I gave him a look and Jimmy White said hastily that no, of course it wasn't possible, even Dr Dermot couldn't have killed them off by voodoo from his vacation. I thought about it myself for a while. Maybe that weaselish little doctor did actually wait until all those old folk were going to take their last journeys.

Was I becoming as paranoid as Jimmy?

Anyway I had plenty to keep me occupied. I had a building firm in Ireland, which was fairly relaxed. Very relaxed. Finn Ferguson often said that when God made time he made plenty of it. Planning permissions were a nightmare; assembling a team was very different from back home. Everyone seemed to be running several jobs in tandem, I would sigh to that nice Hannah Harty sometimes, and she was always very positive and full of practical advice.

Perhaps I should tell the foreman Finn Ferguson that if his wife liked to go to America on a shopping trip, my sisters would look after her and take her to the right stores. It worked like a dream and the woman came back not only with three suitcases of merchandise but with the news that Mark Kovac & Family Building Contractors were huge in the USA. Finn, the foreman, stopped treating me just as bumbling old Chester and called me sir after that. He still would have a beer with me now and then, and often brought a bone for Zloty as well. He would tell me of his worries about the new road that might or might not be built around Rossmore.

Once one of these huge firms got the contract for building the bypass and established themselves in the town of Rossmore, then a little company like Finn Ferguson's would be edged out of the jobs he already had. People would be seduced by big companies with huge earth movers and cranes, and his living would go down the plughole. I assured him that the thing to do was to specialise. To get a name for doing one kind of building very well.

When the Danny O'Neill Centre opened there would be a beautiful glossy brochure about it, which of course Finn could use to get himself more clients.

This galvanised Finn to take a less leisurely attitude to the building, I was very relieved to observe.

'You're a very decent skin, you know, Chester, I mean, sir,' he said. 'A lot of people say that about you. I heard Miss Harty telling Canon Cassidy when he came over here last week, she said you were the angel this place has always been looking out for.'

I liked Hannah and was disappointed that she seemed to

fancy Dr Dermot. I asked her once if she had ever been in love, and she said no, but at the age of fifty-two she didn't think it was a luxury that might come her way. Her mother had always said that Dr Dermot would make a good catch and she had invested a lot of time in trying to realise that. But he was a man independent and set in his ways.

'Or a little selfish maybe?' I suggested. Wrong way to go, Chester.

Hannah Harty defended him. He had worked tirelessly for this place. Nobody could think he was selfish.

I said I was just an outsider; I didn't really know. But I did know. And he was selfish. I saw this more and more.

He would accept a drink from me in the hotel, but never buy the other half. I heard from Hannah how she would make him a steak and kidney pie or cook him a roast chicken because men were so hopeless. But the hotel had a perfectly good dining room where he could have entertained her and yet he never did. He was certainly very arrogant to young Jimmy White, so much so that the young man told me he would have to fold his tent and steal away. There was no living for him here.

Meanwhile my own plans were going ahead. Finn the building foreman now loved me like a brother and had recruited people from all over the country to build the Danny O'Neill Health Centre in Doon. It was growing like a mushroom every day before our eyes.

The people could hardly believe that there would be X-ray facilities and heart monitoring machines and a therapeutic swimming pool, all on their own doorsteps, with a dozen or more treatment rooms planned for those who might want to rent them. It was the medicine of the future, the newspapers said. Already there had been enquiries from a dental practice, a Pilates class, and a yoga class, as well as several specialists interested in the possibility of having a clinic there twice a week. It was all a matter of bringing health care to the people rather than letting patients travel great distances, adding to their distress. I had been hoping Jimmy White would be part of it, but no, he was gone before it was up and running.

Hannah Harty had obviously handed over the bulk of my work to a firm of accountants by now but she still did my own personal books for me. I enjoyed our sessions together.

Finn would come for a Friday drink at the hotel around six and bring me up to date with what had happened during the week, then Hannah Harty would join us, countersign some cheques for Finn, and then she and I would have dinner.

She always had her hair nicely done at the beauty parlour for our meetings. She liked to talk about Dr Dermot and because I'm basically easy going I let her chatter on. She used to meet him on Saturday, so I think the fancy hairdo was really in his honour. But I noticed that there were more and more occasions when Dr Dermot wasn't going to be able to make their Saturday meeting.

He had a case conference about a patient. He had a golf game where they were depending on him. He had friends from overseas passing through. Friends who were never named or introduced.

Hannah had begun to wonder whether Dr Dermot might be avoiding her. I tutted and said surely not, which was just what she wanted to hear.

'And of course you still do his books for him?'

'Well, yes, but he just leaves the material there in a tray nowadays, he's not there himself.' She was very troubled.

'Maybe he's busy, on urgent cases.'

'Ah, Chester, you know Dermot,' she said. 'There's never anything very urgent. I think he's afraid our names are being linked.'

'But he should be proud of that surely?' I said.

She bit her lip, her eyes filled with tears and she shook her head sadly. I wanted to go down and take that annoying Dr Dermot by his thin shoulders and shake the life out of him.

Why should he upset a decent woman like Hannah Harty? A woman that any normal man would be proud to escort around the place. And maybe share a life with.

And as that thought went across my mind, it was followed by another thought. Hannah Harty is much too good for that little weasel. She's the kind of woman that I personally would be happy to spend much more time with. I wondered why I hadn't seen this before.

I hoped that she didn't think she had confided too much in me and therefore could never learn to see me as a person. Well, I would never know unless I moved things on a bit. So I suggested that when she had picked up Dr Dermot's papers tomorrow, she and I might take a drive together.

'That's if he's not there of course,' Hannah said.

He wasn't there, so we drove off to see an old castle that had a waterfall in the grounds. And the next week we went to an art exhibition, and the week after that we went together to the wedding of Finn Ferguson's daughter. By now she was talking a lot less of Dr Dermot, and her name was most definitely up with mine or linked with mine or whatever the expression they used around here.

The three months' visit had turned into six months. And despite the best efforts of Finn the foreman, the building seemed to take for ever. I thought less and less about going back to Kovac's in America. Lots of things were keeping me here. The need to make our grandpa's name connected to a centre of excellence, a place that would be at the heart of the community he had loved so much and mourned so long in America.

I told my brothers that I probably saw this as a permanent position. They were pleased for me and assured me that they could well manage without me and they had long realised that I had found a life that involved me deeply back in Ireland. They didn't realise how much I was involved.

And they hadn't heard of Hannah Harty.

She was such a help to me in so many ways: she found a designer to do a restful decor for the Danny O'Neill Health Centre, she got Finn's new son-in-law to do the landscaping, she gave little dinner parties and invited Ciaran Brown from the bank and his wife, and Sean Kenny the lawyer, and his wife. And Maggie Kiernan and her husband when they could get a babysitter.

She did ask Dr Dermot from time to time but he never was free to accept. And then she didn't ask him any more.

One day he cornered me about the new centre. He hadn't changed at all, he was still very pleased with himself. He had heard it was going to be opened by a government minister. He was laughing at the thought. Hadn't they little to do with their time?

I reminded him that on several occasions I had invited him to take rooms there. I thought that if he had all the referral places on the premises, he finally might actually start sending people for the tests and scans they needed. But he hadn't listened.

He had even ridiculed the idea, saying that he had his own perfectly good surgery, thank you very much.

I explained that I would then be offering the rooms to other doctors, and he said he wished me luck taking money from eejits and losers. But of course I hadn't done that. The Danny O'Neill Health Centre was going to make sure that the people of this place got proper medical treatment, not like my grandpa and his great number of brothers and sisters scattered all over the globe, each one of them in poor health as they headed for a new life in a new land.

But it was only now, when he realised that a real live government minister was going to come and open the premises, that Dr Dermot showed any interest in it.

'I suppose that place will be a licence to print money for you, Chester,' he said to me with his usual sneer.

It was hardly worth arguing with him. He wasn't the kind of

man who would understand that I had put my own money into it, invited others to contribute and gathered a team. The notion that I wasn't in it for a profit would have been beyond his grasp.

'Ah, you know the way it is.' I shrugged. I had learned a few of these meaningless phrases since coming to this land.

'I don't at all know the way it is, I'm the last to know anything around here,' the doctor snapped. 'And a patient told me this morning that you have notions about Miss Harty, that was news to me too.'

'I am a great admirer of Hannah Harty, that is true, your patient was not wrongly informed,' I said pompously.

'Well, as long as it's only admiring from afar, no one would quarrel with that.'

He was actually warning me off, staking his claim to a woman whom he had ignored and humiliated. I felt bile rise in my throat. But I had got as far as this in life by keeping my temper. I wouldn't risk everything now. And I realised that I really did feel a primeval rage against this man as a rival.

But I have seen too many people lose things over rage. I would not give anger its head.

'I have to go now, Dr Dermot,' I said in a voice that I knew sounded choked.

He smiled his superior and hugely irritating smile. 'Well, sure you do,' he said raising his glass at me. 'Sure you do.'

I walked across the square shaking. Zloty came with me to keep me company or to give me courage – I didn't know which. I had never felt so hostile to a man before. Not ever. So that meant that I had never felt so strongly about a woman either. But I had no idea whether she felt anything remotely similar. Calm, gentle, ladylike Hannah, maybe she thought of me just as a pleasant acquaintance.

What a poor specimen of a man I must be. No idea whether this woman liked me, even a little bit.

I found myself walking straight towards the elegant ivy-covered house where she lived alone. Her grandparents would have lived in that house when my poor grandpa was packing his few belongings and leaving the wretched hovel that would now be a tiny part of the Danny O'Neill Health Centre.

She was surprised to see me. I had never called unannounced before. But she welcomed me in and poured me a glass of wine. She looked pleased rather than annoyed to see me. So that was good.

'I was wondering, Hannah . . .' I began.

'What were you wondering now?' She held her head on one side.

I'm just *hopeless* at this sort of thing. There are men who just know what to say, who have words at will. But then Hannah wasn't used to such men, I mean, she had fancied that poisonous doctor. I must just be honest, straightforward.

'I was wondering if you would ever see a future with a person like me.' I said it straight out.

'Someone *like* you, Chester – or you?' She was teasing me now.

'Me, Hannah,' I said simply.

She walked away from me in her elegant drawing room. 'I'm much too old for you,' she said sadly.

'You're two and a half years older than me,' I said.

She smiled as if I were a toddler who had made an endearing remark.

'Ah yes, but before you were born I was waddling around here taking notice.'

'Maybe you were waiting for me to come and join you?' I said hopefully.

'Well, if I was waiting for you, Chester, then I waited a long time,' she said.

And then I knew it was going to be all right. And the rage I had for Dr Dermot died down in me. What had I to be enraged about?

If it hadn't been for him I might never have crossed the street and spoken aloud to Hannah, I might have let it slip away as other possible relationships had slipped away in the past.

'Will I have to go and live in America?' she asked.

'No, I'd prefer to live here. I'd like to see the Centre up and running, I want to know if the big road around Rossmore ever gets built, if the well to St Ann is taken down. I'm fascinated by this place now, and to live here with you would be . . . well, it would be better than I ever dreamed.'

She seemed very pleased.

'But I hope you'll come over and meet my family,' I said.

'They'll be horrified with me,' she said, nervously patting her hair.

'They'll love you and my mom will be so pleased. She said that maybe I'd find a colleen over here,' I admitted.

'Oh, a bit of an ageing colleen,' she said.

'Please, Hannah . . .' I began and she went to draw the curtains of her big bay window that looked out on the square.

Before she closed them I saw Dr Dermot coming out of the hotel. He paused and looked at Hannah's house and then turned and went back to his own lonely place. He had only a short working life ahead of him. Once the Danny O'Neill Health Centre opened in Doon, there would be little demand for Dr Dermot's old-fashioned, blundering medicine. And now he had lost the woman who might have made his last years bearable.

I know that everyone always said about me that I was over good-natured, and always thought the best of everyone.

But truly I felt sorry for the guy.

CHAPTER 8

The Road, the Woods and the Well – 2

Father Brian Flynn went to the station to meet his sister Judy. She hadn't been home for ten years and the time showed very definitely on her face. He was shocked at how pale and drawn she looked. Judy must only be thirty-nine or forty. She could have been in her late fifties.

She saw him and waved. 'Aren't you very good to come and meet me!' She gave him a hug.

'I'm only sorry that I can't offer you somewhere to stay. It seems terrible for you to have to pay for a hotel when you have a mother and two brothers in Rossmore.'

'Will Mam recognise me at all, Brian?'

'Ah, she will in her own way,' he said.

'What does that mean exactly?'

He had forgotten how direct Judy could be. 'I don't know what it means, Judy, it's just something I say to avoid saying anything really, I suppose.'

She squeezed his arm affectionately. 'You were always a pet,' she said. 'I'm sorry I stayed away for so long. There was always one foolish thing or another keeping me over there.'

'But didn't you always write, and you were very good to our mother,' he said.

Judy cheered up. 'Now, take me on a tour of Rossmore showing me all the changes and point me to the best hairdresser.'

'There's a very smart place called Fabian's, though that's not his name at all – I was at school with him, and he was called something else altogether, but apparently they go to him from far and near.'

'Good. I'll remember that. You see, as well as relying on St Ann, I think I should bring up the second line of attack, get some new clothes and a hairstyle as well. A bit of grooming as one might say.'

'You're looking for a husband *here*?' Brian Flynn was astounded.

'Well, yes. Why not? I didn't do too well in over ten years in London.'

'You got a career for yourself.' Judy was an illustrator of children's books.

'Yes, but I am not asking St Ann for a career.' Judy was brisk. 'Lord, would you look at the traffic – it's like Hyde Park Corner.'

'It might not be for much longer. There's great talk of a new road, to take all the trucks and lorries out of the town for one thing. And let the through traffic pass without clogging up our little streets.'

'And will it happen or is it only talk?'

'I think it will happen. That's if you can believe half what you read in the newspapers. There's a lot of debate about it – people coming heavily down on one side or the other.'

'And is it a good thing or a bad thing in your opinion?'

'I don't know, Judy, I really don't. It's meant to be going through the Whitethorn Woods and possibly through St Ann's Well.'

'So I got here just in time,' said Judy Flynn, with a sense of grim resolution that made her brother Brian feel very uneasy.

Judy was astounded at the way every second person seemed to greet Brian as they parked the car and walked along a crowded Castle Street towards the Rossmore Hotel.

A woman came down the steps of the local newspaper office and her face lit up in a smile.

'There you are, Lilly,' Father Flynn said.

'This must be your sister, Father,' she said, pleased.

'It's just as well he hasn't a fancy woman,' Judy said. 'They'd have her identified in ten seconds.'

'No fear of that, isn't Father Flynn a walking saint?' said Lilly Ryan, shocked.

And then Judy recognised her. The woman whose child had disappeared all those years ago. Judy remembered how hundreds of people had gone into the Whitethorn Woods to hunt for a body or to pray at the well. There had been no result from either quest. She felt awkward and she supposed it must have shown on her face. But Lilly Ryan would be used to this after twenty years. Two decades of people shuffling and being unable to mention the great loss for fear of saying the wrong thing.

'I'm trying to get up the courage to visit my mother,' Judy confided. 'I'm afraid our family leaves all the hard work to Brian here.'

'Do it before you do anything else,' Lilly advised. 'If you face the hard thing first it makes it easier.'

'You might well be right,' Judy agreed. 'Brian, can you leave my case in the hotel? I'll go and see her now.'

'I'll come with you,' he said.

'No, I'll do this on my own. Good luck to you, Lilly.'

And they watched as Judy turned into the small side street where her mother lived alone.

'I'd better go after her,' he began.

But Lilly reminded him that Judy wanted to do this alone. So he shrugged and carried his sister's suitcase into the hotel. He would wait in one of their big armchairs until she came back and then he would buy her the stiff drink she would undoubtedly need.

*

Mrs Flynn had indeed no idea who Judy was, and no amount of reminding seemed to bring any recognition. She thought that Judy was a health visitor and was anxious for her to leave.

Judy looked around in desperation but there were no photographs on the walls or in frames on the old desk. Poor Brian had done his best to keep the place in some kind of order and would take his mother's washing to the Fresh as a Daisy once a week, but Judy noticed that the place still smelled bad and her mam was very uncared for. Every month for years now Judy had sent a cheque to her brother Brian, and she knew he had spent it on items for their mam. But the iron sat there unused, the easy chair was half hidden under a pile of newspapers. Mrs Flynn didn't believe in making herself comfortable.

'You must remember me, Mam, I'm Judy. I'm the middle one. Younger than Eddie, older than Brian.'

'Brian?' Her mother's look was blank.

'You remember Brian, surely, he comes in every morning to give you your breakfast.'

'No he does not, that's from the Meals on Wheels.' Her mother was definite.

'No, Mam, they come at lunchtime. Brian comes and gives you an egg every morning.'

'That's what he says.' Her mother wasn't convinced.

'Do you remember Eddie?'

'Of course I do, do you think I'm cracked or something? He wouldn't be told, married that Kitty, no good she was, nor any of her family. No wonder what happened happened.'

'What happened was that Eddie left her for a young one.'

'May God forgive you, whoever you are! Saying such things about my family! It was Kitty who threw my son out and kept his house, you'll note.' Her mother's mouth was set in a hard line.

'And what does Brian say about that?'

'I don't know any Brian.'

'Don't you have a daughter?'

'I do, a young one over in England doing drawings of some sort, she never gets in touch.' So that was the thanks for the weekly letter or postcard, the monthly contribution to Brian. She never gets in touch!

'I'm your daughter, Mam, I'm Judy, you must know me.'

'Would you get away out of that, my daughter's a young girl – you're a middle-aged woman like myself.'

As Judy walked back to the hotel she decided that a visit to this smart hairdresser called Fabian's might be well overdue. She even paused outside a new beauty shop called Pompadours. A course of facials and manicures might not go amiss either. She had put aside a fair sum of money for this visit and St Ann might need a little help to place her satisfactorily on the marriage market.

Brian was a splendid guide. As well as going with her while she made appointments in Fabian's and Pompadours, he showed her a very smart boutique.

'Didn't Becca King work there?' Judy asked.

'For God's sake, don't mention Becca King,' Father Flynn said, looking left and right.

'Why on earth not?'

'She's in jail. She got one of the van men in the shop to murder her boyfriend's new lover.'

'God, and they say you take risks living in London!' Judy said in amazement.

He brought his sister back to meet the canon. Josef and Anna had made little sandwiches in honour of the guest. They kept everything in the priests' house gleaming and the old man himself looked pink and clean. Unlike Judy's mother, he remembered her well. He had been there for her first communion, had looked on when the bishop came to confirm the girls of St Ita's, and although he had long forgotten her infant sins, he had heard her confession.

'I haven't had the pleasure of assisting at your marriage yet,' Canon Cassidy said as he drank his tea and ate his dainty sandwiches.

'No, but it won't be long now,' Judy said. 'I'm going to do a novena to St Ann. I'm going to pray at her shrine for nine days so that she will find me a good husband.'

'And no better woman for doing that than St Ann,' the canon said, his simple faith and certainties all intact.

Father Flynn envied him with all his soul.

'I'd better go and see the sister-in-law,' Judy said with a sigh.

'Don't raise your hopes too high,' Brian Flynn warned her.

'What would annoy her least, do you think, as a gift?' Judy wondered.

'Let me see, flowers would be a woeful waste of money, sweets would rot the children's teeth. Magazines are full of rubbish, a book could have been got in the library. Get her a loaf of bread and a half-pound of ham, she might make you a sandwich.'

'As bad as that, is it?' Judy asked.

'Worse,' said Father Brian Flynn.

He was not in a good humour. He had discovered that there was going to be a public meeting in ten days' time, a big protest meeting, and he was going to be invited to address it. Many of the townspeople had told him that they were eagerly waiting for his words. And he literally didn't have any.

He simply couldn't find it in his heart to stand up and condemn a possible scheme that would improve traffic and the quality of life for a great many people just because it would mean taking down a perfectly awful statue that was beginning to produce dangerously idolatrous feelings amongst the parishioners.

Had life been easier for Canon Cassidy when he was a curate? Or was this the way things always were? If you were a priest maybe it all went with the territory.

But with his usual optimism, he comforted himself that it was still only a rumour about the road. There had been no statement as yet. And also he still had ten days before the meeting. There was plenty of time to work out what to say. In the meantime there were a lot of problems to be faced nearer home.

Like how to deal with Judy if St Ann didn't come up with a husband. Like how they should face up to their mother's failing health. Like how much longer Canon Cassidy could reasonably be expected to stay in the priests' house with the title of parish priest. Or how he could go to see Aidan Ryan yet again in the jail tomorrow and try to tell him that his wife Lilly was not a villainous person who had sold their baby.

And, most immediately, what was going to happen at the meeting this afternoon between the anger-filled Kitty and the tense, strained Judy.

He sighed a heavy sigh and ran his hands through his red spiky hair until it stood up around his head like a mad punk halo.

As it happened Kitty and Judy got on perfectly fine. Eventually.

Judy decided to offer her as a gift a hairdo at Fabian's. At first Kitty laughed a sneering laugh and said Fabian's wasn't for the likes of them. Then Judy said she was asking her to come for solidarity.

'Just to patronise me, you mean,' Kitty had scoffed.

'Not at all. Just because Eddie treated you disgracefully it doesn't mean that Brian and I would. I haven't been back here in years and I wanted to give you a big box of chocolates, then I thought you might just think that they would be bad for the children's teeth, so I decided to get you something you wouldn't go out and buy for yourself.'

'You must be made of money.' Kitty was still grudging.

'No I'm not, but I do work very hard and I saved hard for this trip home.'

'And what brought you home eventually?' Kitty was not yet won over.

'I want to get married, Kitty. It's as simple as that. I can't find anyone in London except married men, and I don't have to tell you what a foolish road that is to go down. You've experienced it from the other side. So I was hoping that maybe if I went for nine days to St Ann's Well . . .' She let her voice trail away.

'You're making fun of me – you're just having a jeer at us, you and your London ways.'

'I'm not as it happens, but honestly, life is too short. If that's the way you want to see it, then there's nothing I can do.'

For some reason it worked. Kitty said in a tone that she hadn't used for a long time, 'If the offer's still open I'd love a hairdo. That young slut Naomi that your brother has gone off with has hair like rats' tails. It would give me a great boost altogether . . .'

Father Flynn had another deputation waiting for him when he got back to the priests' house. A request for support from the other side of the increasingly great divide. A group of concerned citizens were going to have a candlelit procession through the town, campaigning for the rumoured new road that would bring an end to the dangerous traffic that roared through Rossmore. This traffic had already caused numerous accidents and the death of a five-year-old. They wanted Father Flynn to march at their head.

Great, he said to himself, absolutely great, and I haven't even answered the other lot yet.

Then his brow cleared. Maybe this was the answer. He would say that the Church must not be seen to enter local politics. Was this the wisdom of Solomon or was it in fact the refuge of a weak man? He might never know.

In a way he wished the whole thing were out in the open. These shadowlands of rumour and counter-rumour were very disturbing. Each day new fuel was being added to the flames of speculation. People said that big builders had been seen dining in the Rossmore Hotel. That meant that the road had been agreed – it was simply a matter of who would build it.

Farmers with land adjoining the woods were giving themselves airs. The land from which they had once scraped a living might now be worth something in the end. The trick would be to sell now to some speculator. Especially if you had a few acres that might not come under the compulsory purchase order when it happened but would be highly valuable for access. It seemed that everywhere you went, you heard voices. Voices with something to say.

The man that ran a garage was very doleful. If the road came it would kill his business stone dead. It was hard enough for people to park in his premises as things were, and getting back on the road was like Russian roulette.

A woman who had a small guest house on the edge of the town was reported to be putting in new bathrooms and extending her breakfast room, once the new road was given the go-ahead. She would have an unending line of engineers, advisers and consultants looking for accommodation near the site.

There were debates on television about the parlous state of Irish roads; the newly rich country would not remain rich for much longer if European exporters found only Third World crowded lanes and endless delays in delivering their goods to the right destination. Tourism would suffer if visitors couldn't get from one place to another without crawling in their rented cars behind a tractor or some huge lumbering bit of farm machinery.

Places like the Fresh as a Daisy Launderette just couldn't wait for the road to arrive. They had never got any business from visitors anyway. And Fabian's the hairdressers thought they would do better if their clients had room to park their cars.

But the garden centre on the edge of town didn't want the new road. They had a nice little business where travellers from east to west would stop, stretch their legs, visit the café and maybe fill the car with bedding plants or gift-wrapped azaleas for whoever they were visiting. If the new road came no one would need to pass this way any more.

And there were those like the Rossmore Hotel, Skunk Slattery and Miss Gwen in Pompadours who just didn't know.

It was swings and roundabouts of course.

They would lose the passing trade because nobody would pass through any more. But it might mean that there would be more incentive for local people to come out and shop, get beautified, or have a lunch in the hotel, once they knew there would be room to breathe and they wouldn't be mown down by impatient truck drivers on the roads.

And there were the hundreds who had been helped by St Ann. They couldn't believe that their fellow countrymen and women were prepared to turn their backs on the saint, allow her shrine to be dismantled. There was talk of people lying down in front of the bulldozers if they came to the woods, and obstructing all the earth-moving machinery.

It was the least they could do to thank their saint for all the miracles that had been worked through her well. It didn't actually matter that these miracles had not been acknowledged and recognised by Rome like Fatima and Lourdes. People round here knew. And people from far, far away knew.

Didn't they come in droves from miles across the sea?

And still, greedy, money-loving people were prepared to ignore this great blessing, which had given so much to so many, just to get traffic moving faster and earn even more money than they already had.

The canon was completely unaware of the issues and said only that we must pray for guidance in these as in all matters. Josef and Anna confided in Father Flynn and said they thought that the old man needed full-time care.

'It's not that I am looking for more hours, Father,' Josef said. 'It's just that you should know. And of course I am always afraid that one day you will tell me he is going to a nursing home and there will be no job for me any more. I hope I am not being selfish but I want to be prepared.'

Father Flynn said he understood very well and it was indeed a grey area. The canon seemed very happy where he was and it would be a pity to move him. His life had no purpose if he wasn't in the priests' house. Yet of course if he really needed more care, then he would have to have it.

'It's just I was thinking of getting a job helping to build the road,' Josef said.

'You mean it's really going to happen?' Father Flynn was astounded.

'I have Polish friends and they say that it will. They are going to stay with Anna and me, and Father Flynn, you would not believe the great money they will earn building it.' Josef's face was full of hope and dreams.

'Yes, but it's only money, Josef.'

'It's money that will buy a little shop for my brothers back home in Latvia. We have everything we need here but they have so very little.'

For no reason at all, Father Flynn thought of his friend James O'Connor who had been ordained the same day as he had. James had left the priesthood, married Rosie, had two little sons. James worked in computer technology of some kind, he said it was great, easy work, and when you came home from the office you could put it all behind you.

Not at all like parish work. No more of this standing up for the indefensible, or staying silent on matters you cared about. Father Flynn thought he would have loved it.

Just loved it.

Skunk Slattery looked up as Kitty Flynn came into his shop with a good-looking woman he hadn't seen before.

'How are you, Skunk?' asked Kitty. 'We're getting ourselves a few glossy magazines and going off to Fabian's for a makeover.'

'More power to you, Kitty. It's never too late, I say,' Skunk responded, not very gallantly.

'Always the man to flatter you,' Kitty said.

'Are you going to introduce me to your friend?' Skunk asked.

'That's not my friend, Skunk, that's my sister-in-law – don't you remember her?' Kitty said.

'Kitty is another person who'll always flatter you!' Judy said. 'I'm Judy Flynn, by the way. Brian and Eddie's sister.'

'Pleased to meet you, I am Sebastian Slattery,' said Skunk.

'You are not!' Kitty would argue with her shadow. 'You're Skunk – you always were and always will be.'

Skunk and Judy exchanged glances of despair as Kitty burrowed amongst the glossy magazines.

'I'm amazed I never met you before. Will you be around for long?' Skunk asked.

'For as long as it takes,' Judy Flynn said mysteriously.

Naomi approached Father Flynn. Normally she steered well clear of him. Naomi was used to steering clear of people, there were a fair few she had to avoid. Like Eddie's wife Kitty, like Eddie's children, like his mother, and most certainly his brother Brian, the local priest.

'Excuse me, Brian?' she began.

Father Flynn nearly dropped to the ground in shock. 'Yes . . . um . . . Naomi.' What on God's earth could the girl want?

'Brian, I was wondering if you could explain to me how Eddie could get an annulment of his marriage.'

'With great, great difficulty, Naomi,' Father Flynn said.

'No, I mean, it *can* be done obviously, it's a question of how.' Naomi turned her big nineteen-year-old eyes on him.

'It can't be done,' Father Flynn said. 'Annulment is saying that no marriage existed, and I have to tell you that a marriage did exist between Eddie and Kitty, and they have four children as a result of it.'

'It wasn't a real marriage,' she began.

'It was, Naomi. You weren't born at the time. I was there. It

166

happened, you can't say it didn't happen. Now have I said one word to you about your living with Eddie? No, I have not. It's your business, yours and his, but don't go dragging the principles of canon law and the Church into it. Please.'

'He didn't know his mind then, he was only twenty, for God's sake, what does a young fellow of twenty know about taking on a wife and having children? He shouldn't have been allowed to do it.'

'What brought all this on, Naomi?' Father Flynn's voice was level. It wasn't much worse than anything else that was happening around him in his life these days. But it would at least be nice to know why after two years this girl wanted respectability and the approval of Church and State.

'It's just that I want things to be fair and open . . .' she began.

'Really?' Father Flynn was doubtful.

'And, you see, my parents have discovered that I'm not a student any more, they thought I was going to college and they're being a bit troublesome . . .'

'Yes, I'm sure.'

'And so, you see, I told them that I was going to marry Eddie, and now they're all delighted again and getting ready for the wedding, so that's what we have to organise, you see.'

Father Flynn looked at her wildly. He thought that he had become master of the meaningless comforting cliché. But on this occasion he could not summon up one single word to say.

Neddy Nolan brought his father in to see the canon once a week. The two old men used to play chess together and Josef would serve them coffee and biscuits.

'Tell me, Canon, shouldn't we all be voting against this road if we get a chance?' Marty Nolan asked.

'I don't think we do get a chance.' Canon Cassidy's grasp on it was tenuous.

'But you know what I mean, Canon, voting with our feet.

167

Going to the meeting in the square and everything, having banners maybe. Don't we owe it to St Ann?'

'Why don't you ask Father Flynn, he's the brains of this parish,' the old man said.

'I did ask him, Canon, but he just went on about doing what our consciences told us to do.' Marty Nolan shook his head in disappointment. 'That's no use at all, suppose everyone's conscience told them something different. Where would we be then? It's guidance we need.'

'Do you know, Mr Nolan, I think the days of guidance are long gone. I never thought I'd live to hear myself say this but it appears to be true.'

'It's a great worry for us,' Marty Nolan said. 'You see, people are making us offers for the land. Unmerciful sums of money. And I know it has Neddy awake at night wondering what to do.'

'But nothing has been agreed yet. Why would people be offering to buy your land?' The canon was bewildered.

'I'm not sure, Canon, maybe they know more than we know. But you see the problem for Neddy. I mean, his own mother was cured at that well. No amount of money could ever pay for that.'

'Where is Neddy at the moment?' the canon said, possibly trying to change the subject. It worked.

'Ah, you know Neddy, Canon, always the dreamer, he's wandering round Rossmore with his hands in his pockets, interested in everything, understanding nothing.'

'Well, we'd better get on with our game of chess then,' the canon said. 'Was it my move or yours?'

Neddy Nolan was in fact in Myles Barry's law office. 'I've always been a bit slow, Myles,' he began.

'I wouldn't say that at all. Haven't you done very well for yourself, married a grand girl? Aren't you a friend to everyone in Rossmore?'

'Yes, but, Myles, I might not be for much longer. All kinds of people are coming to me and suggesting we sell our property to them.'

'Well, isn't that good?'

'Not really. They must have inside information or whatever it's called. They must know that the road really is coming and will go over our land.' He looked very troubled.

'I know, Neddy, but isn't that the luck of the draw? It couldn't happen to a better family.' Myles couldn't see where the problem lay.

'But I can't sell our land to speculators, people who are buying up bits here and there for no reason, except that they can hold the authorities to ransom by cornering all the available acres. Then when the time comes they can hold out and eventually sell it on again at a huge profit to the government and the builders. That's not the kind of thing we want to be involved in.'

'Well, no . . . no . . .' Myles Barry wondered where this was leading.

'It's just a few of them have told me they are approaching you about it,' Neddy said anxiously.

Myles Barry played for time. 'That's a fact, Neddy. But it's not illegal, you know, to make an offer for someone's land. You name a price and they pay it, and you put the money in the bank, and they sell the land on later for more money, because they'll have lots of little bits here and there to offer. Or you refuse it and take less from the government when the time comes and that's that. It's the system. Where's the problem?'

'The problem is that it's all just about making money,' Neddy said.

Myles sighed and decided to be very direct. 'Yes, it's true some clients have asked me to put in an offer to you but I said you'd need to get a solicitor of your own, and maybe an estate agent to advise you and I couldn't be acting as a sort of an intermediary and twisting your arm over it all.'

'Could you be our solicitor, Myles? I've known you for ever, you were at school with my brother Kit.' Neddy's face was without guile.

'I could indeed be your lawyer, Neddy, but I suggest you get someone more high-powered than me. A big firm from Dublin maybe. There's serious money tied up in this. You'd want a really professional team working for you.'

'Is it that you don't want to let the other people down, Myles, by changing horses and representing me?' Neddy wanted to know.

'No, there would be no conflict of interests. Nobody has mentioned any sums involved. I have seen no papers or proposals. I just said I wouldn't do anything until you got representation, that's all,' Myles said.

'So you could do it if you wanted to?' Neddy was distressingly direct.

Of course Myles Barry could. But there would be much more money in it for him if he were to represent a consortium of local businessmen. He couldn't charge Neddy Nolan and his father proper fees. Especially if things were as they looked and the Nolans were going to hold out. The land would be bought eventually if the road went ahead, which it looked very likely to. Those particular businessmen who had approached him would not have sought out the Nolan farm unless they knew something from the council. Myles Barry had been given to understand that any reasonable demand from the Nolans would be met.

Of course it was speculation. But that's how an economy worked. People took risks; they won or they lost. Only Neddy Nolan would see anything dubious about the whole system.

Myles sat and looked at the gentle man on the other side of the desk. A man who had worked very hard for what he had. It would be great to see someone like that being dealt a winning hand.

Myles Barry was only too aware that the rumours were going to become a reality and the heat was about to be turned on.

Cathal Chambers in the bank had told him about two local councillors, they were fellows who hadn't a bone to throw to a dog, and yet they were coming into the bank these days with large wads of cash which they wanted lodged in savings accounts. It was so obviously vote buying that Cathal was amazed.

Yet what could he do except invoke the law about banks needing to know where any lodged money came from. They looked him in the eye and told him that it was from poker games. The vote about the road when it came would be first at local council level, and then nationally. And it looked like a foregone conclusion.

Myles Barry looked at Neddy. He needed someone to look after his interests. These were dangerous waters that he was entering. But Neddy Nolan didn't want the big boys in Dublin, the firms that would frighten off anyone trying to cheat him. No, he wanted the man who had been at school with his brother Kit – now serving time in an English prison at Her Majesty's pleasure.

'Sure, Neddy,' Myles Barry sighed. 'I'd be honoured to be your solicitor.'

Judy Flynn walked up to the Whitethorn Woods on her own. She wore her best outfit, a navy silk dress with a navy and white scarf. Her newly streaked hair was elegant and shiny. She wanted to show St Ann the raw material for her quest.

In the cave were half a dozen people muttering and praying near the statue. Judy kneeled down and got straight to business.

'I'm going to be completely honest with you, St Ann. I don't really know whether you exist or not, and if you do exist whether you deal with cases like this or not. But it's worth a try. I am going to come here and pray for peace on earth, or whatever you yourself think may be needed, for nine mornings in a row. That's a fair bank of prayers we're building up. And in return you are going to guide my steps towards meeting a man I can marry and have children with. You see, I do drawings all the time for children's books and yet I have no children of my own. And because of doing these drawings I sort of believe in magic, well, a magical world where marvellous things happen. So why shouldn't I find a husband in this place?

'Oh, and you'll want to know why I didn't find one already. That's easy. I looked in the wrong place. I looked in publishing and advertising and the media, that kind of world. Not the right base. What I would like is someone maybe from this town so that I wouldn't feel so alienated and guilty about not being here. And then I could help my brother Brian to look after our mam, I could help Kitty – I'm sure she's been up here asking you to get my brother Eddie to go back to her. Don't do it, it wouldn't work.

'I don't think that marriage is all about appearances and dressing well, but it's only fair to tell you that this is the best I can look. I am inclined to be a bit impatient and short-tempered but I think that I am keeping it under control. And that's it now. I'll say a rosary for your intentions and I'll come again tomorrow. I can't say fairer than that.'

Eddie Flynn came out of the bar in the Rossmore Hotel. Times were very worrying. He had a good business deal possibly going ahead with a gang of people who knew what they were doing. It should bring him in some very badly needed money. And did he need money just now!

Young Naomi had been telling her parents a pack of lies, saying she was a second-year student above in Dublin. Now she was telling them more lies, saying that Eddie's marriage was going to be annulled and that he was going to marry her. It would never happen, not in a million years. The girl was soft in the head.

In many ways it would be easier to have stayed with Kitty. At least there was always a meal on the table when he got home in the evening, there were the children to entertain him. It was all a bit awkward and artificial nowadays, they seemed to think he was some kind of rat who had deserted them. Then Kitty would let him take them to the pictures in the middle of the week, and young Naomi wanted to go out at weekends. And everyone was on his case about not going to see his mam enough.

He was weary of it all. If he went home now, Naomi would be there with pictures of wedding dresses and lists of the people they would invite. Apparently she had had a highly unsatisfactory conversation with Brian about it all and now thought they should go straight through the canon who would surely have a more helpful attitude. And anyway wasn't he technically Brian's boss?

On the other side of the road he saw Kitty. Or was it Kitty? She wore Kitty's anorak certainly but her hair was totally different and she was wearing make-up. He pulled back into the shadows and watched. It was Kitty. But she had done something to herself. Dyed her hair, maybe?

She looked years younger.

He saw her talking animatedly to that poor Lilly Ryan, the one whose baby had been stolen all those years ago and then her husband had turned violent. Eddie watched as Kitty moved along the street. He wouldn't even admit it to himself but life would be a great deal easier if he were going home to Kitty for his tea.

The march against the new road was held right through the town and up to the Whitethorn Woods. Some people carried posters with 'Save Our Saint' on them, others had 'No to the New Road'. Television teams and journalists from national newspapers came to cover it.

Father Brian Flynn knew he would have to make some kind of statement to someone. He couldn't sit like a dummy looking on. But he hated the thought of himself on national television.

'I have such desperate hair, I look like a lavatory brush,' he confided to his sister.

'Go to that man Fabian, he's brilliant,' Judy advised.

'Are you mad – you'd feed a family for a week on what he charges.'

'You don't have a family to feed, go on, Brian, it's my treat,' she said and that was that.

He went into the salon feeling more foolish than he had ever felt in his whole life. He couldn't see what the guy who called himself Fabian actually did to him but he did look a lot more normal afterwards.

So he was interviewed and said that the Well of St Ann was a place of local piety and it was always sad to see parishioners upset and their sensibilities offended.

Then a week later he was interviewed again at the candlelit meeting calling for the introduction of something that would take the heavy traffic away from Rossmore. This time Father Flynn told the interviewer that the death of a child was to be deplored and that the authorities had a duty to do all in their power to make sure that a young life was never lost again in this way.

'I'm sure that anyone who saw both of those interviews will think I am a complete clown,' he said to Judy.

'No, they'll think that when you're in a hole you're right to stop digging,' Judy said.

She was proving to be a much more restful companion than he had feared. She said she knew it was barking mad but she was getting a lot of comfort from that crazy old well. She had also painted her mother's kitchen and got her a kitten, which had cheered the old woman up – but not yet to the extent of admitting that she recognised Judy.

The brother and sister would have a drink together each evening in the Rossmore Hotel. Once they saw Eddie there and waved him to join them. Nobody mentioned Naomi, Kitty or Mother.

It was a perfectly pleasant chat.

'I think we're all getting seriously grown up round here,' Judy Flynn said afterwards.

'Oh, if only, if only,' said Father Flynn. He saw really immense problems ahead once the council's vote was known, which would be any day now.

The voices for and against the road, the voices from the woods, were only gathering their strength – they had seen nothing yet.

CHAPTER 9

Talking to Mercedes

Part 1 – Helen

Ah, there you are, Mercedes. I was having a little sleep there. I dreamed I was back in Rossmore, walking down the crowded main street. I often dream that. But you wouldn't know where it is, it's over in Ireland across the sea from here. Ireland is only fifty minutes on a plane from London. You should go there sometime. You'd like it there, you're religious and it's very Catholic.

Well, it was anyway.

I've always liked you, Mercedes, much better than the day nurses – you have more time for people, you'll make a cup of tea. You listen. They don't listen, it's sit up and wake up and get up and cheer up. You never say that.

You have a nice cool hand, you smell of lavender, not of some disinfectant. You are interested.

You say your name is Mercedes and that you would like to marry a doctor. You would like to send your mother more money. But it took me weeks to find even that out about you, Mercedes, because you only want to talk about me and how I feel.

I wish you would call me Helen rather than Madam. Please

don't call me Mrs Harris. You are so friendly, so interested in my family who come to visit. My tall, handsome husband James, my gracious mother-in-law Natasha, my wonderful, beautiful daughter Grace.

You ask me all kinds of questions about them and I tell you, it's a pleasure to tell you things. You smile so much. And you aren't curious and act like the police, always asking questions. That's what David seems like to me. You know David, he is Grace's boyfriend. I think you sense that about him, you often move him gently on when he is here. You know that he distresses me.

But you I could talk to for ever.

You love the story about the night I met handsome James Harris twenty-seven years ago when I borrowed my flatmate's dress to go to a party. He said that it was the same colour as my eyes and that I must be very artistic. In fact it was the only dress between the three of us that was smart enough for me to wear.

I told you the truth about that, and about how fearful I was about meeting his mother Natasha for the first time. Their home was so big and impressive, her questions so probing. I had never eaten oysters before – it was such a shock to me. And I told you the truth about a lot of things, about how kind they always were to me in the orphanage where I grew up and how they insisted on making my wedding cake. Natasha had objected at first because she thought it would be amateurish but even she was pleasantly surprised.

I went back to see them often at the orphanage. They told me I was the only child in the home who didn't ask about my parents. The others were all very anxious to know details and if it would ever mean their mothers would be coming back to collect them.

But I wanted to know nothing. This was my home. Someone had given me, Helen, away, no doubt for good reasons at the time. What more was there to ask? To know?

I haven't told the Sisters that I am so ill, Mercedes. They couldn't bear it. Instead I told them that I'm going abroad with James and will be in touch later. I have left them something in my will and a letter of thanks. It's important that people be thanked for what they do. Really it is. Otherwise they might never know how much they are appreciated. Like you, for example. I thank you a lot because I am truly grateful to meet someone who will listen to me so well and be so interested in my story.

You who have worked so hard and saved so much would understand how hard I too worked when I did my secretarial course here in London. The others in the class spent ages having coffee and going window shopping, but I studied and practised very hard.

I lived in a flat with two other girls who loved cooking so they taught me how to enjoy it too.

On Saturdays I worked at a cosmetic counter in a big store and I got makeovers and free samples as well as my wages; on Sundays I worked in a garden centre which taught me a lot and so I did flower arranging and window boxes for people who lived near by. By the time I had landed a good job in the City with a really proper salary I was much more accomplished than many girls who had left the orphanage with me. They always told me when I went back there that I looked like a real lady, they were proud of me and I could marry a duke if I put my mind to it.

But I put my mind to marrying James Harris.

I used to read novels about people like James, but I didn't believe they really existed.

He was such a gentleman in every sense. He never raised his voice, he was always courteous, he had a way of smiling that lit up his whole face. I was determined to marry him and I worked hard at that like I had worked at everything else. I hid nothing about my past. I did not want his mother Natasha investigating and discovering things about little Helen from the orphanage, so

I was totally up front about everything. And it paid off. She finally agreed to the wedding and I think that in a way she sort of respected me.

I was a beautiful bride. Did I show you the pictures? Of course I did. I just wanted to look at them once more.

All we were waiting for was a child.

Someone to inherit Natasha's large estate. You don't call it money if you're very rich, Mercedes, you call it an 'estate'. So we were married for three years and no sign of my becoming pregnant. I was anxious, James was concerned and Natasha was incensed.

I went to a doctor in a completely different part of London and had an examination.

I wasn't ovulating, it turned out, so I would need fertility treatment.

I knew only too well how much James would object to this. If it were proven that he was well capable of fathering a child but that his wife could not conceive, things would change between us. If Natasha knew, then the world as we knew it would end.

So I realised there was no way James and I could go together like normal couples who had problems conceiving and could have *in vitro* treatment. There was no way that I could go alone and get a secret artificial insemination. It didn't work like that apparently.

James wouldn't consider surrogate parenting, so there was no point in discussing it. Nor adoption, even if there had been any children to adopt. And I didn't even want to think of Natasha's face on the subject of an overseas baby being brought to our home. A little African Harris! An Asiatic Harris! Don't make me laugh.

No, Mercedes, you are very kind but I'm not upsetting myself, no, not at all. I know that you are always sensitive to my getting upset especially when Grace's David keeps interrogating me about things. But this is not like that. I'm just trying to explain it all to you. You see, I want to tell you this, I need to tell you. Can you think of it as if I am writing you a letter? A letter to Mercedes from Helen.

Yes, I will have a sip of tea, thank you so much, my dear, you are always there when people need you.

So, as I was saying, I had to think what to do next.

Now this was twenty-three years ago, you were only a little toddler then, running around in the sunshine in the Philippines. It is sunny there, isn't it? But I was here in London, worried out of my mind.

I had always been good at finding a solution; I would not be beaten by this. One of the girls at work had been on a holiday in Dublin, over in Ireland, and when they were there they had gone to this place, Rossmore. It was a small town but was very beautiful, it had an old castle and a forest called Whitethorn Woods, and even a wishing well. A saint's well it was, actually. You'd know about that, being Catholic, Mercedes. People went to pray to a saint and they got their wishes answered. They left things there to thank her.

What did they wish for? I wondered.

Everything apparently, the saint had a big job on her hands. People prayed for husbands and for cures from illness. And a lot for babies. There were lots of little baby bootees and things tied to the thorny bushes from people wanting a baby of their own. Imagine!

Well, I did imagine. Day and night I imagined. That is where I would find our child.

These people wouldn't have gone on praying unless there had been some results. So next time James went away on a business trip, I took a couple of days off from my office and sneaked over to Ireland and took a bus to this place Rossmore.

It was extraordinary, the whole thing. It was really very strange. Quite a modern town with nice shops and good restaurants, I even got my hair done in a smart salon. But just a mile out on the road there was this real scene of Third World super-stition. Sorry, Mercedes, no offence but you know what I mean.

There were dozens of people, each one with their own story. There was this old woman praying to St Ann. That's who it was, St Ann, the mother of Mary who was the mother of Jesus, but you'd know all that. We used to have a statue of her back in the Home.

Anyway this woman was asking that her son who was a drug addict would get cured, and then there was a girl praying that her boyfriend would not hear that she had had a stupid fling with another man. A boy saying he simply had to pass this exam as the whole family were depending on him. A fourteen-year-old girl was asking that her father would go off the drink.

So I closed my eyes and I spoke to this saint and I said I'd go straight back to my religion, which I had sort of forgotten about since I met James and Natasha, if she would arrange for me to get pregnant.

It was very peaceful there, and anything seemed possible. And I was so sure she would arrange it. Until the afternoon bus came I spent the day looking around Rossmore. There wasn't much traffic back then, you could walk about easily. I believe it's changed utterly now. Everyone seemed to know each other, greeting half the people in Castle Street, which was the main street. They were all families, I noticed. But, I thought, when I came back to this place with my child one day, I would be part of a family too. I would come back to Rossmore and thank St Ann for her help.

A lot of these people left their children sort of parked outside shops since the prams were too big and bulky to bring in. Passers-by would pause to admire the chubby babies in prams. Dozens of them. Soon I would have our baby in a pram, James's and my baby. Natasha's grandchild. And when we did, we would never leave the child out of our sight.

But the months went on and on, with no sign of any intervention on St Ann's part. I looked back with great rage at my useless trip over to her well and I got very annoyed. I kept thinking of that town where the women just left their babies for all to see in the main street without anyone to mind them. They just left their babies out in the street so casually while so many of the rest of us were aching for a child.

That's when I got the idea.

I would go to Ireland, find a pram and bring our baby home. It didn't matter if it was a boy or a girl. If it were our own child we couldn't choose anyway so this made it all the more natural somehow.

It needed a lot of planning.

You didn't need passports to go to Ireland or anything but still there was more chance of being spotted on a plane or at an airport than on a ferry. So I made my plans to go by sea.

I told James that I was pregnant, and that I had gone not to his and Natasha's family doctor but to an all-women-doctors clinic and that I preferred it this way. He was totally understanding, and gentle with me. And of course utterly delighted with my great news.

I begged him not to tell his mother yet. Said that I needed time. He agreed that it should be our secret until we were sure that everything was on course. After three months I said that I now preferred to sleep alone. He agreed reluctantly.

I read all the symptoms of pregnancy and acted accordingly. I went to a theatrical costumier and got a special mould made to simulate a pregnant stomach. I explained that it had to look good under a nightdress for my stage part. They were very interested in it and I had to be more and more vague about the whole thing in case they wanted to come to the theatre and see me act!

Natasha was overjoyed. When she came to lunch every Sunday she even helped me clear the dishes instead of sitting there like a stone.

'Helen, my dear, dear girl, you have no idea how happy this

makes me,' she said, laying her hand on my stomach. 'When will we feel the baby kick, do you think?'

I said I would ask them at the clinic.

I realised that I would have to go away around the time of the so-called birth of the baby. This would be a problem but I solved it. I told James and Natasha that there was something about approaching motherhood that made me nostalgic for the orphanage, the only home I remembered. James wanted to come with me but I said that this was a journey I wanted to make on my own. And this was a busy time in his antiques business, he needed to be in London. I would be back in a week, long, long before the birth was due. It took a lot of persuasion but they let me go.

I had already begun my maternity leave from the office. I was in charge, I could do what I liked.

I did go to the orphanage where they were delighted with my pregnancy. They were particularly delighted with the timing because apparently my birth mother was in a hospital dying and she wanted desperately to see me just once. To explain.

I said I wanted no explanation.

She had given me life, that was fine. I needed no more. I had just got on with it.

The Sisters and staff were shocked at me. Here was I, with a good job, a wealthy husband, a beautiful home, and now expecting my own child. Why could I not open my heart to a poor woman who had not been so lucky in life?

But I would not be moved. I had too much on my own mind. I was about to go to another country, steal a baby for myself, a child for James, an heir for Natasha Harris. Why should I get involved with the ramblings and remorse of some stranger, which had come far, far too late?

Then I drove on and left my car near the ferry terminal. I wore a wig and whipped out my false tummy and put it in the boot of the car. I had bought a cheap raincoat, a rug and a lifelike doll and then I was ready. They didn't have closed circuit TV so much in those days but I wanted to make sure that if there was a hue and cry nobody would be able to call attention to a woman with a baby boarding a boat for the UK – someone else would be sure to mention having seen her going in the other direction. I sat out in the open air cuddling the doll.

One or two other mothers approached me to have a look at the baby but I said apologetically that she didn't like strangers. You see, I was already thinking of her as my daughter.

Then I got the bus to Rossmore, cuddling the doll very close to me. It was a busy Saturday in the town – I walked the length of Castle Street until my feet were sore.

I did some shopping as well, talcum powder, napkins, soothing creams. There were indeed many prams outside stores on this visit also. Innocent, trusting people in a safe town, some might say. I didn't say that. Criminally careless, neglectful parents who didn't deserve children, was what I said.

I had to be careful.

The bus that I must get would leave at three. It would be two hours to the ferry. I must take the child just before the bus left, not earlier, no point in giving the authorities time to search.

It's strange. I could almost draw a picture of the people in that crowded street that day. There was an old priest, you know, wearing a soutane, the sort of black dress they used to wear, right down to the feet. And he was shaking everyone's hand. Half the population seemed to be out shopping, and greeting each other. I was standing on the steps of the Rossmore Hotel when I saw a little baby in a pram. Just lying there asleep and with a small Yorkshire terrier tied by his lead to the handle of the pram. I crossed the road and it was over in seconds, the doll was in a litter bin and the baby was in my arms wrapped in my rug. The eyes were tightly closed but I could hear a little heart beating close to mine. It all felt totally right as if it was meant to happen. As if in some curious way St Ann had led me to this child.

I got on the bus and looked back for a last time at Rossmore. The bus bumped across the country to the ferry and then I moved with my daughter on to the boat. I must have been well away long before the alarm was raised. And who would have thought to search the ferries at once anyway? I was settled in my car by the time they realised that this was a full-blown child abduction.

I had done what I set out to do: I had got my child.

A little girl who would be called Grace Natasha. She must be between two and four weeks old. It was despicable, leaving a child that age to fare for herself, I told myself. She was better by far that I had come along to claim her, to give her a better life. No one could find me now, I told myself, as I prepared her first formula bottle on a spirit stove at the back of the car.

And the wonderful thing, Mercedes, was that nobody ever did.

I had it all very well sorted out, you see.

I reinstated my false tummy, and left the baby in the car while I checked into a shabby guest house. During the middle of the night I pretended to wake with labour pains and insisted on driving myself to the hospital. In fact I drove back to my orphanage.

I told them that I had delivered the baby myself and needed them to look after me for a couple of days until I recovered from the shock.

One of the staff said that I couldn't possibly have had this baby since I was there a couple of days ago. This was a baby who was two weeks old, not three days. Another wanted to get me a doctor. But these were people I had lived with for seventeen years of my life. I could manage them. And they loved me, don't forget. I had been no trouble all those years there. I had remembered them and come back to visit. I had even sent contributions to their building fund. They weren't going to question poor little orphan Helen, whose own mother was dying.

They knew – of course they knew. These were women who lived with children all day and all night. Maybe they should have reported it, I suppose you could say that. But then they thought that I must have bought the baby. And they knew I was hiding it from my rather grand husband and mother-in-law. So they went along with the fiction.

I burned the false stomach and the wig and the cheap raincoat in their incinerator when nobody was looking. They called James to tell him he had a daughter, and he called Natasha to tell her she had a granddaughter. They even registered the birth. James cried on the telephone. He told me that he loved me more than ever and he would look after us both for the rest of his life. And Grace slept on, delighted with herself and everyone, and never caused anyone any trouble for twenty-three years.

She is so like me, not physically, I know, but the way she behaves. You've seen that for yourself. She is my daughter in every sense of the word.

She is a strong girl with a forceful character. She is just like her mother.

Just like me.

No, Mercedes, I did not enquire about the family who lost her in Ireland. You see, they have different newspapers and everything over there, so I didn't have to read about it.

They all have so many children over there anyway. I don't think about that side of things at all.

No, of course I would never tell Grace, never in a million years.

She's got a boyfriend now, David, of course you know. James isn't crazy about the boy, he doesn't say it but I know. I don't like him very much but he's Grace's choice and so I say nothing, I just smile.

David is Irish as it happens. Extraordinary, isn't it! And Grace has never been over there. Since. Not yet anyway. But I had a real scare yesterday when suddenly out of the blue David started saying that there is this big drama going on in Ireland about a roadway that's going to bypass Rossmore. Huge protests about it, apparently.

'Rossmore?' I said with my blood turning into ice.

'Yeah, a one-horse town back of beyond. Much better bypassed. No one would have any call to go there.' He dismissed the place.

I raked his face in case he knew. Suppose he was actually from Rossmore? Suppose for one terrible moment that it was his sister who had disappeared from her pram? Could it have happened that he and Grace were brother and sister?

I felt very faint. Remember, you were there for me as always.

I didn't pass out as I thought I was going to. I could feel myself coming back to reality. I asked myself, why would he mention that town of all towns unless there was some connection? Perhaps he had been tracking me down for years. I had to know.

'Have you ever been there yourself, David?' I asked, hardly daring to think what he might say.

But no, he said he probably passed through it on the way to the West of Ireland but he had never stopped. He and Grace had been talking about it, because of something there that might be of interest or might not. His voice trailed away. He had only been trying to make conversation.

Grace looked at him adoringly.

'I'll tell you what we were talking about, Mother – David was telling me that there's a sort of shrine there, a wishing well or something. And, you know, people get cured there . . .' She looked at me hopefully.

'No, Grace, and David, thank you, but really I'm fine,' I said. 'Just fine. Those places don't really work, you know.'

'But they say that they work in some fashion, Mother, you know, people get strength, confidence, they feel better. People who go there take what they can from them.'

'I took what I could . . .' I began and then I saw all of them looking at me. 'I took what I could from everything and it made me very strong. I feel absolutely fine,' I said firmly.

And Grace lifted my thin hand and kissed it.

Her grandmother is settling all this money on her in two years' time when she's twenty-five. She will have the whole Harris estate. What would she have had if I had left her in that pram with the dog tied to the handle? I won't be here then of course to see her inherit everything, but that doesn't matter. I gave her a very good start in life. I did everything for her: everything a mother could do. For her, for her father, for her grandmother.

I have nothing to blame myself for. I never told James a lie in my life except this one, and I did it from love. We have had such a wonderful marriage, I know in my heart that he has never told me a lie. Not ever. But as I say, I have nothing to blame myself for.

Stop crying, Mercedes, please stop. You're meant to be helping us to feel strong, not the other way around. Things are hard enough without having the nurses getting all weepy on us.

That's better.

That's the smile I like.

And maybe if there's a little more tea, do you think?

Part 2 – James

Mummy always telephones me at 9 a.m. A lot of people think that's rather odd but I find it quite reassuring. It means that I don't have to remember to phone her and that I am kept up to date with all that's happening in her world, which is always interesting. Full of writers and lawyers, bankers and politicians.

We have always lived a very quiet life, Helen and I, so it's entertaining to hear first-hand about the kind of people you might read about in the newspapers. Helen never answers the phone at that time because we both know it's Mummy. Not that Helen doesn't like talking to Mummy or anything, they get on very well and Helen is utterly charming to her. From the beginning she was the one who decided that we must make Mummy part of our lives, invite her to lunch or dinner with us once a week. Then of course she has always known exactly how to handle her. If Mummy has a fault it is that she's slightly snobby but Lord, does Helen cut straight through that!

She looks at Mummy with big china-blue eyes.

'I'm so sorry, Mrs Harris, but you're going to have to help me here. We didn't ever eat oysters at the orphanage,'. . . or we didn't have fingerbowls or *amuse-bouches* or whatever nonsense Mummy was indulging in at the time. It was completely disarming, Mummy came round to her very quickly – after some initial doubts, shall we say. She was genuinely admiring of someone so direct and unaffected as Helen.

She also knew that I had never loved anyone before and would never love anyone again. I had made it very clear that Helen would be my wife very soon after I met her first, wearing a dress exactly the same colour as her blue eyes. She wears that colour a lot, in silky scarves, in tunics. And also in robes and negligées. Which is all that anyone sees her wear nowadays.

The family, all my uncles and cousins, had always wanted me to work in the City like Father had. But I hadn't the stomach for it. I hated the whole idea. Instead I insisted on serving my time with an antiques dealer. I did the history of art courses and shortly after I married Helen it all took off like a rocket. Helen taught me to dress smartly, rather than in the slightly fuddy-duddy clothes I used to wear, to present myself more forcefully. To give little talks on eighteenth-century furniture. She encouraged me to let the press know when I had something interesting to sell. And the rest, as they say, is history.

My antique shops are all over the country and I am regularly on television, consulted as an expert.

I made my own way and I was very proud of that. As I was proud of marrying Helen. We had our twenty-sixth wedding anniversary a few days ago. Helen even pretended to drink a little champagne tonight in the hospital. We brought in some crystal champagne glasses. She looked quite as beautiful as the day we were married.

And then after that we went to dinner: Mummy, Grace and I. Fortunately Grace didn't insist that the loutish David come with us. We went to a small French restaurant that Helen and I used to go to a lot before she became ill.

Mummy proposed a toast: 'To one of the happiest marriages I have ever known,' she said in one of her tinkly voices. I smiled a gentle, knowing smile.

This was the same woman who had railed and wept at me over a quarter of a century ago, begging me not to marry a girl of whom we knew nothing, a woman with no history, no past, except that she had been given away to an orphanage.

Grace agreed about our marriage. She said her dream was to have a marriage even half as good with David. She said that all her friends reported that their parents were constantly bickering and scoring points. This had never been a part of her life. She never remembered there being any arguments at all.

'Nor do I,' I said, simply.

I didn't taste the food, it could have been chopped-up cardboard. The sense of unfairness welled up in me again. Why was this marriage drawing to a close? Next year we would be talking about my late wife, next month even. What reason could there be that Helen who had never hurt a fly was dying, and others whose lives had been full of malevolence and greed were allowed to live on? Why was I here at this table mouthing clichés to my mother and daughter, when I wanted to be by Helen's bed holding her hand, telling her that it had been a magical time and that I could remember no past before her and contemplate no future after she has gone?

And we would talk about inconsequential things, like planting geraniums near each other in clusters, and I was to send my jackets to be dry-cleaned every week and my shirts to be done at the Chinese laundry, and how I was to wear expensive cufflinks even if it did take three minutes to put them in. I loved her so much and I had never thought of being with anyone else. That's true – I never even thought of it.

But that Filipino woman, Mercedes, the one with the big, sad eyes, kept assuring me that Helen was happy tonight. She had talked about her family a lot apparently and took out pictures of our wedding day, and snaps of Grace when she was a little girl. Helen wanted me to try and live what she called a normal life. To go out and have a happy dinner with my mother and my daughter. As if that were remotely possible. I saw them looking at me, sideways glances, Mummy and Grace, it was a warning sign. I must be more cheerful. I'm tired of being cheerful for other people.

Yet that's what Helen wanted most. She had said it was the one thing I could do to help her, I must keep the show on the road. I must remember to invite my mother around regularly, I must be polite to David, Grace's irritating boyfriend, and not say that she could do better for herself even if I thought it. So with an effort I put my shoulders back, forced myself to identify what I was eating and started to keep the show on the road again.

They were both such handsome women. My mother did not look her seventy-something years, even I didn't know exactly how many. Yes, my mother Natasha Harris was a credit to her hairdresser, her beauty salon and her own good taste in clothes. She wore a lilac dress and jacket, something that had been designed for someone forty years younger, yet suited her perfectly.

Grace with her blonde hair and dark eyes was always striking. But tonight in a scarlet dress with those little straps she looked dazzling. Much too good for that David fellow, too beautiful and too bright, but I was not to go down that road.

She was still talking about David. When was she not? He worked in the City too.

People said he was bright. Bright in the sense of having native cunning. Like a bookie at a race track, not like the accountants, bankers and financial experts with whom Grace moved with such ease.

No, indeed, young David was a different breed.

But there was no doubt that Grace loved him. She had never brought anyone home before this and now it had to be this young lout.

'David was in to see Mother today.' Grace rolled his name around as if she loved saying it. 'He said, wasn't it extraordinary that I looked so different from both of you, that I couldn't sit out in the sun for two minutes without getting burned and yet you both could sit out for a month and just turn golden brown. He's the image of his father, of course, they are like twins, same nose and mouth, same way of pushing his hair out of his eyes.'

I restrained myself from saying that this must be unfortunate for both of them. I managed a weak little sign of interest to encourage Grace to go on speaking about the love object.

'Yes, he was asking Mother, didn't she think it was strange that I was so unlike either of you.'

'And what did your mother say?' I asked, trying to put some warmth and interest into the question. I was barely able to speak. How dare this punk interrogate a dying woman? How dare he confuse her last weeks, days even, with his inane questions?

'Oh, you know Mother, she said she agreed with him, then she wasn't feeling so well so she called for Mercedes.'

'It wasn't the boy's fault, the pain comes and goes for Helen, we were told that,' my mother said. Astoundingly Natasha has always stood up for the young pup.

'And she was fine later, Dad, for the little anniversary ceremony, wasn't she?' Grace's big, beautiful, dark eyes looked at me questioningly.

'Yes, she was fine,' I managed to say.

I managed a lot of things in the next hour. Like smiling at my mother and my daughter, and telling them little stories about happier times. I managed to look as if I cared whether we had an Armagnac or a Cognac as a treat after dinner. And then finally my mother was back in her tall town house, and my daughter back in her flat where undoubtedly that David who looked so like his father would come and sleep in her bed.

And I was free.

Free at last to go and see Helen.

They let you in at any time.

That was the great thing about having enough money for private medicine. I could just push through those big quiet doors into the lobby which looked more like a grand hotel than a hospital. The night receptionist greeted me pleasantly.

'If she's asleep I promise you that I won't disturb her,' I said with my practised and barely sincere smile.

Helen and I had often talked about how life was basically an act. How we have to pretend a lot of the time in life. We sighed over it and told each other that at least we never pretended with each other. But we did. Of course we did. The biggest pretence of all was between the two of us.

She never told me about Grace and I never told her that I knew. That I had always known.

I had known since the day I went into her room that time during the so-called pregnancy when she said she preferred to sleep alone. She was tossing in her sleep in the middle of yet another bad dream, I put my hand on her forehead to reassure her and I saw it, the white garment she was wearing under her nightdress. I lifted up the sheet and saw the beautiful cream and gold negligée pulled to the side and the foam artificial belly attached to it.

The shock was overwhelming. Helen, my wife, lying to me. But it was followed by an aftershock of sympathy and love. The poor, poor girl, how terrified she must be of my mother and, indeed, of me that she would go to such extremes. And what was she going to do when the time came, or rather when she told us that her time had come?

Possibly she had arranged to buy a child from somewhere. But why hadn't she told me? I would have shared anything, everything with her. Why could she not have told me?

I went back to my room that night full of alarm. What did she intend to do without me by her side? I knew that she wouldn't be able to manage it without me, bring to term whatever halfcrazed plan she had dreamed up.

But I also knew I had to wait. I had to let her go ahead. Nothing could be worse than the humiliation of letting her know I had discovered her deception.

The time went on; Helen looked pale and anxious, Mummy put it down to her pregnancy. Only I knew that there was a greater reason. I was very relieved in the end when she said that she wanted to go back to visit her old orphanage, the place where she had been brought up. That was where she would find a baby and pretend that it was ours.

It surprised me, even shocked me, that a place like that, a really respectable institution, would go along with her in such a subterfuge. It was against the law, it was against everything they stood for. They had always been meticulous about the children in their care. Surely they would have found a legal way for Helen to adopt a child rather than be a party to all this deception? But I knew they would always look out for Helen.

There were still women there who had been on the staff when she was a baby herself.

They would have nothing but compassion and pity for her.

So when I heard the news that our baby had been born suddenly, a little girl, strong and lovely, and that everyone was being so helpful, I started to breathe again. I glossed over the whole birth registration business, easily filling in documents here and signing my name there, asking no questions, raising no issues.

I held someone else's little girl in my arms, and even I, a mere man as people would say, realised that Grace was older than the tender age that Helen claimed her to be. I helped to keep people away from the mother and child until it was too blurred and late to know the difference. I reminded everyone that I too had been a very big child at birth and, amazingly, my mother – who is inclined to fight with me on issues like this – agreed and said that I was quite mountainous.

Helen gave no descriptions of the delivery, not even to people like my mother and her close friends who begged her for details. It had all passed in a blur, she said, but now that she held her little Grace to her it didn't seem important, and wasn't she lucky that she had been with people who knew how to help her. Nobody thought it was unusual.

Nobody.

Well, why would they?

They had seen Helen over the last six months swelling gently, planning the birth of her child. Only I knew and I would never tell.

I walked along the carpeted corridors to Helen's room. I had only one more thing to tell her, which was that her secret would be safe with me for the rest of her life. That it didn't matter one damn what that foolish, insensitive boyfriend David said, no one would ever know that Grace wasn't our daughter. But I couldn't tell her straight out. That would be letting her know that I knew.

I would sit and look at her and it would come to me.

I would know what to say.

The room was dark, just a small light and the big shape of the Filipino woman, Mercedes, sitting beside her. Mercedes was holding Helen's hand. Helen's eyes were closed.

'Mr Harris!' Mercedes was surprised to see me.

'Is she awake?' I asked.

She was asleep apparently; she had just had her cocktail of drugs. The palliative care nurse had been half an hour ago.

'I believe that David upset her today.'

'She didn't say, Mr Harris.'

But I knew in my heart that David had made her uneasy, her face had shown great alarm when he was droning on about some place over in Ireland with a wishing wood or a magic well or something. I can read Helen's face like a book. The nurse was impassive.

She saw and heard everything but said very little.

I had to know.

'Did she mention anything? Anything at all?' I knew I sounded unhinged but I had to know if that boy had made her anxious. Now at the very, very end.

'No, no, she told me only of you bringing in champagne for her wedding anniversary.'

Mercedes was looking at Helen in the bed as if she might still hear in spite of all the medication.

So it hadn't turned her whole world around in the fear that her long secret would be discovered. I could breathe again.

I asked, could I sit with her alone. Apparently not. She was to be watched all night. They were worried about her chest.

'Please, Mercedes, I want to talk to her when she wakes,' I begged.

'Mr Harris, when she wakes I will move across the room and you can talk to her where I don't hear you,' she said.

And that's what I did – sat by her bed for two hours, stroking her thin white hand.

They must expect her to die today or tomorrow if there was a twenty-four-hour watch arranged.

Then she opened her eyes and smiled at me.

'I thought you were at dinner.' Her words came out with difficulty.

'I was, it was wonderful,' I said.

I told her we talked about lots of things: that everyone was very happy, and I was happiest of all. I reported Grace telling us that David said, wasn't it odd that Grace had dark eyes while we were both fair and I told him how my father had dark eyes too. Black as soot, so I told Grace that she must have got them from him. And Mummy had agreed and even added that Grace could also have got the dark eyes from Helen's side of the family. It was just that we didn't know them. So David had agreed. And shrugged and gone on to something else.

Helen looked at me long and hard. 'You still don't like him,' she croaked at me.

'I do,' I lied.

'You can't fool me, James, we never lied to each other, not once, remember?'

'I know.'

And then I told her the last lie.

'I don't really *dislike* him, my darling. It's just that I love my little girl so much nobody will ever be good enough for her. She's my daughter, my flesh and blood: nothing can make me think any other man will make her happy like we did.'

And Helen's smile was wonderful. I could have looked at it for ever but something changed in her face and Mercedes was about to go for the Sister.

Before she left the room she said to me:

'You are a wonderful man, Mr Harris, you made her very happy by what you said.' And even though it's utterly ridiculous – when you come to think of it – I felt for a moment that she knew our secret. That she knew all about Grace.

But, of course, that's not possible.

Helen would never have told her.

Not in a million years.

CHAPTER 10

June's Birthday

Part 1 – June

Well, it was obvious from the word go, wasn't it? I was going to be sixteen on 16 June and my name was June. Where else would we go except to Dublin for Bloomsday? It was going to be a magic day, she said.

I didn't really believe in magic days but she was so excited about it that she told everyone she met. 'My daughter's going to be Sweet Sixteen on the day that Leopold Bloom met Molly.' Most people hadn't an idea what she was talking about, but when has that ever stopped Mom?

The planning began almost a year in advance, with hours on the Internet looking for good-value tickets and low-cost accommodation. I swear we must be the only Irish Americans who don't seem to have any relatives in Ireland. I really don't know what Mom did with all her family. Alienate them, maybe. Talked too fancy about how well we were all doing across the Atlantic – which was far from true.

She had been born in this place called Rossmore, miles from anywhere. But most of the family had gone to live in Dublin. Over the years we had prised this much out of her. When she was a child she used to play in these woods and they all went to a holy well to pray for husbands.

'Was it a real wishing well?' I asked.

It had delivered my papa to Mom as a result so she obviously didn't think much of it. Apparently people went there to this day.

Mom had lived in Ireland until she was eleven, for heaven's sake, she must have had some cousins, friends, aunts, uncles. There hadn't been another potato famine since then to wipe them all out or anything. Why couldn't we be normal and go and stay with them?

Oh, no use asking Mom! She would shrug and flutter and say everything was so difficult these days, what with everyone being dispersed and all over the place. But it was never clear who had gone and where and why. It always seemed to me that we were the only ones who had left, everyone else had stayed.

No point in trying to pin Mom down, asking her serious questions. She knew nothing about Rossmore, and didn't really remember her years in Dublin. She brushed it all away, and became more vague and restless and anxious.

It was like mentioning dates and ages and things. It always made Mom uneasy and in the end wasn't really worth it. Mom is forty-four. She says to everyone around here that she is thirty-five, which means that she was meant to be eighteen when she had me and only seventeen when she got pregnant. I don't know how that leaves time for all the college education she says she had, in places far from here where all the co-eds and sorority friends once lived. But it's better not to ask.

I see my papa twice a year when he comes east. He is Italian, very over-excitable, married again and has two little boys. He shows me photographs and calls them my half-brothers. He doesn't meet Mom when he comes to collect me and take me to the motel where he stays. If she's at home she watches from the window upstairs. But she's usually at work. People who sell water

199

features and garden pools are at work all the time, it would appear.

Papa is no help when I ask him about things back in Ireland.

'Don't ask, Junie, don't ask, you just get a different story every time,' he would beg me.

'But Papa, you must know something, I mean, when you and she got married weren't there guests from Ireland at the wedding?'

'A few, but, hey, Junie, you don't want to look back on the past, look to the future, I always say.'

He was about to show me the pictures of my half-brothers again so I headed him off at the pass.

'Okay, this birthday I'm having in Dublin. Did you meet any of Mom's relatives when you were in Dublin?'

'Nope,' he said.

'But why? She met all yours when you went to Italy, didn't she?'

'I never went to Dublin, June honey,' Papa said. 'I always wanted to but we didn't go there. Apparently your mom's grandpa and her father had words one day. Bad words, and her father was a proud young man, so he took his family off to the United States and wouldn't let anyone give a backward look.'

'But wasn't that all years ago, Papa?' I was bewildered that any row on earth could go on this long.

'Oh, you know the way things snowball, they just grow,' Papa said, forgiving everyone as usual.

'But when Mom's father died, when Grandpa was gone, couldn't it have been made up then?'

'Perhaps she felt it would be disloyal to her father's memory. Anyway I never got to see the place, Rossmore, or Dublin. So I'm no help to you.' Papa shrugged.

'I'll tell you all about it, Papa,' I promised.

'Gina and I are giving you a camera for your birthday, June. Take pictures of everything you see and show them to me next visit. You'll have a great trip. Honey, your mom will be so proud

of you whoever you meet. She'll show you a really good time.'
He is so good, Papa is, wants everyone to like everyone else.

I could feel sudden tears in my eyes.

'You never really told me why you and Mom broke up?' I
began without much hope that I'd hear anything.

'Oh well, you know, these things happen, they're nobody's
fault,' he said with a big smile. 'And you know, Junie, nothing
was ever gained by looking back. We'll look ahead, to your wonderful trip to Ireland and then one day you'll come out to the
Midwest to see your little half-brothers and . . .'

I owed him some support. 'I'd love to meet Gina, Papa, and
get to know little Marco and Carlo,' I said and saw his face light
up that I had said their names.

'How was your father?' Mom's voice was clipped and strained.
It had obviously not been a good day selling garden pools. I
longed to tell her how kind and generous he was, so open to
hearing good news from every quarter. But it wasn't worth it, not
if it made her restless and upset. So, like Papa had given in all
those years ago about not visiting Dublin, I gave in too and said
very little.

'He was nice.' I shrugged. 'Didn't have much to say.'

'He never had,' Mom said, pleased. And she was humming a
little tune as she went to get out the big file of info about our
trip. The file she had labelled 'June Sixteen' in big green felt-tip
pen letters.

'What will you do there?' they asked me at school. I didn't
know how to answer for I simply didn't know what we were
going to do. But unlike Mom I didn't care what they thought I
was going to do.

'Will there be a party there for you?' my friend Suzi asked.

I said I didn't know – there might, as a surprise; there might
not.

I'd have a party anyway when we came back. I was hoping we
would go to this place Rossmore where there was a wishing well,

but I wouldn't mention it to my mom until we got there. The only thing I knew we were going to do on 16 June was to go on this James Joyce walking tour. Mom had signed us into this group.

We were to begin out on the coast at a tower, and go to a museum, then have a huge breakfast of kidneys and liver and things, and then go into Dublin City on a little train. It sounded weird but my mom hadn't been happier for a long time so that was good. Anyway after all the fussing, the packing, unpacking and repacking of suitcases, the day came and we went to Dublin.

The flight was crowded, and the bargain economy hotel was okay – not great, just okay. And the stores were all small compared to at home, and the money was different, and I kept asking Mom did she remember it all or even anything about it, and she said she didn't really know, it was all so long ago.

'Not so long, Mom, you're only thirty-five, remember,' I said and for once she didn't rise to it.

'I feel a hundred and thirty-five compared to all the young faces I see around me here, this has turned into a country of teenagers,' Mom grumbled. Her face looked tired and anxious. I decided not to tease her any more.

'You look as good as any of the youngsters, Mom, really you do.'

'You're a good girl, June, you have a lot of your father's Italian optimism in you, I will say that.'

'And what about the O'Leary side of the family? Do I have any of that?' I asked. It was walking on eggshells but if I couldn't mention them in their own home town, where and when could I bring their unspoken name up?

'Mercifully, no,' she said. 'They forget everything but the grudges.'

'Is that why we won't see them?' I was as brave as a lion.

'They are strange people, those O'Learys. We all came originally from this one-horse town called Rossmore and settled in

Dublin. Then I'm afraid *words* were said in a house on the North Circular Road.' My mom's voice was clipped. 'But let's get back to Joyce.'

She had arranged that we see the doorway of number 7, Eccles Street, which she said was the most famous address in English literature, and we could go to Davy Byrne's; on the way there we could familiarise ourselves with some Joycean culture and be prepared before the great tour on Bloomsday itself.

'You do know what it's all *about*, June?' Mom fretted.

I did.

One Thursday in June 1904 a whole lot of Dubliners went walkabout and kept meeting each other and criss-crossing and somehow even though it was only a fictional story it sort of drove everyone mad, and now they all dress up and do it again every year. I'd have preferred to do a tour of Dublin looking for my cousins, the real-life O'Learys, myself. But that wasn't on offer.

On Bloomsday, my birthday day, the city was in fancy dress. They were all dressed like Edwardians in boater hats and tottering on fancy old-fashioned cycles – it was half silly and half fun. I tried to be like my father and see the good side of it all. I tried to be like my friend Suzi who sees every gathering as a source of magnificent and yet undiscovered boyfriends. I tried to take my embarrassed gaze away from my mom who was being deeply foolish, showing off her very limited Joycean knowledge to all the others on the tour. We went from place to place and everywhere there were press people taking pictures of it all and camera teams. Eventually a girl with a microphone who was doing interviews for a radio programme came over to me and asked me some questions.

I told her it was my sixteenth birthday, that I was called June Arpino, half Italian, half Irish, and yes, I did know a bit about James Joyce and I was fairly interested in the tour but that actually I'd prefer to find my cousins the O'Learys.

The reporter was a nice girl with big dark eyes and a friendly manner and seemed interested in my story. Why did I not know where my cousins were?

I told her that they came to Dublin originally from a place called Rossmore miles away in the country. Words had been said, I explained, at a wedding thirty-three years ago in a house on the North Circular Road. My mom had gone to America with her parents shortly after that. Maybe even because of that.

She was really so fascinated about everything I said, this interviewer was, so I told her that I was just reasonably interested in what had happened to Stephen Dedalus and Leopold Bloom and Molly a hundred years ago, but I told her that truthfully I was really much more interested in what had happened to the O'Learys thirty-three years ago and did any of them remember my mom, and was there any chance that the words that had been said that day could possibly be forgotten by now.

She seemed very pleased with this conversation and asked me afterwards for the address of the bargain economy hotel. She told me that it had been a pleasure talking to me and that she wished me good luck, she said sixteen was a great age to be and who knew what could happen before the day was over. I didn't expect all that much to happen actually, just more of the tour, but Mom was having a good time and told everyone that it was my sixteenth birthday.

But it was an okay day. They were nice people on the tour – Swedes and Germans and fellow Americans. They bought me ice creams, they got photos taken with me. My mom smiled all day long. When we paused at the Joyce Centre and bought postcards I sent two to my half-brothers Marco and Carlo. It wouldn't hurt anyone, not a bit, but it would cheer them and Papa and Gina.

Then it was over and we went back to the bargain economy hotel. Mom's feet were very tired, she said she would soak them in cologne before we went out somewhere for my birthday pizza. When we went in the door everyone at the desk was very excited.

They had been having phone calls and messages all day. Never had this bargain economy hotel had such attention. Dozens of people called O'Leary, saying that they were originally from Rossmore and more recently from the North Circular Road, had been looking for us for hours now, and there were a dozen numbers for us to ring. Some of them were in the bar already having a reunion and they wanted to give June Arpino a sixteenth birthday she would never forget.

I looked at my mom in terror. I had done the unforgivable. I had got in touch with people who had Said Words.

I had also, by saying she had left Ireland thirty-three years ago, admitted on Irish radio how old she was. This was as bad as it could get.

Amazingly though, there do seem to be magic days.

'I've been thinking about words all day,' Mom said. 'Joyce was all about words when you come to think of it. Some words are worth remembering for a hundred years, some are worth forgetting much sooner. Come on, June, let's go meet your cousins,' she said and led me to the bar.

Part 2 – Lucky O'Leary

Well, I *know* it's a ludicrous name, but tell me how to get rid of it. I mean, you can't ring a bell and say from now on I am to be known as Clare or Anna or Shelley or something you'd like to be called. But no. It's always been Lucky, and it will always be Lucky O'Leary. That's my curse.

My parents called me Lucretia after an old aunt who had money. She didn't leave them any so it was useless, but Dad always called me his little Lucky because he thought Lucretia was too much to saddle a child with, no matter how great the inheritance might be.

You should have heard the way they used to tease me at school about it.

If I got a bad mark for an essay, if I didn't know the answer when the maths teacher pounced on me, or if I missed a pass in hockey, someone always said, 'Not so lucky, Lucky, now,' as if it was the first time I had ever heard it in my life.

Anyway, I was far from lucky in my hopes of going to work for the summer in a diner in New York. You'd think they'd have been pleased. I didn't want to go and get smashed and have sex with everyone out in a Mediterranean resort like half my class at school wanted to do when we finished our exams. I didn't want a big expensive university career that would bankrupt them. I wasn't asking for my fare out to a place that they would consider wild and dangerous.

All I wanted to do was to wear white socks and support shoes and a pink gingham dress in Manhattan. I wanted to serve pancakes and maple syrup; I wanted to put eggs 'over easy' framed with hash browns in front of the customers. And for them to say, 'Hi, Lucky.'

Or maybe I might even change my name out there and call myself a normal Irish name like Deirdre or Orla.

It wasn't such a mad dream, was it? Earning my own living, doing something respectable, worthy even, like getting people their breakfast. It wasn't as if I wanted to dance naked on tables. But you'd think I wanted to fly solo to the moon. How could I even consider living in a dangerous place like New York City? The matter would not even be discussed. I couldn't understand why we had no relations in America – some marvellous family of cousins where I could go at weekends and have barbecues and clambakes and go to ball games and all the things I loved about America from the movies.

But no. Alone in Ireland the O'Learys seemed to be without any emigrant wing of the family. No parcels of amazing American clothes ever came our way. No uncles and aunts with funny accents and permanently worn cream-coloured raincoats. And my mum and dad didn't even begin to realise what a treasure they had in me. They wanted me to come to this place called Rossmore.

They should have been on their knees thanking God that I was seventeen, a virgin, a non-smoker, only a very occasional drinker. And that all this was fairly rare in my crowd. I would pass my exams, I wouldn't have screaming matches at home. I was even reasonably pleasant to my poisonous sister Catriona even when she prised open my dressing table drawer with a knife to get at my make-up. And to my very annoying little brother Justin who used to bring potato crisps into my room and stink the place out because he thought he had less chance of getting caught there.

So what did they really want as an eldest daughter? Mother Teresa of Calcutta?

Anyway things were pretty glum in the O'Leary household this particular June because of everything. I said very politely, no thank you, I did *not* want to join everyone on a lovely family holiday in Rossmore. I said even more politely that I did *not* think this was throwing their generosity back in their faces, just that I did not fancy walking along a river bank or going through thorny woods or ensuring that Catriona and Justin didn't break their necks at the amusement park. And no, I didn't think that I would make lovely friends of my own during two weeks there. And if they just said yes I'd be right out of their hair and into a lovely New York diner up to my elbows in pancakes and bagels.

And they asked me please not to mention any of this again since it simply wouldn't happen.

So I went up to my room, locked the door against Catriona and Justin and looked at my face in the mirror. I wasn't bad-looking, not gross or hairy or full of spots or anything. I wasn't good-looking either but I had a friendly face – one that would have pleased all the clientele in the diner, specially because I had a good memory and I'd remember people and know instantly if they wanted a cappuccino to go or extra jelly on their toast.

I don't normally listen to the radio, I play CDs to myself. I'd really love a cheap television set in my bedroom but Dad said we're not made of money and not to be ridiculous. But anyway I turned on this radio programme and there was some ancient one solving problems. You know, the way they pretend to be young and hip and with it and get all the words wrong. So some crazy girl had written in saying that her mother was a mad suspicious old bat and she couldn't go anywhere or do anything. So I yawned to myself and said, 'Tell me about it,' but I did wonder why she thought the old one on the radio would have anything to say that would be remotely useful.

The old one said, yes it was desperate that old and young people didn't understand each other but there *was* a solution. Oh yes, I thought, of course there's a solution. Give in, give up, lose the argument, lose hope.

I waited for her to come out with this but instead she said: 'Your mother is lonely, dear, lonely and confused, confide in her, make her your ally.'

Sure, really great idea. I start making my mum my ally and in two minutes she'll say, 'You're not getting round me, do you hear?'

'Tell your mother about your concerns and your worries about the world, ask her about hers. She may not respond immediately but, my dear, she will respond in time. Mothers of teenage girls may look confident but in fact they are often anxious and beached creatures. Be interested, pretend an interest at first and a real interest will follow. You are on the eve of making your mother your great, great friend. Act at friendship first and then as time goes by it will become real . . .'

What kind of a world do these old ones *live* in? Imagine – she's paid serious money to go on the radio and talk all this nonsense. I mean, give us a break here.

Then the old one went on to talk about two best friends who had a fight and she told the one who had written in to make the first gesture to hold out her hand and say, Look, I don't want to fight . . . Which was of course the right advice but she'd prob-ably read it somewhere. Mothers lonely and beached. Huh.

They had had a row, Mum and Dad, we all knew that, it showed itself by over-politeness at supper. I didn't know what it was about and I didn't really care.

'Take your elbows off the table, Catriona, and show some respect for the great meal your mother has made for all of us . . .'

'Don't all talk at once, children. Your father has had a long and *very* tiring day . . .'

I didn't know what it was about, honestly, I didn't care. They sometimes had these coldnesses. But it would pass. I pretended to take no notice. Catriona and Justin, of course, who have the brains of a flea between them, did notice and commented on it.

'Are you having a fight with Daddy?' Catriona asked.

'No darling, of course not,' Mum said in an awful tinny voice.

'Are you going to get divorced, Daddy?' Justin wondered.

'No, Justin, eat your supper,' Dad said.

'Which of you will I go with?' Justin asked, looking from one to the other anxiously.

'Nonsense, Justin, how could a couple with such a wonderful son as you *possibly* get divorced?' I said. I was being sarcastic but Justin doesn't get irony.

'Oh all right then,' he said happily and attacked the rest of his supper.

I helped Mum stack the dishwasher.

'That was good of you, Lucky,' she said.

'Oh you know. Men!' I sighed.

She looked at me suddenly and I thought I saw tears in her eyes. But I didn't want to get soft in the head and make her my great, great friend like the old one on the radio said.

Next morning Dad said I was a terrific daughter, and since he had been saying I was a scourge from on high for the past few weeks I got worried and thought maybe they *were* going to split up.

So I said nothing. I'm getting good at shrugging.

Dad wasn't home for supper next day and Mum was locked up with her sister in the dining room. I tried to listen until I saw Catriona doing the same so I ordered her to go upstairs and not to be so appalling as to listen to other people's private conversations.

Dad came home very late. I tried to listen at their bedroom door but there was nothing to hear. Just total silence.

The next day I decided to do something different. The days were tedious now because we had reached such a stand-off.

Mum had a job working in a children's boutique: it was mornings only, so that she could be home to police us all in the afternoons. I had nothing to do so I went along to the boutique (we were never allowed to call it a shop). She was alarmed as old people always are when they see someone from home. She thought something was wrong.

I told her that *nothing* was wrong, just that there was a new pasta bar near by and that maybe she might feel like us having lunch there together. And her face lit up like the Kish Lighthouse.

During lunch, Mum said, 'It's hard on you, Lucky, having to come to Rossmore with us this year.'

I hadn't told her yet that there wasn't a chance I would go on such a dreary holiday with them. But for some reason I remembered the old one on the radio talking about mothers being beached and lonely. It was worth a try if I could get what I wanted.

'It's probably not all that easy for you either, Mum,' I said.

She looked at me with a long look. 'No, sometimes it's not, Lucky,' she said. She paused as if she were going to say something very important. So I waited. I wondered, would she tell me that Dad bored her to death or she had a toy boy or that I could go to New York, but actually she said none of these things.

'Things have a way of working out, you know,' was what she said in the end. It was so dull and so useless I hadn't an idea what to say.

So I said, 'You might be right, Mum,' and she smiled at me and patted my hand and knocked all the linguini off my fork. I felt like life was over if this was all she could say and I kicked a stone the whole way home, which was stupid because I took the whole front off my fairly new shoes.

Mum was going shopping but I said I had things to do, I was afraid I might kill her stone dead in the supermarket if I went with her. Instead I went home and lay on my bed and wished that I was forty-three, or something ancient with all my life behind me. I turned on the radio and it was some awful thing about James Joyce and all the mad foreigners who come over here.

There was this girl interviewing some Yank girl who was spending her sixteenth birthday traipsing round with her mother, following the whole journey they made in *Ulysses*. Well, I thought, bad all as Mum is – and she is pretty barking mad – she'd never make me do that.

And this one, June, with an Italian name – Arpino or something – said she had had Irish relations called O'Leary and they were originally from the dreary Rossmore, which we were too, from the North Circular Road, which is where Dad's family is from. And suddenly I got this thought. Could she be my cousin?

Could June Arpino and her family get me out to New York to work in a diner?

I listened like mad for more information. She was staying in that budget hotel, the place that looked like a prison in Eastern Europe. I rang the radio station and they told me she, this June Arpino girl, wasn't there, that it was an interview done earlier in the day; but they gave me the phone number of the hotel and said that half the country seemed to have been phoning in and they were all heading for the hotel.

Imagine! Maybe they all wanted her to get them jobs in a diner. People are so odd.

So I might go as well, it would be a laugh.

Mum knocked on the bedroom door. She said she had been

looking at skirts for herself but none of them fitted her for some reason so she had bought one for me instead. It was nice actually, pink velvet – not like the things she usually gets which a child in an orphanage in the nineteenth century would be ashamed to wear.

'Did Dad ever have anyone who went to America, anyone from the North Circular Road?' I asked.

'Yes, his uncle went over an insult or some cracked thing, no one can remember what it was. And no one knows where they are, so they're no use to you, love, for your diner plans, I'm afraid.' She genuinely did look sorry.

'I think I've found them,' I said and told my mum. Amazingly she seemed interested, and pleased. Excited even.

'Let's go,' she agreed.

The hotel was as awful on the inside as from outside. Absolutely full of people, and would you believe it, some of Dad's dreadful cousins were there too, and they were all roaring at each other with excitement, and there in the middle of it all were two Americans who had to be June and her mother.

June was the image of me, we were like sisters. And she was wearing a pink velvet skirt. Mum and the others were screeching away, with Mum telling all kinds of terrible personal details about how she had a fight with Dad and he never apologised and she was sick of always being the one who ended up saying sorry.

So June's mother suddenly weighed in and said that if she had her life all over again she would certainly have made some kind of apology to June's father rather than letting him go off with a trashy young woman and having two more kids . . .

June and I talked to each other so that we wouldn't have to listen to all this historical stuff. She was a whole year younger of course, but with her being American it sort of levelled out – they mature more quickly over there. And we thought, wasn't it *extraordinary* that we were related and had never known the other existed.

Mum rang Dad on her mobile and he turned up half an hour later and the first thing he said was to Mum, that he was sorry he was so difficult and Mum kissed him in front of everyone. And in minutes there he was shaking hands with all of his cousins and telling them Mum was the best wife in the world.

June was just great.

I told her I had two beds in my room if she wanted to stay with me. We might even go down to this mad Rossmore place which had a wishing well never known to fail. My mum said she'd like to have a word with the saint at that well because the first husband she had sent had not turned out to be that great. Maybe he was only a rehearsal, maybe the real husband might be still out there waiting. It was hugely embarrassing at her age of course but June and I could cope.

And June's mother said that of course they could change the air ticket and after their holiday here with us, and the visit to this Rossmore place, then I would go back and stay with them in New York. They knew a terrific diner where I could work. A really respectable family place.

Mum and Dad weren't so sure at the start but June whispered at me that I should remind them that the alternative was going to Cyprus or Majorca and throwing my knickers away at the airport. So that sort of concentrated their minds. It wasn't definite yet. There was still a journey to go down that road. But with my new cousin June I was sure I'd swing it.

I caught Mum looking at me a bit soppily.

'You're not drunk, Mum?' I asked her, anxiously.

'No, not remotely. Do you remember what I was saying to you this morning, Lucky?' she asked in an awful Mary Poppins voice.

June and I had been talking about how easy it was to keep mothers happy if you just talked their language. They didn't know you were parroting it back.

'You said things have a way of working out,' I said.

And Mum's face lit up with pleasure. 'You see, you remember! You really are my greatest friend, Lucky,' she said. 'I'll miss you so much when you go to America.'

And I smiled back. It was a complicated smile, built on many layers.

First it was the smile of huge relief. I had won the battle; I was going to work in a New York diner. My mother had admitted as much.

Then it was the smile of a friend as the old woman on the radio had advised us all. She had said that it would work wonders. She had said in her talk that at first it would be an act, but after a time we would find that we actually meant it. That was an amazing thing about being grown up, time passes quickly.

I was beginning to feel that it wasn't a pretence any more.

When I said all that bit to my mum that she was my greatest friend too, I meant it. I wasn't acting any more. I did mean it.

Maybe I *was* very lucky and didn't need to change my name after all.

CHAPTER II

Tell Me Why?

Part 1 – Emer

Tell me, *why* did I have to get one of those huge digital clocks where you could see the figures from the other side of the Rossmore Hotel? Why couldn't I have had a small travel clock like normal people instead of this big thing the size of a dinner plate beside my bed with red numbers changing every minute?

I have been watching it now for four and a half minutes while it changed from 9.08 and a bit to 9.13 a.m. I vaguely remember setting the alarm for 9.30. I have a sort of cloudy memory of doing that. My thinking was that if I got up at nine-thirty I could be showered, dressed, have a coffee and be on the road by ten.

It's really important that I be on the road in good shape today. I have an interview for the job that I've wanted for years: director of the Heartfelt Art Gallery, a marvellous outfit where I have yearned to work for ages. I had a lot of the right qualifications but there was always someone else in the job. Now the guy who had run it for the last three years was off to Australia. Today I have my interview.

So, tell me *why* had I not gone to bed early, sober and alone?

I can't move, you see, because it would wake him up.

And then he might think I was signalling that I wanted it all over again. I must lie here motionless until I sense the alarm is going off and after one quick blast of its horrific noise I will quench it and leap out of bed all in the same movement and run to the bathroom.

I've got nothing on, obviously, so I'll have to move quickly. There will be no lovely luxurious time while the fizzing drink cures the head and the coffee sends out soothing noises and smells from the percolator. No, it has to be very brisk and businesslike. As if this is the most normal thing in the world to have invited the taxi driver in and gone to bed with him.

Tell me, why didn't I leave him in his taxicab like ninety-nine per cent of the population would have done? *Why* couldn't I have done that too?

I suppose I could blame it on the reception I was at. They had this absolutely rot-gut wine – it practically tinkled down your throat it was so rough. And no food, of course. Not even a biscuit or a crisp to soak it up. It just went on down there in my stomach doing its evil work, sloshing about into every vein and gut and bit of muscle tissue, gradually moving its way remorselessly up to the brain to paralyse it completely. There was that, and of course the fact that I really hated Monica, the woman whose paintings were being shown.

I had always hated her, long ago back at art college, long before she made silly fluttery eyes with Ken on my birthday, at the meal I was paying for. When she knew that I liked him.

And now I hate the way she smiles with her mouth but not her eyes. I hate the way she gets noticed and fêted and admired, and how everyone was standing in line to buy her paintings. There were red dots everywhere to show that they had been sold. Like measles all over her awful chocolate-box paintings.

Well, why did I go, you might ask me? Why did you not stay away and prepare for your interview? Why indeed.

But at the time it made sense to go. I wanted to show Monica that I wasn't going to be frightened away, let her think I was envious, let her think I had cared about Ken and she being friends. Or more than friends possibly. Or anything.

Also, I had got a new hairstyle in preparation for my interview and a new linen jacket which I could wear under my good suede coat. So I thought I should give them an outing. It would do no harm to let Ken see me looking fabulous.

What a bad idea that turned out to be. If Ken feels anything about me this morning it's a huge sense of relief that his cautious Canadian practical streak had triumphed over any tendency he might have had to fancying me. Ken is wrapped in relief this morning. Unlike me. I am wrapped in my own bed with a taxi driver.

From where I'm lying at the edge of the bed I can see the linen jacket with what looks like half a bottle of red wine down the front of it. And my expensive haircut – well, I haven't seen a mirror yet this morning, but it's obviously like a wild bush.

Apart from the terrible wine, it was altogether a dull opening. I mean, the pictures were terrible, anyone could see that. When I get my job in the Heartfelt gallery (that's now *if* I get my job there) I wouldn't countenance hanging an exhibition like that. Nobody liked them – they murmured and said the right things and bought them because they wanted to be well in with Tony who runs the gallery. Tony who might give *them* an exhibition too one day if they play their cards right.

And Monica was so awful to me, so plain rude and insulting, no wonder I took to drink. She seemed to have trouble remembering my name. It's not hard to remember, even slow learners could get to grips with the name Emer. It's not as if the name Emer is challenging or hard to pronounce or anything.

But Monica couldn't manage it somehow. She had to rack her brain when introducing me to people.

'I was at art college with this lady, believe it or not,' she would coo. As if somehow I was so old and decrepit and she was so young no one could possibly believe us to be contemporaries.

Come on, Monica. We are all thirty-one years of age, you, Ken and I. None of us are married.

Ken teaches art in a school, you paint awful sugar and spice pastels, I work in art administration. This very morning I might well land a terrific job in one of the best art galleries in the country. I will be called a director though actually it's a job that could even be described as a curator.

I want that job so much. Tell me, why did I get myself into this mess?

You see, I can't even move to get up and repair myself, try to limit the damage. Find something else to wear. Oh my God. I've just seen that there's spaghetti on that jacket as well as wine!

Yes, naturally we had to go to a pasta bar afterwards. Instead of coming home on the bus like any normal human, I had to cry with delight when Ken suggested a few of us go to this place. And of course Monica came too, said it would be a fun thing to do and brought Tony from the gallery and awful shrieky people. Well, as it turned out I was probably more shrieky than all of them. And one of the waiters came up to me and gave me a bottle of wine because I had painted the sign for his father's bicycle repair shop. And Monica had thought that was a scream. Imagine – Emer does signs for repair shops, how marvellous, isn't she something else?

At one stage I thought Ken whispered to me not to take any notice, that she was only winding me up.

'Why?' I asked him.

'Because she's jealous of you.'

Or that's what I think he said. He might have said that but then again I might have imagined it. To be honest the evening isn't at all clear. There's a heavy bit of mist over the bit where the waiters stood in a line and sang 'By the Rivers of Babylon' and I joined them. And I thought everyone thought I was great. But they might not have thought that at all.

218

And how did we pay? Did we pay? Oh God, tell me we paid.

Yes – I remember it. Ken said that he'd take a tenner from everyone, and everyone thought that was terrific except I seemed to have a window of sobriety and said that he'd need to take fifteen to cover the bill, and I *think* he said, nonsense, that it would be all worth it for the pleasure of seeing me again. And Monica heard and wasn't at all pleased and she put on that vomit-making little baby voice that she does and said that surely nobody expected *her* to pay because she had been feeding them lovely wine all night at the gallery. And Tony got a bit bad-tempered and said that actually *he* had been giving them wine at the gallery all night. And I'm afraid that I said neither of them should fight to claim responsibility over the wine since it was so terrible. And Ken paid hastily with his Visa card and got us all out on the road.

I felt very dizzy when I faced the fresh air and I would have just loved it if Ken had come home with me, not for anything except just to take care of me, make me drink milk or water or whatever I should have drunk. But no, of course, Madam Monica insisted he see *her* home and we all lived in different directions. He got me a taxi, buttoned up my smart suede coat for me and asked the driver to take care of me because I was a very special person.

Boy, did the taxi driver take care of me all right.

But I can't blame Ken, much as I'd like to. He didn't ask the taxi driver to come home and get into bed with me. No, sadly I can't say that that was his fault. It must in some sense have been mine.

But why? Tell me why? I don't normally go to bed with strangers, in fact I never have before in my whole life. Was it something to do with disappointment about Ken? Was he persuasive? Did I fancy him?

Think, Emer. Think and try to reconstruct the journey home. Think silently. Don't wake him.

He was young, early twenties, I'd say. Thin pointy face, a bit like a fox. An evil cunning fox waiting for his opportunity.

'You look as if you had a good evening,' he said as I fell into his taxi, picked myself up hastily in order to wave Ken goodbye and to pretend I was more sober than I was.

'Actually I had a shitty evening if you must know,' I said coldly.

'What would you have preferred?' he asked.

'Not to have gone at all. Not to have drunk that cheap wine, not to have talked to that tiresome woman, not to have looked at her horrifically bad paintings.'

'Sounds terrible all right,' he said. I didn't like him pitying me.

'So what kind of an evening did you have?' I asked him loftily. I think he said it had been an evening like any other really – he was sort of shruggy and resigned over it. I said he had the wrong attitude to evenings.

God, why had I said that, why couldn't I have let him have his own kind of evening like any other instead of going to bed with the passenger? But maybe he did this every evening. What do I know? Very little.

He said something about needing to earn money for a living, and I asked him, did he have a girlfriend? I think he said he had, someone called Hissie or Missie or some awful name. Anyway he can't have liked her much if he ended up here.

He said she was a modern woman, she knew about relationships because she worked in a flower shop, and it was all about guilt and anxiety and lies. She didn't want to get tied down, she let him go his way and he let her go hers. That they both had their eyes open or some such crap.

I said that it was all a heap of lies – that Hissie was mad to settle down with him but she had to pretend not to be, that's how it worked nowadays. I said I knew this for a fact, that I pretended to be cool with Ken but I loved him and if I thought it would work I'd give up any job. But you can't win them all.

'Did you win any part of the evening?' he asked. He was trying to cheer me up.

'Yes, I did, I sang a song with the waiters.'

I sang 'By the Rivers of Babylon' again for him to show him how good I had been, and he joined in at the chorus. Then he asked me if I knew 'Stand by Your Man'. I said I did know it but I didn't entirely agree with the sentiments. But to be a sport I sang it with him, then I suggested 'Hey Jude' and then we were home.

And why, oh why, tell me, could I not have said goodbye to him and thought of it as a good singsong to end a lousy night? Oh no, never do anything the easy way. Instead I must have invited him in with me, and shamefully I can't remember what happened next.

Did I get out my CDs? Was it possible that I could have had more drink? You see, he must have been sober, I mean, he was driving a cab, of course he was sober. Did we go straight to bed?

Oh, if only I could remember what made me do it! Then I might be able to get us out of this situation with marginally less embarrassment than I felt it would involve.

I reached for the huge digital clock just before it burst into sound. Thank God I hadn't woken him. He lay there, a dead weight on the other side of the bed. At least he wasn't snoring or thrashing about.

Where did he park his cab? There's nothing but double yellow lines around here – the traffic is appalling. They are going to build a bypass and the sooner the better. But they haven't built it yet, he'd have had to go miles to find a place to park. Or maybe he left it outside the door in the white heat of passion.

Either way it was his problem.

Did he even give me his name? He must have at some stage. I wouldn't think about that any more, it was too horrifying. Instead I would think what I would wear to the interview. Suppose I were just to button up my suede coat, and drape a scarf over it.

My God, my coat!

Could I have left it in his taxi? It wasn't on a padded hanger on the back of the door where it always lives. Oh no – God, I know you can't be pleased with me. I know it was a wrong thing to take the taxi man to bed with me, very silly and wrong, but I don't do much sinning, not in the great scheme of things. And I had gone to pray at St Ann's Well. I asked the saint to make Ken love me, which she hasn't yet, and I don't suppose she will now. But listen, God, I feel like death, I'll make a dog's dinner of this interview, I've ruined my new linen jacket and now, *now* you tell me that I've lost my suede coat as well.

I was so upset about my coat that I forgot about the taxi driver and not waking him up.

I sat straight up in bed and turned my tortured, hung-over face towards him.

There was no one there.

On the bed beside me was my big suede coat all rolled up. Heavy and obtrusive and taking up an inordinate amount of room in the bed. Pretending to be a taxi driver and frightening me to death.

I leaped from the bed in delight. I had a future, a lot of showering and gargling and finding whatever else in the flat might be clean enough to wear. Then I had to get this job at the Heartfelt gallery, then I would go to the dry-cleaners with all my ruined clothes, then I would call Ken and ask him out to celebrate and I would get him back.

Really, that cheap wine does terrible things to you. Gives you hallucinations even.

As if I would take an unknown taxi driver home to bed with me!

Part 2 – Hugo

It's not that there's anything wrong with driving a taxi. I mean, it's a great job in many ways and you can put in the number of hours you want to. If you're tired you can knock off early, or if you're saving for a holiday you can stay out for an extra three hours a night to help pay for it. There's different people get into the back of the cab every time you stop and you'd need to be a right old curmudgeon not to meet someone you liked a few times a day.

I've driven a woman who was going over to a garden party at Buckingham Palace in London and she was so nervous she had to get out of the cab to be sick twice. I drove an actor who was having trouble learning his lines and we recited them together for forty minutes with the meter still running. I drove a couple who had just got engaged to be married and I had to try on the ring four times and say it was the biggest diamond I had ever seen.

So what's not to like about driving a taxi for a living?

My Uncle Sidney, who drove a taxi and sort of steered me into the business, said he always tried to get one nugget of information from every fare he picked up; that way you got yourself a fine and varied education all while doing a day's work. He came home with information about forecasting the weather, about where to get vegetables half-price when a market stall was just closing down, about how to meet ladies for bridge and other activities through the Internet.

Chrissie, this girl who works in a flower shop, nice girl, I see her around from time to time, she says I'm very funny about the whole taxi driving thing and I should write a book about it. Me, write a book? Me, Hugo? No, that wasn't what I wanted at all.

If the truth be told I would prefer to have been a singer, I fancied myself out on stage in front of the crowds. I'm not afraid of people or shy or anything, this job knocks any nerves out of you anyway. I can read music and play the guitar, but I never got a break, I never made it.

I tried, mind you. I entered talent competitions, I sent sample tapes, then sample CDs. But no one took them. I'm not any worse than a lot of people who did get a chance. I wrote my own songs, I did versions of other people's songs. Nothing worked.

I didn't run with a musical crowd. I know that sounds odd. After all, if you're interested in something, then why not have friends who share the same interests? But somehow I remained pals with the fellows I was at school with.

They liked going to clubs, sure, and liked dancing with birds to good music but they weren't really musical. They never wanted to play it, to be part of it, to be in there making it. So the matter didn't come up much.

They have different jobs here and there and some of them drive cabs too. When we got together we'd talk about that, and about holidays and what teams we support, and sometimes we'd all promise to jog or go to the gym because we're all developing big bums and bellies from sitting in a cab all day. And we'd play football on a Sunday morning and go for a few pints. But one by one they paired off and got married and now when we are all twenty-five or twenty-six I am the only one who hasn't settled down.

So now there's not all that much for me to talk about with them. They go on about raising a house deposit or re-roofing or grouting or laying a decking system. In some ways I envy them because they are all so very interested in it all, and spend the whole of Saturdays fixing up their places. Some of them have had kids who all look exactly the same as each other.

One day I'll marry and have kids but not yet, not till I meet someone right – someone I'd do anything for.

I hope it will be someone involved in the music industry because I haven't quite given up on my dream yet. Nearly, to be honest, but not quite. When you hear these star interviews there was always a bit of luck along the way, they met someone who knew someone who gave them a break.

I still live at home but that's not as wet and wimpish as it sounds for a man of twenty-six.

Well, there's living at home and there's living at home, isn't there? In our house we have a microwave, and a big fridge with three separate shelves marked 'Dad', 'Mum' and 'Hugo'.

My sister Bella, who lives in her own place with two feminists, she said she thought it – our home – was the saddest thing she had ever seen, sadder than a documentary about disabled people because it was only their bodies that were disabled and in our cases it was our minds. We were three sad, sad, dysfunctional people trapped in a pathetic lifestyle. It made her shudder to think of us, three adults who could have had a real life.

Well, I never really knew what she was going on about, to be frank. Our life functioned just fine. I put a nice little sum into the post office for them every month, it was their rainy day fund. My dad worked for a small animals veterinary practice, he was an assistant. That's what he had always been, not a veterinary nurse – he didn't have qualifications – but they relied on him utterly. He could hold the kittens for injections or calm the dogs, or clean up when the hamsters crapped over everything. He just adored animals but sadly Mum was allergic, came out in a bumpy rash and sneezed and got watery eyes. So he kept the animals for work time, and walked other people's dogs in the park most evenings.

My mum worked in a travel agency, she spent her whole day finding cheap holidays for people, she was quite good at it now. She could get great discounts for all kinds of vacations. The West Indies for half-nothing at short notice, a long weekend off-season in Venice . . . But Dad couldn't fly, he had tried once and his ears went funny so he never did it again. Mum had to go on trips with her colleagues, which wasn't quite the same. But they were happy, they were really quite happy compared to most of the world.

Dad was a vegetarian and Mum was always on some kind of nutter's diet so it made sense to have a shelf for each of us in the fridge. And we arranged everything else in the house very well.

We had two television sets, one in the kitchen and one in the sitting room, so there were no heated debates about what we watched. Every third week we each did the washing; there was no ironing, we had everything drip-dry. My sister Bella found that sad too. As if her life with these two dull women who all wore organic clothes and ate organic food and talked organic talk was somehow less drear.

Mum and Dad are just fine and I'd been driving a taxi for long enough to know they were better off than a lot of people of their age. You can see a lot of human misery from the front seat, let me tell you.

Anyway this morning my mum had said she was going to Dubai next weekend for eight days and my dad said that was great, she'd love it, and he might go to a sanctuary for injured animals – he had always wanted to give the time to poor donkeys with their bones coming through their skin and to frightened dogs who often had only three legs and haunted eyes. They both asked me would I be okay and I said I'd be fine. It was my weekend to do the washing anyway so they could just leave everything for me.

'You're a very good boy, Hugo,' my mum said.

'A man really,' my dad said.

'Maybe you'll be off getting married when we get back,' my mum said.

She said it as a joke but I know she was serious. She'd have loved to see me married. I felt a failure to them in a way. When they were my age Bella was five and I was four. I had nothing to show for anything but a reasonable bank balance.

'No, I think I'll be around here until you are old and grey,' I said.

'I hope not, son, it would be nice for you to meet someone you chose rather than living with us, people you didn't choose at all,' my dad said.

And I got a sudden chilly feeling that I never would meet

anyone I knew was right for me because I realised I could never make up my mind.

I just went with things that fell into my lap. Like Uncle Sidney getting me to drive a taxi and going with this girl because she was someone's sister or that girl because she was the mate of some pal's girlfriend. I played football on a Sunday because someone else had set up the team and booked the place to play, I bought my clothes in a place where Gerry, a friend of mine, worked. He always held a few things back for me when they had a sale.

'You could look really well, Hugo, if you tried,' he said to me a couple of times. 'You have that thin pointy face that women go for. You should wear good leather jackets.' But then Gerry is a very cheerful fat guy who says nice things to people all of the time.

He wouldn't know whether I looked good or like the back of the Rossmore to Dublin bus. So I don't go out much testing my so-called good looks.

And oddly, apart from Chrissie, I never really met anyone I'd like to get to know a lot better. And even with her. Well, I wasn't sure.

It would be foolish for us both to get our hopes up if we weren't really sure. I mean, Chrissie was great fun and she was fascinating about flowers and everything but for ever? All day and all night? I don't know.

And neither did Chrissie, to be honest. We had both told each other that nothing was worse than people trapped in loveless relationships. Chrissie saw that all the time. She said that a good sixty per cent of the brides that she dealt with over wedding flowers were all wretched.

I knew that so many of the people I drove were miserable too and seemed to fight all the time. Particularly those going on vacation. They often actually seemed to hate each other.

Anyway the night after my mum had gone off to the Gulf to

get a tan and buy a gold bracelet, and my dad had gone to feed little broken fawns with bottles of warmed milk and bind up the wounds on donkeys' backs, I worked an extra shift. I was thinking it would be really nice to have someone who just adored you and would fight your corner, like happens in the movies.

And then I was going past this Italian pasta place where people were coming out into the street, most of them fairly drinky as it happened. You want to be careful of a fare like that. Uncle Sid always said, turn off the meter but slow down to see if they can stand and pay what they will owe you and especially to keep a beady eye out for those who might get sick in your cab.

A nice young fellow came out and hailed me, he was sober anyway, American or Canadian maybe. Very polite.

'I wonder if I could ask you to take this young lady home?' He gave me a tenner, well above the fare to where she was going.

The *young lady* was weaving round the place, but she didn't look like a barfer – you get the feeling when they're going to throw up – she hadn't that kind of aura about her, if you know what I mean. Anyway she fell into the taxi on her knees, which was a poor start.

He climbed in and straightened her up, very tenderly.

I asked him, was he going to come with us possibly? I was thinking he might be useful at the other end hauling her out again.

'No, I wish I could but, you see, Monica . . . is there . . . and it is Monica's night really and we do live in the same direction. You're all right, Emer – wake up darling, wake up and talk to the nice driver.'

'I don't want to talk, Ken, I want to sing to the driver,' she said mutinously.

'Is that okay, driver?' he asked me anxiously.

'Sure, Ken,' I said. 'I'll sing too.'

'I *hate* Monica, Ken, you're much too good for her, she has a face like a marshmallow and she paints as if she dipped another marshmallow into pinks and blues and yellows. She's a really terrible gross person, Ken, it's just that you can't see that.'

Ken seemed anxious for Monica not to hear this description and he looked at me wildly. I often think this job is a bit like being a diplomat and a marriage counsellor all rolled into one.

'I'll be off now,' I said.

'Take care of her, she's very special,' he said to me. And we were gone. She sat grumbling in the back, asking why if she was so special was he going to take home that Monica who had a face like an almond bun.

'More like a marshmallow really,' I corrected her. She was delighted with me.

'That's exactly what she's like. Exactly. How clever you are to notice.' She smiled happily to herself and repeated it over and over: 'Like a marshmallow,' as if she had not come up with the phrase herself. 'Hey, Ken asked me to sing to you – what would you like?' she asked eventually.

'Why don't *you* choose.' I was polite as always.

She was a nice girl, late twenties maybe, long straight fair hair. She had drunk far too much wine but seemed pleasant about everything except Monica with the flat face.

'Ken is very nice, you see, he knows taxi driving is a dull job and that you might want to be entertained on the way back, that's why he suggested it. I'll sing "By the Rivers of Babylon".' And she did, quite well as it happens.

I suggested we sing 'Stand by Your Man'. She told me that men were foolish and didn't need people to stand by them, what men needed was a wake-up call. But we sang it anyway, and a few more.

Then I was afraid she was going to go to sleep and we might have trouble identifying her house or if it was a flat which one it might be. So I made every effort to keep the conversation going, by asking her, what did men need to be woken up to.

'To the fact that they usually have perfectly good women just within an arm's length and they never seem to see them,' she said crossly. She told me at confused length about this guy Ken and how he had been taken in by Monica's sheer silliness and had wrongly believed that that stupid woman needed looking after. She didn't think that they were sleeping together but you never knew with men. And tonight could be the night. Tonight could be the very night they might do it. In Monica's horrible house at 35 Orange Crescent. She was pretty glum about that.

'Maybe he's too drunk to do it tonight,' I said, thinking that would help.

'No, he hardly drinks at all. He was the sober one who paid too much for the meal for everyone.'

She was brooding heavily about it all. She said she had been to pray at St Ann's Well and St Ann hadn't bothered at all. St Ann had let the truly awful Monicas of this world prowl round and destroy people. Taking them home to ravish them on the way.

'Well, I imagine he just saw her home, you know, and then went home himself,' I soothed her as best as I could.

'But he doesn't see me, that's the problem. What's your name by the way?'

I told her I was called Hugo.

'Hugo – that's a bit fancy, isn't it?'

'Is it? I don't know. I always thought it would look good on a CD or outside a gig where I would be playing. I had my dreams, you know.' I didn't usually talk about myself. I was surprised at myself. But what the hell, she was one drunken woman, I might as well have been reciting the Highway Code.

She was prepared to fight with her shadow. 'Well, why didn't you do something about your dream then?' She was like a small angry terrier dog on the back seat. 'My family wanted me to be a teacher or a nurse, they didn't want me to do arty things, but I fought for it, and tomorrow I have this interview for a huge job, and I hoped that Ken would come home with me tonight and pat me down instead of going to 35 Orange Crescent and patting down that stupid marshmallow as you so rightly called her.' She was near tears now.

I had to stop that at all costs.

'Listen,' I said, 'I suppose men are a bit hopeless, cagey . . . whatever. It's just that we don't want to get into something which may be wrong and there will be a load of grief and aggravation getting out of it. That's all it is really.'

'That's such bullshit,' she said. 'I bet there's some nice girl who has hopes of you, Hugo, some foolish insane girl who thinks you could be a singer if you weren't so cautious, who thinks she might make you happy if you'd let her in. The world is full of women like that. I don't know where we'd stretch to if you put us all in a line. Really I don't.' She shook her head at the tragedy of it all.

I thought I saw her eyes beginning to close in the rear-view mirror.

'I do have a friend, Chrissie,' I shouted, trying to keep her awake, 'but I'm not certain that it's the real thing and I don't think she's certain and it would be silly to get into something we might have to get out of.'

'Oh for God's sake, Hugo, you are one dumb fool. Who can be certain of anything on this earth? I ask you. I never met such a ditherer. In about forty years I'll meet you again and you'll be exactly the same as you are now, older of course and bald and you won't have one of those sharp thin faces that would look so well on a CD, you'll have a fat cautious face and wear a greasy checked cap. But basically you'll be the same.'

I wasn't going to get annoyed with her. I asked her what she thought that I should do. Oho, she knew that too.

I was to go round to Chrissie's house tonight and say I was prepared to give it a go, that life was short and love was good and that we would both give it our best try.

'I might,' I said.

'You won't,' she told me.

'Why don't you say all these things to Ken?' I asked her with some spirit.

'Because I just couldn't bear it if it didn't work,' she said very truthfully.

Then she got out of the taxi and teetered about a bit. I got out to steady her up and help her up the few steps outside the hall door. There was a bit of fumbling with her key but eventually I got her into her flat.

'You're quite a good singer,' she said as she left me. 'Yes, quite good. You'd need to work on your repertoire but you can certainly hold a tune,' she said before she crashed indoors.

It was a quiet night as I was driving around when I saw I was near Orange Crescent. I remembered what she had said about my being a ditherer. I'd show her.

I rang the doorbell.

Marshmallow Monica came to answer it. She wore no shoes but she did have all her clothes on. Maybe I was in time.

'I've come for Ken,' I said.

Ken came out, bewildered.

'You ordered a cab,' I said.

He was very polite but confused, there must have been some mistake. I was adamant. How else would I have known the name and the address, I had come specially, a long way, to collect him.

'Well, perhaps, Monica, since the driver has come for me . . . I should really go with him.'

There was a poutish display of bad temper from the Marshmallow, but I had him in the cab. I would now drive him home.

'Emer loves you,' I said.

'No she doesn't, she loves her career,' he said sadly.

'You're wrong,' I said. 'You're so very wrong. When she wasn't singing she was telling me how much she loved you.'

'She's drunk as a lord of course,' Ken said.

'I think it's the same drunk or sober,' I said. 'And she's going

232

to have some hangover tomorrow, maybe you should go round and straighten her up for that interview she's going to.'

He looked thoughtful. 'Are you into therapy or crisis intervention in your spare time?' he asked me.

'No, I'm into singing. Do you know anywhere I could get a gig by any chance?'

It's a funny old life. It turns out that Ken's students were having a disco in the art college the following night. Their live guy with a guitar had let them down. We had an audition in the cab. I sang three numbers for him and Ken said fine, I was hired and he gave me the address where I should show up. He asked me if I had a girlfriend because there would be a nice do afterwards.

I said I had a nice girlfriend called Chrissie, and maybe he could take Emer to celebrate her having got the job in the gallery. He looked as if he had never thought of doing anything like that.

You know, Emer was right.

Men don't need women to stand by them, that's not what they need at all. They need someone to give them a boot up the bum when all is said and done.

And magic well or no magic well, I'd have been unlikely to get that from St Ann.

CHAPTER 12

The Anniversary

Part 1 – Pearl

I've always loved looking up things, silly facts, useless information. If I only had a computer I'd be at it all day. If we were the kind of people who would go to a pub quiz I bet I'd do well, even win prizes. If I only had the nerve to try and get on *Who Wants to Be a Millionaire?* I think I'd do quite well. Honestly I do. I've often got all the questions right when the real contestants didn't know them.

Brainbox Pearl, they used to call me at school, but that was just at school. Girls in my street didn't go on for what was called further education. My family had come over from Ireland to make a fortune in England like so many Irish did during the 1950s and 1960s. We were originally from a place called Rossmore, which was a very poor sort of place back then. But it had changed utterly now. You wouldn't believe the style some of my cousins lived in back there now. My Bob was originally from Galway, we had met at an Irish ceilidh dance.

My dad worked on the roads and we all got jobs in factories or shops, and were considered dead lucky not to have gone into service in houses like our mothers had back in the old country as they called it. We all married at nineteen. By the latest. It was just what you did.

Just like everyone else here we had two children by the time we were twenty-one. We all went out to work automatically, none of the men we married could earn enough to run a household single-handed. Nobody complained.

We were much more English than Irish. We supported English football teams, Bob and I did. Once a year we took the train and the boat and then another train back to Rossmore. My first cousin Lilly was exactly the same age as I was. They were very poor in those days and she used to envy me what she called my smart clothes.

Smart clothes! My mam had a catalogue on our street, that's how we were dressed. They used to laugh at our English accents when we went back to Rossmore but we didn't mind. Our gran was very nice, she used to make Lilly and me go up to this well in the woods where they had a statue of St Ann and pray that we get good husbands. It was even more important for me to pray hard, because of living in England, where I might meet someone outside the faith.

And it must have worked, the holy well, because of course I met Bob which was great, and Lilly met Aidan which was also great. Back in those days we didn't have the money to go to each other's weddings, but we were both very happy and we wrote each other letters a lot about our lives.

I was expecting Amy at about the same time as she was expecting her first baby, Teresa, so we had a lot of things to write about. Then the most terrible thing happened.

I mean, it's like something that happens to other people, not anyone you'd know. Someone stole Teresa right out of the pram and she was never found and never ever brought back. The poor little dog was barking away and there were hundreds of people in the street but nobody saw anything.

Nothing was ever the same after that. I mean, I couldn't keep talking to her and telling all about Amy after all she had been through. Then after Gran died we didn't go back to Ireland any more. We lived a very happy life here in the north of England and when John was born everything seemed complete.

We did the Pools first every week, and then the Lottery, and we planned how to spend all that money when we won it. There would be a cruise of course first, then a villa on the Mediterranean and a big house on the posh side of town here; there would be a nice small house with a garden for our parents. As for the children! Well, all the plans we had for them!

They were going to go to the most expensive schools, have music lessons, dancing classes, learn to ride ponies, to play tennis. They were going to have everything we never had. And more still!

To be fair to us we did more than dream for our children, certainly Bob and I did. We knew that the big win just might not happen and we desperately wanted them to have more chances than we did. So we had a fund and every week we put aside a sum for them. Ever since they were born. In the post office a nice little sum grew for Amy and John.

I had read in a book that you should give children plain classic names if you wanted them to get on. The names that we liked might be dead give-away, working-class names later on. So Amy and John they were. Two gorgeous children, but then everyone thinks that about their own.

They got a brand-new bicycle each when the time came, not broken-down reconstructed ones. We took them to theme parks and on their birthdays they could ask friends round to the house and we got them burgers and a video. We got John a computer which he kept in his room. I would love to have used it but John was a very knowledgeable fifteen-year-old and I didn't want to mess it up on him.

We sent Amy to a very expensive secretarial college. The fund was stretched greatly for these two things because I worked on

236

the checkout at a supermarket and Bob was a van driver and these are not jobs that pay hugely well. But in fact it was a great investment for the children.

John turned out to be very gifted in technology and got a great job in what they call IT so it had been well worth getting him that computer at an early age. Amy's expensive secretarial course was a great investment as well, she got a very fancy job as a receptionist in a big company and then moved even further upwards to be somebody's personal assistant.

Both of them in London! Imagine!

They came to see us the odd time but of course they didn't bring their friends home any more. They lived their own lives, independent, successful, that's what we had struggled so hard for. I mean, we knew they couldn't bring people back as a matter of course, not to our little terrace. And by the time Amy was twenty-four and John was twenty-three they were both living in flats with other young people, which was as it should be.

A few of our friends asked Bob and myself what we were doing for our twenty-fifth, for our silver wedding. We said we didn't know because we knew the children must have planned something for us. They knew the date well, 1 April, because we always used to celebrate it when they were young.

April Fool's Day!

Imagine, we made the biggest promise of our life on that day, wasn't that typical, we would laugh? We would get them a big ice cream cake, enough for everyone to have second helpings. Our friends in the street and Bob's sister and my cousin had all organised big silver wedding parties when it was their anniversaries. These had been great gatherings where we played the records of songs that were popular back when we were married first.

I wondered where John and Amy would choose.

The family and friends already knew and I realised that they were only asking us about it to make the surprise even greater for

237

us when it happened. Because we were so used to saving for the children's fund anyway, we had put a bit away and I got Bob a new dark grey suit and a smart white shirt, and myself a navy crêpe dress and a matching handbag. Surely we would be smart enough for anything they could spring on us.

The time was getting nearer and there was no hint about what they had planned. In fact Amy was keeping up the fiction in a big way, saying that she and Tim, that was the man she was personal assistant to, if you know what I mean, would be going to Paris that weekend. I pretended to take her seriously. Just as I pretended to think John was going deep-sea diving with some of the guys in his office, he told me that he had bought a new wet suit and all the gear.

Two days before, I began to worry. Two couples we knew had asked us to have supper with them, one in an Indian restaurant, one in an Italian.

They said the day should be marked. And when I said that it would be, I got a look I didn't like. I decided I had better clear it all up one way or another before Bob got too disappointed. He was trying his suit on every second day and admiring himself in the bedroom mirror. I rang Amy at work.

'Oh, Mother,' she said – she used to call me 'Mam' but it was 'Mother' now.

'About your weekend,' I said. 'Are you really going away, love? I mean, this weekend?'

She was on her high horse at once. 'Now, Mother. Please. Up to now you never interfered, you always let me live my own life, don't tell me that now you've joined in the general hue and cry about Tim. His marriage is dead, Mother, there's nothing hole in the corner about our going to Paris. Please don't join in the general chorus against it all . . .'

I told her that I hadn't intended to criticise her trip to Paris, I hadn't even known whether Tim was married or not. That wasn't why I was ringing, certainly not.

'So why *were* you ringing then, Mother?' My daughter could be so sharp. So very hurtful.

I blurted it out. 'Because I wondered, had you forgotten our silver wedding on Saturday?' I said before I could stop myself.

'Your *what*?'

'Your dad and I will have been married for twenty-five years. We thought that maybe you and John were going to . . . well, had arranged something for us, like a party. It's just that the neighbours keep asking and you know . . .'

I heard her catch her breath sharply. 'Oh, Mother, yes. April Fool's Day. Oh God, yes . . .' she said.

And I knew then that she really had forgotten. And that John had forgotten. And that there would be no party.

And it was Thursday, too late for us to invite anyone and make a celebration. Bob's heart would be broken, he had always found it harder than I did that his little girl didn't come home that much and see her parents these days. He had so looked forward to wearing his new suit and he was going to sing 'You Make Me Feel So Young'. He had speculated that they might have rented the room over The Yellow Bird pub because he had heard there was a function there next Saturday.

I thought about Bob's sister, who was always inclined to be a bit critical of our children, and my big-hearted cousin, and the marvellous parties they and their families had arranged. And I thought about my navy crêpe dress and the matching handbag. About the years of sitting in a draught at the checkout at the supermarket to make more money for the fund. I thought about how the fund had paid for that good jacket when she was going to the interview for her first job, and how their friends had always been invited into this house to have birthday feasts for Amy and John. I thought about the long hours Bob had put in on the road when his eyes were red and tired and his shoulders stiff in order to get the bicycles and the radios and then the CD players. I thought about all those journeys to Legoland and the wildlife parks. I remembered the day trips across the Channel to France.

And I felt for one dangerous moment as if I didn't care if I never talked to either Amy or John again.

Then I pulled myself together sharply. What had it all been for, a quarter of a century of saving and working and holding a home together to give them more than we had ever known? It couldn't end in a petulant sulk like this. I had to get them out of this big failure on their part, reassure them that it didn't matter. I must speak quickly before Amy started to apologise.

So I interrupted her just as she was assembling her speech. 'You see, your dad and I are going away together for the weekend so we wanted to be sure that you hadn't made any other plans . . .'

'Mother – I'm so sorry . . .' she was interrupting now. But I must not let her apologise.

Everything would change if she did.

'So, that's absolutely fine, then, and if you are sending flowers could you send them to your dad's sister for us, as we'll be away.'

Amy gulped. 'Yes, of course, Mother.'

'And we'll keep the real celebration for the pearl.'

'The pearl?'

'Well, that's what we always thought, your dad and I, the silver wasn't important for us. But what with my name being Pearl and everything, the big showy party would be on our pearl anniversary . . .' I beamed goodwill and anticipation down the phone.

'Which is . . . um . . . ?' my daughter asked.

'The thirtieth, of course,' I said cheerfully. 'Only another five years, so you and John had better get planning. We'll make that the party of all time.'

Her voice was full of gratitude. 'Thank you, Mam,' she said. Not 'Mother', I noticed.

Then I thought of where I would take Bob for the outing and

booked us a weekend in Blackpool. Bob's sister would be impressed with the flowers. I knew the bouquet would be guiltily enormous. When all was said and done it was much better than allowing myself to wallow in self-pity.

They didn't call me Brainbox Pearl at school for nothing.

Part 2 – Generous John

In the office they used to call me Generous John.

It had all to do with a silly tradition I established; it was just that every Friday I offered everyone a drink of fizzy wine and some smoked salmon on a biscuit at my desk. It started the weekend off well. People who had nowhere to go enjoyed it; those who were going somewhere always stopped by for a while and it was much better than getting smashed in a pub like a lot of other offices did. And for the cost of two or at the most three bottles of something not too pricey. For this and one packet of Marks and Spencer's smoked salmon, a few water biscuits and a chopped-up lemon I got the reputation of being one really generous guy.

We are a good group in our office anyway. It's not an earthshaking place – most of us think we might like to be somewhere more glittery by the time we're thirty.

But come on, it's a job and the place has a good name in the business, so what the hell.

I like it, and I share a big bright flat with two of my colleagues.

My sister rang the office one day and asked to speak to John. 'Do you mean Generous John or the other John?' they asked. She said she thought she must mean the other but she was wrong.

Amy was surprised. 'You're not generous,' she said, accusingly.

'No, but I'm not mean,' I said. She admitted that was true and we talked on easily.

Are we close as brother and sister? Not really. Well, there's the bond of course that we survived our upbringing. And we've lots of shared memories. But we have lived very different lives.

Amy went to one of those fancy secretarial colleges that teaches women to dress well and social skills as well as office procedure. And she learned well, she's as slim as a pencil, wears very smart designer jackets. Very groomed and cool looking. She has only one blind spot – that guy Tim.

Tim has a wealthy wife, a huge house, a couple of kids at ruinously expensive schools. He has a demanding job as CEO of his company, so he wasn't going to risk the package by going off into the sunset with my sister, glamorous as she may be and trophy wife material as she undoubtedly was. But Amy couldn't or wouldn't see this and by the time she did see it, it would all be too late.

I tried to tell her this one night when we had supper together but boy, did it fall on stony and unwelcoming ground. I was told pretty sharpish that it was none of my business, that I didn't understand the first thing about it.

I was also reminded rather firmly that when I looked at myself in the mirror I would realise that I was no great advertisement for true and undying love. I had never had a proper girlfriend at all.

This was not strictly true and I was annoyed by what she said. But Amy and I papered over the cracks and never talked to each other about our private lives again.

Then I met Linda. After that of course I wanted to talk about my private life to everyone.

Linda was a fantastic-looking girl who had been transferred from head office to us for six months. She never actually went back. She was Irish actually but very together – none of all that drippy Irish colleen thing. She was bright as a button and very popular.

And of all the guys she could have had, which was most of

them, she actually fancied me. Which was very pleasing.

One Friday over the smoked salmon she actually asked me straight out how did Generous John spend the rest of his Friday night, and I heard myself saying in this awful voice that whatever Lovely Linda suggested would be fine with Generous John, and we went out to an Italian restaurant. And then we saw a lot of each other.

She took me home to meet her parents. Her father was an Irish banker with some huge job and they lived in a big house with a garden, and an orchard and labrador dogs.

They didn't quiz me about my family – but Linda did.

'When am I going to meet them? Ever? In this century maybe?' she kept asking.

Now I wasn't so stupid as to pretend that my people were classy like hers were or anything, that sort of thing is only laying up heartache ahead. No, indeed, I had told her that I was born in a small terraced house, and my parents were working class. But I couldn't bring her to meet my mother and father. Not yet.

Dad's awful sister Dervla would want to come in and inspect her. My mother's noisy cousin would find an excuse to come round. They would be talking about places back in the Old Country and trying to find links with Linda's family. It would all be too awful.

I would be apologising for them and then hating myself for feeling that way.

No, keep them apart as long as possible. That was best.

Now, meeting my sister Amy, that was another thing. I invited Amy to a sushi bar to meet Linda and she brought the dreaded Tim. He kept running his hand through his hair and saying he had to be at the next place. Amy was looking at him as if she had suddenly been turned into a spaniel dog instead of a highly efficient personal assistant, which is what she was.

When they left I shrugged at Linda and apologised for him. 'I don't know why she puts up with him.'

'I do,' Linda said.

I was amazed.

'Because she loves him,' said Linda as if it were obvious.

And to my huge regret Linda didn't stay with me in my room in our big airy apartment. Girls often stayed overnight; with my room-mates I would have been so proud to see Linda drinking freshly squeezed orange juice for breakfast, wearing my dressing gown.

But no, she was adamant, and I couldn't stay in the flat she shared with another woman either. We could spend the odd overnight in a hotel when we were away somewhere, so it wasn't sex itself that was out. No, it was what Linda called 'dreaded domesticity'.

We must wait until we were sure, she said, and then get our own place.

I kept saying that I *was* sure but she said, nonsense, I couldn't be yet, and meanwhile, could she meet my parents? I wondered, would they be worse at home or if I brought them here to London? It was a puzzler. At least in London awful Aunt Dervla wouldn't be around and half the street would not be peering and examining us. But then they would be so lacking in confidence in London.

I put it off and off.

One day Linda rang from a business trip to say she was only fifteen miles from my home town and she'd love to call and see my parents. I lied to her, I told her they were away. When she came back, I began to bluster about what a pity it was they had missed each other, but she cut straight across me.

'I didn't miss them, John, I went to see them,' she said.

'But they were away,' I gasped.

'They must have come back,' she said.

'And?' I asked.

'And we had tea and cheese on toast and I told them a bit about what kind of work we do, you and I, and your Aunt

244

Dervla came in and she said maybe we would all meet at The Silver sometime. What's The Silver, John? Is it a hotel or a pub or something?'

'I don't know, I suppose so,' I muttered.

Linda had met my parents, been to my house, met Aunt Dervla and survived it. This must be love.

I tried to tell Amy but she was very worked up about a visit to Paris with Tim and she didn't really listen. I wondered, should I ask my parents to London sometime. After all, they had met Linda now so the worst bit was over. And they might not be so ill at ease as if she was a complete stranger. But there was never any real time for it, and there was a lot else going on.

We worked long hours and then on the weekends we wind-surfed all summer long. Some of us were planning deep-sea diving in the autumn. And okay, I did feel a bit bad sometimes when I thought how little they had and how much I had. But honestly, that's the way things are. Look at people out in Africa, they have nothing at all. And we can't cure it. So what's the point about feeling bad all the time?

Linda was always going home to see her family, but it was different for her. And not so far away. She was always telephoning them, telling them nonsensical things. I didn't ring them at my home because Bob and Pearl were really the kind of people who would panic when there was a phone call. Always thought it was bad news, and they'd be warning me to save my money even though I was phoning from the office. And I did mean to book them a show, some musical, you know, that they'd like and an overnight in a hotel. But as I say, the time just passed.

And then I get this phone call from Amy completely from left field, saying that we were meant to have arranged some awful silver wedding party for them. So that was what they meant when they said to Linda that they would be seeing her at the silver. It wasn't a pub at all. It was a bloody twenty-fifth wedding anniversary.

'Shit!' I said several times to Amy, and she was in total agreement.

'If they had only said,' she repeated over and over. 'They never say anything and expect us to be inspired about everything.'

I thought for a moment about the big birthday cards they sent me every year with a linen handkerchief tucked inside or a bookmark or something useless. But then of course people would remember their children's birthdays – when I have children, when Linda and I have a son and daughter, we'll remember birthdays too. Though I must say she's always dashing off for something for people's anniversaries or birthdays at home. But then girls are different.

Which is why it's so annoying about Amy, that *she* should have remembered this goddamned silver wedding. I said, okay, okay, damage limitation, let's do something for them in London, have a dinner, champagne or something, send a limo for them. But oh no. Amy can't be there. She and Tim have some weekend in Paris that just can't be cancelled. She is so selfish, Amy, at times, and foolish. Very foolish.

There was some kind of psychobabble about making the pearl wedding Mum's big celebration, because of her name and everything. A pearl wedding is thirty years apparently.

God knows where we'll all be by then. Linda and I will be married, that's for sure, and Tim will be on to a newer younger model than my sister, that's also for sure.

So I said, let's send a bouquet each to awful Aunt Dervla's house, and I said that maybe they were better off in Blackpool on their own, and I said we'd do a big number for the pearl wedding but somehow I didn't entirely convince either Amy or myself.

I told Linda all about it that evening. She listened to me very quietly. She looked at me as if she had never really seen me before.

I didn't really like the look. It was as if there was some kind of notice on my head.

'What's wrong?' I asked her anxiously.

'Nothing, nothing at all,' she said. 'Go on, tell me more.'

So I went on talking and told her that my mother and father were of course – as she knew because she had met them – the salt of the earth. But what they were was too easily satisfied. It was pathetic, the way they set store by little things. And my mother liked looking well in front of her cousin, of all people, a dreadful woman with no grace, no style, no standards. And they were in awe of Aunt Dervla, my father's bossy elder sister who thought she knew everything but had only been south of Watford twice.

They were perfectly happy with their little house up there instead of finding somewhere proper to live. Times had changed, people had moved on, they just didn't realise it. If the world had been full of people like them we would still be living in caves.

Linda's face showed nothing. Normally she was animated and she agreed or she disagreed. But she sat there blankly and you know the way it is, the less somebody talks the more you talk? I heard myself telling about how my parents had thought chicken and chips was a great treat, how they put up big coloured paper chains all over the house at Christmas so that we could hardly move.

And still Linda said nothing so I told her all about Mum working extra hours to get us new bicycles and awful Aunt Dervla coming to give us milk and biscuits. Little by little I saw Linda moving her feet down from the sofa and slipping them into her shoes, which was odd because we had the flat to ourselves and it wasn't nearly time for her to go.

And then she said she had to be off.

And I said, 'You can't possibly go now – what about the guinea fowl I bought for us to eat with a bottle of really good claret?'

And for no reason at all Linda asked me, had I ever cooked guinea fowl for my mother and father, and I explained that you couldn't cook in their kitchen and anyway they liked such awful things that they would be sick if they had guinea fowl. Her face looked so different somehow.

So I said stupidly, 'What's wrong, Linda? What is it?'

And she looked really sad as she sort of touched my hand before she left. 'Oh John,' she said, 'Generous John, you really don't know, do you?'

And she left.

And I didn't know and I don't know.

I mean, that's what's so difficult about people – you never really know, do you?

CHAPTER 13

Going to the Pub

Part 1 – Poppy

When I was young our gran lived with us and we adored her. She was far more entertaining than our parents and she understood things. She was much more interesting to listen to, having been around for so long and having seen so much. She used to take Jane and myself on long rambles through Whitethorn Woods, always finding something interesting to show us. Like a treehouse built years ago by her brothers, or how to press flowers in a book, or best of all St Ann's Well. She said we must never laugh at the people praying there because one day we would undoubtedly come here to pray ourselves.

That's what happened. When she was young she thought they were all mad to mumble and mutter and leave mementoes but oddly it became comforting once you got older. She taught us to listen to people. Well, she taught me anyway. That's probably where I got the idea of working with older people.

There wasn't much enthusiasm at home.

'You'll have to get some kind of qualification first,' my dad said.

'Old people can be very demanding,' my mum said.

'You'll never meet a fellow if you get stuck in geriatrics,' said my elder sister Jane.

Jane had turned out to be very different to me – she wore blusher and eyeshadow properly and had a steam iron for her own clothes. She took great care of her shoes, always stuffing them with newspaper, and polishing them with shoe cream. My friends and I used to call her Elegant Jane.

So even though they were all against the idea at home I took no notice because to be honest they were pretty negative about everything. I trained as a nurse here locally in Rossmore in St Ann's Hospital and I asked to work in the wards with older people.

And there I met marvellous people and got huge advice about life from them all.

One man taught me all about stocks and shares, another all about planting window boxes, one old lady who had had seven proposals of marriage told me how to attract men and another taught me how to polish copper. So I was well advanced in the ways of the world by the time I saw the advertisement for a matron in a place called Ferns and Heathers five miles outside Rossmore.

It was an old house owned by two marvellous dotty old dears who were obsessed with gardening. When they died it became a nursing home. I was thirty-seven and I had put all the advice I got to good use. I had a small but satisfactory portfolio of shares. Men had certainly fallen in love with me, but unfortunately I had married a man called Oliver who fell in love rather too easily and too often, so I had actually left him after a year of marriage.

I had copper saucepans that shone like jewels. I could make anything grow in a window box and had very successful year-round colour. None of these things were really qualifications for the job of matron at Ferns and Heathers, but I am a well-qualified nurse and enthusiastic so the four directors liked me at the interview and I got the job. A little cottage went with the post. A place with an entirely neglected garden but I'd soon sort that out.

As soon as I was appointed I went to meet the staff and the people for whom Ferns and Heathers was home. They seemed a happy enough group. They had liked the previous matron who had left to work in television apparently.

'I hope that you're not going to use this place as a jumping-off ground to a media career like she did,' grumbled Garry who, I could recognise in ten seconds, was going to be the mouthpiece of any discontent.

'No. If I'd wanted to go that route I'd have gone it,' I said cheerfully.

'Or go away and get married on us?' a frail woman called Eve asked fretfully. I put her down in my mind as a worrier.

'Married? Oh no, I've been there and done that,' I said.

They looked at me open-mouthed. They had probably been used to a more genteel approach.

I asked, would everyone mind wearing name badges for the first three days and that if I didn't know everyone by then, well, it meant I wasn't up to the job. I told them my name was Poppy. I agreed it was a deeply silly name but there's a worse one on my birth certificate so, if they could get their heads round it, Poppy it would be. I said I loved to listen and learn and if any of them had any ideas to add to my store I'd be thrilled.

They seemed to like that. I could hear them saying that I was unusual anyway, as they went off to their tea. I looked around the place that was going to be my new home with some pleasure. It was going to be a real home for me, I realised. The home that I grew up in was becoming ever more remote.

I realised this when I didn't feel any need to ring my dad and mum about the new job. I didn't feel like listening to all the negative things they would say. They would tell me what a huge responsibility it all was and that if any of these people broke their hips it would be my fault.

I certainly didn't ring my sister Jane because she would tell me yet again that there was nothing wrong with Oliver, who was handsome and wealthy, and that I had been foolish to throw him out, and that I should take on board the fact that all men wandered a little. It was in their nature.

I didn't ring Oliver because I never rang him.

I rang my best friend Grania who was also my lawyer who had helped me do the contracts, and I told her that the place was fine and she must come and see me.

'I might be coming sooner than you think,' Grania said. 'My dad has been told he can't live on his own.'

Grania's father, Dan Green, was a marvellous man. I had always enjoyed going to their house. He was unfailingly cheerful with a big red face and a loud laugh.

'I would love to have him in Ferns and Heathers,' I told Grania. I said I'd make a room ready for him as soon as she wanted.

'That's the problem,' she sighed. 'He says he hasn't a notion of going into any kind of home, he's staying put and going to the pub every night for a pint. The problem is that he can't do it any more. That's the problem, Poppy.' She sounded very upset.

'There's got to be a way round it,' I said. Grania's father couldn't be abandoned but then he must not be harassed either. 'Invite him here for tea some day – I won't do the hard sell,' I said.

'I'll try.' Grania didn't have much hope.

One of my first acts at Ferns and Heathers was to reclaim the garden. It had been very neglected.

'A happy matron is a good matron,' I told them. 'And I am deeply unhappy with our garden. I'm getting in a few raised flower beds but I need help planting them.'

Garry said that they paid good money to be in this place and he had no intention of working with earth and dirtying his hands. So I said, fine, of course he must do as he pleased. But when he heard all the laughter and the reading of seed packets and examination of bedding plants, not to mention the glasses of iced tea I prepared for the gardeners, he changed his tune.

As a reward I gave them each a window box and supervised their planting. It became highly competitive and they all asked their visitors to bring them something exotic from the garden centre. By the time the board had its first visitation we were seriously discussing a little fountain which we called a water feature. It was all going very well.

Then Grania brought her father to visit. He was still a jolly happy man, Dan Green was.

But he had been weakened by illness and he was not a fool. He realised that he couldn't live alone for much longer, though he couldn't live with Grania and her big family. We walked together, he and I. I showed him all the planting and said that when the winter came we were going to have painting classes and maybe an exhibition of our work.

'You want me to come and live here, Poppy, don't you?' he said.

'No, I wouldn't be able to swing it for you – it's very hard indeed to get in here, Dan,' I said regretfully.

'I can read you like a book, you've been Grania's friend since you were ten. If I were to go anywhere it would be here but I can't. I really am not able to give up what I like best in life: going to the pub for a drink every evening.'

'You can drink here, Dan. I do, believe me, you could come and have a glass of wine every evening.'

'No, it's not the same,' he said, really testily as if this was an argument he had fought many times before. 'Women never understand about going to the pub. It's the beer, the draught beer, the whole ritual of the thing.'

And he was right, you know. I don't understand it. I don't get this thing of going into a place where you might be bored to death by people telling jokes, or wearied by the barman mouthing clichés at you, or regulars telling endless tales, where you might be assaulted by drunks or feel lonely and isolated because everyone else has a gang and you are on your own. Why not get a few drinks and go to a friend's house or invite them to yours? But it wasn't the time to argue this down to the bone with Grania's father.

I moved to safer waters. I told him about the new big flat-screen television we had and how we were going to make a room into a real old-fashioned cinema, with popcorn and one of the staff with a torch showing people to their seats. I told him how we had set up the library with a huge notice saying 'Silence' and the daily papers laid out there for all to read. People's relatives and friends brought books of every kind and they were properly catalogued too.

I explained that every week a minibus came and took us up to Whitethorn Woods and how I told them my gran's tales, and those from round here shared their own memories, and we collected bark and leaves and flowers. I introduced him to Maturity, the marvellous shaggy dog that had been given to us by Skunk Slattery who had needed to find a home for the animal. Maturity was the perfect old people's home dog, allowing everyone to fondle him and pat his head equally, favouring nobody above anyone else.

I showed Dan the hens in the backyard which were my pride and joy – seven White Leghorns each with a name and a laying record, clucking about happily in a coop. He was quite interested in all this but still he assured me that no inducement would work – Ferns and Heathers was too far from a pub. Nothing wrong with the place apart from its location. It was five miles from Rossmore and civilisation.

'Grania could drive you to one when she comes to see you,' I heard myself begging.

I would love to have had her father here. But no, apparently Grania didn't understand the psychology of a pub either. And a man needed to be able to wander in when it suited him, find his own level. He seemed almost regretful as he was leaving. He had got a smell of some interesting food from the kitchen.

On Thursdays we had a cookery class and a different group each week prepared supper. Tonight it would be nasi goreng after the basic Indonesian food lesson in the afternoon.

So anyway I was very busy, it's always busy here. I didn't think of Dan for a couple of weeks until Grania told me that he had had a bad fall and when he came out of hospital he would need looking after. Please, Poppy, she begged me, would you take him? Just for a couple of weeks until she could see what could be done.

There was only one big corner room available. I had been going to make it into a music room. So now I fixed it up for Dan when he arrived. He was very down, and he showed no interest whatsoever in meeting any of his fellow residents at Ferns and Heathers. There was no sign of his loud laugh and his big red face seemed smaller and more grey. But as it happened I couldn't give him much attention anyway, I didn't have time to worry about these changes in a friend's once happy father. There was too much else happening.

Garry, the voice of any dissident opinion, had led a protest against Dan getting a bigger room than anyone else. Eve who worried about everything said that some of the new books for the library included real hard-core pornography. Oliver my ex-husband said that on mature reflection he had decided that women didn't understand about being free souls and he was happy to return to me on a strictly monogamous one-to-one basis. My sister, the very elegant Jane, said that I was of course insane not to take him back. But that it was clear I had never made a wise decision in my whole life. The board of Ferns and Heathers announced that one of their number was going to cash in his shares and they needed to do a detailed examination of the home in order to establish its worth.

So I sent Garry in to talk to Dan face to face. I knew Dan would explain very forcibly that he had no intention of staying permanently and that this would calm Garry down.

I went to the library with Eve and examined the hard-core pornography, which turned out to be a few innocent bodice rippers. I wrote to Oliver and said that I wished him well in his insights and spiritual journeys but that I would not contemplate a reconciliation. I reminded him politely of the various barring orders that prevented him from visiting me to discuss the matter any further.

I told the board that I would be very happy to bid for a quarter-share in Ferns and Heathers once they had done their valuation. I also said that they were free to come and look at any time just so long as they didn't disturb the residents. And that they would see a fair picture. After all I might want to make the place look rundown so that I could buy the shares cheaply, but then I had to make it look good otherwise I would not keep my job as matron.

It all worked really well. Dan and Garry became fast friends. Eve started a feminist group in Ferns and Heathers to see could anyone understand the psyche of men since they were basically decent, just confused.

Oliver went to my sister's house and droned on and cried on her shoulder so often and for so long on each occasion that far from telling me that I had been idiotic to throw him out she remained fairly wordless about the situation.

And the board came on a secret inspection to see Ferns and Heathers one day when we were out at the woods and pronounced themselves very pleased and asked me for an enormous sum, for twenty-five per cent of the business.

But I was ready for them.

I explained that my buying into it would ensure my continued presence there. I listed the improvements I had made and hinted at further planned developments. I asked them to speak freely to the residents to enquire how they would view continuing to live here if I had moved on. Grimly they agreed that as I had contributed so much already to the whole project, my financial input would be considerably less than they had originally suggested.

'You are quite unorthodox, Poppy,' they said. 'Just make sure that Ferns and Heathers keeps its licence, that it doesn't break any of the rules.'

I didn't think we had broken any rules. The hens were very hygienic, there was no pornography in the library. But there was something niggling at the back of my mind.

It had to do with Grania's father.

Dan was somehow too cheerful.

I would keep an eye on him.

There was no way that he could go out to a pub. The nearest pub was four miles away and if he were to take a taxi I would have known in ten seconds. And yet he had returned to his previous good form and florid complexion.

When he had decided to stay he had gone back to his own place for his possessions.

We had offered to help him install them but he had said no. If he were to have any dignity he must be allowed to put his own few bits and pieces around the place himself.

His new friend Garry would help him, he said.

We believe strongly that our residents should indeed have as much independence and dignity as possible so of course we agreed. There was a bit of hammering but nothing seemed to have knocked down the walls. He had an old sideboard with a mirror at the back of it, some hunting prints, a notice board, a dartboard on the back of the door. Some vague furniture shapes covered with rugs and velvet cloths. Cupboards, chests of drawers possibly?

But his room was so big there was plenty of space for them all. And he said he had brought a few folding chairs in case he invited people in to his room, and two high stools which he used as stands for vases of flowers. I noticed that before lunch several people would drop in to Dan's room for half an hour, and again in the evening.

The women had started to dress slightly better. They had their hair done more regularly by our visiting stylist, even put on jewellery and perfume. The men wore cravats sometimes and slicked down their hair.

Something was up.

It took me longer than it should have to work out that Dan had set up a pub in his room.

He had optic measures which he fitted into his sideboard. The rug-covered furniture turned into a counter. The vases were taken off the high stools, the chairs were assembled around occasional tables.

Eve would have a small dry martini, some of the other ladies had thimble-sized glasses of sherry, and the men mainly had beer taken from a metal barrel, well disguised during non-pub hours as a giant magazine stand.

How did I discover this?

By spying on them.

And what I discovered looked a very happy scene. They were never drunk and it was doing nobody any harm. But of course they were breaking the law. You are not actually allowed to sell intoxicating liquor without a licence. Anywhere. And certainly not at a nursing home where there are all kinds of rules and regulations and none of them include allowing the residents to have a cash bar.

But they were enjoying it so much. It would be a shame to end it. I resolved that I must never know about it.

So whenever any member of the staff began to tell me that maybe I ought to know something, I managed to avoid hearing it. Lord knows what else I might have inadvertently closed my eyes to! Anyway the board continued to visit and I always managed to let Dan know what day they were coming well in advance as they sometimes called on residents to know how they were getting along, and I didn't want them to arrive when the cocktail hour was at full throttle. Eventually another board member sold out and I now owned half the place.

My sister Jane was awfully sulky and not a bit pleased for me when I told her. I wanted to take her out to dinner to celebrate. But Jane was full of shrugs and raising of shoulders and saying it was so odd that a nurse who was more or less trained by the State should have risen so high. I was too busy really to worry about it, I had to make sure not to schedule painting classes at an hour that would cut across Dan's opening times and on the day we had our art exhibition a lot of them went for Dutch courage to Dan's.

The very next day I went for a walk by myself in the woods, accompanied only by the dog.

Maturity loved the woods and found something interesting at every turn. We were near the well so I went in to inspect it.

There were notices around it about the intended road.

'We won't let them take you away, St Ann,' said one of them. Another had a pencil attached and asked people who opposed the huge highway to add their names to a list below. I was going to put my name on it. Most of my people back at the home were against the change. Then I wondered, might it in fact mean that some of them would get more visitors if all that traffic congestion was eased.

At that very moment my mobile phone rang. There was a bit of sighing around me as if to say that nowhere was sacred these days.

It was the home. Three inspectors from the Health Board had arrived unannounced.

I had to think quickly.

I looked up at the statue for some advice. 'Come on, St Ann, you didn't do much for me in the husband stakes,' I said. 'Get me out of this one anyway.' Then I asked to be put through to Dan's room.

'Mr Green?' I said with as much authority as I could muster. 'Mr Green, there's been a little change of plan. I won't be able to join you and discuss your artwork with you as arranged. I wonder if I could ask you all to go almost at once to the dining room. You see, some health inspectors have arrived and I'm not in the building. I'll be back shortly and I want to show them around. It would be a great ease to me if I could know that everyone was heading for lunch. Having of course cleared up all your artwork before you leave, if you know what I mean. Thank you so much for being co-operative, Mr Green.' I hung up.

Dan would do it. Maturity and I raced back to the car and I drove like the wind back to Ferns and Heathers. The inspectors were having coffee and shortbread in the hall. They were looking at the exhibition of local flora in glass cases. They were studying the notices on the wall about upcoming cookery demonstrations, a matinée showing of *Brief Encounter* which was a regular favourite, and a debate on the great new road.

I apologised for not being there and suggested a tour of the premises. As I was leading the inspectors along the ground floor I saw the little line of lunchtime drinkers full of giggles heading for the dining room. Not even the flappers who drank bathtub gin during Prohibition could have had as much fun as they were having.

All I had to do now was make sure that Dan never acknowledged what I had done, how I had saved his little pub enterprise and my home.

'Afternoon, Poppy,' he said cheerfully. Then he nodded at the inspectors from the Health Board. 'Fantastic place this, but my God, she's a stickler for law and order, every by-law has to be observed, fire drill, hygiene, you wouldn't believe it. Still we all like it and that's saying something, isn't it.'

The inspectors were impressed, the gigglers went to their lunch and I knew that we could go on like this for ever.

Part 2 – Elegant Jane

They used to say about me when I was young that I was a perfectionist. I liked the description actually, it meant that I wanted things to be perfect, which I did. But as I got older they stopped using the phrase. Probably thought it meant finicky, picky, hard to please.

And eventually old maid.

Nobody ever said Poppy was a perfectionist. Dear me, no. She always had cut knees or scabs on them. Her hair was constantly falling over her face, her clothes ripped or torn from climbing up in the Whitethorn Woods or sliding down things. And yet amazingly people always liked Poppy. Quite disproportionately in fact.

The house was full of her friends, that loud noisy Grania practically lived in our house for heaven's sake. Oh and crowds more. And it was the same with boys when the time came – which was very early really – she had dozens of them around the place too. When she left St Ita's school in Rossmore she could have gone to university as I did. I have a degree and became a librarian but no, Poppy, who always knew her own mind, had insisted on nursing.

Mother and Father were, I suppose, relieved that it didn't cost them anything but still. What had they worked for and saved for if it wasn't to give us an education? Poppy would come home with hair-raising tales of life on the ward. Honestly, what she had to do all day! How people trusted human lives to my half-crazed sister was beyond me.

When she was qualified (against all the odds; I must say I never thought she'd see it through) she went into a ward for the elderly, most of them mad, poor dears, and completely wandering. Poppy found them fascinating and hilarious. You'd swear she was working with Einstein and Peter Ustinov, not a lot of elderly people who were totally confused and barely knew what day it was.

Amongst the seemingly endless series of young men who all wanted to be with Poppy there was one called Oliver. His people owned a lot of property all over Rossmore. Very, very good looking, a bit of a philanderer, I suppose. He didn't really work because he didn't really need to. And his family were all torn between relief that he was settling down at last and concern that he had chosen as his bride a nurse called Poppy with no background. I warned Poppy that he might not be the entirely utterly faithful type and she said that life was all about taking risks, and after all she might find herself attracted to another man so marriage was just a giant optimistic step.

I didn't see marriage like that. I saw it as something you thought about rather a lot and made sure it was the right thing to do. Oddly, I had never really been close enough to consider seriously marrying anyone, except that time with Keith who was also a librarian and we were really quite well suited but there was a huge misunderstanding there. I don't know what happened.

We were actually talking about getting engaged and I explained about the small square-cut emerald I would like for my ring. It wasn't extraordinarily expensive or anything but it seemed to upset him that I had already chosen it and tried it on. When I was telling him we must have a walk-in closet in the house because otherwise our clothes would get crushed beyond belief he felt . . . well, I don't know what he felt really. But he said he needed more time and then he sort of faded away.

Oliver and Poppy's wedding was just what you'd expect. Haphazard, disorganised, everyone laughing. Lots of champagne and little chicken sandwiches. And a wedding cake. That was all. No proper banquet with place names or anything.

Mother and Father enjoyed it. I didn't.

That loud Grania was braying all over the place, brought her dreadful red-faced father with her. Mother and Father said that Poppy had never been a day's trouble in her whole life.

I thought that was rich.

Poppy? No trouble?

What trouble had I been, I might ask? I lived in my own flat and I did go to see them. Not as often as parents like but enough. From time to time anyway. Poppy and Oliver had a marvellous house, well, compared to my small flat it was marvellous, but of course hopelessly neglected, what with Poppy still out slaving away in a geriatric ward.

I'll tell you, if I had married Oliver and all his money I would have stayed at home, done up that house and invited people in. Then he mightn't have wandered so much.

I knew about his wandering quite early on actually. I saw him nuzzling a girl in a wine bar. Naturally he saw me too and disengaged himself. He came over full of charm.

'We're adults, you and I, Jane,' he said.

'Indeed, Oliver.' I was icy.

'So adults don't run home with silly tales, do they?'

'Unless they see other adults doing silly things in wine bars,' I said, proud of myself.

He looked at me for a while. 'I suppose in the end, it is your call, Jane,' he said and went back to the girl.

I paid my bill and left.

As it happened I did not tell Poppy.

I had tried to warn her before she married him and she had been shruggy and so dismissive – let her find out herself.

She found out about six months later when she came home unexpectedly and opened her bedroom door to find Oliver and an old flame having a nostalgic whatever. She asked him to leave. That very day.

Of course he made a fuss.

She was being doctrinaire, he had said, which indeed in many ways she was. She wanted no explanations, excuses, no promises of a faultless life from then on. She said to him that she just wanted the house, no maintenance, that it was actually a good deal he had got, which he would realise when he came to talk it over with the briefs and his own divorced friends.

And then as if that wasn't all bad enough losing this great catch, Poppy threw up her dull but safe job in the hospital and went to work at a crazy retirement home called Ferns and Heathers.

I mean, what a name! But Poppy, being Poppy, said she liked it. It was better, she said, than calling it St Something as a lot of these places were called, and it made the people who lived there feel they were not being hurtled rather too swiftly towards the next world. And some of these homes for the elderly were called remorselessly jolly names, she said, so she was happy with Ferns and Heathers, and was always down on her hands and knees planting both to make sense of the silly name.

Really, Poppy defied every rule in the book.

Against all the odds the damn nursing home took off and became very successful and Mother told me that Poppy owned a great deal of it nowadays. They said they would like to go and live there when they were old. And Poppy said they should go in nice and early while they still had all their energy for the marvellous things that the residents all did.

I hated going there actually.

I went of course out of solidarity from time to time but really it was looking at the old people's crêpey skin and thinking of their table-tennis tournaments that upset me.

Sometimes Poppy would say in that idiotic way she spoke like an eleven-year-old, 'What exactly is it that you do, Jane, which is so exciting compared to all this?' And of course nobody can answer a question like that.

Mother and Father said there was no stopping Poppy. I don't know why but they seemed to say it with some admiration.

Lots of the old mad people in the home felt very strongly about the bypass that was going to be built around Rossmore. Some of them welcomed it, saying it was progress when they went into town on their occasional visits. It would be easier to cross the road as the traffic would be less. Others were against it and said that their relatives would now fly by and not come to see them at all. Poppy began to organise debates on it at the home and then bring both sides into Rossmore to let them protest on different sides. Is that mad or what? And even Oliver when he called to visit me from time to time said she was a bloody marvel.

I took to keeping big juicy olives and little slices of salami in my fridge in case Oliver called. And I always dressed up anyway so he never found me looking like a slattern. Poor Poppy often looked as if she had been doing hard manual labour all day . . . which in a way she had on those nursing wards. Before she went to that home. And I liked Oliver coming to call, yes I did.

And of course we went to bed together. I mean, Oliver is that kind of person. I mean, there was nothing serious in it. I was his sister-in-law after all or his ex-sister-in-law to be strictly accurate. And I didn't really see him as husband material. No, if St Ann were going to answer my prayers, I don't think it was going to be with Poppy's ex.

He talked rather a lot about Poppy, which was irritating. I said once that we had gone beyond Poppy as a topic of conversation but he looked puzzled. He always wanted to know if she was seeing anyone and I said, you know Poppy, seeing everyone, seeing no one. This puzzled him further and he asked, did she want to know about him.

Now the truth was that if I mentioned Oliver, Poppy would raise her eyes to heaven and sigh. But I didn't pass this on. He seemed to think we were much closer than we were, asking me little titbits about when we were girls. As if I can remember!

I decided to go over to this idiotic place, Ferns and Heathers, to see Poppy, well, really so that I would have something to tell Oliver about her. I wanted him to think we were more loving and bonding than we actually were.

The first thing I saw when I arrived was Poppy's bottom up in the air as she dug at some hole in the ground. Beside her were assorted geriatrics including of all people that loud Grania's red-faced father, Dan. What was he doing here? They were all laughing hysterically at something. I felt that when my shadow fell on them they stopped laughing.

'Why it's Elegant Jane!' cried the awful Dan. And the others looked at me without much pleasure. Poppy came up from the hole in the ground, her hands filthy and streaks of mud on her face.

'Oh hallo, Jane, what's wrong?' she asked. As if there would have to be something wrong for me to come and see my only sister.

'Why should there be anything wrong?' I snapped at her.

They all understood, the old folk, and Dan understood better than most.

'Fasten your seatbelts,' he said. They laughed.

'Light the touchpaper and retire,' said another old man with hardly any teeth. A man who must have retired thirty years ago.

I hated them for seeing our coldness and recognising it for what it was. I hated Poppy for letting them see it.

'Right, folks, I have to go away for a short while. Please stay well away from the hole, for God's sake, I don't want to be digging you all out with broken hips,' Poppy ordered them and led me to her little house in the grounds. She washed her hands, poured me a sherry and sat down to talk to me.

'You still have mud on your face,' I said.

She ignored me completely. 'Is there anything wrong with Dad?' she asked.

'No, of course not, why, should there be?'

'Well, his blood pressure was up last week,' Poppy said.

'How on earth do you know?' I asked.

'I take it every week when I go round on my half-day,' she said.

266

Poppy goes to Mother and Father every week on her half-day? How extraordinary!

'So what is it then?' Poppy asked, looking wistfully out at the garden where she wanted to be, not in here talking to her only sister.

'I was talking to Oliver,' I began.

'Oliver?' She sounded bewildered.

'Yes, Oliver. Your husband, the man you were married to.'

'But not married to him now, Jane,' Poppy said as if she was talking to someone retarded. She talks to those old bats outside on much more equal terms than she talks to me.

'No, but he was making enquiries about you,' I said, wondering how this had got so out of control.

'Like what kind of enquiries?' She was totally uninterested. I so wished I hadn't come.

'Oh, I don't know. Things. Like were you good at games at school, like what we did on your birthday at home.'

'Oliver wants to know all that? Lord, he must be madder than we thought,' Poppy said cheerfully and looking out the window as if she were dying to get back to digging holes.

'I don't think he's mad at all, I think he is very sane. I really believe that he wanted it all to work, you know, when you were married.'

'Yes, of course he did, that's why he brought his old girlfriend back to my bed,' Poppy said in a matter-of-fact way.

'Well, it was his bed too,' I heard myself say idiotically.

'Oh well, of course, that makes it all right then,' Poppy said.

There was a silence between us. I tried to fill it. I wanted to show some interest in this mad place where she worked.

'What were you digging the hole for?'

'Mass burial ground, cheaper than funerals,' Poppy said.

For a moment I believed her. Well, we don't go round making these silly jokes in the library.

'Sorry, it's for a giant palm tree. It's arriving this afternoon –

267

we wanted to have its space ready for it.'

'Then don't let me detain you.' I stood up huffily.

'Don't go – finish your sherry.' She sat there tousled and untidy. I sipped it in silence.

Twice she looked as if she were about to confide in me and then stopped at the last moment.

'Say it,' I ordered her eventually.

'All right, well, item number one, I don't fancy Oliver remotely, so go right ahead if you do. You aren't stepping on any toes. But item two, he's really very boring, clinging and boring. You'll find that. So he's rich and good looking but actually that's not very important in the long run. The rich can often be tight with spending their money and the handsome are often vain. And you end up feeling guilty because you encouraged him. And he hasn't the remotest notion of being faithful. You told me that years back and I didn't believe you. So why should you listen to me now?'

Poppy sat there, assured and mud spattered, with a sherry in her hand and a lot of mad old people outside the window waiting for her to come out so that they could get on with digging a hole.

'And this is better?' I said, indicating the garden, the residents and the whole set-up with a nod of my head.

'Vastly,' she said.

I knew then that I had never understood her and never would. My efforts at friendship and trying to get close, admittedly late in the day, were being thrown back in my face.

As I was getting into my car I heard them cheer at the reappearance of Poppy. Well, it was what she wanted. And she had said the coast was clear.

I got my hair done and bought some smoked salmon – in case Oliver came round.

As it happened he didn't. But he came next evening.

He never brought a gift and he did look at himself in the

mirror quite a lot. And he always stayed just a little too long for me, because I had to get up early for work. Sometimes he would stay the night but that was rather disruptive too.

He never suggested that we go out anywhere. And there *was* something a bit clinging about him. But we weren't married so I couldn't divorce him or get a barring order against him. Even though at times I would have liked to. For a little peace.

There was very little laughter around at the library or at home. The days often seemed long. Compared to that madhouse at Ferns and Heathers where there was never a spare moment in the day and the inmates were laughing all the time.

Was it at all possible that Poppy could have been right? Poppy whose skin had never been cherished, whose hair had never been styled and whose wardrobe was a joke, a bad joke. Surely Poppy couldn't have discovered the secret of life? That would be too unfair for words.

CHAPTER 14

Your Eleven O'Clock Lady

Part 1 – Pandora

I hope it's going to be busy today at the salon. When you have to hang about between clients, time seems to drag a lot. I didn't need any free time to think about the conversation at breakfast.

I was in at 8.45 as usual. Fabian, who is a legend not only in Rossmore but for four counties around, likes to have what he calls 'grooming control' before he opens the door. His salon sinks or swims, he says, by what the staff look like. No grubby fingernails, no down-at-heel shoes, and our own hair must be perfect. We had been warned about that at the very outset. Fabian expected us to have shining, well-conditioned hair every morning, any snipping or trimming he would do. It was one of the perks of the job.

Our uniforms were laundered on the premises so they always looked bandbox fresh. That's a funny word, bandbox. I wonder what it means. Fabian insisted that we all smile a lot and look pleased to see customers. The salon wasn't the place to be if you were going to look glum. Worries had to be left outside the salon. That was an absolute.

Fabian said he could only charge these top prices he does if people felt they were in a special place. No one with hangovers, headaches, difficult children or unhappy love lives had any place on the staff.

Unreal, you might say. And Fabian would agree.

But he said that going to an expensive hair salon was an escape for people, they didn't want to hear of the dull or problem-filled world of ordinary people. So there was to be no talk about the traffic, or illness, or being mugged. An expensive perfume was sprayed around the salon just before opening time and several times again during the day. This was to set the tone of the place. Glamour, peace, elegance, a palace with the power to transform all who came in and paid big money.

The tips were good too, and you could work anywhere you wanted to if you had been a few years in Fabian's. But usually you set up your own place. If you said that you were 'late of Fabian's' people would come to you from far and wide.

Not that I was going to be in a position to set up my own salon. Once I thought I might – and Ian had been behind me all the way, assuring me that I was management material.

But breakfast today had changed everything.

Stop it, Pandora. Smile. Teeth and eyes, Pandora, we are nearly on show.

Pandora is my salon name, and that's what I think of myself as being while I'm here. At home, I'm Vi. Don't think of home. Smile, Pandora, the day is starting.

My nine o'clock lady was in the door like a greyhound out of a trap. She came every Thursday without fail, attached almost surgically to her mobile phone. Fabian was very strict about this. He only allowed phones that vibrated to show there was some-one looking for you. No ringing tones to disturb the other clients.

My smile was nailed to my face. Her conversation was quick-fire and one way, she wanted agreement, nods of affirmation and acknowledgement, all in the right place.

You couldn't let your mind wander here and so no thoughts of

Ian and his guilty, shifty account of where he had been last night was allowed room in my head.

The nine o'clock lady was always in a lather about some aspect of her work. Some fool had done this, some idiot hadn't done that, some bloody courier had been late, some bloody sponsor had been early. Rossmore was the boondocks of the world. All that was needed was immense sympathy, a litany of soothing sounds – and speed. The nine o'clock lady had to be out screaming at a taxi at nine-forty-five.

My nine-thirty lady had been shampooed and was deep in a magazine story about Princess Diana.

'It's a shame they can't let her rest, isn't it?' she said. 'Do you have anything else about her that I could read, do you think?'

She was a regular also, trying out a different style every week until she found the perfect way to look at her daughter's wedding which was going to be a huge affair. The nine-thirty lady had not been invited to get involved in the planning of it all. There was a wedding organiser. Nothing in her whole life had ever hurt her so much. Her only daughter had turned her back on her on this the most important day of her life. Mighty soothing was called for here also. Huge reassurance that it had been a kindness rather than a rejection on the daughter's part. Useless bleatings that it gave her much more time now to concentrate on her own hair, her own outfit, her own enjoyment of the day. The nine-thirty lady had wanted to be in the centre of it, fussing, bossing and driving everyone mad.

'Don't marry, Pandora,' she warned me as she left. 'It's never worth it, believe me, I know.'

I had told her many times in answer to her absent-minded questioning that I *was* married, to Ian. But she didn't remember, and as Fabian said, we mustn't expect them to remember anything about us. They are centre stage when they come in here. We are just a well-groomed, charming set of props. Certainly not the occasion to tell her that she was spot on about marriage.

It was indeed, judging by the way this morning was going, far from worth it.

The ten o'clock was an out-of-town person who had seen a write-up of Fabian's in a magazine. She had come to the town to get fabric for soft furnishings. She had decided to have a hairdo as well. No, nothing new, thank you, she knew what suited her, like she knew what fabrics she needed. The tedium and monotony of her life seeped all over me. I wondered: if possibly my life with Ian was at the moment anxious and unsettling, it might be better than the living death that the ten o'clock lady seemed to be living.

My ten-thirty was a model. Well, actually she was a glamour model, for a photo catalogue for underwear, but she called herself a model. She was nice actually, she came in every six weeks to have her roots done.

'You look a bit peaky today,' she said.

I suppose it was good that she even saw me, most of them didn't. But to be seen and identified as peaky wasn't good. It was a funny phrase, something people said in British soap operas to someone who was about to die or who was pregnant or getting dumped.

Peaky.

Not a good thing to look. I hoped that Fabian hadn't heard. I smiled more brightly than ever, hoping to beat off whatever dull, dead sort of vibes I must be giving off.

'I know, I know. I have to smile like that every night,' the ten-thirty said sympathetically. 'Sometimes I feel like a big bawling session and that's when I have to smile most.'

She was very kind, interested and made me think she cared. I'm sure she's very good at her job, making ladies feel confident about lingerie – I bet they all confide things to her at her work because she sounds interested in other people. I looked around to see whether Fabian was in earshot. We had strict rules about not burdening the clients with our own personal problems.

273

'It's just my husband, I think he's seeing someone else.'

'Believe me, he is,' she said, applying her lip liner.

'What?' I cried.

'Sweetheart, I work for a place that is packed to the gills every night with people's husbands getting the catalogues just to ogle over them. That's what husbands do. It's not a problem unless you make it into one.'

'What do you mean?'

'Listen to me – I know this, they like to look at the pictures and chat up birds. They don't want to leave their wives. They're not sorry they married them, it's just that they hate to think that it's all over and that they are missing out on whatever else is on offer. They sometimes feel that they've been filed away under "Married Man". Cross-reference, "Dull Man". A sensible wife would make nothing of it; the problem is a lot of them make a great, useless fuss about it – weakening everything as a result.'

I looked at her in amazement. How did she get such wisdom? This woman whose modelling name was Katerina but who was probably called Vi, like myself at home.

'You mean, put up with infidelity and cheating and pretend it isn't happening? You seriously mean that?' I asked her.

'Yes, in a way I did mean that, for a bit anyway, until you know definitely it's true – and even if it is you must know definitely if it's going to be the end of the world if he has a bit of a whirl. Soon it could be nothing but a confused memory.'

'But suppose it's not just a bit of a whirl. Suppose he really does love her and not me. What happens then?'

'Well, then he walks,' said Katerina. 'And there's nothing any of us can do. I'm just saying that the very worst scenario is to make a fuss now. Right?' She looked as if she had finished with the subject so I went on to autopilot again, got her hair rinsed and blow-dried it to perfection. As she left she gave me a big tip.

'You'll survive, Pandora, see you in six weeks,' she said and glided like a lithe panther out of the salon.

'Your eleven o'clock lady not in yet, Pandora?' Fabian had a control of the salon that would have been envied by any military leader in a war room. He knew what was going on, or not going on, in every corner. Together we looked at the appointment book. New client. A Ms Desmond. It meant nothing to either of us.

'Find out how she heard of us, won't you, Pandora?' he said, on the ball about work twenty-four hours a day.

'Yes, of course, Fabian,' I said automatically.

Actually I would spend the time trying to find out how this had happened, my five-year-old marriage to Ian unravelling.

First I had accidentally seen the bracelet in his drawer. 'For my darling, to celebrate the new moon, all my love, Ian.' I had no idea what he meant. We hadn't seen any new moon together recently or that I can remember at all.

But it might be referring to something that was about to happen. I checked the diary: there would be a new moon on Saturday next. Possibly he was going to take me away somewhere to celebrate it. I wouldn't spoil the surprise. But there was no mention of an outing on Saturday, instead the rather depressing news that Ian would be away for the weekend on a conference. Still it didn't dawn on me. I must be very foolish. Thick? Trusting? Apply which word you choose.

But last night Ian was very late home from the office and I went to bed at eleven because I was exhausted. I woke at four and he still wasn't back. Now this was worrying. He has a mobile phone, he could have called me. I tried calling him but he had the phone on voicemail. But at that very moment I heard his key in the door. I was so angry with him that I decided to pretend to be asleep and avoid a row. He took ages to come to bed, but I never opened my eyes. At one stage he went to his sock drawer and took out the bracelet. I opened my eyes just wide enough to see him smiling at the engraving and then he put it away. Deep in his briefcase.

Ian always left the house earlier than I did. It took him ages to get to work in his car but he needed it for work. And for who knew what else? He could only have had three hours' sleep. He asked me what time I had gone to bed.

'Eleven o'clock, I'm afraid I was dropping. What time did you come back?' I asked.

'Oh, early hours of the morning, you were sleeping so very peacefully I didn't want to wake you. Such a bloody great fuss on at the office . . .'

'Still, think of all the overtime,' I reassured him, trying to force the suspicion out of my mind.

'Not sure they'll pay anyway and listen, love, I have to go away for the weekend, there's a conference, bit of an honour really – I suppose I should be pleased but I know it's your weekend off so I'm so sorry.' He put on his little-boy face that I used to find endearing. Until this morning when I found it sickening.

He was having an affair.

Lots of things fitted into place now. I had made a list of all these things when he left.

I had an hour before I needed to go out myself but I did not feel like washing up after Ian's breakfast, cleaning Ian's house, preparing Ian's dinner. I put on my coat and headed out the door as soon as I heard his car leave. I got on the first bus that came to the stop. It wasn't going to the part of Rossmore where Fabian's was but I didn't care. I just wanted to get away from the house where I had once been so happy. Once. But it was now like a prison.

The bus stopped at the far edge of Whitethorn Woods and then was going to turn round and go back to wherever it had come from. Like a zombie I walked up through the woods. People said that they were going to be dug up to make a new road but that might just be a rumour. Anyway if the woods did go it would be nice to have a look at them now.

I walked on fighting back the sick feeling of dread in my

chest, the feeling that it was all over and Ian loved someone else. Some horrible, scheming girl.

He had been taken in by her, bought her a bracelet and was going to see the new moon with her.

I had followed the wooden signs to the well. We used to come here when we were kids but I hadn't been since. Even at this early hour there were people praying. An old woman with her eyes closed. Two children with a picture of someone, their mother probably, asking for a cure. It was unreal and kind of sad.

Yet, I thought, now that I'm here, it can't do any harm. I told St Ann the situation. Quite simply. It was amazing what a short story it was really. Boy loves girl, boy finds other girl, first girl heartbroken. There must have been thousands and thousands of similar stories told here.

I didn't feel any sense of hope or anything. In fact I felt a bit foolish. I didn't know what I was asking her.

To afflict this new woman with some awful illness maybe? St Ann wouldn't do that.

To change Ian's mind, really, I suppose that's all I wanted.

Then I walked briskly to the gates of the woods and caught a bus to work.

I travelled with a grim face into Rossmore and all morning I kept remembering more damning proof of the affair. The way he had refused to go bowling last week, normally he couldn't be kept away from it. How he had changed the subject twice when I asked him to do a business plan on buying that corner newsagents near us out in our suburb which was for sale and making it into a salon.

'Let's not be too hasty,' he had said. 'Who knows where we'll be in a year or two?'

Suddenly my thoughts were interrupted.

'Your eleven o'clock lady is in,' one of the juniors called.

Ms Desmond was waiting at the desk. She had a nice smile and she asked me to call her Brenda.

'What a lovely name, Pandora!' she said wistfully. 'I'd love to have been called that.'

Fabian didn't encourage us to tell clients that these were made-up names, in fact he actively discouraged it.

'I think my mother was reading an over-fancy book at the time,' I said, taking the grandeur away from it to reassure her.

I liked this woman. Brenda Desmond handed her coat to the junior and sat down while we looked at her in the mirror.

'I want to look terrific for the weekend,' she said. 'I'm going off to a really gorgeous place in the country to look at the new moon with a new fellow.'

I looked at her reflection in the mirror and told myself that all over this town there were people going away for the weekend with new fellows. It didn't have to be Ian. My pleasant interested smile was still there.

'That's nice,' I heard myself say. 'And are you serious about him?'

'Well, as much as I can be, he's not entirely free, alas, he says that's no problem but, you know, it does throw a wrench in the works. Funny phrase, that, I wonder where it comes from.'

'Probably it's quite a literal thing, like, you know, if a wrench falls into the works of some machine or is thrown into it, it sort of wrecks the whole machine,' I said.

She listened, interested.

'You're right, it's probably quite straightforward. Are you interested in phrases and where they come from?'

She was treating me like a real person with views, not someone who would crimp her hair. But I had to be sure that she was the one before I pulled every tuft of her flat, greasy hair out by the roots.

'Yes, I am interested in words, I was just thinking about the word bandbox this morning. Do you know where that came from?'

'Well, oddly I do, I looked it up once: a bandbox was a light box that held bands, like hairbands, I suppose, caps, millinery, that sort of thing.'

'Does it now?' I was actually interested. Imagine her knowing that! And why should a bandbox be so fresh and clean? But enough speculation. Back to work.

'What do you think you'd like done?'

'I don't really know, Pandora, I'm not much good about hair, I have to work so very hard, you see. We are flat out all the time. So this is a real excitement for me, I called in a sickie this morning, I can't go in tomorrow with a new hairdo or they'd suspect and then on Saturday I'm off for my wicked weekend with a colleague.'

'Where do you work?' I asked her. I could hear the words booming, resounding, echoing in my head.

Please may she not say Ian's company.

She said Ian's company.

My hands were on her shoulders. I could have raised them and put them around her neck and choked her until she was dead. She wouldn't have been expecting it, you see, so it would have worked. She could be lying dead in the chair now.

But I resisted it. There would have been too many repercussions.

Instead I talked about hair.

'You wear it fairly flattish,' I said, amazed that I could function at all.

'Yes. Do you think I should have it higher, and maybe some more shape? What do you suggest?' She didn't want to know what I would have suggested.

I thought of my Ian running his hands through this woman's horrible limp hair, telling Brenda she was beautiful as he so often told Vi she was beautiful. It was almost too much to bear.

'It's quite stylish the way it is,' I said thoughtfully. 'But let me ask Fabian, he always knows.'

I tottered on unsteady legs to Fabian.

'New lady just loves her hair the way it is, think she could be a regular, can you come and tell her she looks fine.'

He peered across the salon.

'She looks ludicrous,' he said.

'Fabian, you asked us to use our initiative to second-guess people, I'm doing that and suddenly now it's wrong.' I looked offended.

'No, you're right.'

He glided over and touched her head in that way he does. 'Ms Desmond, Pandora, who is one of our most esteemed stylists here, asked me to give my opinion. I think the classic style you have chosen is perfect for your face, complements your features and I feel that all you need is a little, tiny trim.'

'You think it's nice?' she asked foolishly and the great Fabian closed his eyes as if to say it was almost too nice to describe. It also prevented him from having to lie to her face.

'Lucinda,' I called to a junior. 'Take my lady and give her a very good, thorough shampoo,' I called. I hissed to Lucinda – who in real life was called Brid – to beat her head on the basin and get lots of soap in her eyes. The child not unnaturally wondered why.

'Because she's an evil tramp and is sleeping with my best friend's husband,' I hissed.

Brid-Lucinda obliged. Brenda Desmond was brought limping, near blinded and aching back to my station. Brid-Lucinda had kicked her for good measure, pretending to fall over her feet. I put the greasiest gel I could find into her already greasy hair and dried it until it looked like rats' tails on either side of her head. I cut it so that it ended up wispy and uneven. When any of the others looked over at it, I shrugged as if to ask, what could I do when these were the instructions I got.

When I had finished and made her as awful as I could, she looked at herself doubtfully in the mirror.

'This is classical, you say?'

'Oh very, Brenda, he'll love it.'

'I do hope so, he's very stylish, you know. What with being French and everything.'

'He's *French*?'

'Yes, didn't I say, they sent him over from the Paris office! Imagine! And yet he does seem to fancy me . . .' She looked childishly delighted.

I looked at her in horror.

'Do you know Ian in your office?' I said suddenly.

'Ian? Ian Benson? Of course I do. He's a great guy, Ian. How do you know him?'

'I know him,' I said glumly.

'He's married to Vi, he's always talking about her.'

'What does he say about her?'

I was so wretched now that I nearly threw myself on the ground and held her around the knees, sobbing out my apologies for making her look like a madwoman.

'Oh everything, he was hoping to take her away this weekend and then they sent him on a conference. It's an honour and everything but he said he'd have preferred to take Vi to this place with a lake and they could have watched the new moon. And made a wish.'

'What do you think he's wishing for?'

'He didn't say but I think he might have been thinking they'd have a baby sometime soon. And that he would get Vi a salon much nearer home. He's been doing endless overtime recently. He's definitely saving for something . . .'

And then she was gone, out there with her horrible hairstyle, about to make a total mess of her weekend with the sophisticated Parisian man.

I think they told me that my eleven-thirty was in but I didn't hear. Like I haven't really been hearing much of anything lately.

You're meant to give something to charity if St Ann grants your request. But she didn't really, did she? I mean, Ian had never stopped loving me at all so we were praying for something that had already been granted. But on the other hand, it had all turned out the way we wanted.

Oh, go on.

It's only money for handicapped children.

It's not the end of life as it had been five minutes ago.

Part 2 – Bruiser's Business

My real name is George. Not that anyone would know it. I have been called Bruiser since I was two. And in the salon I'm called Fabian.

So when anyone calls out 'George Brewster', like at an airport if I am on standby and they are reading my passport, I take ages to answer. Then I leap up guiltily as if I am travelling on forged documents.

At our school, the Brothers in Rossmore, everyone had nicknames and sadly they heard my mum calling me Bruiser so that was that. I wasn't colossal or anything but I was a sturdy thick-set boy, I suppose, so they leaped on that name. In a way it wasn't a bad name to be called. New people I met thought that I had some terrific reputation with my fists and so they kept away from me which was a relief.

I was ten when my mate Hobbit told me that my dad was running around. I was so stupid I thought he actually meant running around, you know, like in circles or up and down the road jogging. But he didn't, he meant going after the ladies. He said he had seen my dad in a car with this blonde one who was much, much younger and they were going at it like knives.

I didn't believe Hobbit and I hit him. Hobbit was annoyed.

'I only told you so that you'd be ready for it,' he complained, rubbing his shoulder where I had thumped him. 'I actually don't care if your dad runs from here to Timbuktu.'

So I gave him two KitKats from my lunchbox as a consolation and everything was all right.

I always had a terrific lunchbox because my mum knew I loved chocolate and peanut butter sandwiches. Poor Hobbit had awful things like apples and celery and cheese and bits of very dull chicken.

Shortly afterwards my mum discovered that Dad was running up and down or whatever I called it in those days and everything changed.

'It's all our fault, Bruiser,' she told me. 'We are not attractive people, we haven't been able to hold your father's attention and interest. Everything must change.' And everything did.

First she kept dragging me up to St Ann's Well to discuss the matter with a statue.

Then I got horrible lunchboxes, worse than Hobbit's, then I had to jog four bus stops every morning before catching the bus. After school I went to the gym with my mum. It was very expensive so we both had to work there in order to be allowed to use the machinery. She used to man the reception desk for two hours and I went round picking up towels.

I actually liked it, I liked talking to the people there, they told me their stories, and why they were there. There was a fellow who had hoped to meet birds but hadn't met many, there was a man who had had a heart scare and a woman who wanted to look well for a wedding, and a singer who had seen a video of herself and said that her backside was the size of a mountain, which it more or less was.

Because I really was interested in their stories they talked more and they told the people who ran the gym that I was a great asset. And though I wasn't really meant to be working there at all, what with being way under age, they gave me more hours. They were afraid to give me money because of the law but they bought me nice things like a good brand-new school blazer from the shop and a camera and it was great.

My mum lost a lot of weight and apparently Dad stopped running all over the place and said that no one should ever underestimate the power of St Ann and a healthy diet. And everything was fine again at home.

It was fine at school too because I had got a lot fitter and when we were thirteen and I went to the disco, Hobbit said that most of the babes there thought I was a fine thing. Which was terrific for me but not for Hobbit.

Neither Hobbit nor I knew what to do as a job, a career, whatever. My dad was a sales executive for electric goods and I sure as hell didn't want to do that. Hobbit's dad and mum ran a corner shop and he hated even the thought of working in it. My mum worked full time in the gym now, she had done a course and she taught aerobics there. But none of that made it any easier for Hobbit and myself to know what we would do. Even Miss King, the careers teacher who came to the school as a consultant, seemed hard pushed to advise us.

She said to me that I was interested in people, I should take that into account. I told her straight out I wouldn't be a social worker, I'd hate it. No, she didn't mean that, she said. Nor teaching. I couldn't *stand* teaching. She nodded sympathetically. She was always nice, Miss King was.

'Some job where you'd be talking to people and making them feel good?' she suggested.

'A gigolo?' I wondered. I just wanted to tell Hobbit that I'd said it.

'Yes, that sort of thing, certainly that's the area where we should be looking,' she said agreeably.

So I didn't tell Hobbit about it after all. Then amazingly Hobbit said that we might do hairdressing, there were loads of babes at the classes in college and we'd be stroking women's heads and all kinds of things all day in the salon.

'*Hairdressing?*' I said.

'We've got to do something,' Hobbit said reasonably.

Nobody liked the idea except Hobbit and myself. My mum said I could have done something more intellectual, my dad said it wasn't for real men. Hobbit's parents said they wouldn't be able to hold their heads up again in the corner shop.

It wasn't bad at all as it turned out. Hobbit got a job at a ritzy salon where he was called Merlin.

Merlin!

I had to remember that when I went in to see him or called him on the phone.

I got a place in a family-style salon way out in the suburbs of Rossmore called the Milady Salon. I liked the owner, Mr Dixon. We all called him Mr Dixon, even people who had been there twenty years.

It was a very middle-aged, middle-class, once-weekly shampoo-and-blow-dry brigade, and a nervous request for a cut, which they called a trim, once every six weeks, discreet colour twice a year. Nothing innovative, no experiments, no chance to show off any style. But basically good people who wanted to look better.

Their eyes seemed big with anxiety as they looked in the mirror. Every hairdo was some kind of dream. A woman might be giving a dinner party, or another might be going to an extravaganza on ice, or to an old girls' reunion. A lot of them were very lacking in self-confidence, which was why they never tried anything new. Sometimes I noticed that they didn't really look all that much better when they left the salon but they felt better and so they walked straighter with more purpose and half smiled at their reflection in the shop window rather than scuttling past it as they had done on the way in.

It had been a bit like that with my own mum.

She didn't look hugely changed after her first weight loss at the gym. She just had more confidence, that was all. She felt better about herself and she didn't bite the head off Dad and ask him where he had been and accuse him of ignoring her. She was just a nicer person to live with and so he was nicer to her. It was as simple as that.

And that's just the way these women at the salon felt too.

I think they liked me, they gave me nice tips, they loved my name Bruiser. They asked about my family and my holidays and if I had a girlfriend. A good fifty per cent of them said I should settle down and the other half said I should take my time. Some of them said I could do worse than visit St Ann's Well, that she was the last word on matters of the heart.

I was taking my time as it happened. Hobbit and I would go out clubbing but we only met awful screeching girls, not settling down material at all. Hobbit, now that he was called Merlin, was full of confidence and ambition. He said to me that I would end up an old man who only knew how to do tightly permed grey heads unless I moved. We needed to branch out, go somewhere that there might be a bit of action, where we might win competitions.

In my head I knew he was right but I hated leaving Mr Dixon and the Milady Salon. It seemed like a betrayal. Mr Dixon said he had five really difficult clients who just loved me. Could I see it in my heart to come in once a month? Merlin said I was raving mad to make a lash for my back like this, but I couldn't not. Mr Dixon *had* taught me everything and paid me well, and I don't think it's right to walk over people who helped you.

So anyway Merlin and I put our savings together and opened our own salon. Rossmore had certainly changed over the years. New affluence meant people had to have the best. There was a young and apparently endless line of clients with money. Girls with tigerish manes, girls with close-cropped, plum-coloured hair, ladies with such heavy frosting that no one could guess at the original colour.

They were leggy and languid and came to the salon twice a week. I marvelled at their wealth and their interest in their hair. It made Milady's seem light years away.

Naturally, my name was changed as well. I was Fabian now. And though Merlin laughed at me for going back to Milady's on the last Friday of every month, I think he half admired me for it as well. Mr Dixon smiled at me as if I were his long-lost son who had come back to the family farm.

They still called me Bruiser there and admired my own very different hairstyle and smart waistcoats. I told them that people were totally mad in the zany salon in Rossmore and liked us all to dress up. They loved hearing these stories and felt safe in their own place. I had more confidence nowadays and so I suggested a little adventure for some of them. Mr Dixon even accepted some of my ideas about slightly more up-to-date decor.

They all asked me about my love life and I told them truthfully that I had been working too hard to find anyone to love. Better not wait too long, they advised, and I nodded gravely.

What I didn't tell them in Milady's was that everyone in the zany place, everyone except Merlin, that is, thought I was gay. Now I had no problems with this, in very many ways it actually worked to my advantage. Women confide in gay men more, as if they were somehow the best of both worlds. Not predatory and about to pounce, not thick and male and wordless; like a girlfriend, really, but not in competition.

It didn't do me any harm; in fact it did me a lot of good. The clients seemed to like it; it helped them to confide in me. They confided. Boy, did they confide. Like that amazing girl Hazel who told me about all her one-night stands and how lonely and used she would feel afterwards. She would never have told me if she had thought me to be a hetero male and possibly a contender.

I did my best for her by toning down her extremely tarty image and making her look somehow more dignified. I suggested a more classy look, and less in the way of bare midriffs. She told me that it was working a treat.

And there was Mary Lou who couldn't get her fellow to commit. He was very happy with her but he wouldn't let her move her things in. And of course no mention of a ring or anything. I said I thought she should be more independent and go on a holiday with girlfriends. No, definitely not a sun, sex, sleeping-with-the-waiters holiday, on the contrary a cultural kind of thing. She was very doubtful but of course it paid off. He was very worried when she looked as if she could survive without him.

So there I was as happy as anything. I was beginning to fancy a beautiful girl called Lara, a designer who came to have her hair done regularly. All the time I went back to Milady's to Mr Dixon, who had after all started me off in the business. Sometimes I brought him a fancy mirror, a turbo hairdryer or a bale of new towels as a gift but I always took my wages from him even though I didn't need them.

Mr Dixon was the old school. You wouldn't want to offend him.

He had come to visit me in our salon once and he took in the whole scene. He said to me later that I was a good lad, the best he ever had, and that he didn't care about my personal habits; it was up to me. My personal life, so to speak.

And I just couldn't explain it all. It was too complicated. Mr Dixon died shortly afterwards and he left me the salon.

I couldn't believe it. But he had no close relations and he didn't want his life's work wound up and sold off to someone who would open a fast-food outlet on the premises.

I had no idea what to do with the place, it was ludicrously old-fashioned and losing money but I knew it had to be kept on as a salon. And I didn't want to dispossess all the old ladies who had been going there for years, by turning it into a proper Fabian salon with all that that involved. Anyway I wasn't giving it much thought at that time. I had other things on my mind.

By then I had fallen totally in love with Lara but she thought I was gay and I couldn't convince her otherwise.

'Nonsense, Fabian, you can't fancy me, sweetheart, you're as gay as a carnival!' she would laugh. 'We're *friends*, you and me, it's only some silly hissy fit you've had with some gorgeous guy and you want to tell him, "I'm going out with a girl, so look at me"!'

'I am not a gay man, Lara,' I said in a level voice, 'I am one hundred per cent heterosexual.'

'And so are Gerry and Henri and Basil in the salon, I suppose,' she mocked.

'No, of course not. But I am.'

It was no use. I told her my name was Bruiser, and she laughed even more. Or George, I suggested in desperation, and she told me to make my mind up.

The nervous woman who was running Milady's kept telephoning me to know what to do about the electricity bill, or whether or not to order more conditioner. Now to top it all off one of my best stylists was having some kind of hysterics in the staff room, roaring and bawling and totally incoherent about having ruined someone's hair and not having understood that her husband was desperate to have children, and about people not trusting other people.

It was all we needed on a busy morning.

Gerry and Basil, who were usually great with tantrums and nervous breakdowns and people howling, couldn't make head nor fist of it. Henri said we should call the paramedics. I went in and sat with her.

'Pandora,' I said gently.

'Vi, my name is Vi,' she cried. I had forgotten. She was always Pandora in the salon.

'I'm Bruiser – that's my real name,' I said. I thought it might help. It didn't.

'Bruiser?' she said in disbelief.

'I'm afraid so,' I confessed.

'Oh my God,' she said. 'That's all we need – you're called Bruiser.'

I decided to get down to the problem. She started to sob again so I got about one word in four: there was Ian who was her husband, there was her eleven o'clock lady, there was poor Brenda Desmond and the Frenchman, and there was the new moon.

I wondered if Henri was right. Maybe she had just gone mad and should be sectioned and locked up. I got her a drink of water and patted her hand.

I was told that Lara was in the salon. I said she'd have to wait. And I went on patting the weeping woman beside me.

'You don't want to annoy Lara,' Pandora-Vi blubbed at me.

'I don't care if we annoy Lara. Lara has annoyed me, she persists in thinking I'm gay, she makes fun of me and sends me up. Let her bloody hair extensions wait until I'm ready.'

Vi looked up with a tear-stained face.

'But that's idiotic, Fabian, just to look at you, anyone would know you swing both ways.' She was red-faced and earnest.

I wanted to give her a good slap, but this was not the moment to argue my sexuality down to the bone with her. She saw the look on my face, however.

'It makes sense to be bisexual when you think it through,' she gulped. 'Less chance of making a mess of things, always another option open.'

'I am not bisexual, Vi. I have sex with women, do you hear, women, girls, birds, babes, broads, whatever. Not enough of them, I have to say, not nearly enough. From now on I'm going to sleep with any woman who has a pulse. And that will show those know-all Laras out there. That will teach them . . .'

I saw Vi's mouth in a round O of horror. She was staring not at me but over my shoulder. I knew it before I turned. There was Lara, listening to every word. Looking very disapproving indeed.

'How dare you make Pandora cry,' she began. 'Big bully. Poor Pandora, what did he say to you?'

Pandora was of course in floods of tears again, triggered by this sympathy. Again I heard a few key words: babies, new moon, Ian, eleven o'clock lady, Frenchman, bracelet. Totally disjointed, completely off the wall. Yet Lara understood at once. There was no problem, she said, we were all to pretend we knew nothing about anything.

Well, that would be easy for me. I mean, I did know nothing about anything.

The eleven o'clock lady could be given a voucher, Vi was to stop taking the contraceptive pill, Ian loved her, the bracelet was for Vi, not the eleven o'clock lady: all was well, nothing to cry about. Main thing was to avoid stress.

It was complete gibberish.

Yet Vi had dried her tears, blown her nose and was actually smiling.

'Hard to avoid stress in a salon like this,' she said ruefully to Lara.

'Go somewhere calmer, somewhere nearer home,' Lara suggested.

'Where?' Vi asked.

'Oh, I'm sure Tiger or Bruiser or whatever he's called here will have a master plan for you,' Lara said but she was smiling at me. A different kind of smile, as if she saw me properly for the first time.

And I did have a plan there and then.

Vi as it happened lived fairly near Milady's, out in the farthest suburbs of Rossmore near the Whitethorn Woods. She could be manager there. She could have babies and bracelets, and new moons, whatever she wanted, and the eleven o'clock lady would be kept away from her. Whatever they wanted. Was that all right, could we all go back to work now? Please?

And we did and I looked at Lara's eyes in the mirror and told her she didn't need hair extensions, her hair was beautiful as it was.

She said, she wondered was there something a bit unprofessional about the way I was stroking her neck. Was it rather like a doctor and a patient and maybe I could be struck off for unprofessional behaviour?

I said I thought not, I thought that different rules entirely apply in a salon and she laughed a warm enthusiastic laugh and said I was not to dream of sleeping with every woman who had a pulse.

She had been there for that bit too . . .

CHAPTER 15

The Intelligence Test

Part 1 – Melanie

You know the way it is: people think that because you're deaf, you're slow. In fact nothing could be further from the truth. If you're deaf you're often as sharp as a tack because you have to pick up so much from the other senses. I look at people's faces all the time and I watch to see what kind of mood they're in. I mean, if you look at the way people can clench their fists, or bite their lips, or just fidget, you know exactly what's going on. I could walk the whole length of Castle Street and Market Street in Rossmore and tell you what kind of a mood the town was in.

So when they all started talking about the intelligence test, well, of course I knew it was important. And the more they said it was nothing to get worked up about, the more I knew it. I'm not a fool, profoundly deaf, yes, but not at all stupid. It was all about this school for girls like me called St Martin's.

'You'd love it there if they have room for you, Melanie,' my mum said over and over. 'It's a kind of legend in education, their girls do so well in life. But if they don't have room then no problems, we'll just go and find another place. There are lots of places.'

But I knew it had nothing to do with St Martin's finding room for me, and I knew that there weren't lots of other places.

If I managed to get the questions right on this intelligence test I'd get in, it was as simple as that.

I had already met a girl who was at school there so I knew all about it, it sounded a great place. This girl who was called Kim said they had fantastic food, and you could be a vegetarian if you liked and even though it was a girls' school there were dances with fellows at them. They would even teach us to dance properly by getting us to recognise the reverberations in the floorboards. They had art classes and an exhibition every year and played a whole rake of games like netball, and hockey, and rounders, against hearing schools as well as other deaf schools. All the girls wore a sort of uniform, any kind of cream-coloured blouse and a navy skirt or navy jeans.

They had all kinds of flashing lights instead of bells, and make-up lessons as well as lipreading and ordinary things.

I was desperate to get into St Martin's.

But my mum and dad were even more desperate. It would be free, you see, on top of everything else. Some rich deaf person had left a fortune to provide an education for girls with hearing problems. Now the money wasn't the main reason they were so keen on it. They mainly wanted it because girls from St Martin's got everywhere. They got to go to university and had great jobs. But it would be a help because my mum and dad hadn't much money and they had Fergal and Cormac to look after too. I know they're not deaf. But they need schooling too.

Dad's business is always threatening to close down. My mum's back is bad and she has to do long hours at the supermarket to keep things going. I knew that Mum used to go up to the well in the woods to pray that I would get my hearing restored, which was kind of ridiculous really. How could they reverse something that had already happened? And if they were able to, then there were a lot of people worse off than I was.

So even though they were doing their best not to pressurise me, they were sick with anxiety in case I wouldn't pass this test.

The test itself didn't really worry me. I didn't think it was going to be very hard. It was going to be general knowledge and fitting shapes into spaces. That wasn't hard. And there would be identifying objects from pictures or drawings. Kim, the girl I knew who was already at St Martin's, said it wasn't too hard. She had problems with a picture of a kite, she said, she never saw one in real life because she hadn't been allowed to go out running after kites in case she didn't hear traffic and might get killed, so she didn't know what they looked like. But she knew everything else so she got in okay.

On the day of the test, I've never seen my mum and dad so worried. My mum kept changing her clothes – the suit was too formal, she said, the frilly dress made her look like a poodle, the jeans made her look as if she hadn't bothered. What was the right thing to wear?

I didn't think it mattered all that much what she wore or indeed what I wore. But she was dead nervous and their bedroom floor was covered in clothes like it never was before. So I didn't say what I was thinking, which was that she could wear a black plastic sack for all I cared – I said that I thought the suit was the best and she could wear a pink scarf to make it look kind of lively. Mum stopped fussing and started kissing me and saying I was a treasure and that I'd obviously get into the school no matter what anyone wore.

My dad cut his face three times shaving and I said it was like going out with someone who had been involved in a massacre. Suddenly his eyes filled with tears.

'You're so bright, Mel. You know marvellous big words like "massacre". They'd be mad as wet hens not to take you in that school.'

We were nervous wrecks when we set out for the place.

We took a train from Rossmore to the town where the school was and then a bus to the gate and we walked up the long avenue. Well, the school looked terrific: as I said, there were these huge sports grounds and there was this walled garden that Kim had told me about where every pupil had a flower bed and they could all grow what they wanted, and I saw through the windows a terrific art room – I could see girls painting a mural and I longed to be part of it all. The school where I was at now seemed so dull compared to it, and it was so hard to get the teachers to remember I was deaf, and so tempting to stop paying attention. But if I were here in St Martin's I'd work so hard, I really, really would. I must not tell them that though. It would sound like pleading or begging.

It would all depend on the test.

When we got in, both my parents had to go to the loo as soon as they got in the door and I stood in the big hall and looked around me. I could just see myself here for the next few years. I imagined having friends that might come and visit me at home and I would go to their homes. They would hate my brothers Fergal and Cormac of course but I would probably hate their brothers and sisters too. My parents would come and visit me here during term time, and see my flower bed, and my exhibit in the art show.

A woman came up to speak to me. She was obviously used to dealing with deaf people. She didn't speak until we were looking at each other.

She was very glamorous looking, with long, dark, curly hair and a big smile. She was very elegant in a tight black skirt and a yellow blouse with a black and yellow brooch on it. She had a book bag over her shoulder and both her hands were free so as well as speaking to me she signed.

This was unexpected.

You see, I thought they didn't sign at this school. I thought they would disapprove of it, and believe it was holding us back. When I went to my lipreading classes three times a week I was told over and over that if I wanted to live in the real world I shouldn't sign.

But then she had signed, and she looked like a teacher. It might be a test. A trick even? It was so hard to know what to do.

But then maybe she might be deaf herself? Courtesy demanded that I should reply in sign language but I decided to speak aloud as well to show I could.

She had asked me, was I lost?

I said, using both ways of talking, that no, thank you, I was waiting for my parents who had both gone to the bathroom and that then we were going to go for an assessment. She said that was fine and she'd see me later because she was going to be taking part in it all.

She looked around the big hall and gave a sort of a little sigh.

'You must like it here,' I said.

'I do. Very much,' she said and there was something sad about the way she spoke as if she was going to be leaving soon. You have to try so hard when you're deaf to pick up the words, you end up picking up loads of other things as well.

My mum and dad were so nervous and they kept getting confused, answering the questions they had to answer, which were just ordinary things for filling in a form. I wanted to scream that *I* was the one being tested, I was the one meant to have the language problems, and that if they could see my mum at the checkout in the supermarket, she was so fast she was like a wizard, and my dad was so reliable in his company that he had the keys to everywhere and if people got locked out they had to come to him. They didn't look like reliable people – they looked like people who couldn't remember if they owned their house or rented it, and they seemed to have trouble remembering what age Fergal and Cormac were.

Anyway the woman with the black curly hair came in to join us and she said her name was Caroline and she would go through a few things with me. She would ask me some questions.

Well, first I thought it was a kind of a joke. They were things like a five-year-old would know about – the colours of traffic lights and about who was the Taoiseach of Ireland and who was Prime Minister of England and the President of the United States and what animal did St George get involved with; then a little harder like in what part of your body would you find a cuticle or a retina. And then a few puzzles about the speed of a train or the length of a platform.

They asked me to tell them about Rossmore and so I told them about all the fuss about the bypass road which would cut through Whitethorn Woods. I said I was in favour of it really because it is so hard to cross the street there at the moment with all the huge lorries, and that really places should want progress rather than looking back. They seemed interested but of course it was hard to know.

Caroline asked, did I want to ask anything myself, so I asked about the signing and what was their policy on it, and she said that a lot of deaf people liked talking in sign because it made them relaxed so St Martin's didn't discourage it, they just used it as a second language. And that seemed fine to me.

Then she said she had a hard question: if a house painter was going to paint the numbers on a housing estate from one to a hundred, how many times would he paint the number nine. I looked at her waiting for the real question. That was it.

I kept looking at her, waiting.

'That's it. There's no catch,' she said. But there had to be a catch. Anyone would know the answer to this one. They couldn't let you into a great school like this or keep you out over something like this.

She asked me to write down the answer on a piece of paper and I did. When she looked at it she nodded and folded it over and involved everyone else in the room.

'What do *you* think?' she asked the Principal.

The Principal said nine. The Assistant Principal said ten. My mother said eleven. My father said definitely eleven, because there would be two nines in ninety-nine.

298

Caroline smiled at them all and asked, 'Do you know what Melanie said?'

They all looked at me and I felt my cheeks go scarlet.

'I'm sorry,' I said, 'I thought you meant every single time he painted the figure nine . . .'

'I did,' said Caroline. 'And you were quite right, the only one in this room who did get it right.'

They all started playing with their fingers: 'Nine, nineteen, twenty-nine . . .'

Caroline put them out of their misery. 'Melanie said twenty times, the rest of you all forgot ninety-one, ninety-two, ninety-three, etc. Well done, Melanie.'

My mum and dad were beaming at me and giving me a thumbs-up sign. The Principal and the Assistant Principal, to give them credit, were laughing and a bit ashamed of themselves.

Then they came to the identifying objects bit.

They were all on cards and to be honest it was very easy at the start: rabbits and houses and sunflowers and buses and things. And we moved on to what might have been the slightly harder things. Now I didn't want to get too confident but these weren't too bad either. Things like a truck, or a food mixer, or a violin, or a saxophone.

But there was one I couldn't work out at all.

It was shaped like a triangle. I turned the card round a bit until I could get a better look at it. No, I still couldn't see what it might be, the drawing was very simple, too simple; there were no real clues.

'I'm afraid I have no idea,' I said apologetically.

Caroline looked disappointed. I could see it in her eyes.

'Take your time,' she said.

But the longer I looked at it the more confused I felt. Who would know what it was? I glanced at my parents and to my amazement I saw they were holding hands very tightly. My dad's eyes were closed and my mum had that slightly exasperated look she sometimes had at the checkout when people were being stupid or fumbling in their handbags for their money. I realised that they knew what this thing was. I couldn't believe it, how did they know? You'd need to be inspired to know.

'No hurry,' Caroline said again. She had big eyes, and she was willing me to know what it was. The others were startled that I didn't know, I could see that.

They shuffled a bit as if to say that maybe my good performance so far had all been sheer luck or getting questions I knew. They couldn't even work out a simple problem about how many nines the guy painted and yet they knew what this thing was.

I stared at the triangle until my eyes hurt. Was this what was going to keep me out of a great school? Did this stand between me and a terrific education? Would I be back in my old school, peering and straining and missing a lot of it? Would I be back in the concrete school yard and not here going to play hockey three times a week and with my own flower bed? I had been planning what to plant in it, tomato plants up against the wall and lots of dwarf conifers and winter pansies in the front for all the year-round colour.

'No, I'm sorry, it really has defeated me,' I said to Caroline.

'Just guess,' she begged.

'Well, it is only a guess,' I warned her.

'That will do fine,' she said.

'It *could* be Cheshire,' I said doubtfully. 'A slice of Cheshire taken from the block but it might be Cheddar. I'm torn between the two of them.'

And then everything changed. They all seemed to be dissolving into tears and shaking each other's hands and hugging me. Caroline had as many tears on her face as Mum and Dad had. Apparently after all my nearly killing myself trying to work out what variety it was, the word 'cheese' was all they had wanted me to say. Imagine. They didn't even know what kind of cheese it was, they just wanted the word. And the fact that I thought this was too easy a question had just settled everything.

They showed us the dormitories and the dining hall, and my mother and father had stopped being nervous and were acting like normal people again.

Caroline said, 'See you at the start of next term then.'

I said, 'You are coming back then?'

She looked at me astounded that I seemed to know there had been a doubt about it although it had been written all over her face and she said yes, she was, that she had just decided it this very day. About ten minutes ago. And she looked a lot less troubled somehow.

As we went home on the train Mum and Dad got out a paper and pen to work out why the painter painted nine twenty times, and I looked at the card with the silly triangle of mousetrap cheese drawn on it, which Caroline had given me as a souvenir of the day.

Part 2 – Caroline's Career

When we were young we had this aunt who came to the house all the time. She was my mum's younger sister but we never called her Aunt or Auntie because she said it made her feel ancient. We always called her Shell.

She was a real glamour puss, Shell was, and she told me and my sister Nancy all kinds of things that our mum wouldn't ever have told us, like that men just loved girls to wear very high-heeled black shoes and to have very big shiny hair and wear bright red lipstick. Shell kept all these rules herself and she was gorgeous and there were always men around her. But never the same man for any length of time, as my mum said, because apparently Shell was a bit flighty. She was always heading off somewhere for a while and always coming back.

Flighty or not, she was dead interested in us and plucked our eyebrows and got us push-up bras. She told Nancy and me that the world was full of opportunities and we must grab them all, which was so different to what everyone else told us. Our mum and dad were always telling us about studying hard and keeping our heads down, and that was what the grannies said too and they said it at school.

But Shell was her own woman. Life was full of promise, she said, and we must be ready to seize whatever came our way. She made us feel great and excited but only one thing worried me.

Shell often said to me, when we were on our own, that I shouldn't bother getting a career or anything. I was a looker, she said, and I'd marry when I was twenty, just let me be sure to get a decent fellow with plenty of money. I didn't like any of this, well, you don't when you're twelve, do you? I mean, saying that because I had a prettier face than Nancy, that I shouldn't study and she should . . . it was a bit . . . I don't know . . . making looks out to be everything or nothing.

But you don't argue with Shell so I said nothing, just nodded and agreed with her.

When I left school I got a place in a training college and learned to teach the deaf. Nancy went to university and studied Economics and Politics. Shell was with a very rich guy at this stage and she gave us both a holiday; Nancy went on an art appreciation tour to Italy and I went on a skiing holiday in a posh resort, which was where I met Laurence.

Laurence was a lawyer in a very well-known law firm. He was a big, handsome, warm man with dark curly hair, and a great smile. And he had everyone around the dinner table in fits of laughter every night. The girls who ran the ski chalet said they would give him a free holiday any time, he was such fun.

He told me the very first night that I was just *ravishing* – that was the word he used – so often I almost began to believe it . . .

Shell had always said that some men were too perfect to be true and that the wise thing to do was to look for their flaws at the beginning, then you wouldn't get so let down later.

Okay, let's look for his flaws, I said. He was very handsome and they say handsome men are vain. He didn't appear to be, but I had to remember that as a possible flaw. He was a little impatient with people who were slow on the slopes or who didn't get the drift of the conversation at dinner. But for me he had all the time in the world, and he was interested in everything about me, my studies, my family, my hopes and dreams – and very interested in going to bed with me.

I told him that I didn't do that on holidays.

'Why did you come on this holiday then?' he asked, irritated.

'To ski,' I said simply.

Surprisingly he accepted that and stopped bothering me about sex. I assumed that I would never hear from him again so was very surprised when he called two weeks after we returned from our holiday.

He lived only fifty miles away from me in a place called Rossmore so we had dinner a few times, and then he brought up the matter of whether I might come away with him for a weekend to a hotel in the Lake District of England.

I said, that would be great, thank you, that I'd love it.

It was great and I did love it.

He brought me to meet his family and they were posh but not overpowering.

And I brought him to meet my family and naturally Shell turned up to inspect him. Out in the kitchen she put her fingers in a bunch up at her mouth and blew a kiss in the air.

'Exquisite, Caroline, that's what he is. Didn't I always tell you you'd be married before your twenty-first birthday and not to bother with a career?'

I looked at her open-mouthed. I *had* a career. I was going to teach the deaf, beginning with my probationary year the following September. What did she mean that I was not going to bother with a career?

But as usual with Shell, you say nothing. So nothing was what I said.

And as it happened things turned out differently. Laurence and I got married in September and there was such fuss getting the house and doing it up, everyone considered it better if I didn't start my probationary year at once. The next year I was pregnant so I couldn't start then.

After that, well, I was looking after Alistair, so it would have been idiotic to try and fit in teaching hours with that. Then when he started going to his first school and I looked for some morning hours teaching, I just couldn't find anything around home. Around Rossmore.

I don't want you to think that I was aching to get out there and be at work or that I was bored, because truly that wasn't the case. There weren't enough hours in the day. Often Laurence would ring and say, could I escape and meet him for lunch; he always told me I was ravishing and he was always admiring me. I loved being with him and making a good life for him.

Money was never short. I had full-time help in the house and a gardener. I went to the gym regularly and to get my hair done at Fabian's and had a manicure; every week we would have people to dinner on a Friday.

Always eight people – like the senior partners at Laurence's work, and business people, and sometimes if there was an extra man we might ask Shell who, according to Laurence, performed very well at a dinner party. I had learned to be a very accomplished cook: I knew ten different starters and ten different main courses and I actually wrote down what I served people so that I would not give them the same thing over and over again. And across the candlelit table Laurence would raise his glass at me.

'Lovely, Caroline, thank you so much,' he would say and the other women at the table would look at me with envy.

We had decided from the start just to have one child but after I held Alistair in my arms I wondered, should we have more.

Laurence was against it and he reasoned it out gently with me. We had always said that one child was fine. Alistair was very happy and had lots of friends – it wasn't as if he pined for a brother or sister. We could have time on our own together, which was what we wanted most. It made a lot of sense, I agreed with him. I didn't think I was being talked into it or anything.

Before I knew it Alistair was eleven and it was time for him to go to boarding school. Now this I didn't want, it seemed inhuman really. But Laurence was very anxious that our son should go to the same place that he had been and his father had been. He brought me to the school several times and we saw where he had smoked his first cigarette, and played his first game of rugby and the library where he had studied hard to get his A levels. He said he had been very happy there and it had made him grow up and he had met most of his friends there, people he still knew. We could come up every second weekend and stay in the hotel and take Alistair and his friends out for a super lunch.

I asked Alistair what he really wanted. I asked him when we were on our own in the garden. I said he could tell me the complete and total truth because it was his life.

He looked up at me with his huge brown eyes and said he would love to go to the school.

So that was that.

That's when I set about getting a job teaching.

I would have loved to get a job in St Martin's. Well, anyone would have. The place was out on its own. They performed miracles there, better than any miracle ever worked at St Ann's Well up in the woods where I took Alistair to play and the dogs to walk. But they had no openings.

Here in Rossmore we did not have a school specifically for the deaf, but there were facilities in St Ita's and in the Brothers. The kids were terrific and like every teacher starting out I made all my mistakes on them and learned a great deal that first year.

I learned how to delegate at home so that the house and

garden were in fine shape without me, and I arranged for the shopping to be delivered every Friday and kept up with the dinner parties.

When my mother-in-law said that I was wonderful to be going out to work – in a tone that meant she thought it anything *but* wonderful – I deliberately misunderstood her and thanked her for her praise.

I tried getting my hair done in Fabian's at lunchtime, and transforming a small dark room which we had once used just for storage into a study for myself so as not to have all my papers and laptop and things strewn around the house. It meant there were no more sudden lunches with Laurence in smart little Italian places, and no long shopping trips with my charge card. I learned like every working wife has learned that if you stay up late and don't do the clearing away, then it's going to be bloody hard in the morning getting it all sorted before racing off to work.

Every second weekend we went to see Alistair and he was making lots of friends and was in a chess club and a birdwatching group, so I became reconciled to the idea that it was the right thing to do for him. We couldn't have found these activities for him at home.

I used to listen to the women at work talking about their husbands and their partners or about the guys they were involved with. Every word that came out of their mouths made me realise just what a jewel I had in Laurence. A warm enthusiastic man, who told me all about his work, who shared everything with me, who told everyone I was lovely or even *ravishing* – he still used that word about me – to my embarrassment when he said it in front of people. I don't even know why I needed to hear their stories to convince myself that he was marvellous.

I listened to their stories of how unfaithful they had found men to be. Many of them, even sophisticated women, had been to St Ann's Well hoping for some kind of magic that would improve their marriages. I just knew that Laurence wasn't unfaithful. And he was just as loving and eager as he had been all those years ago when we were out in the skiing chalet and I was keeping him at arm's length. Sometimes when I was tired, or had to study my notes, or get up early, I wasn't really able for his loving and sort of hoped that he might be tired or sleepy or lose interest for a bit. But when I heard the tales of my colleagues I realised this was a dangerous road to go down.

My sister Nancy often told me that I must be the luckiest woman on earth. As did my aunt Shell. So did my mother, and Laurence's mother.

And so I was.

I just wished he was a little more interested in my job. I was very interested in his. I asked him about cases, and helped look things up in law reports for him. I knew all the partners in his office, the possible partners, the rivals, the allies. I had discussed with him for ever the date of his own possible partnership, which would happen within the next eighteen months.

I persuaded him not to tell Alistair that there was a room with his name on it in the office. He thought it was something that would make Alistair feel secure; I thought it might be something that might make him feel trapped.

Laurence discussed it all with me over a bottle of wine – it was a discussion, not an argument. He was always very reasonable and tried to see my point of view. Possibly I was right and that our son needed more freedom in his life, more chance to have hopes and dreams like we all had. When Laurence talked like that I asked myself why on earth I woke most nights at 3 a.m. and worried.

Surely I had nothing to worry about?

But suddenly when I was thinking about St Martin's School I realised what was upsetting me. Laurence just didn't get it about teaching. He didn't know all the wonderful things they could do there for deaf girls. He tried to be interested when I told him about the school records and how they had placed so many of their pupils in positions that hearing children would have been so glad to reach.

He tried. I know he tried because he knew it meant so much to me, and he wanted to be part of my enthusiasm. If he said once he must have said one hundred times that the more he heard me tell him about my work, the more he thanked the Lord that our Alistair wasn't deaf. And that was not what I was saying, hinting or even thinking.

If Alistair had been deaf I knew that with today's techniques he would still have been able to have a great life. Laurence didn't know this. He thought it was a matter of head shaking and tut-tutting and counting our blessings. Which drove me mad.

A chance came up for me to do a further degree. I needed to do practical work as well and St Martin's School, the crème de la crème of deaf schools, was willing to take me on for six hours' work a week. Suppose, just suppose, that I made a success of that . . . then they almost definitely would offer me a full-time job.

I couldn't have been more excited and was impatient for Laurence to come home so that I could tell him. He was full of some happening at the office, one of the chief partners was resigning. It was completely unexpected and, indeed, out of character. Some story about going to Arizona to find himself. A likely story. The man was off his head.

I remembered him. A dullish sort of person with an equally dull wife who was probably not going to Arizona with him in this search. I listened restlessly to the ramifications of all this, and people moving up and moving over, and someone taking over conveyancing and someone coming in from the cold.

Eventually I began to realise it would be the long-desired promotion for Laurence. He would be a partner at last. I tried to be pleased for him, I assured him that it wasn't like stepping into a dead man's shoes since the boring man going to Arizona to find himself was almost certainly going with someone twenty years younger than his wife and of his own free will.

'It will mean a lot of changes in our lives,' Laurence said sonorously. 'A lot more entertaining for one thing, but you're so brilliant at that, Caroline, and you'll like it, you must be lonely with Alistair away at school.'

I don't know what you would have done but somehow I decided not to tell him about the degree and the practical work at St Martin's. Not that night. This was to be his night. Instead I ran him a nice bath with some sandalwood oil in it and brought him a martini to drink while he was there. Then I got some fillet steaks from the freezer and opened a bottle of wine, dressed myself up in a little black dress and lit the candles. He must have told me twenty times that I was ravishing and that he adored me and that he was the luckiest man in the practice and indeed in the world.

It was four days before I could tell him, and when I did he was astounded.

'But you can't possibly go to St Martin's, Caroline, it's sixty miles away,' he said.

'I have a car, and there will soon be a new road so it won't take long,' I said lightly while beating down my huge disappointment at his reaction.

'But darling, those distances! I mean, I thought . . . I would have thought . . .'

'I'll be well able to do it,' I said, trying hard not to cry.

'But why, Caroline my angel, *why* would you want to take on all this when there's so much for us to do here together?'

I managed to say nothing, which was a very great achievement. What was there to do together? Nothing.

For me alone in the house there might have been overseeing further decoration, repainting, new upholstery. The building of a conservatory, possibly the extension of the paved patio for more guests to drink kir royale at one of our summer dinner parties.

'Why aren't you speaking, Caroline my angel?' he asked me, mystified.

'I feel a bit dizzy, Laurence, I'm going to bed,' I said and pretended to be asleep when he joined me full of concern and a lot of face and arm stroking.

Next day he brought the subject up at breakfast.

But I had had seven sleepless hours thinking about it all and so I was ready for him.

'I'm going to get my qualifications and do my six hours a week in St Martin's, Laurence, and at the end of the year we will discuss whether I shall work there full time or not. It may indeed turn out that they don't want me. Or that the distances are indeed too long. But this learning year is something I can't and will not give up.'

And then I moved on in a seemingly effortless way to talk about a barbecue that we were having the following weekend when Alistair would be home from his school.

I thought I saw Laurence look at me admiringly as he might look at a fellow lawyer who had made a good point at a case conference.

But maybe not. I'm always hopelessly optimistic.

And the year was indeed hard, there is no denying that. I have to say that I remember hours of night-driving in wet weather, with the windscreen wipers clacking and my being on the mobile phone barking instructions about the meal.

Laurence did become a partner and the man who was finding himself in Arizona did indeed go on the quest without his wife but with a very young temp from the office.

My work at the school was magnificent, we taught people to speak. Over and over, we actually gave a vocabulary and a life to the wordless and it was the most exciting thing I had ever done in my life. I loved it in St Martin's and they appeared to like me, and as the exhausting year ended they told me that they would definitely offer me a full-time post there.

They wondered, would I like a bedsit in the school as several teachers had, just in case the weather was bad and the travelling distance, traffic jams and long hours on the motorway were too much?

I said I would let them know. Very soon.

We had a sort of super-glitzy dinner party for the partners and wives, and I must have got in the door twenty minutes before the first guests arrived. I had just time to change my clothes, leave the extra cream that I had bought on the way home in the kitchen, rearrange the place names, and set out the shop-bought canapés on big oval dishes with wild flowers from St Martin's gardens scattered amongst them and flat parsley sprinkled on top.

'Isn't your wife a genius?' one of the partners said to Laurence.

'Lovely, lovely, Caroline.' He raised his glass at me.

'And she has a worthwhile job as well,' one of the wives said in a tinny voice.

'Yes, I can't think why she does it,' Laurence said.

I looked at him, shocked.

'I mean, all it really does is make sure that my income tax situation is even worse than it was. I mean, when they see "wife's earned income", they are all of a flutter and come down on me like a ton of bricks. And I mean, for what in the end? But she will do it. Won't you, darling?' He looked at me indulgently.

I smiled back at him.

I didn't hate him. Of course I didn't. You couldn't hate Laurence. And there were ways in which he was right. Maybe I was just trying to show him I had a life of my own. Possibly it was all a waste of time.

There were plenty of people to teach the deaf. Maybe the deaf were even happier when they were called the deaf-and-dumb; when we weren't trying to get them to breathe properly and force sounds out of them.

Who knows?

I would make up my mind next week. I would put it out of my mind for now.

We talked about the new road. Voices were raised. Some said it was all barbarous, others said it was totally essential. I mentioned the old well in Whitethorn Woods. Voices were raised still higher.

Some said that it was a ludicrous and dangerous superstition, others said it was part and parcel of the old tradition of the country. So I moved them seamlessly on to something we would all be agreed on, like the price of property. I also produced the truffles that I had bought at my lunch hour and brought home and bashed up slightly to make them look uneven, then rolled in cocoa and chopped nuts. Everyone thought they were home-made.

'Lovely, Caroline.' Laurence raised his glass to me again.

'Laurence,' I said, raising my own glass.

My heart felt like lead.

It had probably been a lot of running round after nothing, when I had thought it was a great career. I managed not to sigh at the thought of a dream that had not been achieved. The world is full of people who don't get their dream.

I wouldn't do all the clearing-up tonight. Tomorrow was not a particularly busy day.

Next day when I had left the house gleaming, I drove slowly to St Martin's. I had been asked to sit in on an assessment of a scholarship child. A girl called Melanie who sounded very bright.

It wouldn't be very demanding and what's more I would enjoy it. It might after all be one of the last assessments that I would ever do.

Funny, isn't it, the way you never know when something is going to happen. When I saw what that child Melanie had done already and how much more we could do now with her, there was simply no decision to be made.

We would take her in St Martin's. I knew this as clearly as I knew I would be here to watch her grow in confidence. This is what I wanted to do and would do.

Just as Laurence wanted to run a law practice.

There were no more grey areas. It wasn't going to be the end of the world. There would be no argument, no confrontation. All over the country people were following a dream and having a marriage. It didn't have to be one or the other. We would work it out. Of course we would.

Strangely the bright little girl seemed to understand, it was just as if she could see the machinery in my mind clicking into place.

'You are coming back then?' she asked me casually, just moments after I had decided.

And I smiled the first real smile for weeks. Because now I knew it was settled.

CHAPTER 16

The Road, the Woods and the Well – 3

Eddie Flynn waited outside the church after Mass until he saw his brother leaving.

'Brian, can I have a word?' he began.

'Not if that word is "annulment",' the priest said without stopping in his progress towards Skunk Slattery's for the paper and then back to his house.

'You know it isn't.' Eddie was almost running to keep up. 'Hang on a bit, this isn't the four-minute mile.'

'I'm going for my breakfast, I'm hungry, I have a lot to do today, talk away if you want to . . .' Father Flynn continued to move purposefully along the road, greeting parishioners at every turn.

'You're so well-known here you should go into politics,' Eddie grumbled as they paused for Father Flynn to wish this one success at an examination and that one good luck with his new greyhound.

'Right. A cup of coffee?' he said when they got back to his kitchen.

'I thought you'd have someone to cook your breakfast. Haven't you got a Russian or something working for you?' Eddie seemed disappointed.

His brother had put three pieces of bacon and a tomato in a frying pan and was turning them expertly. 'Josef, who is Latvian actually as it happens, not Russian, looks after the canon, not me.'

'The canon should be in a home for the bewildered,' Eddie said.

'Naomi didn't have much luck with him either, is that right?' Brian Flynn smiled.

'Leave it, Brian. I wanted to ask you about the well.'

'The well?'

'The well, man, it's in your territory, for heaven's sake, the holy well, the sacred well, whatever. I'm asking, will they let it go?'

'Will who let it go?' Father Flynn was confused.

'God, Brian, you're getting very thick, will your lot let it go, the Church, religion, the Pope, all that?'

'Oh, my lot, I see,' said Father Flynn. 'The Pope has never mentioned it to my certain knowledge, or if he has, the burden of what he said hasn't trickled down to us here. Are you sure you don't want a piece of bacon?'

'No, I don't want any bacon, and you shouldn't be having any either, clogging up your arteries.' Eddie Flynn was very disapproving.

'Yes, but then I don't have so many social demands on my life, I don't have to keep so many ladies happy.'

'I'm serious, Brian.'

'So am I, Eddie. The best part of my day is often sitting here peacefully at my breakfast reading the paper. And here you are in my kitchen picking on everything I say or do . . .'

'Some people asked me to join up with them in a syndicate,' Eddie said in a tone of great gravity. He seemed to be waiting for an admiring response.

'But isn't that what you do, Eddie? You're a businessman, you're always joining up with people over this or that.'

'This is my chance to make real money, Brian. And boy, am I going to need real money. Do you know what this wedding is going to cost?' Eddie seemed agitated.

'A simple registry office wedding? Not much surely?' Brian suggested.

'Oh no, we have some dissident priest or other, and somebody is lending him a church to give a blessing in, there are going to be bridesmaids, groomsmen, a huge reception, the whole works. And then all the while I have Kitty sending me notes about school fees. God, I need this break, that's why I have to know about the well.'

'Listen to me, Eddie, I may very well as you say be thick but *what* do you have to know about the well?'

'All right. I'll tell you but it's for your ears only, seal of the confessional and all that. The new road is all ready to go bar the shouting, and we've bought up a lot of land in little bits here and there. Everyone will have to negotiate with us when the compulsory purchase order goes out so we are sitting on a fortune. There's only one snag: some of the lads are afraid the bloody well in the woods is going to balls things up.'

'You may not approve of the well but I wouldn't use that kind of language about it,' Father Flynn said disapprovingly.

'No, okay. But you know what I mean. And I know for a fact that you aren't that convinced by the well either. But is it going to be an issue? That's what we need to know. Nobody wants to take on a crowd of religious nutters.'

'I know nothing about it.' Brian Flynn started to wash the dishes.

'Of course you do, Brian.'

'No, I don't, I have managed to stay out of everything. Deliberately. I would not support either side in the issue. I got out of any involvement so you're asking the one man in Rossmore who doesn't have a view.'

'But you're the one who *knows* whether it will blow up and cause a fuss or if it will just die down. You have the feel for these things and we have to know. Now . . .'

'We being the syndicate who are investing money in land?'

'Don't sneer at it, *Father* Flynn. Plenty of money was spent educating you as a priest, wasn't it? And if I am financially secure that's a weight off your back too.'

'You're not a weight on my back, Eddie, you never were.' Father Flynn was extremely annoyed but he tried hard not to show it. 'Now if that's everything I have to go about my work.'

'*Work?* What work?' Eddie scoffed. 'Sure, nobody is bothered about God these days, you have nothing to do. You've never really done a proper day's work in your life.'

'Fine, Eddie, I'm sure you're right.' He sighed wearily and packed his briefcase.

He was going to visit his mother in her home with a series of old photographs which the counsellor had told Judy might jog her memory about the past.

He was going to take Lilly Ryan and one of her sons to visit Aidan in the jail. Aidan Ryan apparently in a window of calm had relented enough to agree to talk to his wife.

He was going to take Holy Communion to Marty Nolan and another old man out on that road; he was going to open a multi-cultural World Food Day in aid of world famine at St Ita's; he was going to throw in the ball for a match between the Brothers School and St Michael's; he was going to go out to Ferns and Heathers and admire their new prayer and meditation room. They didn't call it a chapel but that's where he said Mass on a Sunday for them.

Maybe Eddie was right and it wasn't really a proper day's work. But it sure felt like it.

Judy Flynn had done eight days of praying at St Ann's shrine. Just one more left.

She had enjoyed her visit far more than she had ever expected she would. It had been a pleasure getting to know Brian again, he was such a good-natured young fellow, as he had always been, and the people here loved him. Her mother was lost in a strange, half waking, half sleeping world but had become markedly less hostile. Poor Eddie was being well and truly punished for having strayed from home – Judy and Kitty had many a laugh over the amazing problems he had on his hands with young Naomi. Kitty said she wouldn't have him back if he crawled the whole way through Whitethorn Woods to ask her.

Judy had tried to assist St Ann in the search for a man by going to the local bridge club in the Rossmore Hotel. She met two handsome men called Franklin and Wilfred. Con men, both of them, talking dreamily about a mobile phone service they were going to set up.

Some day.

They lived with an older lady who never went out because of some scandal, it was too complicated to work out, and anyway they were too shallow for her, so she left them to their plans.

Judy worked out a satisfactory routine to her day. Visiting her mam, spending three hours in her hotel room doing her drawings with no distractions. She would have a cup of coffee with Kitty and then dress herself up for her walk to the well. On the way she would buy a newspaper and then later in the evening she would have a drink with Brian and he would tell her the business of the day. It was a restful way to live. She didn't know why she had been in such flight from it for so many years.

She got her hair shampooed at the smart Fabian's. The young man who seemed to own the place told her that he was in love and hoped that he would marry before the year was out. This surprised her. She had been certain he was gay, but she had learned since coming here that nothing was ever as it seemed.

'I'm hoping to get married too,' she confided to him. 'I've hired St Ann above at the well to help me find a husband.'

'I'd say you'll have no problem there.' Fabian was flattering. 'Beating off the offers is what you'll be.'

She was smiling as she thought of beating off all the offers. She picked up the newspaper in Slattery's and brought it to the counter.

'Just the usual, Sebastian,' she said.

'You're very beautiful when you smile, Judy.'

'Well, thank you,' she said, surprised.

The man they all called Skunk Slattery wasn't known for little pleasantries like this.

'I mean it. I was wondering, would you be free perhaps any evening to have a . . . I mean, to . . . go . . . maybe we could have a meal together?'

'That would be very nice, Sebastian,' Judy said, trying to work out his matrimonial status. She hadn't heard Kitty saying anything about Mrs Skunk but then you never knew.

'If you're not sick of the food at the Rossmore Hotel, they do a very nice dinner,' Skunk said eagerly. There couldn't be a Mrs Skunk if he were taking her somewhere as open as that.

'And what night would you suggest, Sebastian?' she asked.

'Should we strike while the iron is hot? Tonight at eight maybe?' he said anxiously. 'In case you have second thoughts or anything?'

Judy walked up to the shrine with a spring in her step. Everything was going very well. She must ask people why they called him Skunk.

Neddy Nolan said to Clare that eventually he must get in touch with his brothers in England about the land and see that they get something from it.

'I don't see why. Kit's in jail, it can't matter one way or the other to him, the other two haven't been home in years either; we don't even know where they are.'

'But they have a right to share in whatever there is to share if we do have to sell,' Neddy said.

'What right, Neddy? Honestly now, what right? They never

gave anything, never kept in touch, never knew or cared what happened to your father.' Clare was very firm on this.

'But things didn't work out well for them, like they did for me.' As always he saw the very best in everybody else.

'You did it all yourself, Neddy, and you never forgot your father. Now your father is a man who wouldn't have any such sentimentality about the rest of the family,' Clare said. 'They didn't get up to deal with foxes in the hen-run, a sick cow having her calf in the upper field, rebuilding all the hedges and walls. They were never any part of getting your father's meals, clearing up after him and bringing him out to see his friends.'

Her face was full of loyalty to him and Neddy wondered again as he did so often how she could possibly love him so much.

'Anyway, it may all come to nothing, this business about the road,' he said, rather forlornly.

'I wouldn't rely on it, Neddy,' said Clare, who had heard a great deal in the staffroom at St Ita's, at the bridge club in the Rossmore Hotel, and when she left the big bag of laundry in for a service wash at the Fresh as a Daisy. Nowadays nobody was saying *if* the road came, they were saying *when* the road came. There had been a subtle change over the last few weeks.

One of these days her Neddy was going to have to make up his mind. She was not going to influence him. This was something he had to decide on his own. Would he sell his father's farm for a small fortune to that syndicate of gangsters which had people like Eddie Flynn in their number? Or would he hold out in case he alone could stop the march of progress and save the woods and the well that in his big innocent heart he really believed had cured his mother for so many years?

'You're never going to dinner with Skunk?' Father Brian Flynn was astounded.

'Are you going to tell me he has a wife and ten children?' Judy asked in a slightly brittle tone.

323

'Lord, no, who'd marry Skunk?' Brian said and then wished immediately that he hadn't said it. 'I mean, he's never been married so you think of him as always being single,' he said lamely.

Judy was brief and crisp in her response. 'Why do you all call him Skunk?'

'I can't tell you,' her brother said truthfully. 'He was always Skunk as far back as I remember. I actually thought that was his name.'

Lilly Ryan couldn't believe the change in her husband Aidan over the last eleven months. He was very gaunt looking, with a drawn face and large dark circles under his eyes. Their son Donal, who hadn't wanted to come, seemed to shrink back from the man with the wild look.

'Please Donal,' she begged in a whisper. So the boy stretched out his hand unwillingly.

'I hope you are looking after your mam properly.' Aidan sounded very stern.

'Yes, I'm trying,' Donal said.

He was eighteen and wanted to be a million miles from here. He had seen his dad beat his mam in the past. He couldn't bear that his mam was pathetically grateful that they had been allowed to come.

'You can't make a worse job of it than I did,' Aidan Ryan said. 'In front of Father Flynn and you, Donal, I want to apologise for the way I treated Lilly over the past time. I simply have no excuse so I am not going to struggle to find one. Alcohol and the grief over our lost baby is a sort of explanation but it's no excuse.' He looked from one face to another.

Father Flynn said nothing because this was family business.

Lilly was completely lost for words. So Donal answered. In a very grown-up voice he said, 'Thank you for saying all this publicly. It can't have been easy for you. If it were just myself and my forgiveness you were asking for, I would never give it to you, not for a hundred years. I have seen you take the leg off a chair to beat my innocent mother. But life goes on and if my mother asks me to forgive you, I will consider it. We will go out now, Mam and myself, and leave you with Father Flynn and we'll see do you still feel the same next week at visiting time.' He stood up to go.

Aidan Ryan pleaded with him. 'Of course I'll feel the same, son. I'm not going to change my mind.'

'You used to change your mind within half an hour before they locked you up here.' Donal spoke flatly, without emotion. Then he made to leave.

'Don't go!' Aidan Ryan cried. 'Don't go away and leave me for a week not knowing where I am before I know if you'll forgive me.'

'You left my mam for years not knowing what she had done to make you so violent. You can wait a week.' He was propelling his mother out before she spoke, they were nearly at the door.

Father Flynn admired the boy so much he wanted to cheer aloud but he kept his face impassive.

'It was grief, Donal,' said Aidan Ryan. 'It takes everyone in different ways. I grieved so much for your sister who disappeared.'

Donal spoke calmly. 'Yes, it does take people in different ways. In my case I didn't ever know Teresa but I envied her because whoever took her had taken her far from you and your furious drunken rages . . .'

And then they were gone.

Outside in the corridor Lilly said, 'Why didn't you let me speak to him? He's so sorry . . .'

'Speak to him next week, Mam, if he's still sorry.'

'But think of him sitting there all that time . . .' Her eyes were full of pity.

'You sat there all that time, Mam,' he said.

In the visiting room, under the eyes of the warders, Father Flynn sat beside a weeping Aidan Ryan.

'Do you think she'll forgive me, Father?'

'I'm sure of it.'

'So why didn't she say something?'

'She was in shock, Aidan. She needed time to think. You see, how does she know if she can forgive you or not? A year ago you landed her in the regional hospital and then you wouldn't let her come in here to see you. I think that takes a bit of thinking about, don't you?'

The man looked frightened, Father Flynn was pleased to see. This was good. Father Flynn knew that Lilly Ryan would forgive her husband next Tuesday. Donal Ryan probably knew it too.

Let him sweat a little.

Myles Barry, the lawyer, went out to the Nolans' farm. His face was grim.

He had a communication from one of Her Majesty's prisons in Britain. A Mr Christopher Nolan (otherwise known as Kit) had read of the compensation about to be offered to farmers near Rossmore whose land might be acquired in the scheme for the new road. Mr Christopher Nolan wished it noted that his father Martin Nolan was elderly and unable to make any real decision on the matter. And to add that his younger brother Edward Nolan (otherwise known as Neddy) was in fact mentally handicapped. He had not ever been able to hold any position of responsibility or trust. In fact he had proved himself unable to work even on building sites in London. It would therefore not be in the interests of justice if either of these men were to reach a decision that would affect the Nolan family. He, Christopher Nolan, would like his interest in the property recorded and acknowledged.

Myles Barry had never been so angry.

The worthless criminal Kit, having read in some tabloid paper in jail that there was money to be made out of the home and family he had long abandoned, was coming in for the kill.

Myles Barry had to show them the letter or tell them its con-
tents. It wasn't something he looked forward to.

He met Father Flynn who was just leaving the Nolan farm.

'Nothing wrong, is there?' Myles asked.

The priest laughed. 'No, it's not Last Rites or anything. Marty
likes Communion brought to him now and then, he's not able
to get into the church for Mass as well as he used to.'

'I suppose he should be in care?' Myles suggested.

'Hasn't he the best care in the world here with Neddy and
Clare?' the priest said, unaware that Neddy had come out behind
him. 'If I was an old person in Rossmore I'd much prefer to have
that couple looking after me than anyone else. It would be desperate to be left there, like my poor own mother and the poor
old canon who are determined to stay independent but who are
really just struggling to keep going . . .'

Neddy, who had come out to greet the lawyer, joined easily in
the conversation.

'Isn't the canon just fine, Father? Josef was telling me that he
loves being near the centre of the town and in the heart of everything.'

'Yes, Neddy, but Josef wants to leave and go to work full time
on the new road when it comes.'

'If it comes,' Neddy said.

'No, I'd say it's when it comes,' Myles Barry said. 'That's what
I'm here to talk to you about.'

'Oh well, there go my hopes that we wouldn't have to make
any decisions.' Neddy laughed at himself.

The priest got into his car and drove off and the lawyer came
into the kitchen. Neddy kept this house in shining condition.
Myles Barry noted the gleaming surfaces, the scrubbed table, and
the blue and yellow china neatly arranged on the open shelves.

Neddy said his father was having a rest in his own room,
poured the lawyer a big mug of coffee and offered a plate of
home-made biscuits. He had seen a cookery expert do them on

television last week, he said, and thought they looked easy enough.

He was an innocent, certainly, but he was not a foolish man.

Suddenly Myles Barry decided to show to Neddy the hurtful, greedy letter written by his brother Kit from an English jail. Neddy read it slowly.

'He doesn't think much of us, does he?' he said eventually.

'Wasn't I at school with Kit? He was always a bit dismissive of people, you know the way he went on, it really meant nothing . . .' Myles Barry began.

'Was he ever in touch with you since he left school?' Neddy asked mildly.

'No, but you know the way it is, people's lives are different. They go in one direction or another . . .' Myles Barry was wondering why he seemed to excuse Kit Nolan when really he wanted to punch him in the face.

'He never writes to me either. I send him a letter every month, always have, telling him what's happening here in Rossmore, how Dad is and everything else that might interest him. I told him all about the road of course. But I never hear back.'

'Maybe he has nothing to tell,' Myles Barry said.

His anger over Kit was now at boiling point. Imagine, the decent Neddy wrote to that ungrateful brother of his every month for years and what was the result? Kit stirred himself to write to a lawyer to say that Neddy was a halfwit.

'That's true. Every day must be like the day before in there.' Neddy shook his head sadly.

'And you heard from Eddie Flynn's syndicate, did you? I believe they were coming to see you.'

'Oh yes, a confused sort of visit.'

'And what did you say to them, Neddy?' Myles Barry held his breath.

'I told them I couldn't possibly deal with them, and that we would never take that huge sum of money, it was just outrageous.'

'And what did they say to that?' Myles's voice was only a whisper.

'You won't believe it, Myles, but they just offered me more money still! Like as if they hadn't been listening.'

Myles wiped his brow. Never again in his life would he have a client like this. Mercifully.

'So what exactly happens now, Neddy?'

'We get it sorted out when the time comes – when the compulsory purchase order comes.' Neddy was calm about it all.

'You do understand, I mean, I did explain to you, the government won't pay nearly what Eddie Flynn's pals will. You see, those syndicate people are operating from strength – they've bought up little bits of land everywhere.'

'Yes, I know all that, but if I sold it to them it would be theirs and I'd have no say in what happens.'

Myles Barry pondered over whether he should say that Neddy Nolan wouldn't ever have any say in what happened once he sold the land. But it hardly seemed worth it.

'So what will we say to Kit?' he asked despairingly.

'There's no need to say anything to Kit – he doesn't have any rights to anything from this place, only what I choose to give him.' Neddy looked around him proudly at the refurbished kitchen in what had been his father's broken-down farmhouse.

'Well, I agree it sounds as if it would be hard for him to prove any legal claim but of course as your father's son he might be able . . .'

'No, Myles.' Neddy was again very calm. 'No, when I bailed him the second time, I had to go across there to do it. And I found an English lawyer, a very nice old man he was too. But anyway, he made Kit sign a document saying that in return for the bail money he would relinquish his claim on the family estate. I mean, I told this lawyer it was only a few acres of poor land, but still it was an estate technically.' He smiled, thinking of it all.

'And do you still have that document, Neddy?'

329

'Oh I do. You see, Kit skipped bail that time, so I never got our money back, and when he was back in again they wouldn't even give bail so there was no point in his even asking.'

'Could I see this document, do you think?'

Neddy went to a small oak cabinet in the corner. Inside were neat files that would have done credit to any company. Within seconds he pulled out the right piece of paper. Myles Barry looked back into the filing drawer. He saw files marked 'Insurance', 'Pensions', 'St Ita's School', 'Medical', 'Household Expenses', 'Farm' . . . And all this from the man whose brother said he was not the full shilling.

Sebastian Slattery was proving to be an excellent companion. Judy found it very easy to talk to him and he was very interested in her work too. How she set about illustrating a children's story. Were there some stories that she didn't enjoy and did she find them harder to do?

He asked her, did she ever go to France on the Eurostar train? It was something he had always promised himself that he would do when he was next in London. He told her that he had hardly any family himself. He was an only child and his parents were dead. He did have cousins some miles out, in a small village called Doon – a nice place actually. He had been invited to the opening of a building out there called the Danny O'Neill Health Centre, in memory of some Irishman who went to America, and his grandson who was half Polish was doing it in his honour. Maybe Judy might like to come with him as his guest.

'Why do they call you Skunk?' she asked suddenly.

'I don't know, Judy, to be honest. They did at school and it stuck. Maybe I smelled awful then. I don't smell awful now, do I?'

'No, Sebastian, you do not, you smell fine to me,' she said.

At that moment Cathal Chambers the bank manager walked by.

'Evening, Skunk, evening, Judy,' he said affably.

'Oh Cathal, we were actually just discussing this. Sebastian is going to be called his real name from now on,' Judy Flynn said as if she were addressing a class of unruly ten-year-olds.

'Sure, I'm sorry, Skunk, I mean Sebastian, no offence ever meant.'

And Skunk Slattery, who had been called that for over thirty years, graciously forgave him.

Next day Judy got an extensive grilling from her sister-in-law Kitty as they made Mrs Flynn's bed and settled her in a chair. They had got a good routine going now. Mrs Flynn had eventually and grudgingly recognised her daughter, and equally grudgingly got over her unreasonable dislike of her daughter-in-law, which was a considerable advance.

Of course she complained as usual that someone had stolen all her clothes and was not at all comforted when Judy briskly unpacked the clean items from the Fresh as a Daisy.

'Well, come on then! Did Skunk lay his hands on you?' Kitty asked.

'His name is Sebastian and he was quite delightful,' Judy said primly.

'Skunk? Delightful?' It was beyond Kitty's comprehension.

'I told you, he's not answering to that silly schoolboy name any more.'

'It'll take a while to get that message across, Judy.'

'Well, he's starting this morning, he's painting a new sign over his shop,' Judy said.

Mrs Flynn looked from one to the other. 'You could do worse than Skunk, you know, he has plenty put by,' she said.

'You don't choose a man just for what he has put by,' Judy said, reprovingly.

'For what reason would you choose then? Because he's a good tap dancer?' her mam asked and for some reason that they couldn't quite understand they all found this very funny.

*

Cathal Chambers at the bank was concerned because Neddy Nolan had borrowed so much money. Of course he had put the farm up as collateral; still it was a heavy sum. And this from a man who would think twice before buying a pair of shoes in the charity shop.

'Could you let me know what it's all for, Neddy?' Cathal asked.

'It's for my advisers,' Neddy explained.

'But God above, what kind of advice are you getting that could cost all this money?' Cathal was bewildered.

'Experts in their field charge high fees,' Neddy said as if that was any kind of explanation.

'It's just that you wouldn't want cowboy advisers who might bleed you dry or anything.' Cathal was sincere. He was as much out for Neddy Nolan's good as for the bank.

'No, indeed, Cathal, highly professional,' Neddy said with a calm little smile.

Cathal went to see the lawyer, Myles Barry.

'Myles, I don't want to get into the lawyer–client relationship but who are all these advisers Neddy Nolan has?'

'Advisers?' Myles Barry was confused.

'Yes, people he's paying huge fees to apparently.'

Myles scratched his head. 'I don't know who the hell they are – I haven't even sent him one bill, he can hardly have retained another firm of lawyers without telling me. I don't know what you're talking about, Cathal, I really don't.'

Lilly Ryan and her son Donal went to the prison on visiting day. This time they wanted to go without the priest.

'I'll be there visiting someone else in case you need me,' he said.

Father Flynn had an entirely unsatisfactory conversation with poor Becca King, who seemed to be getting madder all the time.

332

She had got a very long prison sentence for being involved in the murder of her rival in love. She showed no repentance at all, just kept repeating that it had to be done. He hoped that she wouldn't ask him again to arrange a prison wedding with that young man she was obsessed with. A young man who wouldn't even come to visit her in jail, let alone marry her there. But no, today it was something different. She had a petition for St Ann, a card that she wanted pinned on to the shrine for all to see.

She showed it to the priest. It was a photograph of Gabrielle King, her mother, and underneath was written: 'Please, St Ann, punish this woman severely for having destroyed her daughter's life. And if any of your loyal followers should see her in the streets of Rossmore, they should spit at her in your name.'

Father Flynn felt very old and tired. He gravely said he would go there this afternoon and do it, he would give it priority.

'It must be in a place where everyone can see it,' Becca called as he was leaving.

'Pride of place, that's what I'll get for it, Becca,' he promised.

As he left, Kate, one of the warders, laid her hand on his arm. 'You are a kind man, Father, not to upset her.'

'You do know that I'm going to throw it away, don't you?' Father Flynn said.

'Of course I do, but you'll wait until you get home and burn it rather than leaving it round here for anyone to pick up,' Kate said.

Brian Flynn put the card in his wallet beside a cheque that had come from London that morning. It was money left by a lady who had died, a Helen Harris. She wanted to thank the shrine of St Ann for having answered her prayers for the safe delivery of a baby twenty-three long years ago. Perhaps the priest could spend it as he thought best to honour the saint.

As he sat there on a wooden bench in case Lilly Ryan might need him later, Father Flynn speculated to himself about the role of a priest in today's society. He hadn't come to any satisfactory conclusion when Lilly and Donal came out.

'All well?' he asked anxiously and felt annoyed with himself at the very question. How could all be well in a family where the father was in jail for domestic violence, a family that had lost a child nearly a quarter of a century ago?

But surprisingly Lilly nodded as if it were a normal thing to ask. 'Just fine, Father. I realise now he's a very weak man. I didn't know this, you see, what with him being so big and strong, and hurting me for being stupid. But he's actually weak and frightened, I see that now.'

'And my mam realises that just because she is understanding and forgiving to him, the State will not be forgiving and allow him to go home. He will have to finish his sentence,' her son said.

'Yes, and Donal was very good, it's not really in his heart but to please me he shook hands with his dad and wished him courage.' Lilly's tired face looked less strained than before.

'So would you say we have a result then?' Father Flynn said.

'Best result in the circumstances,' Donal agreed.

'That's all any of us can hope for,' Father Flynn said.

Clare was taking her pupils to the Heartfelt Art Gallery to do a project. Emer who was the director there was a friend of hers. They would let the girls wander round the gallery and try to answer the questions on the form while the two women had a cup of coffee.

Emer was getting married shortly to a Canadian called Ken whom she had always fancied but thought she had lost. Then suddenly out of the blue he had come to her with bunches of flowers and everything had been perfect.

Father Flynn was going to do a nice speedy job on the service. Emer supposed that the priest was so glad that anyone came into a church at all these days or married anyone of a different sex, he'd agree to anything.

'He's his own man,' Clare said.

'He is indeed,' Emer agreed. 'Did he marry you and Neddy?'

'No, the canon did, but he was there kind of rescuing the canon and bringing him back if he started to wander down too many byways . . .'

'I see your Neddy often these days, he has some kind of business in an office near Ken's up here in the old flour mills they converted,' Emer said.

'Neddy? Business?'

'Well, I assumed so, I saw him today when I was bringing Ken some lunch in his office. And yesterday . . .'

Clare was silent. Neddy had mentioned nothing of any business. She felt a cold lump of dread in her heart. But not Neddy. No, never.

Emer realised what was happening.

'I could have been mistaken,' she said lamely.

Clare said nothing.

'I mean, it's all offices here, little suites they rent out as offices, you know. It's not as if it was flats, apartments. No, Clare, not Neddy. He worships you, for heaven's sake.'

'I think these girls have had enough time, don't you?' Clare said in a very brittle voice quite unlike her own.

'Please, don't jump to conclusions . . . you know men,' Emer begged.

Clare knew men better than anyone in Rossmore.

'Come on, girls, don't take all day,' she said in a voice that was not going to be disobeyed.

She was getting into her car when she met Cathal Chambers from the bank. He greeted her warmly.

'You and Neddy must be making great plans up in that farm of yours,' he said.

'Hardly, Cathal, it's still very uncertain whether there will be a road running through the middle of it or not.'

'So what are all these advisers then, the ones that cost all the money?'

'I don't know about any advisers costing lots of money.'

'Maybe I got it wrong. But you do know you have huge borrowings, don't you?' Cathal's round face was anxious.

'Huge borrowings? Oh yes, yes indeed, I know . . .' Clare said in a voice that would be obvious to anyone that she had absolutely no idea.

There was a time she had thought that Neddy was just too good to be true. Maybe she had been right.

When she got back home her father-in-law was having a siesta out on the porch they had built together. She remembered handing Neddy the nails one by one. Marty was asleep in a big wicker chair with a light warm rug on his knees. This place had meant peace and refuge to Clare, and now it was all over.

Neddy was sitting at the kitchen table surrounded by papers.

'I have something important to ask you, Neddy,' she began.

'And I have something very important to tell you, Clare,' he said.

Judy Flynn stood back to get the full effect of the new sign over Slattery's newsagents. It looked very splendid.

'It may take time for them to stop calling me Skunk,' he said anxiously.

'Well, we have time,' Judy said.

'You don't have to go back for a while yet, do you?' Sebastian Slattery asked from the top of his ladder.

'No, I'm my own boss, but I'm not made of money, I can't go on staying in the Rossmore Hotel for much longer.'

'What about your mam's house?' the newly named Sebastian suggested.

'No, she would be found killed dead with a bread knife in her if I stayed there.' Judy knew herself fairly well.

'Kitty's?'

'Something similar. These are people I can meet just for very short periods of time.'

'Well, what about my place then? You could stay here over the shop for a while until . . . until . . .'

'Until what, Sebastian?'

'Until we get married and look for somewhere nicer for you and for me, for us, I mean . . .'

'Are we going to get married? We barely know each other,' Judy asked.

'I do hope so,' Sebastian said, coming down the ladder.

'Right. I'll move in tonight,' she said.

'Um – I'll have to do up a room for you . . .'

'You mean, we aren't going to sleep together? In your room?' she called across the street to him to the entertainment of passers-by.

'I'll have your terrible Druid of a brother after me, saying I am the wages of sin and all that sort of thing.'

'Don't be ridiculous, Sebastian. Brian will just be delighted to see us happy. He won't go on with all that kind of stuff. You've been away from the Church too long . . .'

Brian Flynn was surprised to see Chester Kovac, the big American who had financed the Danny O'Neill Health Centre in Doon.

'I was wondering if I could prevail on you to marry Hannah Harty and myself quietly, you know, no big ceremony . . .'

'Well, of course I will, and my warmest congratulations. But why won't you be getting married out in Doon where you live? Father Murphy is in charge of the parish there.'

'No, we'd have to ask everyone if we had it in Doon, and we're a bit advanced in years to be making a big show of it. And anyway there's Dr Dermot there – we don't want to be sort of showing off in front of him. It's complicated.'

Father Flynn knew Dr Dermot – a mean, crabbed man. He could well believe that it was complicated.

'I just didn't want you to miss out on a big day, that's all,' he reassured Chester.

'Oh, don't worry about that, Father, we'll miss out on nothing.

337

There will be plenty of people at a big do when I go back to the States for a honeymoon. In fact we will be bringing my mom back here with me for a vacation. Her name is Ann, too, so she is very anxious to visit the well here.'

Father Flynn thought to himself that she had better come fairly quickly if she wanted to see the well and he examined his diary to get a suitable early date for the wedding.

Eddie Flynn was nowhere to be found when the decision to build the new road was announced. The vote in the council had been satisfactorily in favour of building the bypass. Eddie's syndicate had bought every piece of property that might have been central to this plan except the Nolans' farm. The plan said the road would go straight through this property and up through the woods in a straight line, taking the well and the shrine with it.

Eddie had assured the others that buying land from Neddy Nolan was like taking candy from a baby. Yes, true, it was Neddy who was the loser. The compulsory purchase order would not pay anything like what he had been offered by the syndicate. But Neddy had always been soft in the head. The real problem was that Eddie Flynn had not delivered. So he had disappeared.

Kitty and the children barely noticed that he was gone. Naomi, however, was very distressed. She had fabric for brides-maids and flower girls, and she needed to talk to him about it. Why had he done this now? And he had left her no money to be getting on with, and the flat was only paid for for the next two months. It was vexing in the extreme . . .

Lilly Ryan had heard from her cousin Pearl over in the North of England. Pearl was married to this really nice fellow, Bob, and they had two grown-up children. It appeared that something nice had happened in their lives. Their children, who used to be quite cold and distant and maybe a bit ashamed of them, had been much nicer of late. Pearl always wrote very honestly, not pretending or putting on airs. She wondered, could she and Bob come and spend a long weekend in Rossmore. Now Lilly was to say if it was difficult, and she would quite understand.

So Lilly sat down and wrote everything, all about Aidan and his accusations, and how he couldn't cope and that despite his violence he was a weak man, and that he would be in jail for another eighteen months and how she, Lilly, would just love them to visit. When she posted the letter she felt much better, as if she had needed to write out the whole story to make some kind of sense of it. She said that she and Pearl would go up to St Ann's Well for old times' sake when she arrived.

Clare and Neddy sat one on either side of the table. Clare didn't even look at the papers spread out all over the place. She was about to have her first and last row with Neddy Nolan on the day she had been going to tell him that her period was three weeks late and they might possibly be looking at the pregnancy they both longed for. Now it was too late.

Neddy spoke very quietly.

'The permission for the road has been given today, Clare. As we thought it's going straight through here and on up to the well.'

'We knew that would happen, but you refused to sell to Eddie Flynn just at a time when you might actually need money more than any other time of your life.' Clare's voice was cold.

'But I couldn't sell to them or we'd have had no control,' he said as if explaining it to a toddler.

'And what control do you have now? Less money, that's all . . .'

'No, Clare, that's not true, we have all this . . .' He waved at the papers and maps on the kitchen table.

'This?'

'I took advice, I got experts to draw up an alternative plan, another way the road would go so that it wouldn't take away

339

St Ann's shrine. It involved architects, engineers, quantity surveyors, and cost a fortune. Clare, I had to borrow from Cathal Chambers and he thinks I'm into heroin or gambling or something.'

Suddenly she knew that this was indeed what he was doing with the money, rather than feathering a little love nest for himself in the converted flour mills. Her relief was followed by a wave of resentment.

'And why didn't you tell him and tell me, for God's sake?'

'I had to keep it very quiet, have meetings where no one would see me.'

'In the old flour mills?' she guessed.

Neddy laughed sheepishly. 'There's me thinking no one knew!'

He patted her hand and kissed her fingers as he often did. The resentment had gone. Clare felt only the relief that he still loved her. She hadn't known until now just how much she would dread the thought of losing him.

'Will it work, Neddy?' she asked weakly.

Neddy Nolan had hired all these people to make maps and surveys. It was unbelievable.

'I think it will,' Neddy said calmly. 'You see, I hired a public relations expert as well to show us how to get public sympathy. And he will get us a media coach for the two of us for television.'

'For television?'

'If you agree we can go on a big news programme and debate it with the developers.'

'We can?' Clare whispered.

'Oh yes, we can explain how so many people here feel grateful to St Ann and want to keep the well and the shrine. It would make no sense now for anyone to oppose us.'

'But Neddy, couldn't we have done that without you having to hire all these experts?'

'No, that's just the point,' Neddy cried. 'Then we'd only have been pious, old-fashioned, superstitious people standing in the way of progress. We'd only have looked like the old Ireland rooted in history and traditions against the good modern Ireland which wanted to improve life for everyone . . .'

'And now?'

'Now we have a perfectly possible alternative plan. A plan which you and I paid for with our own money, refusing huge financial offers from syndicates and the like.' He nodded over at the little oak cabinet. 'I have every detail of it recorded there. They'll know we are telling the truth and putting our money where our mouth is.'

'And where will the road go?'

She bent over the map with him and he stroked her hair with one hand as he pointed with the other. The new road would still go through the Nolan farm, but would then follow a route that would allow a sizeable part of the woods to remain, the part that held the shrine. There would be a big car park there and a side slip road from the new road to bring visitors directly to the shrine instead of going through Rossmore. And yet the local people could walk there through what remained of the woods as always.

Clare looked at him with admiration. It could well work. A government heading for a General Election, a local council fearful of being accused of taking backhanders, might well want to take this chance of avoiding the huge confrontation that seemed to be brewing. Neddy's solution seemed a perfect way out for everybody.

'I wish you'd told me,' she said.

'Yes, I was going to, but you looked tired, and you have to go into a classroom every day. I just stay here. I have a much easier life.'

She looked around the gleaming house that he kept so well for the three of them. It was not such an easy life, and she knew it. But Neddy never complained.

'Hey, you said you had something to tell me – what was it?' he asked.

She told him that there was an outside chance she might be pregnant. Neddy got up and held her in his arms.

'I was up there at the shrine today and I know it's nonsense but I did say that it was something we both wanted badly,' he said into her hair.

'Well, she had to do something for the man who saved her well,' Clare said.

They were still standing there, arms around each other, when Marty Nolan came in.

'Father Flynn arrived and he couldn't get any answer so I came in to see were you two all right.' He was indignant that he had to be woken from his chair.

As they had their tea and home-made biscuits, the birds started to gather on the trees for the night. And the sun began to set over the woods that Neddy Nolan had almost certainly saved.

And the priest knew that his sister Judy was up there at the well, thanking St Ann and saying she hadn't expected that it would all work so quickly.

So Father Flynn listened, as it got dark, to Neddy's plans.

He was going to buy a house much nearer Rossmore, and then maybe Father Flynn's mother and the canon could come to stay. It would not be like moving too far from the town, he had seen a grand place with a garden that the canon would like. Neddy would look after them all.

And if by any chance they were to get a little baby he would look after the baby too. It would be nice for older people to have a new young life around the place.

And for once Father Flynn could find nothing to say. What he liked to think of as his comforting supply of meaningless clichés had dried up.

He looked at the good honest man in front of him and for the first time for a long time he saw some purpose in a life that had recently been confused and contradictory on every front.

He looked back up at the ever darkening woods.

And it wasn't fanciful to think of them as a very special place, where so many voices had been heard and so many dreams answered.